A WILD EXCITEMENT TOOK
HOLD OF HER . . .

Brandy leaned into Flaming Arrow, caught the back of his head and kissed him with total abandon.

A sudden anger rose in him. He tore his mouth away and shook her shoulders, asking in a voice ragged with desire, "Do you know what you're doing? Or are you only teasing me again?"

Brandy looked at Flaming Arrow with dazed eyes. "No . . . no, I'm not teasing."

"You want me?"

She did want him. She wanted him desperately. "Yes," she answered breathlessly.

Flaming Arrow's pride came to the fore. He wanted more than just a simple agreement. "No. That won't do. You must say the words."

There was just the slightest hesitation on Brandy's part. "I want you."

Flaming Arrow's dark eyes quickly swept over her face, searching for some sign of deception. Finding none, he said, "Remember. If you are lying, you have only yourself to blame, for no power on earth is going to stop me now. You are mine. All mine!"

Also by Joanne Redd from Dell:

APACHE BRIDE
DESERT BRIDE
CHASING A DREAM
TO LOVE AN EAGLE,
Winner of the 1987 *Romantic Times* award for
Best Western Historical Romance

Joanne Redd

STEAL THE FLAME

A DELL BOOK

To my brother, Gerald,
with love

Published by
Dell Publishing
a division of
Bantam Doubleday Dell Publishing Group, Inc.
666 Fifth Avenue
New York, New York 10103

ISBN: 0-440-20825-4

Printed in the United States of America

Published simultaneously in Canada

February 1991

10 9 8 7 6 5 4 3 2

OPM

Summer 1875

The only sounds Brandy Daniels could hear from where she stood by the small stream was the lazy drone of a nearby bee and the sigh of the wind over the prairie. Then the sharp crack of a rifle shot split the air and shattered the serenity of the moment. The unexpected sound made Brandy jump in surprise. She whirled around to face the cavalry camp in the distance, from which the noise had come. But it wasn't the sight of the soldiers running frantically for their horses or for cover that caught her attention. It was the chilling sight of a wave of howling red savages sweeping down on the encampment that made her heart skip a beat and her mouth turn dry with fear.

For a moment, Brandy stood frozen to the spot, too terrified even to move. Then a deep-seated instinct for survival took command of her body. Without a conscious thought even crossing her mind, she threw herself to the ground behind some low-growing bushes. There, lying full-length on her stomach and perched on her elbows, she could see through the lower branches of the shrub the fierce battle taking place in the distance.

The Indians had encircled the camp and were now a swirling, whirling mass of painted, rapidly moving riders. They caught the soldiers so completely off guard that they didn't even have time to throw up a hasty breastworks, much less circle the supply and feed wagons for protection. Only those closest to the wagons managed to take refuge in and beneath them. The rest of the company was caught in the wide open. A few cavalrymen were even startled from the quick naps they had been taking after their noon meal.

To Brandy, watching from where she was concealed behind the bushes, the massacre that followed was a scene straight from hell. Although she couldn't see much because of the thick cloud of rolling dust raised by the Indians' horses, she could hear the battle: the sharp crack of rifles, the whiz of arrows, the pounding of the horses' hoofs, the bloodcurdling war cries, the officers' frantic commands to take cover, the soldiers' angry curses mixed with screams of pain when a bullet or arrow hit them, the pitiful pleas for help from the wounded, and finally, at the end, the nerve-wracking silence until the dust settled and she could see who the victor was. Then Brandy watched in horror while the Indians scalped the dead and set fire to the wagons. The savages' only merciful act had been cutting the mules loose before setting the fire, and for that Brandy was grateful. Hearing the ani-

mals' terrified braying during the brief fight had
been bad enough. Brandy would have never been
able to endure watching them burn to death.

Then a sudden thought occurred to her. Had the
soldiers who had taken refuge in those wagons and
beneath them been dead, beyond all feeling, when
the wagons had been set to the torch? Maybe they
had only been mortally wounded. Scalping didn't kill
a man. Her brother, Paul, had told her as much.
Maybe one or two of the poor men had even been
conscious. The horrible thought made bile rise in her
throat.

For a good hour after the savages rode away, driving the soldiers' horses and mules before them,
Brandy didn't move a muscle. She lay staring out at
the scene in absolute shock at the horror of what she
had just witnessed. Out on the prairie, beyond the
treeline along the stream where she was hidden, the
constant wind set the tall, lush grass into a gentle,
undulating motion that made the Wyoming flatlands
look like a deep green sea. Not a sound could be
heard other than that of the wind, for Brandy lay too
far away to hear the crackling of the fire that remained. But she could still see a few of the more
persistent flames dancing across the charred embers
of the wagons. Heat waves rose from the heaps of
blackened rubble that lay in the middle of the deeply
rutted trail, and scattered all around them in the tall,
waving grass were the bodies of the dead cavalrymen
and their mounts, horses who had inadvertently
been killed during the battle. Above the scene of
carnage, buzzards slowly circled and waited patiently for the last of the flames to die away.

Slowly, ever so slowly, the numbness that had paralyzed both her body and her thinking process receded. The first thought Brandy had was, How could it have happened? How had the Indians managed to catch the soldiers so completely by surprise? Where had the savages come from so suddenly and so unexpectedly? The cavalry had had their Crow scouts out, and none of them had reported any sign of hostile Indians. And then another, much more profound thought entered her mind. She was alive! She had survived the massacre, and it was nothing short of a miracle. Had the attack come ten minutes earlier, she would have shared the fate of the others, for surely the Indians would have seen her walking to the cover of the woods around the stream where she had gone to relieve herself after the column had stopped for their noon break.

Suddenly, a shadow fell over Brandy and blocked the heat of the sun that had been blazing down on her backside. Feeling it, Brandy's spirits, which had been soaring at the realization that she had survived, plunged to the ground, and she stiffened in fear. She knew that whatever caused the shadow had to be tall. Was it a wild animal? she wondered. It had to be. She had watched the Indians ride away in the opposite direction, and even if one had remained for some unlikely reason, it would have been impossible for him to sneak up on her in the wide open, without even a rock to hide behind. But what wild animal could be that large? A chill ran over her as she realized a bear might be standing over her. Petrified, Brandy couldn't even force herself to look over her shoulder.

A hand reached down and caught Brandy's arm, jerking her to her feet. As she was whirled around to face the man who was treating her so roughly, Brandy found herself wishing that it had been a bear that had found her, for she would have rather faced a wild animal than the tall, fierce-looking Indian now looming over her. She didn't understand how he could possibly have managed to sneak up behind her, but she knew by the blue lines slashed across his high cheekbones and the slashes and symbols painted all over his broad chest that he had to be one of the savages who had taken part in the earlier massacre.

Icy fear filled Brandy as the man's dark eyes bore into her. She had never seen such black, black eyes. Nor had she ever felt so threatened. The feeling of lethal danger was so powerful that she found it difficult even to breathe, and her heart was pounding so hard, she feared it would leap from her chest. Then Brandy's inherent strong character came to the fore. Even looking death directly in the eye—as she was firmly convinced she was—Brandy wasn't going to give up without a fight. She struggled to pull away.

Brandy's attempt to free herself came with such suddenness and unexpected strength that it took Flaming Arrow by surprise. Thinking the white woman was terrified and expecting her to cower to him, he had relaxed his grip on her and was momentarily stunned when she broke loose, spun around, and tore off across the prairie. But Brandy's bid for freedom was short-lived. With his exceptionally long legs, Flaming Arrow had no trouble catching up with her, particularly since Brandy's riding skirt was hampering her flight. Within a minute, Brandy once more found herself caught. She whirled around.

"Let go of me!" Brandy shrieked as she struggled frantically to get loose. But the Indian's grasp on her arms was like two iron bands. Desperation gave her a strength she had not known she possessed. She twisted and turned, tried to lash out with her nails, then kicked out wildly. She felt a fleeting moment of satisfaction when the toe of her riding boot made solid contact with the man's shin, and she heard him grunt in pain. The next thing Brandy knew, she was thrown to the ground with a force that knocked the breath from her, and the savage was lying full-length over her, pinning her body down with his and her arms down beside her head with his powerful hands.

With the full weight of the Indian bearing down on her, Brandy couldn't move. She could barely breathe. He felt as if he weighed a ton. Flaming Arrow's face was lying so close to hers that she couldn't see his features. But she could feel his warm breath fanning her face and smell the mint leaf he had been chewing to relieve his thirst shortly before. Realizing she was helpless against his superior strength, she gave up her fight, and her body went limp. "All right," she muttered with a little sob, "go ahead and kill me."

Flaming Arrow leaned back and looked down at her. Seeing him gazing so intently at her, Brandy felt a renewal of her fighting spirit and spat, "What are you staring at? I said go ahead and get it over with. Kill me!"

"What makes you think I will kill you?" Flaming Arrow asked calmly.

"Because you killed all the others. Why shouldn't you kill me too?"

"I had nothing to do with the attack on the horse soldiers."

"I don't believe you! You're wearing war paint just like they were. You're one of them."

"I am painted, yes. But not for war. The men who attacked the horse soldiers were Kiowas. I am a Lakota. Besides, even if I had taken part in the attack, I would not kill you. I do not make war on women, as your people do."

Brandy heard the contempt in Flaming Arrow's voice and briefly wondered at his last words. But she was still distrustful. "You're lying!"

A muscle in the Indian's jaw twitched, and she saw the slightest flare of anger in his dark eyes before he answered in a tightly controlled voice, "I do not lie. Ever! My stripes are blue. The Kiowas' were yellow. We belong to two different tribes."

"Then what are you doing here, if you aren't one of the men who attacked us?"

Flaming Arrow cocked a dark eyebrow at the woman's insolent question. It was *he* who should be asking that question. She was the intruder. "I am the pipeholder, the leader of a raiding party passing through. He who goes before me—my scout—saw the smoke from the fires and reported it to me. I came to investigate."

A sudden dawning came to Brandy. "Wait a minute! You speak English!" she exclaimed in astonishment.

Flaming Arrow's lips curved into a wry smile at the white woman's sudden, belated discovery. "Yes, I speak your tongue."

"But where did you learn it?"

Flaming Arrow rose to his feet, bringing Brandy with him before he answered, "From a trapper who spent his winters with our tribe, mostly in my father's tepee."

Brandy felt a little less threatened now that she knew her life was not in jeopardy. She had never heard of the Lakota. Maybe they were a friendly tribe, and this man would help her. Her courage came flooding back and with it, an inane arrogance, for Brandy was a very spoiled young lady, one who was accustomed to having her every wish fulfilled and every command obeyed. "Let go of my arms."

The white woman's tone of voice grated on Flaming Arrow's nerves. He stiffened, and his dark eyes flashed, for no one made demands on him, not even Chief Crazy Horse. "No, I will not let you go."

There was a finality about the savage's response that made Brandy realize she had more than met her match. And she hadn't missed the brief flash of anger in the man's black eyes, a look that made a tingle of fear run up her spine, or the stiffness in his body that somehow made her think of a coiled snake ready to strike. He was dangerous, she thought, a man no sane person would dare rile. She briefly glanced at his powerful biceps and shoulders, then thought that he could break her in two if he wanted. Brandy was spoiled and arrogant, hardheaded and sometimes reckless, but she wasn't stupid. Although she had never before done so in her life, she knew now that it was time to back off, even though it galled her something awful to have to do so. "And if I said please?"

Flaming Arrow's eyes narrowed. He sensed that the white woman had never retreated from a confrontation in her life or stepped down from her haughty place to say please to anyone. He was frankly suspicious. Was she only being sly? Did she have some trick in mind?

"Please?" Brandy repeated, putting more entreaty into the word.

"Not unless you promise not to try to run away again. I do not have time to be chasing you."

"I won't run away. I was only frightened before. You said you wouldn't harm me."

Flaming Arrow's suspicions weren't altogether put to rest. This white woman was like none he had ever known. Not only did she dare to use a tone of voice to him that none of the warriors in his tribe would, much less a woman, but he had been shocked by her strength and how fiercely she had fought him, like a wild cat, until he had been forced to throw her to the ground and lie on her to subdue her. Warily, Flaming Arrow let go of Brandy's arms and stepped back, half expecting to see her turn and flee again.

When Flaming Arrow stepped away from her, Brandy got her first good look at him, and she couldn't help but stare. She had never seen an Indian this close up, not even the Crow scouts that had been with the cavalry. Until now, her fear that the Lakota would harm her had been almost blinding. But she was more than surprised by what she saw—she was mesmerized. She had always been told that Indians were fierce, ugly creatures. While the tall man standing before her did look ferocious with the paint slashed across his cheeks and while she could almost feel the barely leashed savagery in him, he was far from ugly. In fact, his facial features were the most well proportioned she had ever seen—rugged, yet undeniably handsome. Even his nose was a surprise, for it wasn't at all hawklike, as she would have expected, but strikingly straight and narrow. But most surprising was the man's lips. Although they were thin, there was no hint of cruelty to them. Instead, there was something—a certain . . . sensuality— that made Brandy's stomach quiver strangely.

Not liking the Indian's strange effect on her, Brandy tore her eyes away from his face and directed her attention to his body, then wondered briefly why he was called a red man. On his shoulders and arms and between the paint on his chest, she could see that his skin was bronze colored more than copper toned, actually not much darker than her brother's face had become since he had joined the cavalry. And suddenly another thought came to her. Why didn't the Indian have hair on his chest, as her brother did?

But the Lakota's lack of chest hair didn't detract from his masculinity in the least, nor did his long black hair tied at both sides of his head with strip of fur, a hairstyle that Brandy would have expected to look effeminate on a man. To the contrary, with his incredibly broad shoulders, muscular arms and chest, lean hips, and long legs that fit his tight leggins as if they were a second skin, the Lakota was without a doubt the most perfectly shaped specimen of manhood Brandy had ever seen. He was even more perfect than the marble Greek god she had boldly admired in a museum back east, for which she had earned a severe lecture from her mother on her shocking, unladylike behavior. That his body was a magnificent specimen of manhood alone was disturbing, but the Lakota fairly reeked of self-confidence, self-possession, and command—all strong, manly characteristics, to say nothing of the sexual virility that he seemed to exude. And beneath all this was that barely suppressed savagery, that wild, primitive fierceness that thrilled, excited, and frightened her. All in all, the Lakota's masculinity was quite overpowering, and Brandy suddenly found it difficult to breathe.

While Brandy had been staring at him, Flaming Arrow had been doing a little scrutinizing of his own. He had seen white men up close before, but never a white woman, and he would hardly describe her as a paleface. Her complexion was creamy rather than white, and there was a rosy blush on her smooth cheeks that Indian women lacked or that was hidden beneath the darkness of their skin. Nor had he ever seen eyes the color of hers—a deep, startling blue that took his breath away. Even her hair was a stunning color, the reddish highlights overpowering the brown in the bright sunlight, seemingly glowing with a life of their own.

His eyes dropped to Brandy's body, and again Flaming Arrow was impressed. Although she was taller and slimmer than the women of his tribe, the feminine curves were all in the right places, maybe all the more obvious for her slimness. There seemed to be more of a flare to her hips after her tiny waist, and Brandy's full breasts seemed to jut out in the tight bodice of her riding suit as if daring him to touch them. Staring at the rise and fall of those twin mounds, Flaming Arrow wondered what it would be like to cup that soft flesh in his hands and taste her creamy skin. The thought was arousing. Feeling himself respond, he jerked his eyes away and once more looked at Brandy's face. His gaze came to rest on her rosy mouth with its full bottom lip, a mouth that pouted and bespoke of Brandy's spoiled existence, a mouth that could also drive a man wild to possess it.

Brandy was aware that the Lakota was staring at her lips, and she felt a tingle of excitement rush over her. Suddenly she wanted him to kiss her. Just as suddenly as the strange desire came over her, Brandy was filled with shock. My God! she thought. What in the world was wrong with her? Had the hot sun addled her? Why, he was a wild savage, nothing but an ignorant animal—a magnificent animal, true, but an animal no less, and much below her. Brandy brought herself up to her full height and said in an icy voice, "Stop staring at me like that!"

When Flaming Arrow's dark eyes rose and met hers, Brandy was stunned by the heat she saw in them.

"Why should I stop staring?" Flaming Arrow asked.

Regaining her senses, Brandy answered hotly, "Because it's rude!"

"You were staring too," he pointed out calmly. "Both at my face . . . and at my body."

A flush of embarrassment rose on Brandy's face before she denied it. "I was doing no such thing! I was just . . ." Brandy hesitated, trying to think of a plausible excuse to have been looking at him so intently. "I was just wondering why you're all painted up like that and what those symbols mean. You said it wasn't war paint."

Flaming Arrow wondered if Brandy was telling him the truth. Had she only been curious? He felt a strange disappointment. "No, it is not war paint. I have just returned from a raid on a Pawnee camp to the south of here and was riding back to my tribe with the horses we captured. We paint ourselves for a raid, as well as for war."

"A raid? But isn't that the same thing?"

"No. Our purpose is to steal horses, to count coup if we can get close enough, but not to kill. There is no honor in killing."

Then he was a peaceful Indian, Brandy thought, reassuring herself. But she was curious about something. "What do you mean, count coup?"

"That is when we touch our enemies, either with our hands or with our croup sticks. It is much braver to touch your enemy or, if need be, to fight him in hand-to-hand combat than to kill him with an arrow or gun shot from a distance."

"But you just said you didn't go there to kill but to steal horses," Brandy objected. "You're contradicting yourself."

"No, I am not. It is a matter of intention. We hope the raid can be accomplished without bloodshed. That is why we sneak into their camps while it is still dark and they are sleeping. But sometimes that is not possible, and we have to fight in self-defense. War, however, is an entirely different matter. The killing is planned. We make war only to avenge the deaths of our people."

Brandy was still confused. "Then why do you paint yourselves for a raid?"

"So an enemy who might count coup on us will know that we are great warriors. There is no honor in counting coup on a coward. These blue stripes on my face and chest are my coup marks."

Brandy's eyes swept over the Lakota's face and chest and did a quick count. There were at least twenty slashes. "And those other symbols on your chest? What do they mean?"

"Each hoofmark represents a successful raid I was on; the circles tell how many times I fought behind breastworks; the white squares tell how many times I have been a war party leader; and the red hands tell how many times I have killed an enemy in hand-to-hand combat."

Brandy was stunned. The Lakota's broad chest was covered with symbols, and the six red hands there stood out like bloody banners. She had known from the beginning that he was a dangerous man, but to have him boldly admit that he was a killer unnerved her. There was no doubt that the man standing before her was as warlike as savages came, and she was beginning to have serious doubts about him being friendly to her. She swallowed hard and said, "I've never heard of the Lakotas. Are you a small tribe?"

Flaming Arrow gave a short laugh, then answered, "No, we are part of a great Indian nation, the western group made up of the Lakotas, Dakotas, and Nakotas, the middle group made up of the Yangtons, and the most eastern, the Santee."

The blood drained from Brandy's face. She had heard of the Santee. They were Sioux who had gone on the warpath a decade ago in Minnesota and killed over a thousand whites. Although Brandy had been just a child at the time, the bloodthirsty stories she had heard had left a lasting impression on her mind. And she knew the western Sioux were no less warlike. If anything, they were more so. Paul had told her that they were the most ferocious and feared of the plains Indians, and her brother should know. He had been fighting Indians for the last five years.

Seeing the horrified expression on her face, Flaming Arrow asked, "What's wrong?"

Brandy had to gather her courage to answer. "I—I didn't realize you're Sioux. I thought you might be from a friendly tribe."

Flaming Arrow's nose wrinkled as if he had caught the smell of something very obnoxious. "Sioux is the Frenchmen's word for the name the Chippewas gave my people. It means enemy. We do not use it. We call ourself the Allied Ones. And, no, I am not of a friendly tribe, in the sense that we are on friendly terms with your people. But I have told you, there is no need for you to fear me. I do not make war on women."

Brandy sighed in relief, then asked, "Then you'll take me to Fort Fetterman?"

"No."

"But it's just a few hours away."

"I said no!"

Brandy was a little taken aback by his adamant answer. "Then—then what are you going to do with me?"

Flaming Arrow's black eyes moved slowly down Brandy's length, then back up. His appraisal seemed cold and calculating and made a shiver of fear run through her. "It seems I will have to take you with me."

"Take me with you?" Brandy asked in a shocked voice. "Do you mean take me back to your tribe's village?"

"Yes."

"But why? Why can't you just leave me here? When that cavalry company doesn't show up at Fort

Fetterman, they'll send someone here to investigate, and they'll find me."

"Yes, and you will tell them that a Dakota raiding party recently passed through here, and they will send riders after us, as well as the Kiowas. Then I might have to leave that herd of horses we captured behind in order to escape, and I can't risk losing those mounts. My people need them."

"I won't tell the soldiers that I saw anything of you, just the Indians that attacked us. I promise I'll never mention you."

"I can't risk that. You will have to go with me."

"I give you my word!"

"The white man's word means nothing to me. I don't trust you. You will go with me."

Brandy felt highly insulted. No one had ever doubted her word before, and no matter what, Brandy didn't give her word lightly. Her anger rose. "The devil I'll go with you!" she threw out recklessly.

Flaming Arrow cocked one dark eyebrow in surprise. "Are you saying no?"

"You're damn right I am!" Brandy answered, her blue eyes shooting sparks. "And you can't force me!"

A faint smile crossed Flaming Arrow's lips at Brandy's audacious challenge. Then his dark eyes narrowed. "Can't I?" he asked in a silky voice that should have warned Brandy of impending danger. He scoffed. "You are in no position to defy me. I am in command here. Remember that!"

Flaming Arrow's arm shot out with the swiftness of a striking snake and caught Brandy's wrist. He whirled around and walked swiftly to his horse, which was waiting by the stream, and he dragged Brandy behind him and sent the gravel on the stream's bank scattering everywhere. Brandy tried to resist, kicking and hitting out, then raking her long nails down his arm and clawing the hand that held her. But Flaming Arrow seemed impervious to the burning pain she had inflicted. When they reached his mount, he yanked a long strip of rawhide that hung from his small, flat saddle, caught Brandy's other arm just as she was making a wild swing at his face, and tied both wrists together with speed and dexterity that astonished her. Then Brandy flew through the air as he flung her on his horse. Only out of a sense of self-preservation did she have the presence of mind to spread her legs; otherwise she could have well broken one. As it was, she hit the saddle with such force that she saw stars.

If Flaming Arrow thought his forceful handling of the situation had subdued Brandy, he was sadly mistaken. She wasn't accustomed to such rough treatment, and once she had recovered from her jolt, it only served to fuel her anger. Just as Flaming Arrow was fixing to mount, she kicked out and caught him in the chest. The blow was hard enough to send him staggering backward. Then he recovered and leaped forward, jerking yet another length of narrow rawhide from the saddle. As he bent, Brandy sensed what he was about to do and kicked again. But Flaming Arrow was prepared for her; he simply ducked his head and grabbed her flying leg. With a quick loop, the rawhide circled her boot. Then reaching beneath his horse's belly, he caught her other leg and looped the other end of the rawhide around that boot. Much to Brandy's dismay, she found both her hands and her legs tied, an intolerable indignity.

There was only one weapon left at Brandy's disposal: her tongue. And no one had ever received such a scathing tongue lashing as Flaming Arrow did. He stood and listened with something akin to astonishment as Brandy called him every ugly, obscene name she could think of—a repertoire that turned out to be not only rather long but surprisingly explicit for a woman who professed to be a lady. And when Brandy finished calling names, she made threats, each one more impossible and wild than the last, until Flaming Arrow finally broke out in laughter.

This only made Brandy more furious at him. She glared at him. "What's so damn funny?"

"You are! Your threats are ridiculous. You are in no position to chop off my head, cut out my heart, tear out my liver, or see me burn in hell."

"Don't be too sure about the last!" Brandy retorted. "Have you forgotten the cavalry has Indian scouts? They may figure out that more than one party of Indians passed through here, and they could still follow you when they don't find my body with the others. You see, my brother is expecting me, and he's not without some influence. He's an officer. Maybe I can't kill you, but they will when they catch up with you. Then you *will* burn in hell for eternity."

"It is possible the Crow scouts will see our tracks," Flaming Arrow answered with an unconcerned shrug of his broad shoulders. "But they will know nothing except that we are a raiding party by the large number of hoofprints, and all Indian ponies' hoofprints look alike. We could be a Crow raiding party, for all they know, or Shoshone, their allies. There would be no reason to follow anyone but the Kiowas, whom they will assume have taken you captive, since it is the Kiowas' arrows that are scattered everywhere. Which is why I cannot leave you. Only you could identify us as Lakota, and then they *would* follow us. You see, we are the Crows' enemies. We took the beautiful land we now live in away from them and forced them westward into the Rockies. And your horse soldiers hate us just as much. Neither could turn down the lure of possibly catching us before we reach Dakota Country."

"Dakota Country? But I thought you said you were a Lakota."

"When we speak of the western Allied Ones as a whole, we call ourselves Dakotas."

"Then you're heading for the Sioux reservation?" Brandy asked. Her brother had told her that his company had ridden onto the reservation to remove some miners who had illegally trespassed.

Flaming Arrow's black eyes flashed, and he stiffened. Red Cloud had treacherously accepted the reservation from the white-eyes government after the Dakotas had won the war between them. The white-eyes infuriated him. Flaming Arrow had fought in that war, but he not fought to become a tame Indian, to be fed from sacks and boxes, to be doled out rat-eaten blankets and clothing. Like the others in his tribe, he had fought to remain free, to follow the buffalo and the old way of life. No, he and his party did not go to the reservation. They went to their home deep in the Powder River Country, Dakota Country. "We are *not* reservation Indians," Flaming Arrow informed Brandy in a tight voice between clenched teeth. "We are free Dakotas!"

Brandy knew she had angered Flaming Arrow, but she still persisted. "Then where are we going?"

A mask seemed to come down over the warrior's bronze face, making his rugged features look as if they were carved out of stone. "You will see."

"But—"

"I said you will see!" Flaming Arrow answered in a hard, adamant voice that cut across her protest.

As Flaming Arrow swiftly mounted behind her and nudged his horse forward with the heel of moccasin, Brandy silently fumed at his stubborn refusal to tell her their destination. If they weren't going to the Sioux reservation, then where were they going? Vaguely, she remembered something Paul had written about the unceded Indian country to the west of the reservation. There the nontreaty chiefs and their tribes lived—Sioux who called themself "free" Indians. She concentrated very hard to remember what Paul had said, then recalled that he had written that if the army could ever clear out that nest of wild, ferocious Sioux, the nation's problems with Indians would be brought to an end, for no others posed the threat that they did. Even the fierce Comanches, the Indians who had once been known as the "lords of the plains," had been beaten and put on a reservation the year before. Only the nontreaty Sioux remained to be brought to heel and were of any real consequence among the remaining great Indian nations. The problem was that their fighting force was so numerous, only a major military expedition could invade their territory. And she was at that moment a captive of one of those wild, "free" Sioux. Brandy felt sick. She had survived the massacre only to be dragged off to a godforsaken place deep in Indian country. Her only possible hope for rescue would be for the army to send a major expedition into the area, which just *might* happen to come across her, and even that might be a long time coming. Why, she could very well never see civilization again!

Brandy was reflecting deeply on her apparently grim future when she smelled a hideous odor, one so sickeningly sweet that it was nauseating. The powerful stench roused her from her musing. They were riding past the blackened rubble of the wagons, and she realized what she smelled was burnt flesh. The soldiers' bodies were so charred that they were totally unrecognizable. Again the gorge rose in her throat, and she looked away.

It wasn't until they had put some distance between them and the scene of the massacre that Brandy was able to think logically again. As they rode over a small ridge that overlooked the trail, it occurred to her once more that but for the grace of God, she would be dead. She was forced to admit that things could be worse. At least she was alive. And where there was life, there was hope.

Brandy's spirits came bounding back. She'd be damned if she'd spend the rest of her life in some miserable Indian village at the end of the earth among a bunch of ignorant savages! she thought furiously. Nor would she wait to be rescued, for that would probably never happen. No, she'd find a way to escape, she vowed fervently, some way to get back to her people.

Some way—come hell or high water!

2

As they left the scene of the massacre behind them and rode down the gentle roll of the ridge beside the trail, Flaming Arrow sensed a change in Brandy. She had been very quiet since they had begun their journey, and he'd hoped that he had finally subdued her so that she wouldn't give him any more problems. But when she suddenly stiffened in the saddle and he could see the determined set of her chin, he knew she was far from beaten. He feared it boded no good for him. If he was going to have to take a hostage back to his village, why couldn't he have found a meek, frightened woman who would obey him without question? It would have certainly made things much easier. He had never dreamed a white woman or any woman could be so strong-willed or outspoken. Women were supposed to be retiring, gentle, soft-spoken, docile. It was their nature, just as it was men's nature to be warlike and aggressive. He had a strong feeling that he was going to rue the day he had investigated the smoke and found the white woman. He was already wishing he had ignored it. But that would have gone against his nature, to say nothing of the dictates of his position. As the raiding party's leader, it was his responsibility to see not only to getting the captured herd back to his tribe but to the safety of the men under him. What if the smoke had come from a prairie fire, and they had ridden right into it? No, he had only done what duty had demanded of him—first investigated, then taken the woman with him to keep her from talking. Where he'd made his mistake was in identifying himself as a Lakota. At the moment he had done so, she had looked so terrified that he'd wanted to reassure her. Why he'd had such a strange urge was beyond him. Why should he have cared if she was frightened or not? But he did know he had put himself in a bad situation. What was he going to do with the woman when they reached his village?

There were other options, Flaming Arrow admitted. He could kill her at any time or turn her loose once his party had put a safe distance between them and the horse soldiers. That would seal her death just as surely as if he had done the deed himself. As a white woman, she would never survive in the wilderness. But Flaming Arrow found he could do neither, although he was considered one of the fiercest warriors in his tribe. Killing a woman was beneath him, a cowardly act to which he could never sink.

Flaming Arrow was roused from his thoughts by a wisp of hair that had escaped the hairnet at the back

of Brandy's head. The chestnut tendril was blown by
the wind and lightly trailed across his face. He had
never felt anything so soft and sat perfectly still for a
moment to enjoy the small pleasure. Then he became aware of something else. Brandy's scent drifted
up to him, but it wasn't the remnants of the violet
cologne that Brandy had used that morning that tan-
talized his senses. Rather, it was the exciting womanly essence beneath it.

Once Flaming Arrow became aware of her nearness, everything about her seemed to attack his
senses. He became acutely conscious of the brush of
her back against his chest with every step his horse
took and of the press of her shoulders against his
naked arm as he held his reins before them. But the
softness of her rounded buttocks pressing against his
manhood where she was practically sitting on his lap
became an agony for him. He had to clench his teeth
and exercise all his considerable willpower to keep
his body from responding to that tantalizing stimu-
lus.

Brandy, too, had become uncomfortably aware of
Flaming Arrow's nearness. Just as her feminine softness and sweetness were tormenting him, she had
never been so conscious of a man's body, a body that
was all hard muscle. Every place they touched
seemed to burn right through their clothing, and the
aura of sheer maleness about him seemed to be suffo-
cating. If the saddle had allowed her to, she would
have tried to put distance between them; but it was
even smaller than the saddle the cavalry rode, which
the newspapers had jokingly compared to the size of
a postage stamp. Since there was no place she could
go, she tried to focus her mind on something else. She

concentrated on the Lakota's long, slender hands holding the reins in front of her, but that was another mistake. Before she realized what a dangerous turn her mind was taking, she found herself wondering what they would feel like touching her. No, not touching her, she corrected, allowing her fantasy to go a little farther. He was already inadvertently doing that with other parts of his body. She wondered what it would be like to have him deliberately caress her, stroke her naked flesh, touch her in the most intimate places. A thrill shot through her, and scalding heat filled her.

What was she doing? Brandy wondered, shocked by her own indecent thoughts. She admitted to having a certain curiosity about men—that was why she had stared so long at the silly fig leaf on the marble statue of the Greek god—she had wondered just what great mystery it was hiding. And lying in her bed at night, she had speculated on what the marriage act might involve. She had been wooed enough to know it involved some touching. One or two of her braver suitors had been bold enough to try to touch her breasts. But their caresses had done nothing to her except to leave her feeling revolted. But the thought of this savage caressing her made her heart race and her skin burn all over. Did he possess some dark power? Were Indians devil-worshipers?

While Brandy was thinking her wild thoughts, Flaming Arrow decided to put an end to his agony. He nudged his mount to a hard gallop. Brandy fervently welcomed the distraction, for it took all of her concentration to hold on to the edge of saddle with her tied hands, and the beating her bottom took from Flaming Arrow's hard, muscular thighs was anything but sensuous. Within minutes they came in sight of the Dakota raiding party and their herd of captured ponies. Flaming Arrow slowed his mount, and they rode up to several of his men sitting on their horses in the center of the herd. Brandy looked about her in wonder. She had never seen so many horses in her life. Why, there had to be at least a thousand, and the majority were pintos.

Then Brandy became aware that the Dakotas in Flaming Arrow's party were looking at her intently. Several other warriors rode up from the fringes of the herd, and they, too, stared. It was nerve-wracking to have nine fierce-looking, painted, black-eyed Indians stare at her. She wondered what they were thinking or, worse, what they were planning. The Lakota sitting behind her had told her he wouldn't kill her, but that didn't mean they wouldn't torture her or ravish her. Brandy's busy mind paused. Ravish her? What in the world did it mean? All she knew was that it was something men did to women that was terrible. Damn! Why hadn't she insisted that Paul tell her what it meant, instead of letting him tiptoe around it like everyone else did? He was usually so open with her, since they were very close. Why hadn't she taken the time to at least look it up in the dictionary? Anything was better than the unknown!

Suddenly a bloodcurdling cry rent the air, and the sharp, unexpected sound made Brandy jump. Then she froze in fear as one of the warriors jerked his knife from its leather scabbard and raced his horse toward her and Flaming Arrow. The long blade gleamed in the sunlight, where he held it poised above him for the kill. Brandy knew with certainty that that knife was meant for her. She saw murder in the man's eyes.

"Stop!" Flaming Arrow called out in his tongue, then seeing the warrior had no intention of obeying him, he jumped from his mount and ran to meet the man and his horse. As the enraged warrior's pony raced by him, Flaming Arrow reached up, caught the man's other arm, and jerked him from his mount. There was a brief scuffle, then Flaming Arrow forced the man to his knees. He twisted the man's arm behind his back and told him to drop the knife he still clutched in his other hand. For a moment it looked as if the warrior were going to refuse—his dark, hate-filled eyes were locked on Brandy. Only when Flaming Arrow increased the pressure on the man's arm, almost breaking it, did the brave finally relent and drop the weapon.

Brandy was trembling from her near brush with death. Flaming Arrow pushed the warrior to the ground and said angrily in his tongue, "You are a disgrace to this party! Only cowards kill women."

"She is a white-eyes," the man answered.

"She is a woman, and she is *my* prisoner," Flaming Arrow turned and looked at the men who had crowded around, and he said, "You are being fore-warned. If any one of you makes any attempt on this woman's life, I will personally kill you. I have given her my word on this."

The man whom Flaming Arrow had thrown to the ground rose to his feet and said, "Then let us rape her, as the horse soldiers did my wife before they killed her."

Flaming Arrow's anger was replaced with compassion. He knew why Red Hand had wanted to kill the white woman. Red Hand was a Southern Cheyenne. Horse soldiers had mistaken his village for a Kiowa village and attacked it—Kiowa warriors had killed several white people in a raid shortly before. Red Hand and most of the warriors had been away hunting at the time of the attack. Only old men, women, and children had been present. The entire village had been obliterated in a frenzy of blind hatred—the women raped, all the dead Indians' bodies defiled in some manner. By the time the Cheyenne warriors returned, the white-eyes' bloodlust and senseless killing had been spent and the officers were once again in control of their emotions and their men. They had captured the returning braves while they were still in shock and then placed them on a reservation in an area so dry and desolate that only snakes and lizards could survive. Red Hand and some of the other warriors had escaped and come north to live with the Northern Cheyenne and Dakotas, but they still burned for revenge. Flaming Arrow could well understand, but he could not—would not—allow his men to rape the white woman. Even though it was a common, accepted practice among the plains tribes, done, just as the white men had done, to punish and degrade, Flaming Arrow personally thought it as cowardly as killing the woman.

She was not the enemy. Women did not make war. For the men to take their anger and hatred out on her was unjust. Besides, he knew the white woman thought he had meant he would not harm her when he had said he would not kill her. She had said as much. And by not correcting her, he had given his promise on that as well. He would still be breaking his word if he let them harm her. "No, you cannot rape her, or harm her in any way. I have put her under my protection."

"You took her to warm your pallet, to ease your loins?" Red Hand asked with a sneer.

Flaming Arrow stiffened, and the look that came into his black eyes made shivers run up the spines of the Indians who had dismounted and were watching the confrontation. Red Hand was a fool to challenge Flaming Arrow on anything, they all thought. Did the Cheyenne not realize that Flaming Arrow was one of the most respected and feared warriors in their tribe, a man who was surely destined to become a great war chief because of his leadership qualities, fierceness, courage, and fighting skills? They watched with bated breath.

Flaming Arrow fought back the anger that was surging to the fore and answered in a hard voice, "It is not your place to ask why I brought her with me. I am the leader of this party. No one questions me or my authority. But nevertheless, I will tell you. I did not bring her with me because I wanted to. She was with a group of horse soldiers who were all annihilated by a war party of Kiowas. He who goes before us saw smoke—it was from their wagons burning. The woman survived because she had hid in some bushes. She knows we are a Lakota raiding party. I brought her with me to keep her from telling the horse soldiers who will come to investigate when the others do not arrive as expected. It would have been too dangerous to leave her behind."

No one asked Flaming Arrow how the white woman knew who they were—either because it never occurred to them, or because they didn't dare. But Red Hand still lusted for revenge. His eyes glit-

tered as he said in an excited voice, "Then we will
attack the soldiers when they come to investigate."

"We will *not* attack the soldiers," Flaming Arrow
answered in a firm voice. "We are a raiding party, not
a war party. The horses we have captured are important to our tribe."

"We can leave them here with one or two of our
men while we attack."

"Are you insane? There are only ten of us, and only
five carry rifles. The horse soldiers will be at least a
hundred, and they will be well armed. They will not
be caught off guard like the others. They might even
bring one of the guns that sounds like the wood-
pecker and spits bullets like lightning."

At the mention of the Gatling gun, the Dakotas
nodded their heads in approval of Flaming Arrow's
prudent decision. The Indians were helpless against
the white man's awesome, superior weapon, which
could cut them down like grass beneath the hooves of
a stampeding buffalo herd. Only Red Hand was not
satisfied by Flaming Arrow's wise logic. He swooped
up his knife where it lay in the grass, assumed a
fighting stance, and said to Flaming Arrow, "I think
you refuse because you are a coward."

Every Lakota watching sucked in his breath
sharply and waited, expecting Flaming Arrow to accept the challenge and draw his knife. Flaming Arrow stared at Red Hand, an inscrutable expression on
his face, as a minute ticked by, a length of time that
seemed an eternity to everyone, including Red
Hand, who was beginning to regret his recklessness.
Finally Flaming Arrow spoke. "And I think you are a
fool to think you can goad me into a fight with you or
into rashly attacking the horse soldiers when I know

it would be suicide. No. We came to capture horses. Nothing else! The day will come when we will fight the horse soldiers, and you will have your revenge, Red Hand. But this is not the day."

Flaming Arrow deliberately turned his back on Red Hand, proving without a doubt that he had no fear of him, and he said to the other men, "We have lost enough time. Mount up!"

Flaming Arrow's command came with such authority that every man, including Red Hand, who was beginning to look a little sheepish, scurried to obey.

As the others rode off to take up their positions, Flaming Arrow walked into the herd, caught a sorrel stallion by its mane, and led it over to where Brandy was sitting on his horse. He yanked another length of rawhide from his saddle, fashioned a loop in the center, which he slipped over the horse's lower jaw, and tossed the two free ends—his reins—over the animal's neck. Brandy might have found the procedure interesting had she not still felt shaky after the Indians' attack and the confrontation between Red Hand and Flaming Arrow, for she sensed she would be in great danger if anything happened to Flaming Arrow.

Flaming Arrow saw Brandy's ashen face and knew she was frightened, but he gave no hint of it. He himself had mixed feelings about her, feeling both compassion and resentment that she had put him in the position in which he found himself now. Of all the parties he had led, his authority and decisions had never been questioned before today—and it had started because he was trying to protect her, a white woman, no less. Yes, he knew he was going to regret bringing her with him.

Flaming Arrow flew to the back of the stallion, slipped the reins over the head of the horse Brandy was sitting on, and galloped off without so much as a glance or word to her. As they rode to the front of the herd, scattering horses from their path in all directions, Brandy came to her senses and called out, "Wait! Aren't you going to untie me?"

"No," Flaming Arrow called back.

"Why not?"

"I told you before, I do not trust you."

"But I don't even have a horn to hold on to. I might fall."

"You can't fall. Your legs are tied, remember?"

As if she could forget, Brandy thought bitterly, and gritted her teeth. With her feet tied together, the insides of her legs were being rubbed with every jogging gait the horse took. She couldn't even lift them and give herself temporary relief; her bottom stung each time she bounced on the lumpy, grass-filled saddle. She was miserable, and it was all because of the man riding before her, the brute who had overpowered her and taken her prisoner. She glared at his back with impotent fury.

That was only the beginning of what turned out to be a long, excruciating day for Brandy. They rode over the prairie through what seemed an endless sea of grass for hours and hours and hours. The only trees in sight were those in the distance that lined what she knew was the North Platte. Brandy was amazed at the endurance of the little Indian pony she was riding, for no thoroughbred could have maintained that grueling speed for so long. The remarkable animal even seemed impervious to the sun beating down on them.

Brandy wasn't impervious. Her hair was plastered to her head with sweat, and her clothing was wringing wet. Her sunburned face stung like fire, and every muscle in her body ached, for although she was a fairly accomplished rider, she had never ridden so long or so hard, and certainly not astride. The rawhide around her wrists had rubbed them raw, and it seemed that no part of her body didn't hurt. Her throat ached from thirst, and her lips were so dry, they were cracked. Her head was throbbing from the almost deafening pounding of the herd's hooves all around her. She prayed for darkness to come and the agony to end. But when the sun did finally go down, Flaming Arrow kept going, racing through the night into the early hours of the morning.

By the time Flaming Arrow did halt, Brandy was so exhausted she was numb all over. He walked up to her and found her slumped in her saddle and staring out into space as if in a trance. He was shocked by her condition. He had deliberately driven the herd and his men hard and long to get them as far away from the scene of the attack as possible. The few times he had glanced over his shoulder to see how the white woman was doing, she hadn't appeared to be faring too badly since she could glare at him as angrily as she had. But he hadn't had a good look at her for some time, despite his exceptionally keen night vision. Feeling a twinge of guilt, he quickly untied her legs and wrists and lifted her to the ground. Then he took his water skin from the back of the saddle, and he cradled her shoulders in his arms and lifted it to her lips.

Most of the cool water ran down Brandy's neck and chest. It took her a moment to orient herself and figure out who was holding her. Then, realizing he was offering her the water she had been dying to have for hours, she took a few painful swallows, then spat, "You bastard! If you were going to kill me, why didn't you just get it over with when I asked you to?"

Her words sounded more like the croaking of a frog than a woman's voice, but Flaming Arrow understood. From the corner of his eye, he saw the balled-up hand coming at him, but Brandy's fist never made contact. In midflight, she fell into an utterly exhausted sleep, and the arm fell limply to the ground.

Flaming Arrow lowered Brandy to the ground, stood, and relieved the horse she had been riding of its saddle and reins. Only then did the well-trained animal move away a few feet to munch on the grass. Lowering himself and sitting on his heels, Flaming Arrow pulled a piece of jerky from a leather pouch tied to his saddle and ate it, alternating bites of the hard, dried meat with gulps of water as he stared thoughtfully at the woman lying beside him. As exhausted as she was, she had found the strength to curse him and try to hit him. This amazed him. He glanced at her hand and saw it was still clutched in a fist. Even asleep, she was defiant. Despite himself, Flaming Arrow smiled, and he had to admit to a certain grudging admiration for her spirit.

Placing his water skin to the side, Flaming Arrow lay down on the hard ground beside Brandy, without benefit of even a blanket to keep off the dew. So did his men scattered amongst the grazing herd. It was as it had always been for the bronzed plains raiders. The grass was their pallet, and the dark, star-studded sky their only cover.

3

Brandy was awakened the next morning when Flaming Arrow nudged her shoulder with the toe of his moccasin. She opened her eyes and saw him standing above her.

"Get up!" Flaming Arrow commanded. "We will be leaving shortly."

Brandy looked around her groggily but quickly regretted it. Even that slight movement had made a sharp pain shoot up her neck. And she saw that the sun hadn't even risen yet. In the predawn light, only a pearlized glow lined the eastern horizon. "Are you crazy? It isn't even morning!" she objected. "No one gets up at this ungodly hour."

Flaming Arrow crouched beside her, looked her straight in the eye, and said in a firm voice, "Let us get something straight between us. I did not bring you along with me because I wanted to. I brought you because I *had* to. I will not have a weak white woman slowing us down. Now, get up!" Flaming Arrow rose and motioned to one side, saying, "There is a small stream over there where you can wash. But don't dally, and don't try to escape. I will be keeping an eye out for you."

Flaming Arrow turned and walked away, and Brandy glared at him until he was out of view. Her eyes moved as far to the corner as they could, but she didn't make another move. She had already learned how painful that could be. How dare he talk to her like that, with such a superior attitude! she fumed. And how dare he call her weak just because she was a white woman. The arrogant brute! She'd show him!

Although she was stiff all over and every muscle in her body screamed in protest, Brandy forced herself to rise and limp to the small stream. She furiously blinked back the tears that the movements brought her. When she reached the stream, she managed to kneel and splash a few handfuls of water on her face, but any further attempt at bathing was simply beyond her.

As Brandy walked back to the herd, she spied Flaming Arrow before he saw her and was thankful for it. She'd rather die than have him catch her limping. He'd call her weak again. It took every bit of willpower she had to straighten up and walk normally to her horse.

Flaming Arrow had already saddled her horse. As he handed her a piece of jerky, she looked at it in surprise and asked, "What am I supposed to do with this?"

"Eat it. It's dried meat, your breakfast."

"You mean we aren't going to build a fire and cook real food?"

"I said, that is your breakfast."

"But I haven't had a hot meal in twenty-four hours! I'm starving!"

A hard expression came over Flaming Arrow's face. "I told you I will not have you slowing us down. Nor will I make any special concessions for you. Indians do not pamper and spoil women. You will eat what we eat and sleep when we sleep."

Brandy was highly indignant. Now he was calling her spoiled as well as weak. "I've got a better idea!" she threw out angrily. "Why don't you just give me a horse and point me in the direction of Fort Fetterman? By the time I reach it, you'll be too far away for the soldiers to chase you. Then I won't be slowing you down!"

Flaming Arrow laughed and said, "That is the most ridiculous thing I have ever heard." He motioned to the south and said, "Look out there. Do you really think you could find Fort Fetterman in all that open space? It takes more than just pointing out the direction to find a place. You could miss the fort by fifty miles. Then you would get lost and wander around in the wilderness until you died of thirst or a wild animal killed you."

Brandy looked in the direction Flaming Arrow had motioned. There was nothing there as far as she could see but grass—not even a solitary tree. She glanced quickly around her and saw that even the Laramie Mountains, which had been in distance ever since she had left the fort named after them, had disappeared. She no longer had any landmarks by which to orient herself. Apparently they had ridden much farther than she had realized. What Flaming Arrow had said was true—she'd never find her way back without getting hopelessly lost. At least not from this point. If she tried to escape she would have to wait until she found a trail or river to follow, or something to guide her. But the fact that she couldn't possibly make it back by herself at the present time didn't lessen her anger at Flaming Arrow for insulting her. "So what do you care what happens to me?" she asked in a biting voice. "You'd be rid of me."

But Flaming Arrow did care. He didn't want the white woman's death on his conscience. "I do not wish to see you dead. If that is what I wanted, I would have killed you when I found you. No, you go with us." Seeing Brandy was about to object, he added, "And do not argue with me anymore. My mind is made up!"

Flaming Arrow turned and walked away, tossing over his shoulder, "Now eat your jerky and mount. We are leaving shortly."

Brandy was furious. If she'd had a knife at that moment, she would have gladly sunk it into Flaming Arrow's broad back. He complained about taking her with him, but he refused to let her go. Not for one minute did she believe that business about him not wanting to see her dead. He was just throwing his weight around again, being a big bully.

Brandy tossed the jerky to the ground and paced beside her horse. She toyed with the idea of disobeying Flaming Arrow's order to mount; the adrenaline her anger was pumping into her bloodstream made her completely forget how tired and sore she was. Then she remembered how quickly and efficiently the Dakota leader had handled her refusal the day before, and she admitted that defying him in that manner would be folly. And she'd be damned if she'd be humiliated by having him manhandle her in front of his men. Grumbling beneath her breath, she mounted, sucking in her breath sharply at the pain when she swung her leg over the horse's back.

Brandy had barely come to rest on the lumpy Indian saddle when Flaming Arrow rode up beside her. She had not seen him approach and was startled when he said, "I will not tie your hands and legs today since you seem to have learned your lesson."

"Oh?" Brandy asked haughtily. "What lesson was that?"

"Not to hit or kick me."

Brandy would have dearly loved to hit or kick Flaming Arrow, but to do so would cause herself more pain than him. She glared at him, and when he leaned over and picked up her horse's reins, she asked, "Aren't you going to let me guide my own horse?"

"No. I don't trust you not to try to escape."

"I thought we had already settled that, that it would be foolish of me to try to find my way back."

"It is settled in my mind, but I am not sure of yours. As impulsive as you are, you may change your mind."

There he went again, Brandy thought hotly, making assumptions about her. "And where did you get the idea I was impulsive?"

"Anyone who has not eaten for as long as you and does not know when they might eat again does not throw food away without first giving it serious thought. That was impulsive, if not simply foolish."

As Brandy opened her mouth, Flaming Arrow cut

off her words, saying, "No! We have wasted enough time talking. Now we ride!"

With that, Flaming Arrow galloped off, leading Brandy's horse behind him in what would be another long, grueling day. But Brandy discovered something that morning. She could actually doze in her saddle if she made a determined effort to block out the beating her bottom was taking, the sun blazing down on her, and her gnawing hunger. When they stopped at noon to change horses, she was tired, but not nearly as exhausted as she had been the night before. This time, she wasn't so foolish as to refuse the jerky Flaming Arrow offered her.

Flaming Arrow watched the white woman sitting on the ground hungrily chew the tough strip of meat. Her face was beet red, her hair wringing wet, and trails of sweat trickled down her temples and neck and disappeared beneath the V of her blouse. She had taken off her riding jacket in deference to the hot sun, but nothing else, and the worst heat of the day was still ahead of them. "You should strip off one of those skirts, and your leggins too," Flaming Arrow pointed out. "You are already burning up, and this afternoon will be even hotter. Why do you wear so many clothes, anyway? Our women wear leggins only in the winter, to give their legs extra protection from the cold."

"What are you talking about?" Brandy asked. "I'm not wearing any leggins."

Suddenly, it occurred to Brandy what garment Flaming Arrow meant. He must have seen the bottoms of her knee-length drawers when her skirt hiked up as she sat astride her horse. The other skirt he mentioned had to be her petticoat. "Oh, those aren't leggins. And that other skirt is a petticoat. They're both underwear—clothing that's not meant for outer wear."

"Then what purpose do they serve?"

"Purpose?"

"Yes, purpose. My people never do anything without reason, including what they wear. Things are worn either for protection from the elements or for decorative purposes."

"They're worn for the sake of modesty," Brandy answered, then added sarcastically, "but a savage like you wouldn't understand that."

There was just a brief flash in Flaming Arrow's dark eyes, then he answered in a tight voice, "Of course I understand modesty. Indians do not walk around naked. That is why we have our breechclouts. But what need do you have for a breechclout if you wear a long skirt? No one can see anything. That is why our women do not wear them. So how can you claim it is worn for modesty's sake?"

"Breechclout?" Brandy asked in astonishment. "What in the world makes you think I'm wearing one of those silly aprons?"

Flaming Arrow frowned, then asked, "Aprons?"

"Yes! That piece of material you're wearing at both the front and back. My people call them aprons. You talk about me wearing useless clothing. What purpose does that have?"

"It covers me." Flaming Arrow lifted the front flap of his breechclout, and Brandy realized that he wasn't wearing a pair of buckskin trousers beneath it. The rawhide leggins were just pieces of leather that fitted his legs and the sides of his hips. There was no front or back to them. They were held together by a thin strand of rawhide that tied at the front of his breechclout. For the life of her, Brandy couldn't help but stare at the strip of material that covered Flaming Arrow's loins. The fig leaf on the marble statue of the Greek god had teased her curiosity, but it had been a successful covering. Not so with the breechclout. It hung heavily between Flaming Arrow's thighs, and the material was stretched so tight that she could clearly see the bold outline of his manhood. Suddenly her heart raced wildly as a curious excitement filled her.

Brandy wasn't the only one affected by her avid staring. So was Flaming Arrow. In his tribe when a woman did that, it was an open invitation to join her in her pallet. Could the white woman possibly desire him? he wondered. He had to admit that despite all her faults, she was very beautiful. What would it be like with her? A sudden scalding heat flooded his lower pelvis.

Brandy saw the stirring of Flaming Arrow's manhood beneath the material and was frankly shocked and a bit frightened. She jerked her eyes away, and a belated flush of embarrassment rose on her face.

Keen disappointment filled Flaming Arrow. Was she truly embarrassed by her own boldness, or was she teasing him? He dropped the flap of his breechclout and said accusingly, "You were staring at my body again."

The flush on Brandy's face deepened, a heat that infuriated her. "I wasn't staring at your body. I was looking at the cloth. I expected you to be wearing buckskin trousers."

"Like the trappers and mountain men wear?"

"Yes."

Flaming Arrow's brow wrinkled as a sudden thought occurred to him. "Is that how your leggins are made, like the white men's buckskins?"

"If you mean are they sewed in the center, yes."

"Then take off the skirts and wear your leggins. Not only would it be cooler, but riding would be much easier without all of the material of your skirts bunched up around you."

Brandy was horrified. "Strip down to my drawers? Absolutely not!"

"Why not?"

"Because they're my underclothes. It's simply not done. Why, it's an outrageous suggestion!"

Flaming Arrow's dark eyes narrowed. "I think you are just being stubborn."

"I'm being no such thing!" Brandy answered hotly. "We shouldn't even be discussing my underwear."

"Why not?"

"Because it's highly improper. Respectable men and women never mention something as personal as their underclothes."

Flaming Arrow laughed and answered, "That is silly. They are nothing but clothes—stupid clothes at that."

Brandy flew to her feet. "I don't give a damn what you think of them! And as far as I'm concerned, the subject is closed."

"No, the subject is not closed," Flaming Arrow answered in a hard voice. "You will remove those skirts. I will not risk your getting ill from overheating."

"Because I'll slow you down?" Brandy asked in a voice dripping with resentment.

"Yes."

"I didn't get ill yesterday," Brandy pointed out.

"You are in more danger today. You lost salt both yesterday and this morning. Look at you. You are soaking wet. You have never been in the wide open in the sun for this long. It can not only make you ill, it can kill. Now, take off those skirts."

Flaming Arrow's logic had no effect on Brandy. All she heard was his commanding tone of voice, a tone she felt bespoke of his bullying arrogance. Her refusal was no longer a matter of modesty. She wasn't worried about being seen in the serviceable heavy cotton drawers that she had chosen especially for this trip, since she'd known she would be doing a lot of riding. No, It had become a matter of refusing to be dominated by the tall, infuriating warrior standing before her.

Flaming Arrow saw the defiance in Brandy's eyes before she even opened her mouth or made a move, and he knew she was going to resist. With a swiftness that stunned her, he caught her arm in one hand and the skirt in the other; then with a swift, powerful yank, he ripped the garment from her.

Brandy came alive with fury. She kicked and swung her free arm wildly, but Flaming Arrow had been expecting her retaliation, ducked her flying fist, and sidestepped her feet with a calm deftness that angered her all the more. The ripped skirt was joined by the petticoat. For a moment, Brandy continued to struggle, but a glance at the shredded garments at her feet made her realize that any further resistance was pointless. "You savage bastard! Someday you'll pay for this. I swear you will!"

"I am only doing what is best."

"For me? The devil you are! You don't give a damn about me! All you care about is proving how strong you are, how you can force me to do what you say with your superior strength."

"If I could reason with you, I would, but you are totally unreasonable and unbelievably stubborn. Therefore, I do what I have to do. Now, get on your horse! We are leaving."

Flaming Arrow whirled around, caught the mane of his mount, and flew onto the stallion's back in an effortless movement as graceful as a ballet dancer's. It served only to increase Brandy's resentment of him. Then he sat with an inscrutable expression on his face, waiting for her to obey.

Brandy would have loved to refuse, but she knew it was pointless. Resistance accomplished nothing with this man. And to think he had the audacity to call her unreasonable and stubborn! she fumed. Why, he was the most unyielding, infuriating man she had ever had the misfortune to meet!

Rigid with anger, Brandy turned and walked to her horse, looking not in the least defeated. Watching her, Flaming Arrow again marveled at her perverse nature. She was the most hostile woman he had ever met, fighting him at every turn. He had an unsettling feeling that he was winning only skirmishes, and he feared it might be a long, tiring war.

He wondered if the white-eyes was worth the effort of saving. Perhaps it would be best to leave her on the wide-open prairie to meet her fate, for there was no doubt in his mind that she would keep his household in a state of constant turmoil. But to waste such vast beauty and such spirit—as exasperating as it could be—went not only against his personal convictions but would be a crime against nature, something that the Dakotas took very seriously. For that reason even the most ferocious animal was spared if at all possible. And he couldn't deny that she was beautiful and very desirable. His treacherous body was constantly reminding him of that.

Flaming Arrow briefly considered what it would be like to make love to her, if somehow, in some way, they could set their differences aside and meet in common passion. Would he discover that she had been worth saving? It was such a tantalizing thought that it made his powerful muscles tremble.

But Flaming Arrow was a realist at heart. It wasn't within his nature to entertain sensual fantasies. He knew passion was a shallow emotion, that once it was spent there was often nothing else there, that it did nothing to satisfy the soul. And undoubtedly that would be the case with the white-eyes as well. It would be a purely physical experience that left him feeling somehow cheated and wishing he hadn't succumbed to his baser instincts. Then he would only end up being sorry.

With that disappointing thought still on his mind, Flaming Arrow turned his horse and rode off.

Brandy's anger at Flaming Arrow
kept her adrenaline flowing and her dress kept her
cooler, so Brandy fared better that afternoon than
she had the day before. But she was still grateful
when the Dakota leader called a halt at sundown.
Wearily, she dismounted and walked gingerly a short
distance away from the herd. There she paced, trying to walk the stiffness out of her legs and longing to
give her numb buttocks a brisk rubbing.

Then Flaming Arrow strode toward her, and she
felt a strong twinge of pique, for he didn't look the
least tired, or sore, or hot, and he had been riding
bareback, no less. He stopped in his tracks and looked
at her. Brandy thought he must be staring at her
sweat-stained blouse, her dusty knee-length drawers,
and her high riding boots. Her hair hung about her
sunburned face and down her back in long, unruly

strands, for somewhere along the way, she had lost her hairnet. She knew she looked a sight, but he didn't have to remind her of it. The rude bastard! She drew herself up to her full height and stared back, her eyes glittering with resentment.

But Flaming Arrow wasn't thinking how badly Brandy looked. He was staring at the way the setting sun behind her picked up the reddish highlights of her hair, making her face look as if it were surrounded by a fiery halo. Even when he saw her blue eyes flashing, it did nothing to break the spell. If anything, it only made her appear more beautiful. His gaze dropped to sweep over her body, noting that the damp, limp clothing clung to every luscious curve like a second skin. Then realizing that he was gaping like a moon-struck adolescent, Flaming Arrow came to his senses, jerked his eyes away, and said tersely, "You can rest over there away from the herd."

Brandy heard the hard edge to Flaming Arrow's voice. Having no idea that it was from anger at himself for being so susceptible to her beauty, she assumed he was just being bossy again. She gave him a withering glance, then looked in the direction he had motioned. Her eyes widened in surprise, for she hadn't even noticed the trees in the distance when they rode up. Knowing that there must be a stream nearby where she could wash up, she hurried away without giving Flaming Arrow a backward glance.

She found the narrow, shallow stream nestled among rustling cottonwoods that lined each bank. After the heat of the afternoon, it was like finding a treasure. She bathed her face and arms in the cool water, then yanked off her boots and socks and waded in until the bottoms of her drawers were wet. She was sorely tempted to dunk herself in the stream but knew it would be foolish to reveal herself to the Indians' eyes, for wet, the white material of her blouse and drawers would conceal nothing. Damn that domineering brute! she thought angrily. If he hadn't ripped off her skirt and petticoat, she could have bathed with her clothing on and still maintained her modesty.

Muttering darkly beneath her breath, she waded from the stream and sat beneath one of the trees, watching as several of the Indians gathered wood and started a fire. Soon a dozen sage hens were roasting over the flames, and the tempting aroma of cooking meat filled the air. But despite how hungry she was, Brandy was too tired to stay awake until the hens had finished cooking. She dozed off where she sat leaning against the trunk of a tree.

Feeling a hand gently shaking her shoulder, she opened her eyes. Flaming Arrow was crouched beside her.

"I brought you something to eat," he said, holding out half a roasted hen.

Brandy hated to accept anything from the domineering savage, but the tantalizing smell of the food was too much for her. She took the meat and ate it hungrily, not caring in the least that she had no plate or eating utensils, or that Flaming Arrow had touched it with his bare hands.

Flaming Arrow had fulfilled his obligations to his captive in bringing her food. There was really no reason for him to stay by her side. But he found he didn't want to leave. He sat down across from her and watched as she ate; then as she tossed the bones away and wiped her hands on the tail of her blouse, he asked, "What is your name?"

"I hardly see what that matters!" Brandy answered tartly.

There was a pregnant pause before Flaming Arrow replied, "I asked you a simple question, and I expect an answer."

"And if I refuse to answer?" Brandy asked with a defiant glitter in her eyes.

Why did she have to make a battle out of everything? Flaming Arrow thought in exasperation. "Your defiance is beginning to get tedious."

Brandy gave a haughty flip of her head and turned it away from him.

Flaming Arrow reached out and caught her chin, forcing her to turn her head to face him again. "I am not accustomed to having my questions ignored. You will answer, or else. Now, what is your name?"

Flaming Arrow's voice was soft, but the steel in his words and the determined look in his eyes made Brandy reconsider. Or else what? she wondered. Would he torture her? Surely he wouldn't go that far. He hadn't really harmed her. Not so far.

"If you do not tell me your name, I will be forced to call you *winw*. That means 'captive woman' in my tongue."

Brandy liked neither the harsh sound of the word or its reminder of her predicament and reluctantly relented. "It's—it's Brandy," she answered with a surly tone of voice and a look that could kill. "Brandy Daniels."

Flaming Arrow had never been able to understand why whites used both a first name and a surname. One name was sufficient and served its purpose. But it really didn't matter. Neither word meant anything to him. He dropped his hand from her chin and remarked, "Crooked Nose, the trapper who spent his winters with us, told me that the white-eyes use names that have no meaning. It seems a strange custom. Even the baby names my people use have some meaning, if only to signify the first thing the mother sees after she gives birth."

"But my first name does have a meaning," Brandy informed him. "It's the name of a liquor made from fermented grape juice."

"You were named after firewater?"

Brandy wrinkled her nose in distaste. "Well, not exactly. Brandy and firewater aren't the same. Brandy is made from wine. It's much more sophisticated."

"And what does that word mean? 'Sophisticated'?"

Brandy quickly searched for an explanation and, for lack of a better definition, answered, "It means uncommon . . . refined." Seeing Flaming Arrow frown, she added, "It doesn't matter what it means. That's not why my father named me Brandy. It was because the color of my hair reminded him of its color."

"Ah," Flaming Arrow said, finally understanding, "you were not named after firewater because of the way it burns one's throat and stomach, but because your hair is the color of fire." He glanced up at Brandy's hair and remembered what it had looked like in the sunset. Then he nodded in approval and said, "Yes, you were well named."

Brandy had mixed emotions about her name. She liked it because it was unusual, but she didn't particularly fancy her red hair. Red was such a vulgar color.

She much preferred to think of her hair as more brown.

"Brandy."

As Flaming Arrow softly tested the word, a shiver ran through Brandy. With his deep, masculine voice, the word took on a sensuous sound. It was almost as if he had reached out and caressed her. She was feeling stunned when Flaming Arrow asked, "Where are you from?"

"From a place I'm sure you've never heard of. St. Louis."

"I've heard of St. Louis. That is where Crooked Nose took his furs to sell. He said it sits just below where the Big Muddy and the Father of the Waters join."

Brandy didn't have to ask what "Big Muddy" and "Father of the Waters" meant. Everyone in St. Louis knew those names, for the trappers were as likely to call the Missouri River the Big Muddy and the Mississippi River the Father of the Waters as the Indians. Hearing the familiar sectional names brought on a wave of homesickness

"You said you have a brother at Fort Fetterman and he is expecting you?" Flaming Arrow asked, breaking into her thoughts.

"Yes, he's a captain."

"Why did he allow you to come out here when it is so dangerous?"

"He didn't feel it *was* dangerous," Brandy answered, highly resenting Flaming Arrow's criticism of her brother. "Nor did his commanding officer. There have been no Indian uprisings to speak of. They thought I'd be perfectly safe since I was being

accompanied by soldiers. And of course the fort itself
is a bastion."

Flaming Arrow bit back a scoff. The Dakotas had
forced the horse soldiers from their forts on the Boze-
man Trail in Red Cloud's war. The outposts were not
as invincible as Brandy thought. But he didn't bother
to correct her or remind her that she had narrowly
escaped being killed by Indians and was now in the
hands of one. Flaming Arrow thought it should be
quite obvious to the white woman that her brother
and his commanding officer were both grossly mistaken about there not being any danger. Flaming
Arrow shook his head in disgust. He could not understand the white-eyes. No Indian would endanger his
women and children by placing them so close to the
enemy. That was one reason they had retreated before the white tide, to protect their families. Yet the
officers brought their loved ones with them and allowed visits from other relatives. In Flaming Arrow's
opinion they were not only foolish but incredibly
stupid.

While Flaming Arrow pondered these thoughts,
Brandy had been thinking that he looked both dangerous and ruggedly handsome. The firelight played
over his strong painted features and brought out the
luster of his black hair. Not even the feathers attached to his braided scalp lock detracted from his
masculine appeal. Briefly, she wondered why she
had never met a white man who attracted her the
way this man did. Just sitting close to him made tingles run up and down her spine, and despite her
anger at his arrogance and domineering attitude, she
was filled with curiosity about him. "What is your
name?"

"Flaming Arrow."

"And does it have a special meaning?"

"Yes, it is the name I took when I returned to my village after seeking my vision."

Brandy frowned, then asked, "Vision? What does that mean?"

"It is the Dakotas' way of responding to the call of the Mystery."

"Mystery?"

"The Great Spirit."

"I still don't understand."

"A youth goes into the wilderness where he fasts and prays for four days and nights, waiting for his vision to come. From it, he will know what his power is, his special wisdom, his protection. Many times he will receive predictions of his future."

Brandy was skeptical. It sounded like a bunch of hocus-pocus to her. "And what if he doesn't have a vision? Does he make one up?"

A shocked expression came over Flaming Arrow's face. "No! Never! If he does not have a vision, he has to buy someone else's. But it never has the power that his own vision would bring."

Brandy might have scoffed at the idea of buying someone's vision, but Flaming Arrow seemed so deadly serious and sincere about his beliefs that she couldn't belittle them. "And so your vision was a flaming arrow?"

"Yes."

Flaming Arrow stared into space as he recalled the day he had stood on the ledge of the mountain cliff where he had gone to seek his vision. It had been winter and he had not been allowed a fire, but he'd worn only his breechclout and had been painted with white clay, which symbolized purity. He had fasted and prayed for three nights and three days, terrorized off and on by a pack of hungry wolves—for he had been allowed no weapons other than stones that happened to be lying nearby—and had begun to despair of having a vision. Then he had seen a dark cloud laced with bolts of jagged lightning, from which a flaming arrow emerged and streaked across the sky. At the time he had been disappointed. He had hoped his vision would be of some animal whose cunning or strength or courage he could exemplify: an eagle, or wolf, or better yet, the all-powerful buffalo. He'd had to seek the aid of one of the medicine men to interpret his vision, for he had no idea what attributes an arrow possessed or how to mimic one. Since the arrow had been a fire arrow, an instrument of war, the medicine man had assumed that it meant he was destined to become a great warrior, and since that day Flaming Arrow had strived to fulfill what the Great Spirit had planned for him, volunteering for every war party, raid, and dangerous mission he could and constantly honing his fighting skills and horsemanship.

There were many who thought Flaming Arrow had already been successful in his endeavor. Because of his acts of courage and bravery during Red Cloud's war on the white-eyes and the raids on the camps of his Indian enemies, he had already earned enough feathers for a war bonnet and was one of the few warriors allowed to wear the coveted buffalo horn bonnet. Even Chief Crazy Horse, respected by all the Dakota tribes as one of their greatest war chiefs, singled Flaming Arrow out by choosing him to lead the most dangerous raids. But Flaming Arrow thought differently. He sensed that his greatest test was yet to come and that there was much more to his vision than had met the eye.

"And how old were you when you sought your vision?" Brandy asked, breaking into Flaming Arrow's thoughts.

"Nine winters."

"Nine?" Brandy asked in shocked disbelief. "Why, you were just a child!"

"Perhaps a white man would still be a child, but not a Dakota. It is at that age that we throw off our baby names and baby ways and enter our manhood."

Flaming Arrow gazed off into space, deep in thought about the true meaning of his vision. It was a puzzle that he often contemplated but had never truly grasped. He had even repeated his spiritual ordeal several times, hoping to gain more insight into his dream, but it had always been the same, and Flaming Arrow had always been left with the strong feeling that the vision was incomplete.

Brandy watched Flaming Arrow as he gazed off, looking as if he had forgotten she existed. His ignoring her both disappointed and piqued her. She was accustomed to having men fawn over her, and she had secretly hoped when he asked so many questions that he might be taking more of a personal interest in her. She wondered how old he was. Probably in his midtwenties, about the same age as her brother; yet the Dakota leader seemed much more self-confident and self-reliant. Nor did her brother possess the same aura of command and quiet authority that Flaming Arrow did even though Paul was an officer and leader of men. No, the Dakota seemed much more mature than Paul. Flaming Arrow seemed more sea-

soned, more experienced, wiser. Was it because Indians assumed the responsibilities of manhood much
earlier in life? But the other Indians in the raiding
party hadn't impressed her. She was forced to admit
that Flaming Arrow was a cut above most other men,
white or red. And there was something else about
him, something subtle that she couldn't quite put her
finger on, something that she had not sensed in any
other man she had met. Then it came to her with the
suddenness of a thunderbolt. There was about Flaming Arrow a hint of greatness.

It was a profound thought, particularly since
Brandy wasn't accustomed to deep thinking. Then
she scowled—she was allowing herself to become too
enthralled with her captor. Not only was she attracted to him physically, but she was admiring him
as a person. Why, it was unbelievable! He was still an
uncivilized savage and the most infuriating man she
had ever met—rude, uncaring, domineering.

In hopes of distracting herself from her unwanted
attraction toward Flaming Arrow, Brandy jerked her
eyes away from him and gazed back out at the Indians' camp. The Lakotas had finished eating and were
quietly talking among themselves. Several times that
night they had glanced in her direction, but their
looks were always quick and surreptitious, as they
had been ever since Flaming Arrow had protected
her from the irate Cheyenne's attack the day before.
She wondered if Flaming Arrow had ordered them
to keep their eyes to themselves, for they had certainly done enough staring at first. Why, even the
Indian who had threatened her seemed to be making
a point of ignoring her when he thought Flaming
Arrow might be watching, and his sneaking glances

seemed more resentful than hateful. Brandy wondered just what her relationship with Flaming Arrow really was. He protected her, provided her with a mount, fed her. Would she continue under his protection when they reached his village, or would she have to fend for herself? And how long would it be before she could get her bearings and attempt an escape? Was it true what her brother had said about Indian women, that they were crueler than the men and enjoyed torturing captives? A million similar questions came flooding in about her uncertain future, and for the first time since her capture, Brandy was beginning to feel real apprehension.

Flaming Arrow was still gazing off into space. "When will we arrive at your village?" she asked.

Flaming Arrow tore himself from his musings and answered, "The day after tomorrow."

"So—so soon?"

Flaming Arrow didn't think it was soon. They had been averaging a good sixty miles a day and had been in the saddle for over a week already. "Yes, we will be crossing the Powder River tomorrow morning. Then we will be in Dakota Country. From there, our summer camp is just a little over a day's ride." Watching the expression on Brandy's face, she did not look at all relieved to have the grueling trip soon over with, as he would have thought. He scowled and asked, "Is something bothering you?"

Brandy longed to ask what would happen to her when they reached the camp, but she couldn't summon the nerve. She'd die before she'd allow her arrogant captor to know she feared what lay ahead of her, that she not only needed his protection but wanted it. "No, I was just curious," she quickly fabricated.

Flaming Arrow's scowl deepened. He sensed she was lying. Then he said, "It is time to sleep. We will leave even earlier tomorrow."

As Flaming Arrow stretched his full length out on the ground beside her, Brandy asked in surprise, "You're going to sleep here? Beside me?"

"Yes. I slept beside you last night also."

Brandy didn't remember falling asleep the night before. Tonight, tingling sensations rushed over her at Flaming Arrow's nearness, for she could feel his heat, and her heart raced.

Flaming Arrow thought she was going to object. He would not tolerate that. It wasn't the admiring glances that the others had been casting in her direction when they didn't think he was watching that bothered him. He knew they wouldn't dare try anything with his captive, no matter how beautiful and desirable they might find her, so he didn't need to sleep beside her to protect her. No, Flaming Arrow thought Brandy meant to object because she considered herself so much above him, and that was something the proud warrior would not accept. "Do not argue with me. Lie down and sleep."

Flaming Arrow's sharp command broke the spell his nearness had woven, and Brandy's resentment at his dominating attitude surged to the fore. She shot him a cutting glance, then lay down, deliberately placing her back to him, her demeanor serving only to confirm Flaming Arrow's suspicions. He, too, rolled on his side, placing his back to her.

It was a long time before either slept; both seethed with anger at imagined slights. Brandy was the first to succumb to slumber, but without her skirt or petticoat or jacket, the damp night air was cool. Instinctively, she sought the warmth of Flaming Arrow's body, rolled over, and cuddled up to him.

Flaming Arrow sucked in his breath sharply as Brandy pressed her body against his back. Every soft, seductive curve seemed to burn a hole in his skin, and against his will, his manhood hardened and rose. Cursing himself for insisting upon sleeping next to her and Brandy for being so alluring, he started to rise, but then Brandy shivered, slipped an arm around his waist, and snuggled closer. Flaming Arrow realized Brandy was simply cold, and much to his disgust, he couldn't deny her the heat of his body. It was a concession—this caring for her comfort— that disturbed him as much as his unwanted physical attraction to her. There was no place for a woman— particularly a white captive—in his life. What had he gotten himself into? And more important, how was he going to get himself out of this awkward predicament?

5

The next morning the usual haze hung over the prairie, and about midmorning, after the sun had burned off the heavy dew, the raiding party crossed the Powder River. That wide waterway was much shallower than usual at this dry, hot time of the year. As her horse waded across the river, Brandy studied its course, wondering if she could use it as a guide to escape, until it dawned on her that the river didn't run east, the direction she needed to travel, but north.

Shortly thereafter, Brandy noticed a lofty range of mountains in the distance and wondered if they were the Rockies. If so, she had traveled much farther west than she had ever dreamed. That noon, when they stopped for a brief rest, she asked Flaming Arrow about the mountains.

"They're the Big Horn Mountains," he answered. "Our summer camp is in their foothills."

"What direction do they run?" Brandy asked, wondering if she could use the mountains as a reference point to aid her in her escape.

"They run north and south."

"And what's over there?" Brandy asked, pointing to the east.

"More prairie."

Brandy could see her questions were making Flaming Arrow suspicious. Not wanting him to know she was even considering trying to escape, she changed the subject. "I thought there were supposed to be big herds of buffalo out here, but I have yet to see one."

"They run more to the east of here, and the herds are not as big as they used to be before the white man came. When I was a child, it wasn't unusual for herds to stretch as far as the eye could see. But the white man came and killed them for their hides or for sport. Our Cheyenne brothers have told us of places to the south that are covered with bones of the buffalo your hunters killed at random and then left the meat to rot in the sun. Miles and miles of nothing but bleached bones. Now all the buffalo there are gone, and the Indians are forced to either starve or live on a reservation. That is why the Dakotas are so determined to keep this country free, so that the herds can be preserved. Without them, my people would cease to exist."

"You could always turn to farming, like the eastern tribes do."

"What eastern tribes? The few that are scattered on the miserable little pieces of land the whites do not want? They starve there too," Flaming Arrow answered, his voice heavy with bitterness. He gazed off to the east, then said, "A long time ago, the Allied Ones were an eastern nation. We were woodland Indians who lived in log lodges and raised corn and hunted game. But other tribes coveted our land. They forced us west to the land where the Father of the Waters begins, where we lived for a while. Eventually, because we were being pushed farther and farther west by both the Chippewas and the white man, the Dakotas split from the Santee and moved to these arid plains, a land that no one wanted. We survived because we learned how to hunt the buffalo, and it became our life. We no longer needed corn for food, or deer for clothing, or wood for shelter. Everything we needed came from the buffalo, and like them, we roamed free, free as the wind. That was our new way of life, and we became many and powerful. Then the white man came to this land too. At first he did not want the land itself, only to cross it. We gave him permission to build his trail and his forts to protect it. Then the iron horse came and with it towns and farmers, scaring away the buffalo. The whites wanted another trail, across the Powder River Country, and we refused. This was the only place left where the buffalo could still roam. But the whites tried to take it anyway, and we fought for it for two years and won. Red Cloud touched the pen at Fort Laramie in which your people agreed to abandon the new trail and its forts and to set aside all of the land west of the Big Muddy, including the Black Hills and the Powder River Country as Dakota Territory, as long as the buffalo roam, a land that was strictly forbidden to all whites. But Chief Crazy Horse, Sitting

Bull, Gall, Spotted Eagle, and other Dakota chiefs refused to sign. We have learned that treaties with your people are meaningless. You only make them to break them. No, we do not need a treaty to tell us this is our land. We took it from the Crow, and we will hold it. Nor will we return to our old way of life and become farmers. That life is behind us for good. We have fought for our land and our way of life, and no one shall take it away from us. No one!"

Flaming Arrow turned and walked away, leaving Brandy to reflect on his impassioned discourse. She knew that her government had made a treaty with the Sioux, but she had no idea it had involved so much land or what the terms had been. Her government had given the Sioux from the Missouri River to the Rockies? That was an awful lot of land. But she didn't doubt Flaming Arrow's words for one minute. Deep down, she knew he spoke the truth, that lying was beneath him. She recalled what he said about her people making treaties only to break them. But surely that couldn't be true, she thought, not if her brother had been sent into the Black Hills to remove those prospectors. No, the government was living up to their end of the bargain. Then, remembering something she had overheard while she was at Fort Laramie, she frowned. Something about the army escorting a geological party into the Black Hills. What would a group of geologists be going there for, Brandy wondered, unless it was to investigate the reports of gold being discovered? But what difference did it make to her government if there was gold of any appreciable amount there, if it was Indian land? Brandy felt a sinking feeling. As much as she hated to admit it, she thought she knew the answer to that question. If there was really gold there, if the land was valuable, her people would want it. Like it or not, Americans were a greedy bunch. Just look at the way they had swarmed into California, then Colorado, then the area around Virginia City when gold or silver had been discovered. They had been an unstoppable human tide and along with the prospectors had been the scum of the earth that preyed on them. Brandy strongly suspected her government's motives in exploring the Black Hills, and she feared that what might be in store for the Dakotas was another broken treaty. Despite the fact that she was being held against her will by an Indian, she felt a twinge of shame in her nation's behalf.

That afternoon, as they drew nearer and nearer to the Big Horn Mountains, the terrain changed from the monotonous flat prairie that Brandy had seen for the days on end since she had left Omaha to a gently rolling land covered with lush green grass and laced with crystal-clear streams. All around her were herds of grazing antelope and graceful pronghorns that scattered to the wind on their approach, racing away at an unbelievable speed. They passed through valleys wooded with aspen, cottonwood, willow, and chokecherry, where wild raspberries and plum and cherry trees grew beside the streams and white-tailed deer and elk watered. Brandy thought she had never seen such beautiful country, with the towering mountains hovering over all, and she watched in awe that evening as the sun set and turned the green hilltops to gold and cast long, melancholy shadows over the meadow where they had camped.

A hush fell as the sun sank below the horizon, and

it still prevailed when Flaming Arrow brought Brandy her evening meal, the hindquarter of a roasted rabbit. As he handed the still-steaming piece of meat to her, Brandy said, "I can understand now why your tribe treasures this land. It's really lovely."

Flaming Arrow looked around him in mute appreciation, then said, "It is not only for its beauty that we prize this country. It abounds with game."

"Yes, I noticed that too."

Brandy took the meat from him, and as he turned to walk away, she said, "Wait! I have something I want to ask you."

Flaming Arrow turned and waited patiently for Brandy to speak. Brandy fidgeted nervously with her meat, then asked, "Will we be reaching your village tomorrow?"

"Yes, at midday."

"Then aren't you close enough that you could send your men on without you?"

Flaming Arrow frowned, then asked, "Why would I do that?"

"You said you couldn't take me back to my people because you couldn't risk losing the herd. But those horses are perfectly safe now." Brandy saw the frown on Flaming Arrow's face deepen and hurried to say, "My father is a banker, a very wealthy man. He'll pay you very well for bringing me back."

"I have no use for your money."

Brandy hadn't really thought she could bribe Flaming Arrow with money, but she was desperate and would try anything. The more she thought of what might happen to her the next day when they arrived at the Indian camp, the more apprehensive she became, and she knew she was in no position to attempt an escape yet. "All right, so you don't want money. But you have no use for me either. I'll just be someone you'll have to feed, to look out for."

"No, it will not be as it has been on the trail once we reach my village. You will work for your keep."

"But I don't know how to work for my keep," Brandy answered, still hoping that she could reason with Flaming Arrow. "I've never worked a day in my life. Don't you see? I'm useless, I'm weak. I'd only be a hindrance to you." Brandy paused, giving Flaming Arrow time to consider her words, then said, "Take me back just as far as the fort! All you would have to do is put me on the road to it. By the time I got there, you'd have plenty of time to get away, particularly as skillful a rider as you are. You wouldn't really be in any danger, and you'd be getting rid of me."

Flaming Arrow was tempted—he still hadn't figured out what to do with Brandy. But her suggestion was impossible. Dakotas didn't return captives, regardless of the reason they had taken them. The others would consider him weak if he gave in to the white woman's pleas, and he'd be the laughingstock of his village. No, he wouldn't let the woman ruin his hard-earned reputation as a fierce warrior. "No, I will not take you back. I will never take you back."

"But why not?" Brandy cried out in exasperation.

"Because you are my captive, and Indians do not return captives. It is our way."

"Then you intend to keep me your prisoner for life?" Brandy threw out, angry that Flaming Arrow had refused to listen to reason.

"For life" was a long time, and Brandy's words gave Flaming Arrow pause. Then he replied, "Perhaps. Perhaps not. We shall see."

Flaming Arrow spun on his heels and walked away, leaving Brandy to reflect on his ambiguous answer. It was an answer that grew increasingly ominous the more she pondered it. She wished he would return so she could ask him what he meant, but Flaming Arrow made no appearance as the evening wore on. He seemed to have disappeared into the grazing herd, swallowed up by the purple night. Finally, when the fire had burned down to nothing but a pile of glowing coals, Brandy lay down and tried to sleep. At first, it was her apprehension that kept her awake, then the cool night air. She lay curled in a tight ball, shivering and feeling absolutely miserable, wondering why to-night was so much cooler than the night before. She longed for something to cover up with, then thought of a solution. Remembering a nearby cottonwood that was hardly more than a large scrub, she rose and sought it out.

An hour later, Flaming Arrow found Brandy sound asleep beneath a pile of thickly leaved branches she had broken and placed over herself. To spare himself the agony he had experienced the night before with her body pressed so close to his, he had deliberately avoided lying beside her. But Flaming Arrow had found that he couldn't sleep for worrying about her being cold. He had brought his small saddle blanket to cover her, a piece of a trading blanket that was hardly a foot square and that would not give her near the warmth that the covering she had made for her-self did.

Brandy had said that she didn't know how to care for herself, but she had proven she could if she put her mind to it. He would have never thought a white woman could be so resourceful. And she was not weak, as she had claimed. He was amazed at how well she had held up during their grueling trip. Nor had she made unreasonable demands upon him, as he would have expected a spoiled white woman to do. All she had asked was for him to take her back to her people, a request that seemed perfectly natural.

Unfortunately, it was the one request he could not grant her.

6

The next day, the raiding party stopped beside a small stream and, while the herd of horses grazed nearby, prepared for their entry into their village by repainting themselves. As they remounted, Brandy could sense their excitement, and as incredible as it seemed, they somehow reminded her of children at Christmastime. All except Flaming Arrow, that is. He seemed even more serious than usual.

They crossed several other shallow streams, the clear water gurgling as it tumbled over the rocky beds, before they entered the Indian village that lay on a broad grassy meadow surrounded by a thick woods. Brandy was surprised at how large the camp was—there were at least three hundred tepees. Their entrances all faced east, and a good half had the sides rolled up to provide for better ventilation in

the heat. Flaming Arrow led the procession through
the camp, still holding the reins to Brandy's horse as
it followed behind his mount. Trailing behind them
came the captured herd and the rest of the raiding
party. An air of festivity hung over the camp as the
Indians rushed from their tents to greet the returning warriors with shouts of welcome. Children
raced here and there, and caught up in the excitement, the camp dogs barked furiously.

As Flaming Arrow weaved his way through the
maze of tents and the villagers crowded around
them, Brandy had never felt so self-conscious in her
life. The Dakotas stared at her as if she were a crea-
ture from another planet, and a few even pointed
rudely at her. Sensing she didn't belong here, several
of the dogs ran to her mount and began jumping at
her, snapping at her feet and legs with their sharp
teeth. With her high riding boots, they did no harm,
but it was unnerving. Brandy didn't dare to kick out
at them, for fear their owners would take insult and
retaliate. She was greatly relieved when Flaming Arrow turned and gave a sharp command to the dogs,
sending them scurrying back into the crowd.

They rode up to a tent in the middle of the village,
marked by two standards of fluttering eagle feathers
stuck in the ground, and came to a halt. As Flaming
Arrow slid from the back of his horse, the Indian
sitting on a buffalo blanket before the tent rose to his
feet and walked to him. Since the Indian had on a
war bonnet whose double tail of feathers swept the
ground, Brandy assumed he was important and studied him. She judged him to be about ten years older
than Flaming Arrow. Something about him—something more than his short, muscular body that be-

spoke power, something more than his dark eyes that shone with a peculiar gleam, something more than his erect, kingly stance—told Brandy that he was a cut above other men.

Brandy watched as Flaming Arrow and the chief conversed. She felt a moment of acute nervousness when the shorter Indian gave her a brief but very through once-over, then relief when he turned his full attention to the herd. She waited while the chief walked to one of the captured horses and examined its teeth, as well as its withers. Then he smiled broadly and said something to Flaming Arrow that must have been a compliment, since a rather embarrassed expression came over the handsome Dakota's face. Then, looking very pleased, the chief walked down the line of horses, stopping here and there to examine the animals and congratulate the other members of the raiding party. The men in the crowd of excited onlookers followed and did their own appraisal of the loot their raiders had brought back.

Flaming Arrow walked back to where Brandy sat on his horse and said, "You may dismount now."

Brandy looked about her and felt even more apprehensive. It seemed that the entire female population of the camp had crowded around them, and she feared what their intention might be or, for that matter, Flaming Arrow's. Could he mean to turn her over to them? she wondered. And if that were the case, what would they do to her? "Why—why do you want me to dismount?" she asked nervously.

"So the boys can take my horse with the others to graze."

Brandy glanced over her shoulder and saw that several boys were beginning to lead the horses away.

She dismounted. Flaming Arrow had already turned and was walking away. Completely forgetting about the jacket she had tossed over the back of the saddle, she hurried to catch up with him, acutely conscious of several of the Indian women following them. With his long legs and quick stride, Brandy never fully caught up with the tall Dakota. The next thing she knew, the crowd of women circled her and began to roughly handle her blouse. Convinced they were attacking her, Brandy screamed at the top of her lungs and tried to fight them off, swinging her arms wildly. The Indian women grabbed handfuls of fabric and hung on with the determination of bulldogs with a bone. The blouse was ripped to shreds before Flaming Arrow whirled around, saw what was happening, and barked a command to the women to stop what they were doing.

He shoved the women aside and stepped up to Brandy, asking sharply, "What is wrong with you, screaming like that?"

Brandy was stunned by his angry expression. "Wrong with me?" she asked in stunned disbelief. "Why, they attacked me!"

"They did not attack you. They were only curious about your clothing."

Brandy looked down at where her blouse was ripped to shreds. Anger filled her, and outrage came to her defense. "Curious or not, they had no right to touch me or my clothing!" she flared out. "Look what they did to my blouse. It's ripped! Totally torn apart!"

"Sh! Keep your voice down!" Flaming Arrow said in a tight voice, embarrassed by Brandy's outburst, for Indian women didn't raise their voices or let their emotions get out of hand. "There is no need to get hysterical."

"I'm not hysterical. I'm angry! I'm tired of people ripping my clothes from me. First you. Now them!" Brandy glanced around, then recklessly tore off what was left of her blouse and tossed it at the women, saying, "Here, take it, damn you! It's useless to me now."

Brandy whirled and stormed away. Flaming Arrow glanced quickly at the women around him and saw that they were occupied with tearing the remains of the blouse apart. He shook his head in disgust and hurried to catch up with Brandy. Taking her arm and turning her, he said, "You passed my tepee. It's back here."

Brandy glanced only briefly at the tepee Flaming Arrow indicated, then angrily responded, "I don't give a damn where your stupid tent is!"

Flaming Arrow suddenly became aware of Brandy's state of dress. She had deliberately worn thicker drawers for her trip, but not so her camisole. It was made of the thinnest silk and, damp, concealed absolutely nothing. Flaming Arrow stared at her full creamy breasts with their rosy nipples. The tempting flesh rose and fell with her quick, agitated breaths just a few inches from his chest. Her flashing blue eyes only made her all the more alluring, and Flaming Arrow was stunned by the wave of desire that swept over him. It took all of his willpower to overcome the impulse to throw her to the ground and take her right then and there.

Brandy saw the hot look that came into Flaming Arrow's eyes and mistook it for anger. "I don't care if you don't like what I said! I'm not going into that tepee. I'm tired of you ordering me around. Go ahead and make me, force me like you have everything else, you—you filthy savage!"

Flaming Arrow stiffened at the insult, which did much to cool his sudden ardor. He dropped his hand from where it lay on her arm and stepped back, saying in a carefully controlled voice, "I have no intention of forcing you into my tepee. If you prefer, you can stand out here in the hot sun all day."

Flaming Arrow turned and walked away. Brandy glared at his broad back. Then, after he had disappeared in the maze of tepees, she saw that the Indian women who had torn her blouse had followed them and were watching her curiously. It was then that she realized they had meant her no harm, that she had let her fear of the unknown get the better of her. Her anger was replaced with embarrassment at knowing she had made a fool of herself. More to get away from their stares than from the sun blazing down on her, she sought the shelter of Flaming Arrow's tepee.

Pushing the hide covering over the oval entrance aside, Brandy stepped inside and looked about her with surprise. Not only was it a good fourteen feet in diameter—much larger than she would have thought—but the walls were translucent, so that a pleasant light entered. Nor was it musty smelling, as she had expected. Fragrant leaves scattered on the grass around her sweetened the air.

In the ground in the center of the tepee was a shallow depression for a fire, and above it, a fire hole in the ceiling, from which the sun cast a small circle of bright sunlight. At the back of the tepee was a wide pallet made of a buffalo blanket stuffed with grass, and above it, hanging from the bare poles, was an assortment of small weapons and leather pouches. A large parfleche lay at one side, and at the opposite side was a backrest made of woven willow branches.

Brandy jumped as the hide door was pushed aside and an old woman with long gray braids stepped into the tepee. The woman was just as startled to see Brandy as Brandy was to see her, for Swift Rabbit had not known Flaming Arrow had brought back a captive, much less a white woman. Unlike the others who had run to greet the men returning to the village, the old woman had rushed to prepare Flaming Arrow's tent, then brought him food, for she wanted him to remain pleased by how well she took care of his needs. For a moment, the two stared, each wondering who the other was. As it dawned on Swift Rabbit who Brandy had to be, her eyes narrowed menacingly.

Brandy had misinterpreted the other Indian women's curiosity, but there was no misjudging Swift Rabbit's look. Without a shadow of a doubt, the old woman had taken an instant dislike for her. Brandy watched warily as the elderly Indian set a wooden bowl of roasted meat and a water skin down on the pallet. Then, with a look that could kill, Swift Rabbit stepped from the tepee.

It took a few minutes for Brandy to recover from the uncomfortable encounter. But as a tantalizing aroma came from the meat in the bowl, she walked to the pallet, sat down on it, and helped herself to a hunk. The venison had a stronger gamy taste than the sage hen or rabbit she had eaten, and it was a little too rare for her taste, but Brandy was so hungry that she ate it anyway. Then, suddenly feeling very tired, she reclined on the pallet and fell asleep.

It was dusk when Brandy awoke. She looked grog-gily around, wondering what had awakened her. See-ing a dark shadow hovering over her, she sprang to a sitting position, her heart racing in fear. Since he had washed the paint from him, it took a moment for her to recognize Flaming Arrow, and when she did, she almost collapsed in relief and muttered, "Oh, it's you."

"Of course it is me. Who else would enter my te-pee?"

Something in Flaming Arrow's tone of voice made Brandy suspect he thought she was being hysterical again. "It could have been that old woman," she an-swered defensively.

"Are you talking about Swift Rabbit? She wouldn't harm you."

"I wouldn't be too sure about that. She took an instant dislike for me."

"You are imagining things," Flaming Arrow an-swered. Crouching in front of the small pile of fire-wood he had brought in, he began to work with his flint to light a fire.

Brandy had an excellent view of the Dakota's bare, muscular thighs, for Flaming Arrow had removed his leggins and was wearing only his breechclout, moc-casins, and a bear-claw necklace. Brandy had never seen so much bare male flesh. The fact that it was all hard muscle beneath a sleek, bronzed skin made it all the more distracting. She struggled to concentrate on the conversation, then said, "I'm not imagining things."

Flaming Arrow shot her a look of disgust, but Brandy said, "I realize I made an unnecessary distur-bance this afternoon, but I didn't know what to expect when we arrived here. I'd heard that Indian women torture captives. So when they surrounded me and started grabbing at me, I thought they were attacking me."

Brandy's sudden screaming that afternoon had unnerved Flaming Arrow. Indian women did not scream, any more than Indian children cried. But he had not realized the white woman had been so frightened, and he was forced to admit that her fear wasn't totally unfounded. Warriors sometimes did turn their captives over to the female relatives of slain comrades, and those women's vengeance on their enemies knew no bounds. Sometimes their methods of torture were so cruel, so barbaric, that it horrified even the men of his tribe. But no Indian woman would dare to touch someone's captive without his express permission. "You are in no danger here."

"You're not listening to me!" Brandy retorted. "I tell you that woman hates me. If looks could kill, I'd be dead. Who is she? Your mother?"

"No. My parents are dead. She is a widow woman. I provide her with meat and hides for clothing, and in return she keeps my tepee and cooks my food." A sudden thought occurred to Flaming Arrow. "Perhaps your beliefs are not totally unfounded, but I do not think she hates you as much as she fears you."

"Why should she fear me?"

"Because she is afraid that you will replace her in caring for my household and I will no longer provide for her."

"But I couldn't replace her. I don't know a thing about keeping house or cooking, much less Indian housekeeping."

"I will have her teach you."

"You're crazy if you think I'm going to be your slave!" Brandy answered indignantly.

"I did not say you would be a slave," Flaming Arrow answered in exasperation. "You will work for your keep, just as she works for hers."

"And just what is my keep?"

"Meat, hides for clothing and shelter, protection from the enemy."

"You're the enemy, remember?"

Brandy's persistence in arguing about everything wore on Flaming Arrow's nerves. "Enough!" he said sharply, coming to his feet. "Swift Rabbit will teach you, and you will learn if you want to eat."

"And what if she refuses to teach me?"

"She won't. I will explain to her that I will continue to provide for her. I will even offer her extra hides for teaching you."

Brandy heard a scratching noise at the door. Flaming Arrow said something in his tongue, and Swift Rabbit entered, carrying another pallet. She placed the pallet on the ground at one side of the tepee and smoothed it out. As she rose from her chore, Flaming Arrow spoke to the old woman. From the resentful look on the old woman's wrinkled face, it became obvious to Brandy that they were discussing her. But her expression became less hostile, if still rather forbidding, and Brandy assumed that Flaming Arrow had set her fears that he would cease to provide for her at rest.

When Swift Rabbit started to step from the tepee, Flaming Arrow said, *"Pila maye."* The old woman smiled at him and nodded her head, which surprised Brandy, for she could have sworn Swift Rabbit's face would have cracked in two if she smiled. She had never seen such a stern-faced woman.

As soon as the hide flap over the door fell back in place, Brandy asked Flaming Arrow, "What does that mean? *Pila maye.*"

"Thank you."

Brandy was surprised that Indians practiced courtesy among themselves. Then a sudden thought came to her. "She can't teach me if we can't communicate. Or does she speak English, too?"

"No, she doesn't. But there are other ways of communicating until you learn our tongue."

Brandy had no intention of learning his tongue—she wouldn't be around that long. But she would have to pretend to learn it if it meant surviving until she could escape. As a matter of fact, Brandy realized, it would come in handy to learn how to build a fire and cook. She'd need to know these things on her trip back to civilization.

Flaming Arrow wondered when Brandy gave him no further argument but appeared to accept his dictates. He puzzled over her uncharacteristic behavior for a moment, then asked, "Are you hungry?"

"No, I ate some meat earlier."

"Then we will retire for the night."

Brandy's head snapped up at Flaming Arrow's calm announcement. "Retire? Are you saying you intend to sleep here too?"

"Of course I intend to sleep here. This is my tepee, and that is my pallet you are sitting on." He motioned to the second pallet that Swift Rabbit had just brought in. "This is yours."

Brandy could have guessed when Swift Rabbit brought in the second pallet what the sleeping arrangements were, but things had come at her too fast. The idea of spending the night with the handsome Dakota in the confines of a small tepee seemed much too intimate. "You can't sleep here," she blurted. "It's too—too intimate."

"I slept beside you on the trail," Flaming Arrow pointed out.

"That was different. It was in the wide open. The others were there."

Flaming Arrow's dark eyes narrowed. "Are you afraid to be alone with me?"

Suddenly Brandy was acutely aware of Flaming Arrow as a man and the fact that she was very much alone with him. His masculinity and the strange magnetism he exuded seemed overpowering, but she couldn't admit to her fear. "No, it's not that," she lied quickly. "It's just that—that it's not done in my society. An unmarried man and woman simply do not sleep in the same room. It's considered indecent."

"Why?"

"Because—because something might happen," Brandy answered, giving him the same vague answer her mother had given her.

Flaming Arrow frowned. "Are you afraid I will violate you?"

Violate her? Brandy thought with alarm. What did that mean? Was it the same as ravish? It sounded much worse.

Flaming Arrow saw Brandy's face turn pale and the wild look come into her eyes. For a moment, he felt a surge of anger that she would think he would sink to such a lowly act; then he was forced to admit that Indians had gained somewhat of a reputation as rapists, and the emotion was quickly replaced with pity. "I have never forced a woman. Any woman! You have nothing to fear from me."

Flaming Arrow's answer only confused Brandy, for he had forced her to do many things.

Still misinterpreting her bewildered expression as one of fear, Flaming Arrow walked to her and sank to one knee on the pallet beside her. "I told you, I will not harm you."

He touched the side of Brandy's face, meaning to be comforting and reassuring, but as soon as his fingertips touched her soft skin and he gazed down into her wide blue eyes, he became achingly aware of her femininity and her desirability. Without even realizing what he was doing, his hand slid down to cup her chin and lift it. Then he was kissing her.

Nothing in Brandy's past experience had prepared her for Flaming Arrow's kiss. She had been kissed by several men who had courted her, but their kisses had been wet and messy, disgusting her. Flaming Arrow's lips were incredibly warm and sensuous as they moved lightly over hers, testing, seeking, tasting. She had never known a man's lips could feel so wonderful, never dreamed that they could actually taste—exciting! When Flaming Arrow's tongue blushed across her lips and the tip flicked at the corner of her mouth, a sudden weakness invaded her. She caught his broad shoulders for support and melted into him.

Encouraged by her embrace, Flaming Arrow's heart raced in gladness. She desired him too! he thought with excitement. Still kissing her, he gently lowered her to his pallet, his arms slipping around her as he crushed her soft body to his hard length. Her womanly scent filled his nostrils as he savored the intoxicating sweetness of her lips, feeling as if he were drowning in sheer sensation. Brandy's full breasts with their budlike nipples pressed against his chest, and her soft thigh lay between his rock-hard ones like a burning brand against his skin, igniting his passion even further.

Brandy jumped when Flaming Arrow's tongue shot into her mouth. No one had ever kissed her so boldly. His tongue searched her mouth, swirling around hers one moment, then skillfully stroking its length the next, sliding in and out, in and out, and she felt as if she were whirling in a warm vortex at his masterful possession. She shivered in delight as he ran his hands down her arms, across her back, over the swell of her hips, leaving what felt like a trail of fire in their wake. When one warm hand cupped her breast and his fingers brushed across the nipple, her heart raced with excitement and a heat flooded her pelvis. She arched her body into Flaming Arrow's, seeking to assuage that terrible burning that seemed to be centered at the very core of her womanhood.

When Brandy arched her back, Flaming Arrow shifted his weight slightly and pressed the long, hot, throbbing proof of his arousal against her softness. The rock-hard flesh seemed to scorch her right through her drawers and his breechclout, and Brandy stiffened. She recognized what it was. She had seen it stirring when Flaming Arrow had showed her his breechclout. But now, it seemed enormous and terribly threatening, and her fear brought her to her senses. What was she doing, letting this savage kiss her and touch her so intimately? she thought wildly. She tore her mouth away from Flaming Arrow's and pushed on his broad shoulders, saying, "No! Stop it!"

Brandy's sudden resistance angered Flaming Arrow. He knew he had not mistaken her embracing him and pressing her body against his. Had she only been teasing him? Or had she gotten so caught up in her passion that she had momentarily forgotten he was an Indian? The last thought angered him even more, and he glared down at her, very tempted to take her against her will. But just the thought of forcing her to submit filled him with self-disgust. He let out an oath and rolled from her, coming to his feet with the ease and grace of a cat. Then seeing her staring at his erection, which tented the flap on his breechclout, he said in an angry voice, "If you do not want me to complete what I started, stop staring at me like that!"

Brandy jerked her eyes away.

"And cover yourself! That flimsy garment you are wearing does nothing to hide your breasts."

Brandy looked down and saw that what Flaming Arrow said was true. The small fire he had lit gave just enough light to penetrate the sheer material, and for all practical purposes her chest might as well be naked. Instinctively, she crossed her arms to cover herself. Then her anger rose. "How dare you talk to me like that! I didn't tear my clothes. You did, and those rude women. And how dare you accuse me for what just happened. I didn't attack you. You did me!" she finished in an irate voice, totally forgetting that she had encouraged him, had actually delighted in his kiss and touch.

"Ah!" Flaming Arrow cried, throwing his hands up in disgust. "I did not attack you! I kissed you. There is a big difference between the two. And I only did so because I thought you were agreeable to lying with me, that you wanted me too. But you need not worry. It will not happen again."

Flaming Arrow turned and stormed from the tepee, and it took Brandy a while to recover from his "attack." Then she reclined on the pallet with a light trade blanket pulled up to her chin and relived the episode, recalling every thrilling sensation his lips and hands had brought her. She was secretly forced to admit that it had been wonderful, until the end. Once again, the unknown had frightened her.

She tried once again to piece together the man-woman puzzle that had teased her for years. Remembering how Flaming Arrow had pressed his hot, hard flesh between her legs, how she had burned down there, and what he had said about her being agreeable and wanting him, she suddenly thought she had solved the mystery. But it was shocking. Surely that was not what went on between men and women. He couldn't possibly put that part of him in her. But then she remembered little whispered snatches of conversations between her mother and her friends, little hints of disgust, little snickers, and the acute embarrassment of her mother and brother when she had tried to get them to tell her what went on. And Brandy knew it was true.

Brandy could feel only revulsion, until she remembered that that was not how she had felt when Flaming Arrow had kissed and touched her. It had been absolutely wonderful. What would have happened if she had let him continue? she wondered. Would that, too, have opened doors to wondrous sensations beyond her wildest dreams?

Then Brandy remembered that Flaming Arrow was an Indian, a lowly barbarian who was much beneath her, and outrage rose in her. How dare he think that she would submit to his indecencies willingly, how dare he think she actually desired him! But no sooner did her outrage pass through her than she was fantasizing again, becoming aroused all over. She *was* shameful, as her mother had accused her when she had stared at the fig leaf on the statue, Brandy thought. But the admission did nothing to stop her from thinking about it, and above all, she was filled with an insatiable curiosity about what it would be like with the handsome, wildly exciting savage.

Much later that night, Flaming Arrow returned to the tepee. He had deliberately waited until Brandy was asleep in hopes that she would not be so tempting, and he was determined not to make the mistake of succumbing to her desirability again. Not only was forcing a woman completely unacceptable because of his principles, but Brandy's spurning him had wounded his pride. He knew he was considered one of the most physically attractive men in his tribe, pursued by maidens, divorcees, and widows. The latter group were more than willing to share their pallets with him and even complained that he didn't seek out their company more often. So he assumed there was nothing lacking in his skills as a lover. It irked him to no end that Brandy had rejected him simply because he was an Indian, and that he was attracted to her angered him even more. He should feel just as much disdain for her.

When Flaming Arrow stepped into the tepee, he

was relieved to see that Brandy was asleep and covered with a trade blanket. Her thick hair was spread out around her like a cloak. He walked past her and stripped off his breechclout, then sat on his pallet. Before he could recline, however, Brandy stirred in her sleep, and the blanket slipped to her waist. In the reddish light cast by the glowing embers of the fire, Flaming Arrow saw that one strap on the camisole had slipped down, and the breast on that side was fully exposed. Her arms were thrown above her head, her long thick hair was spread out around her like a flaming cloak, her mouth was partially open in sleep, and her lovely breast was revealed to him— Brandy looked very provocative, and Flaming Arrow found he couldn't tear his eyes from the tantalizing sight. Again his passion rose, hot and heavy in his loins.

Muttering an oath beneath his breath, Flaming Arrow turned his back to Brandy and lay down facing the side of the tepee. But he couldn't get the memory of her out of his mind. It seemed to be branded on his brain. When he recalled how silky and soft her skin had been earlier, his hands actually itched to take her in his arms and finish what he had begun. For well over an hour, Flaming Arrow tossed and turned, trying to suppress his unwanted desire. That he was unsuccessful was a great truth to come to terms with, for rigid self-control was one of Flaming Arrow's major strengths. Finally, he rose, grabbed his breechclout, and quickly donned it; then, without even a glance in Brandy's direction, he walked from the tepee and paced for the rest of the night.

By the time dawn came, Flaming Arrow had come to terms with an undeniable truth. Under no circumstances could he keep Brandy in his tepee. No matter how much she exasperated him with her obstinacy, outspokenness, and irritating white ways, she possessed a desirability against which he had—for some unknown reason—absolutely no defenses. He had to get rid of his captive, one way or another. If he didn't, he'd disgrace himself.

Then an idea came to Flaming Arrow, a solution to his dilemma that brought him a sigh of vast relief. Smiling, he turned and headed for the nearest stream to bathe and, facing eastward toward the rising sun, to commune with the Mystery, something that he had done every day of his life since he had reached his manhood.

7

There was a jauntiness in Flaming Arrow's stride as he walked to his brother's tepee later that morning, for he was confident that the solution to his dilemma would work. He smiled, thinking how elated Yellow Fox would be.

When Flaming Arrow reached his brother's home, he stopped and greeted his comely sister-in-law, Morning Star, who was busy scraping a deer hide tied to an upright frame a short distance from the tepee. Then he entered the structure and found Yellow Fox finishing his breakfast. Yellow Fox greeted his brother warmly and motioned for Flaming Arrow to make himself comfortable on the willow backrest across from him. When he had done so, he offered Flaming Arrow a piece of meat from a wooden bowl between them.

"No, thank you. I have eaten," Flaming Arrow answered, then waited rather impatiently while Yellow Fox finished the piece of meat he was eating. Both brothers were muscular, and they shared the same handsome features, but other than that they were nothing alike. Flaming Arrow was tall and slender, while Yellow Fox was short and stocky, and although Yellow Fox was the older of the two, Flaming Arrow was much more mature and much more serious-minded. Yellow Fox, although an excellent provider, was something of a tease and not nearly the warrior his younger brother was. He was also more vain about his personal appearance, spending hours grooming his long hair and never appearing in public without his part painted red.

"I saw the Pawnee herd you brought back yesterday," Yellow Fox commented after he had finished his meal. "You have done well."

Flaming Arrow had seen Yellow Fox in the crowd when he had ridden in and nodded to him. "I'm sorry I didn't have time to visit you yesterday, but after I took my captive to my tepee, Chief Crazy Horse conferred with me until dusk." Flaming Arrow hoped his brother wouldn't ask why he had not come to visit then. He was loath to admit to Yellow Fox that he had been worried about Brandy—a lowly captive—then had been too humiliated and angry because she had spurned his advances. He'd never lied to his brother—or anyone for that matter—

Yellow Fox knew it was common practice for the chiefs to question the leaders of parties returning from raids for information, but he had never heard of such a conference that lasted so long. Why, it had been more like a war council. He knew his brother shared privileged information with the tribal leaders because of his elevated position in the tribe, and Yellow Fox rarely asked questions, but in this instance he not only wanted to know but felt he had the right to know. "There are rumors going around in the camp that Red Cloud has received an offer from the white-eyes to buy the Black Hills. He betrayed us once by putting his mark on the white-eyes treaty, then by agreeing to live on a reservation. Is he preparing to betray us again?"

Seeing a closed expression coming over Flaming Arrow's face, Yellow Fox quickly said, "No, do not refuse to answer my question. I realize the tribal leaders tell you things that are confidential, but this is something every Dakota has a right to know, not only those that live on the reservation. The Black Hills belong to us all. They are a sacred place."

Flaming Arrow knew that what Yellow Fox had said was true. The Black Hills, a small mountain range, had been thrust high into the sky by powerful forces aeons ago, a richly timbered, well-watered island of land among the dry, alkaline plains. They were charged with deep and mystical meaning for the Dakotas, a place where the spirits dwelt. Yellow Fox did have a right to know what was going on, particularly if there were rumors going around. In all likelihood, the truth was much more assuring than what his brother had heard. "It is true the white-eyes want to buy the Black Hills, but I do not think Red Cloud will betray us this time. I have been told that he intends to ask an impossible sum for them, an amount so high that the white-eyes will be forced to refuse. But that does not mean that the white-eyes will not break their agreement with Red Cloud and try to take them by force, as you well know. That is why Crazy Horse questioned me for so long. Since the meeting to discuss this will take place in just a few weeks, he wanted to know if I had noticed any build-up of horse soldiers while I was passing through the area. I did not. The only horse soldiers I saw were the column that the Kiowas killed between Fort Laramie and Fort Fetterman. Crazy Horse seemed to be reassured by that. The white-eyes do not appear to be preparing any moves against us at least at the present."

Yellow Fox was relieved that Red Cloud did not plan to betray the Dakotas the second time. Perhaps it was as some of the reservation Dakotas claimed: the great chief still fought the whites, but his resistance was more concealed and cunning than that of the nontreaty chiefs. But Yellow Fox wasn't surprised that Crazy Horse suspected the white-eyes would try to take the Black Hills despite Red Cloud's agreement with them. Yes, it was just as the free Dakotas had known all along. The white-eyes' word meant nothing. They wanted all of the Dakotas' land, and the Dakotas would have to fight again to keep it. But that fight would not come until later, and right now, Yellow Fox was curious about something. "Is it true what the others in your party told me? That the white captive you took was with the horse soldiers the Kiowas killed?"

Flaming Arrow was glad Yellow Fox had brought up Brandy. It made what he had come here for look less deliberate. "Yes, and now that you have mentioned her, there is something I want to tell you. I would like to give her to you."

Flaming Arrow's calm announcement stunned Yellow Fox. For a moment, he just stared at his brother.

Then, when he had recovered from the surprise, he asked himself why Flaming Arrow was giving the woman away. Yellow Fox had seen the white woman. She was beautiful, a woman any man would be delighted to have on his pallet—which is exactly where most female captives eventually found themselves. Did Flaming Arrow not find the white-eyes desirable? It seemed impossible, but Yellow Fox had to admit that his brother was a little strange sometimes, so committed to becoming a superior warrior that he lived and breathed it. But that didn't explain why Flaming Arrow wanted to get rid of his captive. Even if she didn't warm his pallet, she could be useful to him.

"Why do you want to give her to me?" Yellow Fox asked, breaking his long silence. "She can be trained to care for your household."

"I know," Flaming Arrow answered. "I'd already instructed Swift Rabbit to teach her. But this morning, I thought more deeply on it. I don't need the captive. Swift Rabbit provides for my needs very well. She could be helpful to Morning Star."

Swift Rabbit provided for all of Flaming Arrow's needs but one, Yellow Fox thought. His manly needs. For those, Flaming Arrow sought out the young widows and divorcees of the camp. He repaid them handsomely with meat and hides, but Yellow Fox seriously doubted that payment was necessary. All the women in the camp idolized his brother, even the very married and the very old. That Flaming Arrow had never married was a puzzle that had teased Yellow Fox's mind for some time. Flaming Arrow was twenty-seven, a few years over what was considered the marriageable age for Dakota men, and could have his pick of women in the tribe. His bachelor state was particularly baffling to Yellow Fox since the Dakotas considered it every man's responsibility to take a wife and reproduce, and Flaming Arrow took all his other responsibilities very seriously. And Flaming Arrow could certainly provide for a wife. He was one of the tribe's best hunters and most successful raiders. Why, Flaming Arrow's herd of horses numbered second only to that of Crazy Horse himself. Had Flaming Arrow never found a woman who attracted him? Did he not feel his manly needs warranted a woman in his tepee all the time? Yellow Fox knew Flaming Arrow didn't seek physical comfort from women often.

"Well?" Flaming Arrow prompted, breaking into Yellow Fox's musing. "Will you take her?"

Yellow Fox frowned suspiciously. Flaming Arrow seemed much too anxious to get rid of the white-eyes. Perhaps his brother did desire her but would not sink to forcing her, and keeping her in his tepee was too uncomfortable. "Let me think on it for a moment," Yellow Fox said, stalling for time so he could explore his suspicion more thoroughly.

The longer Yellow Fox thought, the more convinced he became that Flaming Arrow secretly wanted his captive and that his younger brother needed a dalliance with the white-eyes. Flaming Arrow was far too serious, too intense, and there was much more to life than raiding and warring. A woman to ease his loins and keep him company might help him relax the rigid controls he kept over himself and learn to enjoy life. And surely, as manly and attractive as Flaming Arrow was, he could break down the captive's resistance. Force wouldn't be necessary. There was always seduction.

Yellow Fox wondered how he could refuse Flaming Arrow's offer without arousing his brother's suspicions, for as tempting as the white-eyes was, he loved his younger brother and had no qualms about putting Flaming Arrow's needs above his. If need be, Yellow Fox would give his life for his brother, as was fitting in the Dakota culture. But Yellow Fox knew he would have to be very careful about how he phrased his refusal. Flaming Arrow would highly resent him trying to interfere in his life in any manner, particularly in his love life. But Yellow Fox had no doubts about his ability to manipulate Flaming Arrow if he put his mind to it. Had he not been named after the fox for his slyness?

Then Yellow Fox remembered an idea he had been toying with but had not fully decided upon. This was the means for gracefully refusing. Smiling with pleasure at his own cleverness, he answered smoothly, "I am afraid I am going to have to refuse your generous offer. You see, I am considering taking a second wife since Morning Star is with child. With three adults and a child in my tepee, my lodgings would not hold another person comfortably."

"When did you find out you were to be a father?" Flaming Arrow asked in surprise.

"Morning Star told me a week ago. But I was already suspicious, since she has not been to the women's lodge for three moons now."

"I am very happy for you both," Flaming Arrow said with all sincerity. "You have wanted a child for some time."

"Thank you. We are both very pleased that Wakan'tanka has blessed us."

Flaming Arrow nodded his head in agreement, for the Dakotas believed children the greatest gift the Great Spirit could bestow on someone. "But Morning Star having a child is all the more reason for you to accept my gift. The captive can help her with the heavy work, and then the baby, when it comes."

"Yes, I thought of that," Yellow Fox answered. "That is why I thought to take Morning Star's younger sister for wife. She could help Morning Star, and Morning Star could move to the exalted position of first wife. Since she is honoring me by bearing me my first child, Morning Star should not have to work so hard anymore." Yellow Fox paused; then, with a conspiratorial wink, he leaned forward and confided, "But just between us, there is another reason why I would like a second wife. I do not care to remain celibate until the child is weaned. Morning Star's sister would share my pallet until Morning Star and I could make love again." Yellow Fox deliberately paused a second time, then, pretending something had just dawned on him, he said in an excited voice, "But then, the white-eyes could serve that purpose, too, couldn't she? Share my pallet? And she is much more beautiful and desirable than Morning Star's sister."

Yellow Fox saw a fleeting flash of anger in Flaming Arrow's eyes and knew he had guessed the truth. Flaming Arrow wanted the white woman, wanted her enough to feel jealousy, wanted her enough even to feel anger at his brother for talking about taking her to his pallet.

Flaming Arrow was stunned by the surge of jealousy he felt. The emotion was totally foreign to him. But much to his dismay, he couldn't take back his offer to give Brandy to his brother. That was unheard of among his people. "Then I must warn you," he responded in a tight voice. "The white-eyes is very warlike and very strong. She will not be easy to force to lie with you."

Yellow Fox laughed and said, "I will not have to force her. I will seduce her. You may not realize it, but the women think me very charming. And I am patient. I will woo her into my pallet. I have plenty of time. The child will not be born until next spring."

Flaming Arrow paused. He had never dreamed Yellow Fox would want Brandy, or any other woman. He was very much in love with Morning Star and had always been faithful to her. He had never stopped to consider that Morning Star would become pregnant or that Yellow Fox would be so against a year or two of celibacy that he would take another woman into his tepee. And could his brother actually seduce Brandy? He did seem to have a way with women. Why, it was uncanny the way women had pursued Yellow Fox before he had married.

Yellow Fox was enjoying teasing his brother and watching him become increasingly frustrated. Then he decided it was time to relieve Flaming Arrow of his worries. He said in a tone of voice he hoped sounded disappointed, "On second thought, I think I still should refuse your offer. Morning Star would not mind her sister sharing my pallet. When we married, she knew that I would probably take her younger sister for a wife someday, since that is our custom. But I do not think she would like me to take the captive to my pallet or even into our tepee. She might think the white-eyes too threatening, since she is so very beautiful."

The look of relief that came over Flaming Arrow's face almost made Yellow Fox laugh. "Yes," Flaming Arrow agreed and hurried to say, "and now that we are both giving this more consideration, I don't think it would be a good idea either. The white-eyes is very stubborn. I doubt very seriously that she would take orders from Morning Star or that Morning Star would want anyone so unruly in her household. You see, she's very argumentative and outspoken."

Yellow Fox knew Flaming Arrow well enough to know that he would be bored to tears by an ordinary woman on a steady basis, just as he would be bored with a mount that had no spirit. From what Flaming Arrow had told him about the white-eyes, she was far from docile. Yellow Fox was intrigued. Yes, perhaps she was just what Flaming Arrow needed—a woman who would stimulate him, a woman who would bring him out of his self-imposed rigid shell. But Yellow Fox couldn't help but tease his brother just a little more. "If the white-eyes is that disruptive, why don't you sell her?"

Flaming Arrow knew that any man in the village who would buy Brandy from him would do so because they desired her. He couldn't sell her for the same reason he couldn't give her to his brother. The thought of any man touching her softness or kissing her infuriated him, particularly since he'd had a taste of her intoxicating sweetness the night before. Aware that his brother was awaiting an answer, Flaming Arrow replied vaguely, "I will think about that."

Yellow Fox bit back a laugh. He knew Flaming Arrow's answer had been deliberately evasive, some-

thing that he had never done before. Flaming Arrow
had always been totally honest with him. Already the
white woman's influence was making him more human.

Flaming Arrow stayed awhile longer to visit with
his brother, but he couldn't concentrate on their conversation. As soon as he could excuse himself, he said
his good-byes, then walked to the meadow where his
herd of horses were grazing. He caught his war horse
and led the animal to his tepee. When he stepped
inside, he was relieved that Brandy was not there.
Apparently, Swift Rabbit had gotten an early start on
their lessons, and for that, Flaming Arrow was thankful. He wasn't prepared to face Brandy just yet. He
needed time to adjust to the turnabout of events:
that, like it or not, the tempting captive had become
a permanent fixture in his life. Snatching his bow and
a quiver of arrows from where they hung over his
pallet, he walked from the tepee, flew gracefully
onto his horse's back, and rode from the camp, seeking the quiet and solitude that hunting had always
brought him.

While Flaming Arrow was riding out of the village,
Brandy was on the other side of the camp digging in
the prairie on her hands and knees for what Swift
Rabbit called *tusenah*, a sort of wild turnip. Her once
well-manicured nails were broken and caked with
dirt, and her hair hung about her in damp, limp
strands. Laboring beneath the hot sun, she was burning up in the buckskin dress Swift Rabbit had
brought her that morning and was regretting her
own stubbornness in insisting that she wear her underwear beneath it, for the additional garments only

made her hotter. But at least she'd had the sense to
wear the moccasins the old woman had given her
instead of her riding boots, as she had been tempted
to do at first. Undoubtedly, the boots would have
made her all the more miserable too.

Brandy sat back on her heels and wiped the sweat
from her brow. She glanced around the prairie and
saw other women digging in the tall grass. Not a one
looked as tired or hot or filthy as she did. She supposed the Indians were used to it, but it seemed
there must be an easier way to obtain vegetables.
The grass's unbelievably long roots twisted around
the turnips, and the ground was as hard as a rock in
places.

A shadow fell over Brandy, and she knew it was
Swift Rabbit's. The old woman was a slave driver.
Brandy wouldn't have tolerated Swift Rabbit pushing her so mercilessly for a moment, but she was
learning valuable lessons on how to survive in the
wilderness. Brandy looked up and saw the Indian
motioning for her to pick up her basket and follow
her. Wearily, Brandy retrieved her half-full basket
and rose.

They walked into a nearby woods, and Brandy relished the cool shade. They picked berries for over an
hour, then wild artichokes called *panghai;* then they
dug once again in the ground to gather *mdo,* the root
of a slender vine that reminded Brandy of a narrow
sweet potato. When Swift Rabbit led her out onto the
prairie to pick—of all things—sunflowers, Brandy re-
belled, until Swift Rabbit pulled a few of the seeds
from the center of the huge flowers and made as if to
eat them. Brandy could hardly believe that the Indians ate flower seeds, but then, she could hardly be-

lieve they actually ate any of the peculiar-looking things in her basket.

Finally, the two headed back to the camp and Swift Rabbit's tepee. Before it lay a deer that Flaming Arrow had killed. Brandy then got a lesson, one that totally sickened her, in how to skin and butcher a deer. When Brandy had finished, she was not only nauseated and filthy but bloody all over, and from the way Swift Rabbit was shaking her head, she knew the old woman was disgusted with her. But Brandy couldn't have cared less. She was exhausted.

As tired as she was, Swift Rabbit still wasn't finished with her. She taught Brandy how to build a fire, using a flint to spark the kindling, then how to cook what Brandy assumed was a kind of stew, since Swift Rabbit tossed both the vegetables they had gathered and hunks of venison into the black kettle over the fire. By that time it was late afternoon, and Brandy thought the terrible day was finally over. Not so. Swift Rabbit motioned for her to follow to the woods to gather wood for the next day.

By the time they had both collected an armful of firewood, it was all Brandy could do to shuffle behind Swift Rabbit back toward the camp. She actually feared she might fall asleep on her feet if she couldn't lie down soon. When they came to a stream, Brandy came to a dead halt, looked at it longingly for a moment, then tossed down her firewood.

As she headed to the stream, Swift Rabbit jumped in front of her and pointed sternly toward the camp.

"No, you old witch!" Brandy responded with considerable heat. "I'm going to take a bath."

Brandy shoved past the old woman and walked to the stream. She kicked off one moccasin, then the other, then grabbed the hem of her dress, yanked it over her head, and threw it aside. Just as she was about to step into the stream in her underwear, Swift Rabbit caught her arm, whirled her around, and shook her head violently. She motioned to the setting sun, then to the east, then made washing movements on her arms. Brandy realized she was telling her they would bathe in the morning.

"No, I am not waiting another minute, and that's final!" Brandy said in an adamant voice, pulling away from Swift Rabbit.

Brandy waded into the water until it was at her hips, then sat, luxuriating in the feel of the cool liquid all around her. She dropped her head back so her hair could get wet, too, then briskly scrubbed it with her fingertips, wishing she had some soap.

Swift Rabbit yelled something to her and motioned for her to get out.

"No! I'm not through yet."

The old woman snorted, tossed her head in disgust, then turned and walked away. For a long while Brandy sat in the water, letting it wash the dirt and sweat from her and soothe her aching muscles, while the shadows cast by the trees all around her got longer and longer. A deer came to the stream, hesitated when it saw Brandy, then cautiously took a drink, shooting Brandy a curious look as it bounded away. Finally, when it was almost dark, Brandy left the stream, stripped off her camisole and drawers, and washed them. She slipped on her buckskin dress and moccasins and walked back to the camp carrying her dripping-wet underwear in one hand and ignoring the pile of firewood she had tossed down earlier.

When Brandy appeared at the old woman's tepee,

Swift Rabbit was standing at her fire, dishing up a bowl of stew. Brandy walked past her and hung her underwear from a line strung between two poles that was ordinarily used for drying strips of meat. Swift Rabbit looked at the dripping underwear scornfully, shook her head in disgust, then offered Brandy the bowl of stew.

Brandy remembered the beautiful deer she had seen at the stream and wanted to refuse the food. But the delicious aroma of the stew got the better of her, and she'd had nothing to eat but a bowl of thin gruel that morning and a handful of berries. She accepted the bowl and scooped out the vegetables with her fingers—the Indians had no eating utensils—then drank the broth. For a moment she stared at the large piece of meat left in the bottom of the bowl. She told herself that she wouldn't touch it, but she found she couldn't resist. The rest of the food had just teased her appetite. She reached in, picked it up, and ate it, and she felt absolutely no remorse when the act was done.

Swift Rabbit took the empty bowl from Brandy and handed her another full one, but larger. Then she picked up a smaller bowl of roasted sunflower seeds and walked off, motioning over her shoulder for Brandy to follow. They wove their way through the maze of tepees in the dark, and the ones that had fires lit inside them looked like giant candles. When they reached Flaming Arrow's glowing tent, Swift Rabbit stepped aside and waited for Brandy to enter first.

When Brandy stepped inside the tent, Flaming Arrow was sitting on the ground beside a small fire, sanding a gooseberry stick that was destined to become an arrow with a piece of pumice. She was immediately conscious of his near-nakedness in his breechclout and the powerful muscles on his arms and shoulders gleaming in the flickering light. Then, as he looked up with those black, black eyes of his, her stomach quivered peculiarly.

Swift Rabbit shoved her from behind, and Brandy almost stumbled into the fire. She looked over her shoulder and gave the old woman a furious glare. Swift Rabbit was pointing at Flaming Arrow. Brandy realized she meant for her to give Flaming Arrow the bowl of food, but still she hesitated. Serving the overbearing savage in any shape, form, or manner galled her. When he held out his hand, she shoved the bowl at him, saying, "Here! Take it! But the next time, she can serve you!"

"She is teaching *you* how to care for my household, or have you forgotten? That includes cooking for me and serving me."

"Oh, yes, now I remember," she answered, her voice dripping with sarcasm. "I'm earning my keep, aren't I?" Her eyes darkened with anger. "I broke my back digging up the silly vegetables in that stew, lugged the water, toted the firewood, built the fire, and cooked your damned meal. And what did you contribute? A deer! All you did was go out and kill one lousy little deer. I hope you didn't exert yourself."

"What else would you expect me to do but provide the meat?" Flaming Arrow responded calmly. "The other is woman's work. And if I am not mistaken, it is the same with your people. Men do not build fires and cook if they have women to do it for them."

It was a point that Brandy couldn't dispute. In her

home back in St. Louis, the cooking had been done by servants—*women* servants. She seethed in frustration while Flaming Arrow looked her over, then asked Swift Rabbit, "Could you not find a better dress than that for her to wear? It's filthy and covered with bloodstains."

"It wasn't that way when I gave it to her this morning," Swift Rabbit answered defensively. She shot Brandy a disgusted look, then said, "She is impossible. She will never make a decent servant for you. She could not dig without getting herself filthy, and you should have seen her skinning and butchering that deer. You would have thought she had wallowed in it by the time she was through. She was covered with blood from head to toe."

Flaming Arrow was surprised to learn that Brandy had skinned and butchered the deer. Not only had she not mentioned it, but he would have thought she would balk at such a messy chore. In fact, he was surprised that she had done all the things she had, considering she had never done a day's work in her life. Then he said, "She is not covered with blood now."

"No, she stopped at a stream on the way back to camp this evening and bathed. I told her it was not our way, that we bathe in the mornings, but she would not listen to me. And she did not bring her firewood with her when she returned either. She can be very stubborn."

Flaming Arrow was very well aware of how obstinate Brandy could be. Then Swift Rabbit gave Brandy a hard look and said, "If she gets stubborn on me again tomorrow, I shall take a stick to her."

"No!" Flaming Arrow said firmly. "You will not whip her!"

"Then how will I make her obey? That is how we handle the other captives in this village."

"The other captives are Indian. They understand our ways. She does not. It will only make her more stubborn."

"Then how will I make her obey me? I cannot teach her if she will not obey."

Flaming Arrow was determined that Brandy would not be whipped or hurt in any manner. He didn't stop to consider that by forbidding this, he had placed her out of the realm of an ordinary captive. "It seems to me that she is obeying the better part of your commands if she has already learned so much. What do you intend to teach her tomorrow?"

"How to make jerky and how to tan a hide," Swift Rabbit answered. "And what if she won't obey me? What if she turns lazy on me tomorrow?"

"Then I will handle it."

Brandy knew Flaming Arrow and Swift Rabbit were discussing her, and it infuriated her to be talked about as if she were nothing but an animal or a piece of merchandise. She broke into their conversation, saying hotly, "Hasn't anyone ever told either of you that it's rude to talk about someone in front of them when they can't understand you?"

"What tongue would you have us speak when we are discussing your progress?" Flaming Arrow replied calmly. "Swift Rabbit does not understand yours."

His logic infuriated Brandy all the more. "Then step out of the tepee if you're going to discuss me. Or better yet, translate for me."

"No, that is an unreasonable and time-consuming request. Until you learn our tongue, you will just have to tolerate it. Perhaps it will be an incentive to make you learn quicker."

Flaming Arrow turned his attention back to Swift Rabbit, thanked her, and bade her good night, clearly dismissing her. Scowling deeply, the old woman handed him the bowl of roasted sunflower seeds and said good night.

After the old woman left, Brandy sat on her pallet and watched Flaming Arrow eat his food. Despite her pique at him, she thought that he looked very handsome and appealing with the firelight playing over his features. His physique really was splendid, she thought in silent admiration as her eyes drifted over his broad shoulders and chest. Then she frowned, noticing some scars just below each nipple on his chest. What could have caused them? she wondered. "Were you attacked by some wild animal?"

"What makes you ask that?"

"The scars on your chest."

"No, I was not attacked by an animal. Those are my *ne-wä-gwa-wa-che-pe* scars, my Sun Dance scars."

"You worship the sun?" Brandy asked, her expression clearly showing her disapproval.

"No, we dance *in* the sun. We worship the Great Spirit, just as your people do."

"But how does dancing in the sun make scars?"

"Wooden skewers are placed beneath the skin on the chest. They are tied by a long strip of rawhide to the sacred pole in the center of the sun lodge. We dance until the skin tears. It is how we take on the agony of our people, how we free ourselves from human darkness, how we—" Seeing the horrified expression on Brandy's face, Flaming Arrow stopped in midsentence. Then he said, "I do not expect you to understand the meaning of our ritual, but that is how I got the scars."

Brandy was revolted by Flaming Arrow's admission of self-mutilation in the name of God. But when an uncomfortable silence fell between them, she realized she had offended him and regretted it, which puzzled her. He was a savage, someone who had shown no concern for her feelings when he had taken her captive and brought her back to this camp, and an admitted killer. So why should she give a damn about him? But despite all this, Brandy discovered that she didn't want to alienate him, and she had to admit to a certain grudging admiration for him. He was like no man she had ever met, not only devastatingly attractive and exciting, but self-possessed, intense in his beliefs, and incredibly strong. Yes, he was everything she had ever dreamed a man should be, and more, much more.

While Flaming Arrow picked up the stick he had been working on and began to smooth the arrow's shaft once more, Brandy became even more conscious of him. She couldn't help but stare at his sensuously shaped mouth and remember how it had felt on hers, the lips warm and mobile. Then she directed her attention to his hand as it slid up and down the narrow stick, recalling how those fingers had caressed her, had cupped her breast and teased her nipple. Then she noted his scent drifting across to her, which she hadn't noticed before. He smelled of a combination of wood smoke, leather, trees, and some faint, exciting masculine odor. She felt a peculiar tingling sensation and a warm curl deep in her belly and wished, with something almost akin to desperation, that he would take her in those powerful arms of his and kiss her again.

Flaming Arrow was feeling the effects of Brandy's nearness too. He had told himself he had only to school himself with strict self-discipline to make himself immune to her desirability. He wasn't a child. He was a man who exercised exceptional self-control every day of his life. He was determined not to allow her to chase him from his own tepee. He would simply ignore her, just as he had ignored the agonizing pain when he had danced the Sun Dance and the gnawing hunger when he had fasted before spiritual rituals. But the longer Brandy stared at him with those searing blue eyes—dark, liquid pools that he seemed to be drowning in—the more Flaming Arrow's heat rose. He was tormented by her mouth with its pouty lower lip and ached to take the enticing flesh into his mouth and suck on it.

As Brandy broke eye contact, Flaming Arrow sighed silently in relief. But the respite from his torment was only temporary. Brandy spied the brush he had tossed down on his parfleche after he had groomed his hair that morning, cried out with joy, reached over, and picked it up. Then as she brushed her long, reddish tresses, Flaming Arrow felt a stab of desire, for the movements were incredibly provocative. Her proud, full breasts rose and strained against her dress each time she lifted her arm, and her hair crackled with static electricity that somehow seemed to fire an answering spark deep within him.

Seeing the flush rise on Flaming Arrow's face, Brandy assumed he was angry at her audacity in using something as personal as his brush without asking. She stopped her arm in midair and said, "I suppose I should have asked your permission first. It was just that I was so happy to see a brush after all these days. My hair is a rat's nest of tangles."

But Flaming Arrow wasn't looking at Brandy's hair. He was staring at the brush she held out between them. There, caught in the porcupine tail that served as its bristles, was a long dark hair from his head, and next to it was a reddish one from Brandy's head. The two strands were twined around one another and were moving with the electrical current from Brandy's hair, twisting and turning in a sexually suggestive manner that ignited Flaming Arrow's seething passion.

Flaming Arrow felt his manhood stir, and he knew he was on the very verge of disgracing himself. He had told Brandy he would never touch her again, but if he didn't put distance between them fast, his thin control was going to shatter. He slammed to his feet and walked swiftly to the tepee door.

Stunned, Brandy asked, "What's wrong? Surely you can't be that angry because I used your brush."

Flaming Arrow realized his sudden departure must look a little strange. He stopped at the door, holding the skin flap aside, and looked over his shoulder, saying, "It is not the brush. You may keep it."

"Then—then what's wrong? Why are you leaving so abruptly?"

"Nothing is wrong. I always go for a long walk before I retire."

With that, Flaming Arrow ducked beneath the skin flap and stepped from the tepee. As he walked past his war horse, which he had staked at the back of his tepee in case of a sudden Crow attack, he was filled with self-disgust. First he had been evasive with his brother, and now he had told an out-and-out lie— something to which he had never thought he would sink. He had been only too correct when he'd feared he'd rue the day he found the white woman. But he had never dreamed how profoundly she would affect him. Not only had she made his life more complicated, his seductive captive had brought him low.

8

Over the next two weeks, Swift Rabbit kept Brandy busy from dawn to dusk teaching her Dakota women's tasks. Brandy learned how to make jerky by slicing the meat into paper thin strips and then drying them on a line strung in the sun, how to scrape and tan a buckskin by using an obnoxious concoction of fat and deer brains, how to make soap by boiling soap root with ashes, how to make paint from plants, how to make moccasins and sew on beads and quills, how to weave a basket from willow branches, and how to snare small animals and birds in the event the men were gone, and how to clean her buckskin dress with white clay. Added to this were the daily backbreaking chores of gathering wood, wild vegetables, and fruits, toting water, and standing over a hot fire in the blazing sun to cook the large game that Flaming Arrow delivered to them, either boiling the tough meat until it was finally tender in the big black trading kettles or roasting it on a spit.

During this time, Brandy saw very little of her handsome captor. Where Flaming Arrow busied himself during the day when he wasn't hunting, Brandy had no idea. In the evenings he stayed in the tepee just long enough to eat his meal, then hurried away for his nightly walk. Brandy had no way of knowing what time he returned at night, although she tried several times to wait up for him. But she was just too exhausted from all her hard work, and she always fell asleep. What's more, he was always gone in the morning when she woke up. She wondered if he was deliberately avoiding her, and that thought not only piqued her, it hurt. She thought of him constantly, day and night, and was particularly tormented by the memory of his kiss. As the time passed, she began to think that that night he had taken her in his arms had been nothing but a figment of her imagination. Why, she could be dead for all he cared.

One evening, after Flaming Arrow had hastily eaten his meal and left, it occurred to Brandy that maybe he wasn't taking an evening walk. Maybe he was courting a maiden, or visiting one of *those* women. Although she hadn't wanted to bother to learn the Lakota tongue, Brandy had picked up quite a bit of the language, enough to know that her suspicions about what went on between men and women were true, for the Indian women spoke very frankly about sex and it seemed to be their favorite topic of conversation. She had learned that there were experienced women in the tribe who were free with their favors, and as long as they and the man were discreet in their liaisons, this was an acceptable practice. But it wasn't at all acceptable to Brandy. Even though the women had made it quite clear that the man might not have any particular feelings for the woman other than simple lust, Brandy was filled with jealousy at the idea of Flaming Arrow visiting one of those women. And the thought that he might be contemplating marriage to some young, beautiful maiden with whom he was falling in love was too painful to even consider.

After Flaming Arrow had departed, Brandy sat in misery while these disturbing thoughts ran through her mind. Then she decided she had to know the truth, rose, and left the tent to follow him. She caught sight of Flaming Arrow a good distance away, striding past the glowing tents with that graceful walk of his that made him look as if he were floating on air, and hurried to catch up. She was so busy craning her neck to keep the tall warrior in view that she didn't see the rawhide tether tied to a war horse staked behind one tent. She tripped over the rope and fell flat on her face, painfully skinning her elbow. When she rose, there was no sight of Flaming Arrow.

Disgusted, Brandy decided to bathe her injured elbow in a nearby stream before making her way back to Flaming Arrow's tepee. She left the village behind and picked her way through the dark woods until she found the stream. Then a sudden impulse came over her. She decided to take a real bath, one without her underwear for a change. No one would see her in the dark. She quickly stripped and waded in, then dallied far longer than she intended in the cool water.

Flaming Arrow left his brother's tepee, where he had been visiting every night. It was a new ritual since his return to the village that bewildered his sister-in-law and confirmed Yellow Fox's suspicions that his younger brother was fighting his attraction to the white-eyes tooth and toenail. Flaming Arrow departed earlier than usual that night and decided to take a walk beside the stream, where he wouldn't be distracted by the camp noises as he thought over Crazy Horse's plan. Cutting through the thick woods, he came to a dead halt as the stream came into view and he caught sight of something with his excellent night vision. He sucked in his breath sharply at the arresting sight of Brandy coming from the water, her pale skin seeming to glow with a life of its own despite the darkness.

As Brandy stepped on the sandy bank, she sensed someone's presence in the dark shadows. She stopped and glanced around wildly, her heart suddenly racing in fear, for she had no idea if the presence was human or animal or if it posed a danger for her.

"There is no need to fear," Flaming Arrow said softly. "It is just me."

Brandy sighed in relief as she recognized Flaming Arrow's voice. Nor did she feel the slightest bit of alarm at his catching her totally unclothed. As pitch dark as it was, he couldn't possibly see anything other than a vague outline. After all, that was all she could see of him. She carefully picked her way to where she had dropped her clothing, asking, "What are you doing out here?"

Flaming Arrow frowned. Was it his imagination, or had there been a sharpness to Brandy's voice? But why would she be angry with him? "I might ask you the same thing."

"I decided to take a bath," Brandy answered, dropping to her knees and groping in the dark for her underwear.

Flaming Arrow stepped forward, bent, and swooped up her camisole. He handed the garment to her and said, "I thought you bathed earlier in the evening."

Brandy didn't answer. If he had seen what she had been blindly searching for, he could see her nakedness. She jumped to her feet, holding the flimsy garment before her, and said, "Go away!"

"Why?"

"Because I'm not clothed, that's why! You have no business being here."

"I had no way of knowing you were bathing here, and you did not tell me to go away when I first walked up. Why are you so outraged now?"

"Because I didn't think you could see in the dark."

"And now you think I can?"

Brandy didn't think it. She knew it! She could feel his hot gaze sweeping up and down her body. She thought to turn and run, but suddenly her knees felt incredibly weak, and for the life of her, she couldn't say a word. His presence, his powerful masculinity seemed to be smothering her.

"You are correct," Flaming Arrow said in a husky voice when Brandy failed to answer his question. "I can see you. I happen to have very good night vision." Once again his smoldering gaze swept over her, stopping at the rosy circles of her nipples, then dropping to linger at the dark patch between her ivory thighs.

Brandy felt mesmerized as Flaming Arrow
stepped up to her and took the camisole she held in
front of her from her grasp. As he pulled her into his
embrace, she gasped at the heat of his bare chest and
his taut belly against her skin. Then his mouth closed
over hers in a hungry, demanding kiss that sent her
senses reeling dizzily, and she melted into him, her
arms snaking around his broad bronze shoulders.

Flaming Arrow's powerful heart raced wildly as he
lowered Brandy to the soft grass and lay halfway over
her, his mouth still locked on hers in that fierce, passionate kiss. Then Brandy began to kiss him back.
Her small tongue dueled with his, stabbed provoca-
tively, then retreated elusively before he could catch
it in his lips. A shudder of raw desire ran over him,
while a peculiar roaring filled his ears. But as wildly
exciting as Brandy's kiss was, Flaming Arrow wanted
to dominate her, to place his brand on her forever.
Snarling against her lips, his strong tongue plunged
deep into her mouth, plundering its sweetness with a
ferociousness that bordered on savagery, his lips
grinding against hers as his hands swept over her
body possessively.

When Flaming Arrow finally broke the torrid kiss,
Brandy felt as if she were submerged in thick molas-
ses. Her breath came in ragged gasps, and her heart
pounded so rapidly, she feared it would burst. She lay
perfectly still as he dropped a trail of searing kisses
down her throat, then across her shoulders to the rise
of her creamy breasts. Even when his warm hand
cupped one mound, Brandy felt powerless to move.
Every muscle in her body seemed to have melted,
and she was tingling all over. Then as his lips touched
her aching nipple and his warm tongue brushed

across it like a wet lash, she did move, a spontaneous jerking of her entire body as a shot of mind-boggling, intense pleasure ran through her. Again, she wrapped her arms around him, her fingers slipping into the soft hair at the nape of his neck and holding him closer as he played at her breasts, his mouth sucking, his tongue licking, his strong, artful fingers massaging until she thought she would go out of her mind at the wonderful sensations he was invoking, the warm curl in her belly spiraling outward until it was a terrible burning between her legs.

Brandy was so enthralled with Flaming Arrow's ministrations at her breasts and the burning at the core of her womanhood that she hardly noticed his other hand trailing down her hip, then across her lower stomach. Not until his fingers slid through the dark curls at the apex of her thighs did she suddenly become aware of his bold intimacy. Her eyes flew open, and somewhere in the back of her foggy mind, she thought to object. But before she could even whimper in protest, Flaming Arrow's skillful fingers were working their magic, gently exploring the aching lips; then they found and sensuously stroked the tiny bud there, swooping down on the most sensitive spot of her body with the sureness of a honey bee seeking the nectar of a fragrant flower. As Flaming Arrow's deft fingers continued their sensual assault, Brandy moaned and arched her hips, her legs spreading of their own accord as shock wave after delicious shock wave coursed through her body, each one more powerful than the last, until she saw a burst of stars behind her eyelids.

The sound of Brandy's throaty moans and the feel of her wet, throbbing flesh against his fingers excited

Flaming Arrow even more than the taste of her lips and breasts. As her entire body convulsed in pleasure, his erection lengthened another inch, straining painfully against the tight confines of his breechclout. All too aware that the material was the only barrier between him and the hot, womanly depths in which he ached to bury himself, he rolled to his back and jerked impatiently on the strip of rawhide that held his breechclout in place. As the string gave way, he brushed the material aside. He rose over Brandy, straddled her legs, and held himself poised over her, supporting his weight on his elbows as he kissed her lightly. Then he whispered against her lips in a voice roughened with desire, "I want you."

Still feeling dazed from the release his fingers had brought her, Brandy opened her eyes to see the dark form of Flaming Arrow hovering over her. It took a moment for his words to sink in. Suddenly she became aware of just how far their lovemaking had progressed, of her sprawled legs, of him poised above her; and his words, instead of exciting her, filled her with self-disgust. Why, she was no better than those other women, she thought, spreading her legs to a man simply because he desired her and she desired him! And how many other women had he said those words to? Not *I love you*, but *I want you*. Well, maybe it was enough for those other women, but it wasn't enough for her. No, for her, there had to be more.

Brandy shoved on Flaming Arrow's shoulders and cried out, "No! Stop this minute!"

Brandy's sudden turnabout was the last thing Flaming Arrow had expected. His black eyes flashed angrily. "What do you mean? No? Stop? You loved what I was doing to you. Admit it!"

"No, I didn't!"

"You lie! You moaned in pleasure. You pressed yourself against my hand. You embraced me. You kissed me back."

A humiliated flush rose on Brandy's face, for she knew she had done all those shameful things. "That doesn't mean anything. I didn't know what I was doing. You took me by surprise."

"By surprise? And what does that mean? That you temporarily forgot I was an Indian?" Flaming Arrow asked, his voice heavy with bitterness.

Surprisingly, Flaming Arrow's being an Indian had nothing to do with Brandy's sudden reluctance. She no longer considered him beneath her. For her, there had to be more than desire, regardless of who the man was. "No, that doesn't have anything to do with it. I just don't want to do it, that's all."

"You don't want to do it," Flaming Arrow repeated in a hard voice. "You only want to tease a man, to drive him wild with passion, then refuse?"

"No! I didn't mean it that way either. I told you, I didn't realize what I was doing, and now I just want you to stop."

Flaming Arrow didn't think he could stop. Every muscle in his body was screaming for release, particularly the powerful, throbbing one whose tip was so close to Brandy's womanhood that he could feel her scorching heat. He ground his teeth, struggling to bring his raging passion under control. Then, so suddenly Brandy cried out in surprise, he sprang to his feet, bent forward, and jerked Brandy to hers. "I think you lie. I think you are a tease. Twice you have tried to make a fool of me. But do not try it again. I warn you. The next time, I will take you with"—he paused as his dark eyes bored into hers—"or without your consent!"

Flaming Arrow pushed Brandy away from him, sending her stumbling backward, picked up his breechclout, and stormed away. Brandy stared at where his shadowy form disappeared in the inky darkness, feeling shaky at how near she had come to submitting to his ardent advances. Then, remembering that he had accused her of deliberately teasing him, anger came to her defense. How dare he! she thought hotly. She had been minding her own business when he had all but attacked her, not once, but twice, catching her by surprise and sweeping her off her feet. And he had almost succeeded with his passionate kisses and indecent caresses. If she hadn't come to her senses, it would have been too late.

Supported by the outrage she had whipped up in herself, Brandy dressed and rushed back to the tepee, determined to wait up for Flaming Arrow and give him a piece of her mind. But she didn't have to wait up for him. She found him saddling his war horse beside the tent, which so surprised her that she was momentarily speechless.

Flaming Arrow mounted and walked his horse up to her, then said in a tight voice that told her he was still angry, "I will be gone for several days. Swift Rabbit will look after you."

Brandy's outrage disappeared like a puff of smoke in a brisk wind. Where was he going? she wondered. On another raid? Or off to war? Both were dangerous. A sudden fear for his life seized her. "Where are you going?"

Flaming Arrow didn't make explanations to anyone about his coming and going. Besides, he was angry at the white-eyes for spurning his advances. But he heard the fear in Brandy's voice and, despite his negative feelings, responded to it, once more finding himself wanting to reassure her. "Crazy Horse has asked me to accompany him and several other chiefs to Red Cloud's reservation, where they are to meet with commissioners from your government who want to buy the Black Hills. Crazy Horse does not trust the white-eyes. He thought, since I know English, that I might mingle in the crowds and pick up information that might be helpful to us."

So it was just as she had suspected, Brandy thought. Now that her people had discovered the Black Hills were valuable, they wanted them. Then she asked, "Crazy Horse? Is he the man you reported to that day you brought in the captured herd?"

"Yes, he is the war chief of this village."

Brandy had heard of Crazy Horse. Her brother had told her that the old mountain men called him "the strange one" and that, had Crazy Horse been white, he would have been called the greatest cavalry commander the world had ever known. Yes, she had known that day she had seen him that the chief was a cut above other men. "Why are you leaving in the middle of the night?" she asked. "I should think Crazy Horse would wait until daybreak."

"That is when he and the party he has chosen *will* leave. I go before them so that I can blend in with the reservation Indians before they arrive. Crazy Horse does not want anyone to associate me with him. He hopes the commissioners and those in their party will be less cautious around the supposedly tame Indians and let something slip."

"Will it be dangerous?" Brandy asked, then hated

herself for inquiring, fearing she might be giving her
innermost feelings away.

Would it matter to her if it was? Flaming Arrow
wondered. It would please him immensely to know
she cared enough to worry about him. But that would
be even more foolish than wanting her to desire him,
he reminded himself brutally. "Only if I am caught
spying on the white man, and I do not intend to get
caught."

For a long moment, Flaming Arrow sat on his horse
and gazed down at Brandy. Brandy gazed back. They
seemed to be locked in some strange vacuum of time,
each forgetting their anger and secretly yearning
that the other would kiss them good-bye. Then Flaming Arrow's horse nickered impatiently and broke
the spell for him. He scoffed at himself for being yet
again a fool and nudged his mount forward.

Long after Flaming Arrow had ridden away,
Brandy stood beside his tepee and gazed out where
he had disappeared, the steady night breeze ruffling
her long hair that hung around her shoulders. The
fear she had felt for him at first had been dispelled,
for she knew he could more than adequately look
after himself. Besides, the meeting he was going to
was a peaceful one. No, what Brandy felt now was
loneliness.

She wondered at the strange emotion. How could
she feel lonely when she hardly ever saw him anyway? Yet his presence was so powerful that she had
known he was there all the while, somewhere in the
camp, somewhere nearby, and had found solace in
the knowledge. But even so, he had just ridden off
now. It was too soon for her to miss him.

The exciting savage was beginning to get to her,

she admitted. Not only did he attract her physically, invoking shocking yearnings, but she was worrying about him and missing him, something that she had never done for any man, other than the brother she adored. Yes, Flaming Arrow was dangerous to her, very dangerous. If she wasn't careful, she'd lose not only her virtue but her heart too. The first would be humiliating enough—giving her body to a man who felt nothing for her but lust; but to put herself in a position where a man could trample on her affections was something Brandy would never tolerate. She had far too much pride for that.

With these troubling thoughts on her mind, Brandy turned and entered the tepee.

9

         By the next morning, Brandy had come to a firm decision. The few days Flaming Arrow would be gone would be an excellent time to make a bid for freedom. It was more than a yearning to return to her people and her old way of life with all its comforts that was driving her. She was desperate to escape Flaming Arrow before she succumbed to his powerful seductive magnetism.

  During the day, Brandy began to collect things that she might need for her journey back to civilization: strips of jerky, roasted sunflower seeds, dried plums and grapes, a snare for catching small animals, a skinning knife, a flint, several lengths of rawhide rope, a small pot, the hairbrush Flaming Arrow had given her, her old riding boots, and a water skin. She rolled these things in the trading blanket that lay on her pallet. Then Brandy cut off a third of the pallet and sewed the loose ends of the buffalo skin together with an awl and a piece of sinew, as Swift Rabbit had taught her, to fashion a rough saddle for her trip.

Brandy looked around the tepee, wishing she had a weapon other than the knife, but Flaming Arrow had taken his rifle with him. Then she spied the bow he had left sitting beside his pallet. She walked to it and picked it up. When she tried to pull its string back, she was shocked. She couldn't even begin to budge it, no matter how hard she tried. She'd had no idea it took so much strength to fire an arrow. The times she had seen Flaming Arrow test the fit of a new arrow in his bow, it had looked so easy. No wonder the Dakota had such powerful wrists and arms.

She heard someone step into the tepee, and Brandy whirled around and saw Swift Rabbit. Brandy glared at her, for the old woman hadn't even had the courtesy to announce herself by scratching on the tent before she entered. As Swift Rabbit stared at the blanket roll and the crude saddle, Brandy's nerves began to crawl. Did the old woman suspect that she planned to escape?

Swift Rabbit didn't leave Brandy in suspense for long. She looked the young woman directly in the eyes and asked in her tongue, "You go away?"

Brandy saw no purpose in denying it. The evidence spoke for itself. "Yes, back to my people."

"It is a long way."

"I know, but I'm going anyway."

During the time Brandy had been in the camp, Swift Rabbit had secretly come to admire the young woman's determination and spirit. And she had never dreamed that a white woman could work as hard as an Indian. The old woman now thought she

knew why Brandy had been agreeable to learning
the Indian ways, but that didn't change her opinion
of Brandy one iota. If anything, it only meant the
white-eyes was resourceful and cunning—attributes
that Swift Rabbit respected. And the girl had courage, if she was going to attempt to get back to her
people. Neither Swift Rabbit herself or any Indian
woman that she knew of would ever dream of taking
such a long journey alone. Even for their spiritual
rituals, Indian women did not venture far from the
protection of their camps.

When Swift Rabbit remained silent, Brandy stuck
her chin out and said defiantly, "You can't stop me."

Swift Rabbit might have tried to do just that, since
Flaming Arrow had distinctly instructed her to
watch over his captive and had thereby made the girl
her responsibility. But after what she had learned the
night before, Swift Rabbit wanted Brandy gone as
much as the white-eyes. She had stumbled across
Flaming Arrow and Brandy by the stream and had
seen him attempt to make love to her. The old
woman had been shocked, for she'd had no idea that
Flaming Arrow was attracted to the white-eyes. He
had seemed to be avoiding her. But his desiring
Brandy put an entirely different light on everything.
If Flaming Arrow were to become so enraptured
with the white-eyes as to make her his wife, Brandy
might insist that he stop supporting Swift Rabbit.
After all, she had not been very kind to the white-
eyes, driving her the way she had. It seemed only
natural to Swift Rabbit that Brandy would seek revenge. Nor did Brandy's refusing Flaming Arrow
bear any weight with Swift Rabbit, for the old
woman was so positive of Flaming Arrow's masculine

appeal that she was certain he would eventually overcome the white-eyes' resistance. "I have no intention of stopping you. I plan to help you."

Brandy was shocked by Swift Rabbit's answer until she remembered that the old woman had felt threatened by her in the beginning. Apparently Flaming Arrow's assurance that he would continue to provide for her had not fully reassured the Indian woman, and Swift Rabbit still felt the need to protect her security so much that she was anxious to get rid of her. But Brandy was still wary. She cocked her head and asked suspiciously, "How can you help me?"

"I can get you a horse."

Obtaining a mount was the only thing in her plans for escape for which Brandy had not found a solution. The herds were guarded at night for fear of a Crow raid, and she didn't dare try to attempt an escape in the broad daylight. "You'd steal a horse for me?" she asked in surprise.

"I would not have to steal it. Flaming Arrow gave me three horses to use when I am moving his household. I will give one to you. But it will not be safe to bring it into camp. That might arouse suspicion. You will have to meet me by the stream where you bathe after dark." Swift Rabbit paused, giving the saddle Brandy had fashioned a disgusted look, then added, "And I will bring a saddle too. A woman's saddle. It will be more comfortable than that."

Brandy had to struggle to keep up with what Swift Rabbit said. She had never had to decipher so much of the Lakota language at one time. She hadn't even realized there was such a thing as an Indian woman's saddle. By the time she had comprehended everything, Swift Rabbit was already halfway through the entrance, saying over her shoulder, "At the stream, tonight."

Brandy left the tepee as soon as darkness fell, and she found Swift Rabbit waiting beside the stream for her with a little pinto mare that was already saddled. In the light of a sliver of a new moon, Brandy tied her rolled blanket and its contents to the back of the saddle while she admired it, for it looked nothing like the tiny, lumpy saddles she had seen the men ride. The cottonwood saddle had a high pommel and cantle, with sideboards and metal stirrups, and it was padded with soft buckskin. There was even a saddle blanket, decorated with beads, and the mare was wearing a chest ornament of the same design. Brandy was elated, then felt a twinge of guilt. Slipping the water skin around the pommel, she managed to set her resentment toward the old woman aside and admit to Swift Rabbit, "I feel bad taking your pretty saddle."

Swift Rabbit wished Brandy hadn't mentioned feeling bad. She was beginning to experience a little discomfort herself for helping the white-eyes escape. In the first place, Flaming Arrow would be furious with her if he ever learned of it. But what was really gnawing at Swift Rabbit's conscience was her serious doubts that the girl would ever make it back to her people. She strongly suspected she was sending the white-eyes to her death. "I have other saddles."

Brandy frowned at Swift Rabbit's gruff answer, for she had no way of knowing that the old woman had spoken so sharply in an effort to hide her real emotions. To Brandy, it seemed to only confirm how anxious the Indian was to get rid of her. She turned to mount, but every time she tried to put her foot in the stirrup, the mare shied away. Finally, she asked, "What's wrong with this horse? She won't let me mount."

"That is the wrong side to get on a horse."

"It is not!" Brandy said indignantly. "I know what side to use."

"Indians use the other side."

"Are you insane? Telling me to mount on the right side?" Then realizing she had spoken in English, Brandy said in the Lakota tongue, "I used this side when I rode Flaming Arrow's horse."

"That stallion is a war horse and is specially trained. They can be mounted from any direction, even the back. This is just a plain Indian pony."

Exasperated at the Indians' strange custom, Brandy walked around the pony, ducked beneath its long neck, and mounted. Picking up the reins, she looked down at Swift Rabbit for a moment, then grudgingly managed to say, "Thank you for helping me."

Swift Rabbit's guilt momentarily got the better of her. "You should not thank me. You may be going to your death."

It was a sobering thought, and for just a brief moment, Brandy had doubts. Then she asked, "Do you know of any trail I can follow?"

"Dakotas do not use trails. Knowing which direction to travel comes from within us, like the geese that fly away each fall and return each summer. But I will tell you something my husband once told me. If you ride toward the rising sun, always keeping the mountains behind you, eventually you will come to the Big Muddy."

Brandy's eyes lit up with excitement. The Missouri! Yes, once she reached that river, she could find her way home. All she had to do was follow it southward.

Once again, she looked down at Swift Rabbit and felt a twinge of regret at leaving her. The emotion surprised Brandy, for over the past weeks she had spent the better part of her waking hours silently cursing the old woman for being so severe with her. But toiling beside the Indian day by day, learning new and sometimes difficult things from her enforced mentor, had formed a sort of strange bond. Brandy was forced to admit that while she had never particularly liked the stern old woman, she had come to respect her. Brandy had never met anyone so persevering and was amazed by Swift Rabbit's energy and physical strength, particularly in view of her advanced age. Why, Swift Rabbit could work circles around her or, for that matter, around any of the servants back home.

Swift Rabbit was also feeling a twinge of regret and was even more astonished by it than Brandy. It shouldn't be that way, Swift Rabbit told herself. The girl was her *toka*, her enemy. She should hate her. But deep down, Swift Rabbit had to admit that she didn't. Somehow, in some twisted way, she had begun to hope that the white girl might become her friend.

Both women found their emotions hard to deal with, and neither was forthright enough to admit their feelings to the other. They stared at each other silently for a long moment, then finally Brandy turned her mount and rode away.

* * *

Brandy rode just far enough that night to put a reasonable distance between herself and the camp, then she rested until dawn, when she climbed back into the saddle. She fared amazingly well the first day of her long journey, covering almost as much territory in one day as the raiding party had. Her month in the Indian camp had stood her in good stead. Not only had it accustomed her to the heat, but the hard labor she had performed had developed muscles and brought forth a physical stamina she had never known she possessed. That evening as she sat by the fire she had built and roasted the rabbit she had snared, she was feeling very good about herself. She had been totally self-sufficient that day, in complete and total control of her destiny for the first time in her life, something that very few women of her class could claim. Why, she seriously doubted that many white women of any station had done what she had done that day. Her success was heady stuff, and it wasn't until she retired, lying beneath a sky filled with glittering stars with only the thin covering of her blanket over her, that the full significance of her leaving the Indian camp finally hit her. She would never see Flaming Arrow again, never hear his deep voice, never watch his graceful, catlike walk, never feel the heat of his dark eyes upon her, never know the excitement of his arms around her and his warm lips on hers. She reminded herself that he had forced her to go with him, bent her to his will. She tried to whip up an anger at him, but her ploy didn't work. Her high spirits plunged to the ground, and it was a long, long time before she finally slept.

* * *

Two days later, Brandy reached a river that she assumed was the Missouri because of its width. She turned her horse to the south and followed it, traveling across a grassy land dotted with high buttes that towered into a cloudless, searing-blue sky. The farther she rode, the more arid the country became, until the river narrowed into little more than a trickle and the grass grew only in an occasional brownish tuft here and there. But Brandy still followed the river, convinced that it was the Missouri, thinking that the country she was passing through was only a temporary bad stretch. By the time Brandy realized she was following the wrong river, it was too late to correct her mistake and turn back. She was hopelessly lost in a desertlike land filled with curiously carved ridges and mounds from which rose grotesque rock pinnacles and columns of variegated colors, and criss-crossed with deep canyons with dry stream beds.

For days, Brandy wandered in the badlands, unaware that she was traveling in circles. Each morning, she reoriented herself and headed eastward, but by midday, the sun was a searing globe in a blinding white sky, its light reflected on the gray sand creating a fierce glare that was painful to the eyes, and Brandy lost all sense of direction. Eventually, she even lost count of the days she had wandered aimlessly in this land where there was no water, no vegetation, and no living thing except snakes and lizards, where the alkaline dust burned her eyes and nostrils, where the wind blew constantly, grating on her nerves. On the fifth day she ran out of water. The next evening, her lips cracked and bled from thirst and her stomach gnawed with hunger, and she remembered her brother telling her of a cavalry patrol that had been lost in the desert. The men had killed their horses so that they could drink the animals' blood and eat their meat. Brandy seriously contemplated doing the same, but she found she didn't have the courage to kill the mare. The little Indian pony had served her well and, having been her only companion for ten days, had become like a friend to her. Perhaps if the mare died first, it would be different, but Brandy knew that wasn't likely. The pony was much sturdier than she. By the next morning, Brandy found she no longer had a choice. The mare had disappeared during the night, apparently gone on its own quest for water.

That day, Brandy didn't even bother to try to find her way out of the badlands. She was simply too weak. She knew she was going to die, just as those people whose bleached bones she had seen scattered here and there over the past few days had died. And they hadn't all been Indians, either. She knew that at least one group had been white, for the remains of a wagon were nearby. It was then that she was forced to admit to a profound truth: She had been a fool to think that she could ever make her way back to her own people. Now she would have to pay the price for her foolishness. And for what? To save her precious virtue? Given the choice, she would choose her life over her virtue anytime. Besides, living with the Indians hadn't been all that bad. She'd had food, shelter, the necessities of life. And she really hadn't missed the comforts of home all that much. She had even had the opportunity to meet an extraordinary man.

Brandy tried to retract that last thought, but she couldn't. In the face of death, there was no place for duplicity. No longer could she practice self-deception. Flaming Arrow *was* special, a man like no other she had known, and she had been a fool to run from him. Had he been white, she would probably have knocked herself out trying to snare him, despite his infuriating domineering tendencies. Somehow, some way, she would have brought him to heel—or at least made him meet her halfway. No, she wouldn't have let her stupid pride keep her from getting what she wanted. She had let someone wonderful slip through her fingers because he was an Indian, and yes, she admitted as long as she was being brutally honest with herself, she had denied herself a wonderful experience when she had refused to let him make love to her. Now she would go to her death and never know what it was like with him—or with any man, for that matter.

A sudden thought came to Brandy. Maybe Flaming Arrow would come after her when he returned to camp and found she was missing. Did he want her enough to do that? Her spirits soared. Then doubts crept in, and her hopes crumbled. Why should he, when there were so many other women in the camp who were willing? Besides, he'd never find her in this desolate, godforsaken country.

A profound regret filled Brandy, and she squeezed her eyes shut. Had there been moisture in her body, a tear would have slipped down her cheek. Oh, she thought bleakly, if she could only turn back the hands of time! How different her behavior would have been! She wouldn't care that Flaming Arrow desired her but did not love her. She would neither expect nor demand more than desire from him. She'd gladly be his slave of love.

For the remainder of that day, Brandy lay in the hot sand beneath the blazing sun and slowly grew weaker and weaker, disoriented and plagued by hallucinations. The most tormenting hallucination was that a tall, dark-eyed, ruggedly handsome savage was hovering over her.

10

But Brandy's vision of Flaming Arrow standing over her was not a hallucination. It was real. When the Dakota found her and looked down at her, he was filled with dread, thinking she was dead. Then, seeing her open eyes and her shallow breathing, he exhaled the breath he had been holding, turned to his horse, and quickly took his water skin from where it hung on his saddle.

Brandy still thought she was hallucinating when Flaming Arrow knelt beside her, cradled her shoulders in his arms, and held the bag to her lips. The man in the vision that was taunting her couldn't possibly be the same one who had captured her and insolently held her against her will. This man's dark eyes were filled with concern. She refused to drink, so Flaming Arrow all but forced the liquid down her throat. Still disoriented, she coughed half of the water back up and swung her arms wildly at him. The Dakota muttered an oath as he thought, Even on the brink of death, she fought him.

"Stop it!" Flaming Arrow said harshly. "Do you want to spill what little water we have left? Behave yourself and drink!"

Brandy suddenly became still. She recognized that deep male voice and its domineering tone. Surely her ears couldn't be playing tricks on her as well as her eyes. Then, feeling the steady thud of Flaming Arrow's strong heart against her shoulder, she realized he was real. He had come after her, she thought, and a shot of pure joy streaked through her. He had actually come!

The next time Flaming Arrow put the water skin to Brandy's lips, she drank willingly—too willingly. When he pulled the bag away, she made a weak protest, and he said, "No, don't drink too much too fast. It will make you ill."

Over the next two hours, Flaming Arrow patiently gave Brandy carefully measured sips of water, slowly hydrating her. When she was able to keep the liquid down, he offered her a strip of jerky. Too weak to chew, she shook her head and muttered, "No, I can't. Just give me water."

"You need nourishment as well as water." His gaze quickly swept over her. She looked much thinner than when he had last seen her. "How long has it been since you have eaten?"

Brandy couldn't remember when she had eaten her last jerky, and there had been nothing in this desolate place to snare. "I don't know," she admitted.

Flaming Arrow shook his head in disgust, then

broke off a piece of the jerky and held it to her lips. "Just suck on it."

"No, it's too hard. My tongue is sore and cracked."

Flaming Arrow put the piece of dried meat in his mouth, chewed on it until it was soft, then held it out to her. Seeing that she was about to refuse again, he said in a hard voice, "Take it. My saliva will not kill you. It didn't when I kissed you. It won't now."

It was a point that Brandy couldn't refute, yet it seemed extremely intimate to take food that had been in his mouth. Reluctantly, she accepted the softened jerky, and as she sucked on it, she wondered at her hesitancy. He had put his tongue in her mouth when he had kissed her, but he had been motivated by mindless passion. This act had been deliberate and motivated by—what? Care? Was that why it seemed so terribly personal, his caring for her as if she were a baby? And did he care? Another shot of joy ran through her.

Flaming Arrow disappeared for a short time, and Brandy dozed off. When she awoke, it was dark and a fire was burning. She sat up and gazed groggily at the flickering flames. Flaming Arrow was removing a piece of meat from the spit he had been turning. "Where did you get the wood for the fire?" she asked.

"From a wagon I found a few miles from here."

Brandy remembered the wagon and the skeletons scattered all around it and remembered how close she had come to meeting the same end. A shiver ran over her.

Flaming Arrow walked around the fire to her and handed her a thin strip of roasted meat. Brandy accepted it and ate it hungrily, then ate another piece, and she asked, "Where did you find something to eat out here? I haven't seen anything but snakes and lizards."

"That was snake you just ate. Rattlesnake."

Brandy's eyes filled with horror, and her hand flew to her mouth. Seeing her, Flaming Arrow said in a stern voice, "Don't you dare gag and lose that! That is perfectly good nourishment, and it may be the last fresh meat you see for a day or two. Even snakes are scarce out here."

Brandy forced down her rising gorge. As much as she hated to admit it, she knew that what Flaming Arrow said was true. She would be foolhardy to reject the meat. It really hadn't tasted all that bad, rather like chicken. It was more the idea of eating snake, than anything else.

Seeing her fight to control her revulsion and retain the meat, Flaming Arrow felt another wave of relief wash over him. To lose her now from nothing but sheer foolishness on her part would be unbearable after he had searched so long and hard for her. He stepped back around the fire and sat down, then gazed silently across the flames at her. He recalled the day he had returned from Fort Laramie to find her missing. His first reaction had been anger, for he had warned her not to try to escape. But when her trail had led into this arid, desolate area, and he had realized how much danger she was in, he had been filled with an emotion that was totally alien to him. For the first time in his life, he had known real fear, but he had stubbornly refused to delve too deeply into his feelings. All he would admit to was that he *had* to find her.

While Flaming Arrow was musing over these thoughts, Brandy had lain back down, shocked at how weak she still felt. Then, lulled by the sound of the crackling fire and feeling its welcome warmth creep over her, she closed her eyes and fell asleep.

Flaming Arrow scrutinized Brandy for a long moment as she slept. Then he rose, walked around the fire, and sat down beside her. He pulled her blanket up around her and tucked it in. He started to rise to bed down on the other side of the fire, but he discovered he couldn't, which baffled him. He knew she didn't need his body heat to warm her. She had her blanket and the fire for that. Nor did she really need his protection. There were no wild animals out here, and even if there had been, the bright light of the fire would have kept them away. His strange need to protect her, to care for her, was perplexing enough, but his desire to just be close to her was even more disconcerting. Mysteriously, she seemed to hold him to her side as if by some invisible tether. With something bordering on helplessness, he lay down beside her.

The next morning, Flaming Arrow produced the little mare that Brandy had used to escape with from behind a nearby sand dune. She was filled with gladness to see the pony she had become so fond of and softly cried out, "Oh, thank goodness, she's alive! Where did you find her?"

"A few miles back. She looked familiar." He paused, giving Brandy a piecing look, and said, "If I'm not mistaken, this is one of the ponies I gave Swift Rabbit."

Brandy knew by the glitter in Flaming Arrow's black eyes that he suspected Swift Rabbit had aided her in her escape and was not pleased with the old woman. Strangely, even after her close brush with death, Brandy didn't want Swift Rabbit to get into any trouble because of her. After all, the old woman had warned her. Pasting an innocent look on her face, she said, "Oh, really? What a coincidence! I stole Swift Rabbit's saddle—it was sitting right outside her tepee—and I had no trouble sneaking it away in the dark. But I had no idea it was her horse I was taking too. She must have been furious with me when she discovered they were both missing."

Swift Rabbit had not said a word about either her horse or her saddle being missing, which was why Flaming Arrow was so suspicious. The old woman usually jumped at any opportunity to blame or criticize Brandy. "How did you manage to steal the pony with the guards all around?"

"I guess I was just lucky. The mare had wandered away from the rest of the herd," Brandy lied adroitly.

Flaming Arrow was forced to believe Brandy's story, for he couldn't imagine why Swift Rabbit would help the girl escape after he had given her his word he would continue to provide for her, much less why Brandy would lie to protect the old woman. The two certainly weren't friends. He was left to assume that Swift Rabbit hadn't mentioned the missing saddle and mare for fear he would blame her for being careless, making it so easy for Brandy to escape. Putting his suspicions aside, he saddled the mare and helped Brandy mount. Then he flew to the back of his own horse, caught Brandy's mare's reins in one hand, and rode off.

That day, the traveling was just as tedious and the sun just at hot as it had been before, but somehow it didn't seem as bad to Brandy as it had been. She had all the confidence in the world that Flaming Arrow would lead her from this hostile area with its glaring gray sand and its maze of strangely twisted rock formations. Knowing that they would soon be leaving this miserable country made everything much easier to bear. But late that afternoon, when she saw the bluish mountains jutting abruptly from the desert floor, she was startled. How in the world had they managed to reach them so soon? she wondered. Why, it had taken her days and days to travel that far! What had happened to the broad prairie she had crossed?

Seeing the perplexed expression on Brandy's face and guessing her thoughts, Flaming Arrow circled back and brought his horse beside hers. "If you are thinking that those are the Big Horn Mountains before us, you are mistaken. Those are the Black Hills."

Brandy was shocked by Flaming Arrow's announcement. If those were the Black Hills before her, how had she missed them on her journey eastward? The range seemed every bit as large as the one that overlooked the Dakota village she had fled. But the last mountains she had seen had been the far-distant Big Horns, and that had been days and days ago. Had she been so addled by the blazing sun that she hadn't even noticed the Black Hills and ridden right by them?

Again, Flaming Arrow guessed her thoughts. "We are backtracking. The Black Hills are to the east of the area where you were lost."

"But why are we going east, not west?" Brandy asked in confusion. Then as a sudden thought occurred to her. "Are you taking me back to my people, after all?"

Flaming Arrow stiffened in his saddle and answered in an adamant voice, "No! I told you I will never take you back!"

A part of Brandy was vastly relieved. Deep down, she didn't want to leave Flaming Arrow. But another part of her bristled at his domineering attitude, for despite all the vows she had made when she thought she was dying, she still resented his being so overbearing. She wanted staying with him to be her decision, not his. She wanted him to ask her, not command her. The two conflicting emotions struggled within her, and eventually resentment won out. She glared at Flaming Arrow and asked in an angry voice, "Then why are we going there?"

"We are going to the mountains so you can rest and regain your strength. It will be a long trip back to my village, and your ordeal has left you in a weakened condition."

"I'm not in a weakened condition!" Brandy retorted. Now that her ire had been stirred up, she took insult at everything he said. "There is nothing weak about me, damn you!"

There she goes again, Flaming Arrow thought, his own anger rising. Arguing about everything—just aching for a fight. Why had he bothered to come after her? She was the most exasperating female he had ever met. And at that moment she didn't look in the least weakened, not with her beautiful blue eyes spitting fire. No, she seemed to thrive on conflict. But this time he was determined not to give her the satisfaction of quarreling with her. Wordlessly, he turned his horse and rode away, leading Brandy's mare behind him.

Furious that he had turned his back on her, Brandy shrieked, "Did you hear me? I said I'm not weak!"

Flaming Arrow ignored her, acting as if she didn't even exist. Since he held the reins to her horse and she was too weak even to dismount, Brandy was left to glare at his broad back and seethe in silent frustration. But as the day wore on, even seething required energy that she really couldn't spare, for her ordeal in the desert *had* drained her. By the time Flaming Arrow led her mare into the rugged mountains and stopped beneath a stand of towering pines, it was night, and she was so exhausted she was hardly aware of her surroundings. When he reached up to help her dismount, she collapsed into his arms, dead to the world.

When Brandy awoke the next morning, the first thing she became aware of was the pungent odor of pines. The second thing she noticed was the gurgling sound of water running over the stones in a nearby stream. She sat up groggily, saw the small fire Flaming Arrow had built, then looked about her.

Their camp was on a steep mountainside, surrounded on both sides and above by a thick pine woods. Gazing out at the rugged mountains, she saw that the bases of the gigantic rises were made up of exposed rock formations, some of which looked very dramatic. Some were so weathered by aeons of water and wind that the stone seemed almost polished. The farther up the mountain she looked, the denser the forest was, until the towering jagged crests were a solid verdant green.

Catching sight of a movement to one side of her, she turned and saw Flaming Arrow stride into the clearing. Brandy had completely forgotten her anger at him the day before and thought how handsome he looked with his impressive physique and his rugged, clean-cut features. No man—absolutely none—could possibly walk as gracefully, as silently as he did. With his feline stride, the aura of sheer power he exuded, his corded muscles rippling beneath his bronze skin, he reminded her of a sleek tawny cat. Yes, she admitted in silent admiration, he was truly a magnificent animal.

Flaming Arrow came to a halt beside the fire and looked at Brandy warily, half expecting her to be angry and to lash out at him. When she only stared at him, he ventured to say, "Good morning."

"Good morning," Brandy answered.

Her pleasant answer surprised Flaming Arrow, pleased him, and puzzled him. Had she declared a truce? If so, what were the terms? Still a little wary, he knelt by the fire, set his bow down, skewered the two rabbits he had shot and dressed, and put them to roast over the fire. Then he gazed across the dancing flames at Brandy. The dark circles under her eyes were almost gone. Yes, he had been correct to bring her here, he thought. After a day or two in these mountains, she would be completely back to normal. He slipped the quiver with its arrows from his back and sat cross-legged on the ground.

Brandy cocked her head and listened to a bird singing joyfully in a nearby tree. "Why do they call these mountains the Black Hills? The ground isn't that dark."

"It is not the color of ground for which they were named. They are called the Black Hills because of their dark evergreen forests."

Brandy gazed out at the thickly timbered moun-

tains. From a distance they did appear black, and the
bluish haze that hung over them only enhanced that
impression. Then her breath caught as she saw a doe
and her spotted fawn bound across the clearing just a
short distance away. No sooner had they disappeared
into the woods than she spied another deer—this one
a big twelve-point buck—farther down the mountainside. Suddenly there seemed to be game all
around them in the woods. A rabbit hopped through
the underbrush, a bevy of quail scurried from the
cover of one bush to another, and squirrels ran up
trees and flew from limb to limb. She caught sight of
an animal nibbling on a low-hanging pine branch on
the mountain across from them. In some ways it
looked like a deer, but it was much larger. "What is
that animal?" she asked.

Flaming Arrow glanced in the direction Brandy
was looking. "An elk. They prefer to spend their sum-
mers in the forests, where it's cooler."

"I don't think I've ever seen so much game in one
place. Why, you don't even have to look for it. It's
almost impossible to believe that just yesterday we
were in a desert where there was no vegetation, no
life of any kind, except"—she shivered in revulsion—
"snakes and lizards."

"Yes, that is one reason the Black Hills are so special to my people. They are completely surrounded
by a hot, dry, desertlike land. The mountains jut
above that area like an oasis in the sky, not only
bounding with game of all kinds but cooler and wet-
ter than any land between the Father of the Waters
and the Rockies."

"I can understand why you treasure these mountains. They are beautiful," Brandy answered. She be-

came aware for the first time of a strange serenity within her, then said, "And so peaceful, so—utterly peaceful."

Was that why she was behaving so amicably? Flaming Arrow wondered. Had she come under the unique magical spell of these mountains? "Yes, that is another reason the Black Hills are special to my people. It is a mystical place, a sacred place, a place where the spirits dwell."

"Spirits? Do you mean ghosts?" Brandy asked, wondering why she felt no apprehension.

"No, not evil spirits. Good spirits. Healing spirits. There is no place here for anger, for hate, for any of the ugly human emotions. That is why my people are so determined to hold this land. We revere it. It is our link to the Mystery."

That reminded Brandy of something. "How did your meeting with the government officials who want to buy this land go?"

Flaming Arrow frowned. "At first it did not go so well. There were many angry Dakotas there. One, Little Big Man, and his followers surrounded the commissioners with their guns leveled, saying this was as good a time as any to begin a war. Then your horse soldiers formed into a line of battle across from them and drew their carbines. It was Chief Spotted Tail who averted a battle. He told the hotheads in the war party that they could have their fight right then and there if that was what they wanted, but he would not back them. Of course it was not what they wanted, and they backed down."

Brandy imagined the commissioners had been a little unnerved by the close call, particularly since they would have been in the line of fire between cavalry and the threatening Indians. "Then what happened?"

"Later, the commissioners and Red Cloud sat in council. He told them what he wanted for the Black Hills. Needless to say, the white man did not agree to Red Cloud's demand."

"What was his demand?"

"Six million dollars."

"Six million?" Brandy gasped. "No wonder they refused to buy! Do you have any idea how much money that is?"

"No, and it does not matter. The point is that we will not sell these mountains at any price, and now the white man knows that. The commissioners did not even bother to haggle. In fact, they left with surprising swiftness."

Brandy frowned. If Flaming Arrow thought the matter closed, she feared he was sadly mistaken. And if Red Cloud thought he had pulled a clever coup on the white man, he, too, was in error. The great Dakota chief simply didn't understand her people. She knew that the commissioners must have been embarrassed by being put into a position where they couldn't possibly pay the demanded price, and that they'd been frightened by the Indians too. Brandy would stake her life that they would never forgive the Dakotas for humiliating them, not if they were as pompous as the government officials she had met. Somehow, some way, they'd get their revenge.

After they had eaten, Brandy rose and announced, "I'm going to have a bath."

As she walked off, Flaming Arrow rose to his feet. "No, not that way."

Brandy turned. "I know the stream is in this direction. I can hear it."

"The stream, yes. But it is too shallow for bathing. I will take you to a place where there is a deep pool."

Flaming Arrow led Brandy into the woods in the opposite direction. There, nestled against a high cliff covered with grapevines, a pool of crystal-clear water sat in a deep depression of pure rock. The variegated colors of stone reminded Brandy of a beautiful Roman bath she had once seen in a picture. Seeing her surprised expression, Flaming Arrow smiled. "Feel the water."

Brandy knelt beside the pool and dipped her hand into it, expecting it to be ice cold. But to her surprise, it was warm, very warm.

"It is fed by several hot springs," Flaming Arrow informed her. "I think you will find the water much more relaxing than a cold bath. But do not stay in too long at one time. The heat can weaken you."

Brandy could hardly wait for Flaming Arrow to disappear into the woods so that she could strip and sink into the pool. It seemed years since she'd had a warm bath. When she did slip beneath the water, she thought it the most wonderful thing she had ever felt, even more luxurious than the baths she'd had back home, for not only was the water deliciously warm, but the springs that fed it shot forth with such force that they massaged her tired and aching muscles and relaxed her. She bathed, using the sand from the bottom of the pool to scour herself. Then she removed the two strips of beaded buckskin that held her long hair at both sides of her face and sank into the pool, laying her head back and letting the warm water run through her reddish-brown tresses. It felt so good that she dallied longer than she should have, even though the water had a rather strong sulfurous odor to it. When she finally left the pool, her skin was a red as a beet, and she was feeling just a little light-headed.

Brandy sat on the side of the pool and let the air cool her, then ran her fingers through her long hair to dry it. While it was still slightly damp, she tied it to both sides once again, donned her buckskin dress, and carrying her boots, walked back to the camp.

She met Flaming Arrow coming down the trail to the pool. He came to halt and asked harshly, "What took you so long?"

The tone of his voice irritated Brandy. "I wasn't aware that there was a need to hurry," Brandy replied tartly. "I thought the whole purpose of coming here was so I could relax and regain my strength."

Flaming Arrow had meant for Brandy to relax and enjoy her bath, but when she had taken so long, he had become worried. There were dangerous wild animals in these woods, bears and mountain lions, and he had been tormented by fears that she would be attacked by one. He quickly glanced over her to reassure himself of her well-being. Not only was she in one piece, but there was still a rosy glow to her skin from the hot water and her hair shone in the sunlight like a fiery halo, making her look very beautiful and very desirable. A new emotion replaced the anxiety he had been feeling, and his passion rose and swept over him like a tremendous tidal wave. Never had he wanted her as much as he wanted her at that moment, and it angered him that he was so vulnerable to her beauty and her powerful sexuality.

"That is still no reason to take so long at your bath,"

he answered curtly, striving very hard to force his unwanted desire back down. "You can relax back at the camp. There is danger lurking in the woods. Wild animals."

"I'm not afraid of wild animals!" Brandy answered with a defiant toss of her head. "If I had been, I wouldn't have run away."

When Brandy tossed her head, it made the reddish highlights in her hair dance like flames, and Flaming Arrow's passion for her rose yet another notch. "Then what about me?" he asked, his voice dropping to a husky timbre. "Don't you realize the danger of your standing there looking so beautiful and desirable? Have you forgotten what happened the night I caught you coming from your bath?"

Brandy had thought the hot look she saw in Flaming Arrow's eyes came from anger, but now she knew differently. He was furious, yes, but he was also aroused. The memory of the night when he had kissed her and touched her so intimately was imprinted on her brain as if it had been burned there. A sudden answering heat enveloped her, and her heart raced. A terrible need for him to kiss her again rose in her—but he just glared at her. She felt weak with longing, so weak her legs seemed to turn to jelly, and without even realizing what she was doing, she swayed toward him.

Flaming Arrow recognized her leaning toward him for what it was—an open invitation. Despite his firm resolve to resist the temptation, his defenses crumbled, and a helpless groan escaped his throat. He reached out and pulled her to him, flattening her breasts against the hard planes of his chest and molding her pelvis and legs to his. Then, his dark eyes blazing with both desire and fury at himself for giving in to desire, he looked down at her and muttered against her lips, "Don't you know what you do to me, how enticing you are, how you tempt a man beyond his endurance?" He ground his hips against hers, letting her feel his eager readiness for her so there would be no doubt in her mind about her effect on him. "You are a witch! An accursed seductress!"

Flaming Arrow's lips came crashing down on Brandy's in a hard, demanding kiss. His tongue shot into her mouth like a fiery dart, for he was determined to give her no respite, to brand her as his, to force her to his will by the sheer fury of his passion. When Brandy kissed him back, her small tongue dancing sensuously around his, and pressed her trembling body even closer, he realized she wasn't resisting, and his lips softened and became more coaxing.

The sudden switch from fierce demand to tender seduction had a devastating effect on Brandy. If there had been any doubts in her mind, any remaining reservations, they would have been swept away by the feel of his artful tongue sliding in and out, in and out, in an endless, breathtaking kiss that brought her to her tiptoes. She leaned even farther into him. Then, feeling a wild excitement take hold of her, she caught the back of Flaming Arrow's head and kissed him back with total abandon.

Flaming Arrow's senses spun dizzily. As he felt Brandy press insistently against his throbbing, rigid manhood in what seemed like a silent appeal for yet more of him, somewhere in the back of his foggy brain he wondered if she were only playing games with him again. A new anger rose in him, anger di-

rected fully at her. He tore his mouth away and shook
her shoulders, asking in a voice ragged with desire
"Do you know what you're doing? Or are you only
teasing me again?"

Brandy looked at Flaming Arrow with dazed eyes
and muttered, "No—no, I'm not teasing."

"You want me?"

The question penetrated Brandy's passion-dulled
mind, and she couldn't deny it. She thought she
would die if Flaming Arrow didn't continue and
finish what he had started. She did want him.
She wanted him desperately. "Yes," she answered
breathlessly.

Flaming Arrow's pride came to the fore. He was
determined not to give Brandy the opportunity to
humiliate him by spurning him again. He wanted
more than just a simple agreement. "No. That won't
do. You must say the words."

After just the slightest hesitation on Brandy's part,
she whispered, "I want you."

Flaming Arrow hardly dared believe his ears. His
dark eyes swept over her face, searching for a sign of
deception. Finding none, he said, "Remember· If you
are lying, you have only yourself to blame, for no
power on earth is going to stop me now. You are
mine. All mine!"

With that, Flaming Arrow swept her up in his arms
and carried her back to their camp.

11

As Flaming Arrow carried Brandy through the dark forest to their camp, she had no doubts about her decision to allow him to make love to her. Some of her willingness came from deep within her, from her need to express growing feelings that had nothing—yet everything—to do with passion. But a great deal of her acquiesence had to do with the amorous fire Flaming Arrow had lit within her, a fire still smoldering in his sensual presence. Never in her life had she been so acutely aware of his exciting masculinity or his closeness. She could feel his powerful arms around her back and beneath her knees. The rock-hard muscles of his chest pressed against her side, seemingly to burn her right through her buckskin dress. One of his hands, the long slender fingers splayed, lay to the side of her right breast, tantalizingly close to where she longed for him to caress her. Her head lay on his broad shoulder, her cheek against the thick strand of long, silky hair he kept tied to the side of his head, her mouth so close to the bronze column of his throat that she could almost taste the saltiness of his skin. His unique scent surrounded her, stimulating her titillated senses even further, and his strong heart seemed to be beating in unison with every sure step he took, each bringing her closer and closer to that eagerly awaited moment when he would make her his. By the time Flaming Arrow walked into the sun-splashed clearing where their camp sat and dropped her feet to the blanket beside the burned-out fire, Brandy's anticipation of what was to come was so intense that every nerve in her body was strung as taut as a guitar string, and her lips were aching for the feel of his.

Flaming Arrow's desire had not cooled in the least. It was a raging inferno of need inside him. It took all of his considerable willpower to keep from throwing her to the ground and taking her by storm. Only briefly did he wonder why he didn't do just that— simply slake his lust on her. She was his captive. It was his right. It wouldn't be rape—she had admitted she was willing. But strangely, Flaming Arrow didn't want a quick coupling. He wanted to savor this long-awaited joining, and once more, he wanted Brandy to enjoy it too.

His hands trembling from the rigid control he was forcing upon himself, Flaming Arrow slid his fingers through the hair at both sides of Brandy's head and cupped the back of her head, lifting it for his kiss. The feel of her soft lips against his was as hot as a branding iron, and Flaming Arrow had to further steel himself to go slow. He nibbled at her lips and the ultrasensitive corners of her mouth—then he took the full bottom lip into his mouth and sucked on it, drawing a moan deep from Brandy. The throaty sound shattered the rigid control he had held over his desire. A primitive groan escaped his lips as he tightened his embrace, and his mouth captured hers in a deep, possessive, ravishing kiss that gave full rein to his passion and sent Brandy's already reeling senses wildly spinning into space.

Their lips still locked in that passionate kiss, Flaming Arrow drew her to the blanket and laid his body halfway over hers. Brandy gloried in the feel of him pressing against her, and she snaked her arms around his broad shoulders, drawing him even closer, lost in the breathtaking wonder, the heart-slamming excitement of his heady kiss. Her hands feverishly explored the muscles on his back and shoulders as if she couldn't get enough of him, as if she were trying to absorb him through her fingertips.

Brandy was drifting on a warm, rosy cloud, oblivious to her surroundings, when Flaming Arrow slipped her dress over her head. He sucked in his breath sharply at the impact of seeing her naked, for in the bright light her creamy skin had an almost translucent sheen to it. There wasn't a flaw on her body. He leaned back on his side and drank in her beauty, hungrily eyeing the soft shoulders, the high, full, rose-tipped breasts, the tiny waist, the gentle flare of her hips. His gaze drifted lower and lingered on the dark, reddish triangle between her rounded thighs and found the unaccustomed thick mat of curls—for Indian women had only a smattering of hair there—curiously very erotic. His mouth turned dry, and his pulse pounded in his temples. It was all he could do to force his eyes away to sweep over her long, graceful legs.

While Flaming Arrow was staring so boldly at the juncture between her legs, Brandy regained some semblance of awareness. An embarrassed flush crept up her body, for she suddenly felt very exposed in the broad daylight. She was just about to roll away from Flaming Arrow to cover her nudity when his eyes rose to meet hers. The naked, hot desire she saw in his dark eyes seemed to pin her to the spot and left her feeling incredibly weak.

"You're beautiful, absolutely beautiful," Flaming Arrow muttered in a ragged voice, one hand trailing up her side to cup a soft breast.

It was hard for Brandy to tell which had the most devastating effect on her—the husky sound of Flaming Arrow's voice, or the brush of his fingers across her nipple, making the aching points stand at attention. Both left her quivering with need. He kissed her lips softly again and again, then dropped light, nibbling kisses down her throat and across her shoulders, descending ever so slowly, inch by inch, tormenting Brandy until she felt she would scream in frustration before he reached what she knew was his ultimate goal. As his warm, wet tongue circled one throbbing crest, then took it in his mouth and sucked and nipped, she cried out in sheer gladness and moaned as warm, delicious sensations flowed over her, awash in a shimmering warmth that ebbed and flowed.

Flaming Arrow's hands slowly swept down the entire length of Brandy's body, his fingertips so light that the caress took her breath away and seemed to leave every nerve ending he had touched sensitized.

Then, as his hand slipped between her thighs, Brandy knew that he was offering her even more delights. She opened to him, a strangled cry escaping her lips as his fingers caressed the soft, moist folds and found the core of her womanhood, circling and teasing. The shimmering warmth turned to a blazing heat as wave after wave of exquisite sensation flowed over her, each wave more intense than the last, until a liquid fire raced through her, burning her clear to the soles of her feet as the spasms shook her.

The feel of her beneath his fingers, hot and wet and throbbing, drove Flaming Arrow wild. Impatiently, he stripped off his leggins with his other hand, then with a quick flick of his wrist, untied the string that held his breechclout in place. As soon as the material fell away, he rose over Brandy. His knee nudged her legs farther apart as he positioned himself between her thighs.

It took a moment for Brandy to realize that Flaming Arrow had removed his hand. She opened her eyes and saw him kneeling between her legs. Slowly, dreamily, her eyes roamed over his handsome features, the exceptional breadth of his shoulders, then down over his muscular chest and taut belly. Then she froze, her eyes locked on the bold, rigid flesh between his thighs. With the tip glistening in the sunlight, it seemed enormous. Why, he'd never be able to put that inside her! she thought wildly.

Flaming Arrow mistook the fear he saw in Brandy's eyes for revulsion. He cursed himself for a fool. He should have taken her in the shadows of the forest instead of in the glaring sunlight. Now she would refuse him again, and he didn't think he could stop, not this time. "If you are thinking of refusing me, don't! I told you no power on earth could stop me —not even myself."

"I don't refuse," Brandy answered, confused by her feelings, for although the sight of his erection frightened her, it also curiously excited her. "It's just that it's so big. I'm afraid you'll hurt me."

Flaming Arrow took Brandy's remark about his size as a oblique compliment. As an Indian male, he believed that the size of his organ was a direct measure of his manliness, and he was proud of it. That, and knowing that Brandy was more frightened than repulsed, made him lengthen yet another inch.

Brandy stared even harder, for she could hardly believe what she had just seen. Why, he seemed to be growing right before her eyes. She could see it throbbing, seemingly in unison with that strange throbbing between her legs. But still . . .

Flaming Arrow saw Brandy stare at him even harder, and the pulse beat in her throat quicken. He suspected that looking at him was arousing her, but she was still hesitant. "I will not hurt you," he said in a soft, reassuring voice. "Perhaps a little at first, but not that much." He dropped his hand between her legs and dipped two fingers inside her. "See, you are wet. You are ready for me. You body will stretch to accept me."

As Flaming Arrow moved his fingers slightly, placing them just inside the portal, a new bolt of fire shot to her loins. Brandy blushed as she felt a rush of wetness down there, bathing Flaming Arrow's delving fingers even more. Yes, she thought, there was no denying her body wanted him. Shamelessly, it had spoken with a voice of its own. But . . .

The thought was never completed. Flaming Arrow

was a man of action and characteristically took matters into his own hands. He leaned forward and
kissed her with such fiery passion that Brandy's
senses were quickly sent reeling and all hesitation
fled, just as the Dakota had calculated it would. As his
hands stroked her and excited her to a feverish peak,
she wasn't even aware when he slowly, ever so
slowly, entered her. Even when her virginal barrier
broke, the brief pain was obliterated by the wonderful sensations his mouth and hands were invoking.
Not until he lay deep inside her and stopped kissing
her did Brandy come to her senses. Suddenly aware
of his hot and throbbing length within her, she was
surprised that the only discomfort she felt was a
vague aching and a feeling of pressure. Unbelievably,
her body had stretched to accommodate him.

Then Flaming Arrow began his movements—slow,
sensuous movements that lit fires and awakened
nerve endings Brandy had never dreamed she had.
She felt consumed in a terrible heat. Then Flaming
Arrow moved faster, harder, deeper, rocking their
bodies in a primitive rhythm as ancient as time itself,
and her eyes filled with wonder as a whole new bar-
rage of sensations attacked her senses. Her body became an agony of throbbing anticipation—an anticipation that grew more and more urgent. She
wrapped her legs around Flaming Arrow's narrow
hips, drawing him even deeper and bringing a hiss of
pleasure from him, holding on for dear life, her
senses expanding until she feared her skin could no
longer contain her and a roaring filling her ears.
Then suddenly, Flaming Arrow stiffened above her,
groaned, and collapsed weakly over her. To Brandy's

dismay, the sensations vanished, leaving her feeling strangely disappointed.

Flaming Arrow rolled to his side and pulled her to him, laying her head on his shoulder. Brandy was grateful that he was still paying her some attention—she could not have borne it if he had left her as soon as it was over. She would have felt used, as well as cheated. Brandy wondered why she did feel cheated. Flaming Arrow had certainly introduced her to some wondrous feelings with his lovemaking, and it had really been quite exciting. But somehow she sensed that in the end, he had received much more pleasure than she. Was that the way of the world? she wondered. Was it meant to be better for the man? She supposed that shouldn't surprise her. It seemed to be a man's world. They got to do all the exciting things, while the woman was expected to live a humdrum existence in the background and be there at their beck and call.

As Brandy was nursing her resentment at men enjoying everything in life more than women, Flaming Arrow asked, "Do you regret what we have done?"

The question hit Brandy square in the face and took her somewhat aback. But she didn't regret it—it had seemed so right between them, and it had been a thrilling experience. It was just that the ending seemed to have fallen short in some unexplainable way. "What made you ask that?"

"You seem withdrawn. Do you regret it?"

Damn, why did he have to be so perceptive! Brandy thought. "No, I don't regret it."

"Then what is wrong?"

"I guess I'm just a little . . . disappointed," she admitted. "I thought the end would be better."

Flaming Arrow was glad Brandy didn't regret their lovemaking. He certainly didn't. It had been the most exciting experience he had ever had, and the white-hot climax had been almost frightening with its intensity. He had feared that if Brandy regretted it, she would refuse him the next time, and he still wanted her, perhaps even more. He breathed a silent sigh of relief. "That is understandable. It was your first time. Your body is inexperienced, your muscles unaccustomed to lovemaking. It will take time before you experience it to the fullest."

A thrill ran through Brandy to learn that there was more, and she belatedly realized she should have known it. She had felt that she was on the brink of discovering something wonderful when Flaming Arrow had stopped. Suddenly, she wanted to know what that something wonderful was. "How soon can we do it again?" she asked, then blushed at her own audacity.

Her direct question took Flaming Arrow aback for a moment. An Indian maiden would have been more coy. It appeared Brandy was as outspoken and brutally honest about sex as she was about everything else. A smile crossed Flaming Arrow's face as he realized that her anxiousness could be taken as a compliment to his skill as a lover. Apparently she hadn't been all *that* disappointed.

"I think we should wait until your body has had time to get over its soreness."

Brandy did feel soreness between her legs, but not enough to make her want to wait, and she was frankly disappointed. Then she was filled with self-disgust. What had gotten into her? It was bad enough that she had acted like a brazen hussy and freely given herself to a man—her captor, no less—but now she was practically begging him to make love to her again! Did she have no pride left at all? And what must he think of her? That she was utterly shameless?

Deep down, Brandy didn't want Flaming Arrow to think badly of her. She wanted him to admire her. That was why she had gotten so angry when he had implied she was weak. Where did she stand with him? she wondered. Although she had thought she would be content to be his lover, she wanted to be more than just his mistress. Did he have any feelings other than lust for her? She swallowed hard and summoned her courage to ask, "Why did you come after me?"

Again, Brandy's point-blank question took Flaming Arrow aback. Without even thinking, he answered, "You are my captive. My people do not let captives escape, any more than we take them back to their people."

"It was just a matter of saving face with the others?"

The hurt in Brandy's voice touched a chord deep within him. He had given her the same excuse he had given those in his tribe when he had announced he was going after her, but it no longer held any credibility. He was forced to admit that there was a much deeper reason he had gone after her. "No, that is not the only reason I came after you. I desire you. You know that."

Brandy had secretly hoped for more, but something told her not to push too hard. For the time being, she would have to settle for his passion. But it was a beginning, and Brandy was determined she would eventually have more. She vowed she'd make him fall in love with her.

Shortly thereafter, Flaming Arrow donned his breechclout and left the camp to search for game for their evening meal. Brandy returned to the hot springs to bathe, letting the healing waters sooth the soreness between her legs. She spread her buckskin dress on the ground and cleaned it with wet clay, then returned to the camp.

It was dusk when she walked into the clearing, and the setting sun edged the dark mountaintops around them in silver. Flaming Arrow had built another fire and was roasting a turkey over it. As Brandy sat on the blanket beside the fire, he asked, "You have been back to the pool?"

"Yes. It's quite a luxury," Brandy admitted. "It's going to be hard to leave behind." She gazed out into space thoughtfully. "How do you suppose the water is heated?"

"There is much heat beneath the earth in places out here. Why it is there I do not know. But in a region to the west of the Big Horn Mountains, hot water shoots into the air for hundreds of feet and there are huge pits of boiling clay. When steam jets from one mountain, you can hear it from miles away. It is heavily timbered like this area, with sparkling clear streams, ice-cold lakes, and high waterfalls. It, too, is a place filled with mystery, a sacred place among my people, among all Indians."

Brandy thought she knew what place Flaming Arrow was speaking of by his description of the geysers. She had read a newspaper article several years before that said the government was making the area a national park because of all of the unusual natural phenomena to be found there. It seemed the white man had claimed yet another of the red man's sacred places; the fierce Dakota sitting across from her didn't realize the whites were encroaching there too. Again, Brandy felt a twinge of shame for her people.

Later that night, Flaming Arrow again made love to Brandy. He began by kissing her until she was weak and breathless, then announced in a husky voice that this time she would experience sublime ecstasy. It was a promise Flaming Arrow kept.

He lay beside her and softly kissed her bared shoulders, then lavished butterfly kisses over her breasts. His long silky hair brushed back and forth across her skin as sensuously as his lips and tongue. As his mouth closed over one turgid peak, she gave herself up to sensations, arching her back to give him better access, glorying in the hot, spine-tingling waves swamping her, gasping when his hand cupped the other breast and his fingers rolled the nipple and tugged, increasing the incredible pleasure twofold.

This time when he stripped off his breechclout and bared himself to her in the flickering firelight, Brandy felt neither fear nor hesitation. An unbearable excitement filled her, and without even thinking, she reached for him. But she was shocked by the heat she encountered and surprised by how soft the skin felt. Then, as he stirred beneath her touch, lengthening yet another inch, and the moist tip nuzzled her palm, her hand closed around him, sliding down the long, rigid length and back up.

"Hoh!" Flaming Arrow cried out in a mixture of wonder and sheer pleasure.

To Brandy's ears, the cry had sounded almost painful, and she hesitated.

"Don't stop!" Flaming Arrow said in a ragged voice, his hand closing over hers and guiding it.

As Brandy's hand again slid up and down his length, a long shudder ran through Flaming Arrow. It brought an answering thrill to Brandy's body, exciting him, exciting her. Faster and faster, her hand moved and her heart raced, her breath came in shallow gasps, until Flaming Arrow stilled her hand and muttered urgently, "No more!"

Flaming Arrow rolled her to her back and knelt poised over her. Brandy was more than ready for him. She felt the hot, insistent tip of his manhood against the throbbing heat of her arousal, and her already racing heart pounded like a jungle drum in intense anticipation. As his rigid heat slowly pressed into her, her thighs trembled in eager welcome, and her entire concentration was focused on the sensations flowing over her. It seemed as if every nerve ending in her body had suddenly rushed to that burning, aching part of her. His slow, careful penetration was an agony for her, the expectancy so intense, she thought she would scream. When he stopped to nuzzle the fragrant valley between her breasts, his wet, hot tongue lathing the aching tip, she sobbed in frustration, then sharply sucked in her breath as he moved yet another inch forward.

Brandy thought she couldn't possibly stand any more of this exquisite torture. Then he began his movements, slowly moving in and out, in and out, and shock wave after shock wave traveled up her spine with each powerful, masterful stroke. As he increased his tempo, a frenzy seized her. She clung to him, melted around him, arched her hips and met him thrust for thrilling thrust, driven by an ungovernable urgency, feeling herself on the verge of some earth-shattering discovery. Suddenly, it peaked, and time stood still. She held her breath, her body trembling all over, until the unbearable pressure burst through, sending blinding flashes of light through her brain and rocking her body in spasms of ecstasy.

Flaming Arrow hovered over Brandy and watched the expressions on her face as he carried her up that rapturous ascent, determined that she would have as much pleasure as he from this joining. Not until her eyes flew open with the wonder of it and he heard her joyous cry and felt her hot spasms contract around his own feverish, pulsating flesh, did he allow his steely control to break. With one powerful, deep thrust, he followed her into his own shattering release.

For a long while they lay, their ragged breaths rasping in the night air, locked in that sweet embrace, Flaming Arrow's dark head buried in the crook of Brandy's soft neck. Then he kissed her ear and raised his head to look down at her face.

Brandy gazed up at him dreamily and stroked his broad shoulders that glistened with perspiration in the firelight. She smiled blissfully, then muttered in an awed voice, "Oh, that was beautiful. Absolutely beautiful. Thank you."

A strange knot formed in Flaming Arrow's throat, preventing him from uttering a word. He felt an unfamiliar moistness at the back of his eyes. Totally bewildered, he kissed Brandy's lips softly and rolled to his side, placed her head on his shoulder, and gazed up at the stars.

He had meant to give Brandy pleasure, had placed it like a gift at her feet. But Flaming Arrow didn't understand why he had felt driven to please her, and why pleasing her had touched him so deeply. He had never felt such happiness, nor such utter contentment.

12

Two days later, they left the Black Hills, much to Brandy's disappointment. Their brief visit to the lovely mountains had been so beautiful that she wished they could have stayed there forever, just the two of them. It had been rather like Adam and Eve in the garden of paradise before the fall. Flaming Arrow had made love to her several times on the second day, taking her to a heaven of their own making. Even when she hadn't been feasting on the new, exciting sensual delights he brought her, there had been something special about their time together, although very little had been said between them. Instead, it had been a quiet companionship, a sharing of a peaceful solitude that seemed to infuse them with a strange sense of tranquillity that made verbal communication not only unnecessary but unwanted, as if each sensed that breaking the pristine silence might risk shattering their fragile new relationship. Yes, Brandy hated to leave. She feared that she and Flaming Arrow would never again experience that privacy or that special closeness.

It had been that very closeness that had made Flaming Arrow decide to depart a day earlier than he had originally planned, for deep down he feared it. He didn't know if it was the magic of the mountains themselves or Brandy that cast a spell over him, but he no longer seemed to have any control over himself. Ever since he had gotten a taste of her heady passion, he couldn't seem to get enough of her. He could have stayed in these mountains forever and just made love to her. He was beginning to think there was much more to her name than her father had intended. She *was* like firewater—not only intoxicating but addictive—and Flaming Arrow knew only too well how susceptible to liquor Indians were. It could bring him to his downfall, rob him of his manhood, leave him weak and powerless. Already she was working her sorcery on him. Not only did she leave him reeling with mindless passion, but once she had temporarily sated it, the strange contentment he felt in her presence seemed to erode his sense of obligation to his people. He had no business dallying here with the white-eyes. He was needed back at the village.

Despite Flaming Arrow's determination to force himself to keep his previous commitments, he did tarry on the trip back to the Dakota village, taking the longest trails and stopping earlier than necessary each evening. It took five days to reach their destination, instead of the three it should have taken if they had rushed back. When he and Brandy finally rode back into the Indian camp, he came face to face with his brother.

Yellow Fox glanced from Flaming Arrow to Brandy, then commented to his brother, "You have been away much longer than I expected. She must have gone far."

Flaming Arrow wasn't about to admit to his brother that he had deliberately taken his captive to the Black Hills to rest after he had found her, then dallied. Yellow Fox would laugh at him for letting the white-eyes get the best of his emotions. "She was lost in the badlands. It took me a while to find her."

Yellow Fox's eyes swept over Brandy. "She does not look any the worse for her ordeal."

Was his brother suspicious? Flaming Arrow wondered, noting a glimmer of amusement in Yellow Fox's eyes. "She is strong," Flaming Arrow answered, then not wanting to appear too complimentary, he added, "for a white-eyes."

Yellow Fox glanced at Brandy's untied hands and said, "She came back willingly?"

Flaming Arrow frowned. Brandy had been willing —a little *too* willing, she had wanted her freedom fiercely enough to try to escape. She mentioned his taking her back to her people only once since he had found her. Had his answer been so determined, so adamant that she had finally accepted her fate? Had she let him make love to her because she felt she could no longer fight off his advances, that she would be wise to surrender to him and make the most of a bad situation? After all, for all her faults, he knew Brandy wasn't stupid. She was, at heart, a survivor, someone whose fierce determination and endurance he could appreciate. But the thought that Brandy might have entered a more intimate relationship with him just to make her captivity more endurable didn't sit well with Flaming Arrow. Deep down, part of him wanted her to want him for himself; yet another part of him, one much more superficial, was suspicious of her motives, fearing that she would coldly and calculatingly use his seemingly unquenchable desire as a weapon against him. He shot her a sharp glance. Then, aware that his brother was still waiting for an answer, he belatedly looked him in the eye and said, "She has realized the folly of trying to escape. Her foolishness almost cost her her life. She will not try it again."

That Flaming Arrow and his brother were discussing her as if she were a piece of merchandise had brought forth Brandy's underlying resentment. But when Flaming Arrow called her foolish and pronounced that she would not try to escape again, using a tone of voice that seemed to smack of arrogance, she suddenly came alive. Her brilliant blue eyes flashed like lightning. She opened her mouth to object, but Flaming Arrow, fearing she would humiliate him in front of his brother by defying his authority over her, cut across her words with a commanding, "No! Hold your tongue!"

"Why should I?" Brandy threw back angrily, her body rigid with fury. "Because I'm your captive?"

"Yes. It is not fitting for you to speak in front of my brother without my permission, and most certainly not to defy me. You will show both him and myself the proper respect."

Brandy was surprised to learn that the man standing before them was Flaming Arrow's brother. She had not known he had a living relative. But this news did nothing to temper her anger. "The devil I'll show either of you any respect! That needs to be earned, not demanded. No! Hell will freeze over before I'll grovel to either one of you!"

Flaming Arrow was furious with Brandy for showing her temper in front of his brother. The fact that she had flared out at him in English meant nothing. Yellow Fox understood the language as well as he. Flaming Arrow longed to throttle her, but he didn't dare even touch her. Using force on a woman was considered unmanly among the Dakotas, but Indian women knew their place and kept it. Totally exasperated, he thundered, "Silence! I will not tolerate any more of your outburst!"

Brandy didn't know that Flaming Arrow would not touch her, but at that moment he looked angry enough to kill. A shiver ran up her spine, and she thought it prudent to back down for the time being. That didn't stop her from giving Flaming Arrow a withering glance before she turned her horse and rode off.

Glaring at her back, Flaming Arrow said to his brother, "I apologize for my captive's behavior. She has much to learn of our ways."

Yellow Fox was more intrigued than anything else. "Do you suppose all white women are so outspoken, so utterly fearless, so—so—"

"So disrespectful?" Flaming Arrow supplied when Yellow Fox hesitated. He frowned, then answered, "No, I think she is just more stubborn than other women, and more—"

"Fiery?" Yellow Fox asked, saying what he had meant to say before Flaming Arrow interrupted him.

That, too, Flaming Arrow thought, for she was cer-

tainly volatile. Her flare-up had been totally unexpected, from out of the blue. But he answered, "No,
'uncontrollable' is a more apt description."

"Ah, yes. She is wild, as free-spirited as the mus-
tangs that roam our prairies." He paused, giving
Flaming Arrow a thoughtful, piercing look, then continued. "But remember, my brother, the wildest
mustang makes the best mount. You will just have to
tame her."

Flaming Arrow would have compared Brandy to a
wildcat rather than a mustang. But the principle was
the same. She did need to be tamed, to be mastered,
to be taught once and for all who held the reins, and
the sooner he made her realize her place in the nature of things, the better. There could only be one
lord, one master in a relationship, and naturally that
was him. He was the male. It was his right.

Flaming Arrow was in the same frame of mind
when he approached Brandy that night: She had to
be tamed, brought to heel. Brandy was still angry
with him and she sensed his intent to dominate her,
so she tried to spurn his amorous advances. It was a
futile effort on her part, but not because of his superior strength. He didn't have to overpower her. The
desire for him that burned just below the surface
came to the fore with a suddenness and swiftness that
stunned them both.

Their coming together was a fierce, wild union as
their mutual desire ignited in a white-hot, consuming fire. This time, there was no sweetness, no tenderness, no gentleness in Flaming Arrow's lovemaking. He stripped her of her clothing in a lightning-
flash movement; then his hands roamed roughly over
her body, his kisses fierce and demanding. Brandy

surrendered nothing. She bucked and twisted beneath him, returning every feverish nip, every savage, burning kiss, her own hands boldly exploring.
They were combatants more than lovers, struggling
for supremacy, each demanding complete and total
surrender. They rolled from the blanket onto the
ground, their bronze and white legs entwined, their
animal groans and moans filling the tepee, their
breaths hot and ragged. The ground shook, and the
air around them reverberated with the sounds of
their frenzied, wild lovemaking.

Flaming Arrow's mouth crashed down on
Brandy's, his lips hard and bruising, his tongue
thrusting, then plundering her mouth. Brandy met
his ferocious kiss, and her own scalding tongue rav-
ished him back. They rolled again, still locked in
that sweet-savage kiss, until Flaming Arrow finally
pinned her to the ground. For a brief second, he rose
poised over her, and then with a cry that was half
triumphant and half growl, he wrenched her legs
apart and drove his hot, rigid flesh deeply inside her.
Brandy lurched, as if she had been impaled on a bolt
of lightning, and the shock waves of electrical heat
coursed up her spine until they burst in a white-hot
spray of lights in her brain.

But if Flaming Arrow thought he had finally succeeded in mastering her, he was sadly mistaken.
Brandy met him stroke for stroke and searing kiss for
searing kiss. She surrendered only when he withdrew, then devoured him as he devoured her. Two
hearts pounded frantically against each other as their
sweat-slick bodies strained and their hips pounded
with feverish urgency. And then suddenly, they
were perfectly still, frozen together on that lofty

apex, no longer struggling for supremacy but sharing a breathless and trembling anticipation of what they knew was coming. They tumbled over in a shattering explosion that hurled them into a fiery shower of swirling, brilliant flashing colors, followed by total oblivion.

As he slowly floated back down, his body still trembling with aftershocks, Flaming Arrow felt stunned by the shattering experience and was filled with awe. Brandy's reaction was a soft purr of utter contentment. When he finally found the strength, Flaming Arrow lifted his head and saw Brandy had drifted off to sleep. He was glad, for he hadn't any notion of what he could possibly have said to her.

He rolled onto his back and stared at the smoke hole at the top of the tepee. He knew he had failed miserably in mastering her, but strangely, the knowledge didn't distress him, nor did he any longer have the desire to do so. He didn't really want to break her spirit, to bend her to his will, to dominate her. Broken, subdued, she wouldn't be Brandy, but would be just like any other woman—meek, dull, predictable. It was her ungovernable spirit that made her so special, so unique.

It was an astonishing discovery for Flaming Arrow —that the very thing that most exasperated him about Brandy was also what most attracted him. But nonetheless he knew it was true. Not only was she the most desirable woman he had ever met, she was by far the most fascinating and exciting. But Flaming Arrow didn't know how his strong Dakota heritage was going to come to terms with this truth, for he still firmly believed that the male was supreme. It was a dilemma that kept his mind reeling for the better part of the night.

Flaming Arrow was gone from the tepee when Brandy awakened the next morning. Shortly thereafter, Swift Rabbit arrived and told her that the village was packing up to leave for their fall buffalo hunt and that she would teach Brandy how to take down Flaming Arrow's tepee.

Brandy glanced out of the tepee and saw a horse with a travois tied to it. On the travois was a pile of buffalo hides and household goods that belonged to Swift Rabbit. With swiftness that was astonishing, Flaming Arrow's tepee was brought down, a travois fashioned from the longer poles, and all his household belongings loaded onto it. Then the travois was tied to the little mare Brandy had taken on her attempted escape.

Swift Rabbit pointed to the pile of goods on her own travois and said, "You may use that saddle for your horse, unless you prefer to walk. I will ride the spare horse."

Brandy wasn't surprised by Swift Rabbit's dictate. After all, she was the captive. And even if she hadn't been, it was only right that Swift Rabbit have the spare horse due to her age.

Brandy took the saddle Swift Rabbit had offered her and placed it on her horse, then mounted and looked around while she waited for Swift Rabbit to mount. The entire camp was in a frenzy of activity as the women and girls dismantled the tepees and packed. The boys not deemed old enough to travel with the men brought the horses from the herd in the distance, while the younger children ran wildly through the camp, playing tag and raising even more dust to add to the thick cloud of gritty material that hung over the camp. Peering through the dust, Brandy saw the men of the village riding out in the distance. There they went, she thought with renewed bitterness, gleefully riding off while the women did all the work.

The camp pulled out. The men rode in front of the procession, and the women and children followed behind, some riding horses and some on foot. Here and there, a child or an elderly member rode in a travois, while black-eyed babies, swaddled to the chin in cradles, were lashed to the sides of the horses or to their mother's back. For the first hour or so, the Indians chatted excitedly as they rode or walked, then when the sun grew hotter and they trudged across one rise of seared grass after another, they traveled in silence. The only sounds were the constant moan of the wind across the prairie, the scraping of the travois, and the incessant bark of the camp dogs who never seemed to tire.

A squad of adolescents riding ahead broke from the column and angled off at a gallop, shooting their arrows. Brandy squinted her eyes against the glare of the bright sun but could see nothing of the game they were shooting at. "Is there a herd of buffalo ahead?" she asked Swift Rabbit, riding beside her.

"No."

"Then what are those warriors shooting at?"

"They are chasing an imaginary enemy. They are not warriors yet, not until they count coup. They are only braves."

Brandy couldn't care less what the young men were called, but she did felt a twinge of disappointment. She had hoped they had sighted a buffalo herd.

She was eager to see one of the beasts. "How long does it usually take to find a herd of buffalo?"

Swift Rabbit shrugged her shoulders. "Sometimes a few days, sometimes weeks."

"Weeks?" Brandy asked in a shocked voice. "But I thought buffalo were all over the place out here."

"We are looking for a large herd, one big enough to supply us with enough meat and hides to last us the winter. Winter is almost upon us, you know."

Brandy could hardly believe winter was just around the corner the way the sun was beating down on her bare head. "If that's the case, you should have started hunting a long time ago."

"No, we could not have hunted earlier. The buffalo were mating then. If we had, there would be no calves next spring. This is the perfect time. The grass is the thickest and the buffalo the fattest. Also, the bulls have not yet left the herds."

"Left? Where do they go?"

"They winter by themselves."

"You mean the bulls go off and leave the cows and calves unprotected?" Brandy asked, feeling a tinge of outrage in behalf of the female buffalo.

"The cows do not need them for protection. A female buffalo can fight off a wolf as easily as a bull, and the cows are much faster runners. They always lead the herd in a chase. Besides, I do not think the cows particularly want the bulls around. The bulls are nasty-tempered animals."

Rather like their human counterparts, Brandy thought, still smarting a little at Flaming Arrow's attempt to dominate her the night before. She looked out over the prairie, which was reddish brown in its fall dress. "So we wander around out here until we run into a herd?"

"No. Members of the hunting party have gone ahead as scouts. Warriors who belong to the Buffalo Society."

"Buffalo Society?"

"Yes. It is a secret organization that is not really all that secret, except for some of its rituals. Everyone knows who belongs. It is quite an honor to be asked to join. Only the bravest men and the best hunters are invited, and only they can wear the buffalo horn headdress. Besides acting as scouts, they patrol the camp at night to make sure no man tries to sneak off and hunt alone, and they generally preserve order on the marches."

"Why should they care if someone goes off and tries to hunt alone?"

"Ordinarily, a man may hunt as he pleases, but not on a tribal hunt. He might scare the entire herd away, in which case the entire tribe suffers."

That made sense, Brandy thought, glancing to the side. From the corner of her eye, she caught sight of a figure walking about fifty feet from her. In utter disbelief, she turned to Swift Rabbit and whispered in a shocked voice, "That's a man over there—dressed like a woman!"

"Yes, he has been proven guilty of cowardice, and that is his punishment. He must dress like a woman and live like a woman, and he can never marry."

"I've never seen him with the women."

"No, we do not want anything to do with him either. For the better part, he is an outcast."

"Isn't that a rather harsh punishment?"

"His cowardice led to the deaths of three other warriors. No, we do not consider it harsh."

Brandy's curiosity was aroused. "And what happens to a man if he is caught trying to sneak off and hunt alone?"

"His tepee is torn down, his belongings are destroyed, and he is banished."

"I'm surprised he isn't killed," Brandy remarked.

It was Swift Rabbit's turn to look shocked. "Dakotas do not kill as a means of punishment. Banishment is the worst punishment we can inflict on one another. Killing is for our enemies. The only time we sanction it for punishment is for traitors."

"What about murderers?" Brandy persisted. "What punishment do you give them?"

"A murderer is almost unheard of among the Dakota, as is a thief, but they, too, are cast out. For a Dakota, it is the worst possible punishment to be sent away from the tribe in disgrace. The respect of those he lives with is everything to a Dakota. Without honor, he is nothing."

For a few moments, the two rode in silence, Brandy pondering over everything Swift Rabbit had told her. Then Swift Rabbit cast her a curious look. "Why did you not tell Flaming Arrow I gave you the horse and my saddle?"

Brandy didn't hesitate to answer. "Because I knew he would be angry with you if he knew, and I saw no point in getting you in trouble."

The old woman's only response was a snort, but unknown to Brandy, she had succeeded in gaining Swift Rabbit's eternal gratitude.

13

For the next ten days, the tribe moved back and forth over the length and breadth of the Powder River Country in search of buffalo. The men led the way, and the women and children trudged after them in the hot sun and breathed the choking dust stirred up by the men's horses. Each morning, the women dismantled the tepees and packed up, then each evening, they threw them back up. Brandy became as adept and speedy as the best of them. She could pull down the twenty-six poles and seventeen buffalo skins in less than three minutes and load the entire household onto the travois in less than twenty. Then in the evening, despite how exhausted she might be, she would put it back up again in less than fifteen minutes with the help of Swift Rabbit, for no one could throw up a tepee without someone to help with the poles.

During all this time, Brandy never saw Flaming Arrow, and she assumed that he must be one of the scouts searching for buffalo. She missed him much more than she wanted to admit, and the nights were the worst. She lay on her lonely pallet, tossing and turning, torturing herself with memories of his love-making, which always left her aching for his kiss and touch. The Dakota had awakened a deep need in her and then left her to deal with physical yearnings that couldn't be satisfied without him.

On the morning of the eleventh day, they came to a wide river, but instead of crossing it, they followed it downriver. Curious, Brandy asked why they had deviated from their usual pattern, and Swift Rabbit told her that one of the scouts who had submerged his head in the stream thought he had heard buffalo blowing water in the distance. Brandy was amazed to learn that sounds traveled farther in water than air. Shortly before noon, word arrived that the scouts had found a herd about five miles away, and camp was hastily made. No sooner had the tepees been raised than the men built fires to purify their weapons in sweet-gum smoke and painted themselves and their horses for their hunt. The women kept busy sharpening their butcher knives and scouring their big pots and kettles. An air of festivity hung over all, and the preparations for the big event became feverish as the tribe's excited anticipation rose higher and higher.

Brandy was helping Swift Rabbit build a fire when Flaming Arrow suddenly appeared before them. She looked him over quickly, her eyes hungrily taking in every detail. He looked even more handsome than she remembered. Wearing only his moccasins and his brief breechclout, every powerful muscle and sleek tendon was revealed to her. The lightning he had painted on his arms for strength and the eagle feathers tied to his scalp lock only added dash to a man who radiated excitement as the sun radiated heat waves.

Flaming Arrow was taking in Brandy's beauty. It had been unnecessary to make a special visit to relay his instructions to Swift Rabbit. The old woman had taught the white-eyes the Dakota way exceptionally well and needed no coaching. But it gave him an excuse to see Brandy. Now seeing her, he realized coming had been a mistake. Much to his disgust, his body was becoming aroused, something that absolutely could not happen. The hunt took precedence over everything.

Flaming Arrow jerked his eyes away from Brandy and said to Swift Rabbit, "Be sure to take the white-eyes with you to the hunt so she can be taught how to butcher the buffalo."

With that, Flaming Arrow turned and walked away. Brandy stared at his broad back, feeling hurt and angered. Her eyes dropped to his half-exposed buttocks, the powerful muscles contracting and relaxing with each step he took, and she remembered what they had felt like beneath her hands during their last frenzied lovemaking. Feeling heat envelop her and knowing he had aroused her without even trying infuriated her all the more. "That bastard! How dare he ignore me like that!"

Swift Rabbit didn't know what the English words Brandy had said meant, but she knew the girl was furious by the expression on her face and her flashing eyes. "What has angered you?"

"Him!" Brandy answered, motioning to Flaming

Arrow. "He walked up here, gave you an order, then walked away without even a word to me. That's the second time he's treated me hatefully in front of others, acting as if I don't exist."

"It would be unseemly for him to acknowledge you in public. You are his captive."

"Oh, yes! How could I forget that I'm nothing but his slave?" Brandy responded, her voice heavy with bitterness. She glared at Flaming Arrow, then spat, "Well, I won't be his slave anymore—not in his home or his pallet!"

Suddenly realizing what she had divulged, Brandy glanced sharply at Swift Rabbit to see if she had caught her slip. The old woman had and remarked calmly, "You have given nothing away that I did not already know. I know you share his pallet."

"How?"

"There was a change in the way you looked when he brought you back, a certain glow about you. You had the look of a woman who had been well loved."

"Not well loved. Well used!" Brandy threw back, tears glittering in her eyes. "But he'll never use me that way again. If he tries to, I'll scratch his eyes out!"

"I think you are more hurt than angry with him. And I think you are wrong when you say he uses you. I have seen women who were used. They have bruises on them, and there is a look of pain and humiliation in their eyes."

"But he *does* humiliate me. If he cared, he'd treat me more civilly in public."

"You are thinking as a white-eyes. That is not the Dakota way."

"I *am* a white-eyes! How else do you expect me to think?"

"You are a white woman who is in love with a Dakota warrior."

Brandy was shocked by Swift Rabbit's words. She had never admitted the depth of her feeling for Flaming Arrow, and to do so now would seem like a betrayal to herself. "I'm *not* in love with—"

"No! Do not lie to me!" Swift Rabbit said, cutting across Brandy's words. "Lie to yourself, but not to me. I am not a fool." The old woman paused and looked deeply into Brandy's eyes, as if she were trying to peer into her soul. "And I do not think you are a fool either. You have shown wisdom in too many other things. A wise woman would learn the Dakota ways and accept them if she wished to capture and keep Flaming Arrow's heart."

Swift Rabbit paused, then asked, "Do you remember that I told you that the respect of others is everything to a Dakota?"

Brandy nodded.

"Then you must realize that Flaming Arrow will not tolerate anything that humiliates him in front of others, that he will not break any tribal taboo. He will do nothing that might endanger the high respect that is given to him by the others in this tribe. This is true of any Dakota male, but even more so of Flaming Arrow, for he has strived for many years to be a perfect warrior. Someday he will be chief. A great chief."

Brandy had sensed from the very beginning that there was a hint of greatness about Flaming Arrow, but that didn't make it any easier for her to accept what Swift Rabbit was telling her. "That may well be, but I come from a society that believes both men and women should be respected. He treats me as if I don't even exist."

"Ah, but that, too, is the Dakota way. Single men and women do not mingle freely in public. For a man to address a single woman before others is almost a public announcement that they are courting. Even husbands and wives are reserved to one another in public. And no matter what, a Dakota woman never humiliates a man in public. She treats him with the utmost respect."

The news that Flaming Arrow's behavior toward her was a part of the Dakota manner in male-female relationships did nothing to temper Brandy's anger. She didn't like his overbearing attitude and rudeness, regardless of the reason. "You mean you women grovel to your men. You let them humiliate you, but you do nothing in return. No, I can't do that. I won't do it!"

"How did Flaming Arrow humiliate you?"

"I told you! He ignored me!"

"But even if you had been an Indian maiden, he would not have acknowledged you. I told you—that is our way."

"Oh, women are supposed to be seen, not heard? Has it ever occurred to you that your men are totally dominating you?"

"I said that that is the way it is in public. What happens in the privacy of a couple's tepee is another matter. A Dakota wife may interrupt her husband. She may correct him. He may"—Swift Rabbit shrugged her shoulders—"or he may not listen. But that is the way it is with your men, too, is it not? Do they not try to dominate your women? Do women not have a 'place' in the white man's world?"

Brandy knew white men weren't any better; their word was as much law as the Indians'. It seemed that trying to dominate females was an irritating trait of all males, that they all wanted to be lord and master. "Yes, there's a woman's place, but I don't fit into it in my world either. I want to be treated like an equal. It would be very hard for me to step back."

"Yes, you are an unusually strong-willed person. So is Flaming Arrow. He has to be, if he is to be a leader. It is inevitable that your wills will clash. But if you are wise, you will take care to see that they do not clash in public. A woman who loves a man will go out of her way to save face for him, and face is very important to a Dakota male. That is our way, whether you approve or not, and Flaming Arrow is Dakota to the bone." Swift Rabbit turned away and said over her shoulder, "Enough of that. Now sheath your knife, tie your travois to your horse, and mount up. The hunt will begin soon."

Brandy glanced around and saw that the hunters were already mounted and forming lines five-abreast. Flaming Arrow sat bareback on his horse in the first line, a full quiver of arrows over his left shoulder. But for once, it wasn't the handsome, exciting warrior that caught Brandy's attention. She gaped at his pony in astonishment. Not only were its legs painted with lightning streaks for strength and speed and its eyes circled with red for keenness of sight, but the entire animal was painted. Of course, all the horses were painted—a few with stripes, dots, or geometric patterns—but Flaming Arrow's mount was a very striking blue color. Once she recovered from the stunning sight, Brandy had to admit that the animal looked quite impressive with the colorful feathers in its mane and tail and the powerful, fierce-looking warrior on his back. Taking note of the horse's ears, she said to Swift Rabbit, "Why is Flaming Arrow riding that horse? It isn't his war horse. That pony's ears are notched."

"That is his runner, a horse that has been chosen for its speed and trained for buffalo hunting. If you will notice, all of the runners' ears are notched. That is how they are singled out from other horses, and it takes an exceptional pony to keep up with a stampeding buffalo. A fleet runner is valued as much, if not more, than the war horse."

Brandy watched while the hunters rode forward, then asked, "Why are those long ropes dangling from the runners' necks?"

"If a rider is knocked from his pony during the hunt, he can try to catch the rope and pull himself back up on his horse before he is trampled to death."

A chill ran over Brandy at the thought of being pounded to death beneath the hooves of a herd of stampeding buffalo. "How would a rider get knocked off?"

"When a buffalo tries to hook, it often veers suddenly and bumps into the horse. That's why a hunter can't get any closer than his bow's length to the buffalo, for then he would be within hooking range. Both the hunter and the horse have to know exactly what they are doing."

"A bow's length!" Brandy exclaimed in horror. "Are you telling me they get that close?"

"Yes, they must shoot the buffalo straight down between the shoulders to kill him instantly, so as to put the arrow through the heart. Otherwise the hunter just wounds it, and a wounded buffalo can run

for miles, even one with an arrow in its lungs. A
wounded buffalo is also very dangerous and unpre-
dictable. The pain enrages them."

An icy fear clutched Brandy's heart. Flaming Arrow was facing that kind of danger. But then her fear
was replaced with anger. "Why don't they shoot
them with rifles, like the white man does? They
wouldn't have to get close. Why endanger themselves unnecessarily?"

"But it is necessary. Bullets cannot be marked. Arrows and buffalo spears can be, with notches and
different colored feathers. Each hunter has his own
markings. That way each man can identify his kill."

"I thought you said this hunt was for the benefit of
the entire tribe. I should think the hunter would
share his meat with everyone."

"The hunters do share anything in excess of what
their families might need, and that is why only the
best hunters are allowed to participate. The tribe
cannot afford to risk a hunt being anything less than
totally successful because of less skillful hunters, and
since everyone knows they will get meat, no one
objects to being excluded. But the hide is a different
matter—that belongs to the hunter." Again, Swift
Rabbit turned her back on Brandy and cut her short.
"Now hurry, before we are left behind."

A few minutes later, the party left the camp. The
soldier warriors rode ahead to watch for enemy
tribes during the hunt, and then came the hunters,
followed by the women who would butcher the buffalo. The rest of the women, the children, and the
elderly stayed behind to keep the fires going.

It seemed a long ride to Brandy, up a rolling grassy
hill, then down, then up another, as the late Septem-

ber sun beat down on them. Then, at the top of one
rise, the men reined in and gesturing excitedly at
something ahead. Knowing that they had sighted the
herd, the women crowded in behind them to get a
look at what they had been seeking for days on end.

At the first sight of the herd, Brandy sucked in her
breath, her eyes wide with wonder. The herd was
immense. It seemed to stretch to the horizon and
made the prairie look as if it were covered with a
huge reddish-brown and purplish-black patchwork
quilt. Noting that the shaggy beasts were grazing
lazily as if they didn't have a care in the world,
Brandy asked Swift Rabbit, "Why aren't they running? If we can see them, surely they can see us."

"No, buffalo are very nearsighted. It is their sense
of smell that they must rely on to warn them when
danger is near. That is why we approached them
from their downwind side."

The warriors who were not participating in the
hunt spread out and took positions where they could
watch for the possible approach of enemies, since the
Dakotas were not the only tribe of Indians out in
search of buffalo before the winter set in. Crow and
Pawnee hunting parties thought nothing of encroaching on the Dakotas' hunting ground. Once the
sentries were in place, the hunters formed one long
line; then, crying out, *"Iluka hey!"* they charged.

Brandy thought it unbelievable, but the herd just
stood there and continued to graze as the Dakotas
swept down on them. She assumed the buffalo were a
little deaf too. Several outlying cows were felled, and
the Dakotas were actually riding within the herd
itself before the slow-reacting beasts finally realized
the danger. Then they bolted and raced away with a

speed that seemed incredible for such large, cumbersome-looking animals.

Running with their heads down, their huge, shaggy shoulders thrust forward, and their short tails stuck straight up in the air, the ground shook from the tremendous pounding it was taking. The buffalo's peculiar rolling gait made the prairie look as if it were undulating. Brandy kept her eyes glued on Flaming Arrow as he plunged into the herd. He raced his horse up to the side of the quarry he had chosen, a prime four-year-old bull that was six feet tall at the shoulders and two thousand pounds of terrified animal energy. She gasped when Flaming Arrow rode so close to the beast that his legs actually brushed against its side. When he raised his bow, positioned his arrow, then shot, she held her breath, for he had to rely entirely on his knees to hold onto his racing mount. He seemed at that moment very vulnerable.

For a moment it appeared that Flaming Arrow had missed his mark. The buffalo kept right on running. Then suddenly, it toppled over as its hooves seemed to go out from under it, and it did a half-flip in the air. Flaming Arrow didn't even know when the big beast crashed to the ground and the impact raised a cloud of dust. With supreme confidence that he had killed the animal, he had raced his runner forward after more prey without so much as a backward glance.

Brandy stood on the rise with the other women, who were yelling encouragement to the hunters below, adding their voices to the almost deafening sound of thousands and thousands of hooves on the ground. She could understand why everyone had been so excited about the hunt. It wasn't just the prospect of obtaining food. The sight of a hunter racing his colorfully painted pony up beside a speeding buffalo, with feathers on his head and in his mount's flying mane and tail, was a beautiful sight. Knowing that he and his mount were pitting their speed, strength, and skill against a huge, wild animal was electric with danger, for the buffalo with their immense size, their bloodshot eyes, their hot breath steaming from their flaring nostrils looked very much like awesome, terrifying dragons to Brandy. The air was charged with so much excitement that she could almost taste the men's intense anticipation and the buffalo's fear, could feel the tremendous power generated by the herd.

Then the buffalo sped over the next hill and disappeared, leaving the dead behind in a cloud of thick dust. Swift Rabbit broke the spell and said to Brandy, "Come. Now it is time to work."

When they were out in the open where the carcasses lay, Swift Rabbit quickly identified one of Flaming Arrow's arrows jutting from a huge beast, and the two women struggled with its massive weight to turn it onto its side and butcher it. It was a tedious, bloody, back-breaking chore to dress one huge buffalo after another, then load the big chunks of meat onto their travois. Moving the hides alone worked up a sweat on the two women, for they weighed 250 pounds with the thick mane of purplish-black hair on the bulls still attached. After they had butchered three buffalo, Swift Rabbit told a group of women crowded around them that they could have the meat from the rest of Flaming Arrow's kill. As the excited women rushed off, Brandy sank gratefully to the ground, exhausted. Then she noted that everyone seemed to be ignoring a huge bull with a long-flowing beard lying nearby. "Why isn't anyone butchering that animal?" she asked.

"The first kill in every hunt is never butchered, but is offered as a thanksgiving to the Mystery. Did you not notice that some of the other women moved the carcass and placed it where its head would face east, the holiest of all directions?"

"No, I didn't," Brandy answered. Then she saw a cow lying nearby that was also being ignored and asked, "And that one? Why isn't it being butchered?"

"That is what we call a mourning cow, because it has fetlocks. They are never eaten. To do so would bring death to the family."

Brandy wasn't surprised that the Indians offered the first kill to the Mystery. Since she had come to live with them she had learned that they were a deeply religious people. Communicating with the Great Spirit was an integral part of their daily lives. What did surprise her, however, was to learn that a superstition kept them from taking the mourning cow's meat. They were such a practical people, wasting absolutely nothing that nature gave them, and the buffalo was a classic example. Every part of it would be used: the hides for clothing, tepees, and parfleche, the thick manes for stuffing, the bladder for pouches, the brains for curing hides, the sinew for sewing and stringing bows, the bones for knives, paintbrushes, saddle trees, and scrapers, the horns for drinking vessels, the hooves for glue, the skulls for religious ceremonies, the scrota for rattles, the tails for medicine switches, and on and on. Even the buffalo chips were used for fuel, burned when there was no wood available on the treeless prairies.

Brandy wasn't allowed to rest for long. Swift Rabbit soon urged her to her feet to help some of the other women who were occupied with dressing the buffalo. Shortly thereafter, a few of the hunters arrived, as the hunt had been ended for that day. The men stood and anxiously watched while their wives butchered the beasts. When the liver was pulled from the carcass, they grabbed it and ate it raw, for this was considered the greatest delicacy and the right to devour it belonged to the hunter who had killed the animal. Watching the gruesome scene, Brandy felt her gorge rise, and her face turned ashen. Swift Rabbit saw Brandy's reaction from where she was wielding her knife on another buffalo, and she shook her head. Although the white-eyes had come a long way in becoming Indian, she still had a way to go if she was that squeamish.

The sun was setting when the women returned to the camp with their heavily loaded travoises, whose poles had left deep ruts in the ground. The entire village greeted them with revelry: the adults jumped and whooped, and the excited children shrieked and ran helter-skelter everywhere, the drums beat, and the aged grinned toothlessly from ear to ear. They were also met by the ravenous camp dogs, who in actuality were half-tame coyotes and had to be beaten away from the raw meat with big sticks. Half of the buffalo meat was thrown into the waiting kettles, and a boisterous feast followed. Most of the Indians did not even wait until the buffalo was thoroughly cooked before they gorged themselves.

Brandy didn't wait for the meat to cook either. She didn't even bother to eat. Instead, she slipped away to a nearby stream to bathe, for although she had been angry with Flaming Arrow earlier, she fully expected him to come to his tepee that night since he was no longer scouting for a herd. The more she thought about him making love to her while she was washing the caked blood and sweat from her, the more excited she became. By the time she reached the tepee, she was more than primed for the night. Every nerve and muscle in her body was taut with expectation.

But Brandy was doomed for disappointment. She waited far into the night, but Flaming Arrow didn't appear, and when she finally admitted to herself that he wasn't going to come, she surrendered to a combination of sexual frustration and profound hurt. Then she did something that she had never done, not even as a child. She cried herself to sleep.

14

After the buffalo hunt, the Dakotas didn't pack up and move on but stayed where they were camped on the broad, empty prairie. The men again worked on their weapons while the women cut the remaining buffalo meat into thin strips and strung it on lines to dry in the sun. On the third day, the tribe moved closer to the herd, which had wandered about twenty miles away to graze, and another hunt took place. Over the next two weeks, the tribe repeated this pattern of preserving the meat and then killing more buffalo until Chief Crazy Horse declared that the tribe had enough to last the winter, and the hunt for that year was ended.

That night there was a special thanksgiving celebration. There was not only feasting but a dance. Brandy attended at Swift Rabbit's insistence—the old woman felt that the white-eyes had more than earned her right to be there since she had worked just as hard as anyone else. Only the members of the elite Buffalo Society danced at first, and the painted warriors' long hair hung free and swirled about their faces and shoulders beneath their buffalo horn head-dresses. As the men drummed their feet on the ground, chanted to the beat of the tom-toms, and whirled around, Brandy had to admire the gorgeous feather bustles at the back of their waists, called crows. Despite the fact that the only light was that of the flickering fire, she could see that no two were alike, and it seemed as if each man were vying to pick the most colorful combination. When it occurred to her that one of the shadowy figures dancing around the fire was bound to be Flaming Arrow, her awe was replaced with bitterness, for although Brandy had seen the rugged, exciting Dakota at a distance in the camp, he had yet to come to his tepee. Each night had been a miserable repeat of the first, until Brandy had convinced herself that Flaming Arrow no longer desired her and had even abandoned the comfort of his tepee to avoid being in her company. She was hurt, bewildered, and anxious, for she didn't know what would become of her if he should remove her from his protection. And then anger had come when she remembered that she had foolishly given away not only her body but her heart to a man who had soon tired of her. How naive she had been to enter-tain ideas of making him fall in love with her! All he had ever been interested in was slaking his lust, and now he didn't even feel that much for her.

To Brandy's horror, she felt tears threatening at the back of her eyes. She turned to flee before any of the others could see. But Swift Rabbit caught her arm and asked, "Where are you going?"

Brandy refused to turn to her for fear the old woman would see her tears. Keeping her back to the Indian, she answered, "To my tepee."

"But the women will soon join in the dancing. Don't you want to see that?"

Without a doubt Flaming Arrow would be dancing with one of them, Brandy thought morosely, feeling yet another stab of pain. "I'm not interested," she answered sharply, jerking her arm away. "I'm tired, and I'm going to bed."

Brandy shoved her way through the tight crush of spectators, passing some small boys on the fringes of the crowd who were mimicking the dancers; the beaded, lizard-shaped pouches that held their dried birth cords around their necks swung from side to side as they wildly twisted and turned. Leaving the circle of light that the huge bonfires in the center of the camp had cast, she rapidly walked around the scattered, darkened tepees until she came to Flaming Arrow's at the back of the encampment, furiously brushing away a tear that spilled over. Once inside the tent, she lit a small fire, more to ward off the chill of the night than for light. Then she stripped, lay down on her pallet, and pulled her blanket up tightly around her shoulders, hoping that sleep and oblivion would come quickly for a change.

It didn't. For what seemed ages, she lay there, listening to the noises coming from the festivities in the distance. She knew from the change in the music that the men and women were dancing together. Instead of just drums and rattles and a steady, rhythmic thumping of feet, she could distinctly hear the soft sound of a lute and a muted shuffling of feet. Also, the Indians were now chanting a monotonous *"hi-yi,"* a repetitive drone that played on her nerves.

Suddenly, the hide that served as a door to the tepee was thrown open. Startled, Brandy bolted to a sitting position and barely stifled a cry of alarm before she saw Flaming Arrow standing there. The fire had burned down to a pile of red coals, and the rosy glow it cast brought out the copperish tone of his smooth skin and emphasized his high cheekbones and the planes of hard muscle on his chest, taut belly, and long, corded legs. Droplets of glistening water clung to his loose black hair and his broad shoulders from where he had bathed, and there was a fierce-looking gleam in his black eyes. He looked very primitive, very dangerous, very exciting, and altogether breathtakingly magnificent. Brandy's body responded to him with a will of its own, her nipples hardening and the secret woman's place between her legs suddenly burning.

When she became aware of his blazing gaze on her bare breasts and saw the tenting of his breechclout, a thrill ran through her. That he possessed so much power over her that he could make her body betray her suddenly infuriated Brandy. She jerked the blanket up to her chin to hide her nudity and cried, "What in the hell do you think you're doing here? Get out! Get out this minute!"

Flaming Arrow was clearly stunned by her angry outburst, as a dumbfounded expression came over his face. Then his dark eyes narrowed suspiciously. "Is this a game you play? Like the last time? Do you intend to resist me again?" He sighed deeply. "Your game grows tiring. I grow weary of always having to fight you. Tonight, I would like a warm and willing woman instead of a wildcat."

"I'm not playing any games! I never have. And there won't be a repeat of the last time either," Brandy answered hotly, her blue eyes flashing dangerously, "because I'll never let you touch me again!"

"And why this change?" Flaming Arrow asked in a terse tone of voice, a hard expression coming over his face.

"Why?" Brandy cried even louder, making Flaming Arrow flinch. "I'll tell you why! Because I won't be treated the way you've been treating me, even if I am a captive. I won't let you ignore me for weeks and then, when the whim happens to hit you, use me to satisfy your—your disgusting animal urges!"

Flaming Arrow had just gone through a very trying time himself and was in no mood to be denied, much less to endure her show of temper. He, too, had been plagued with memories, not only of their torrid lovemaking but of Brandy's intoxicating beauty. His nights had been pure hell as he had tossed and turned for hours with unfulfilled desire, and during the days, visions of her loveliness seemed to be everywhere he looked. Even when he had painted his runner, he had been thinking of her. He had picked blue because it was the color of the heavens and therefore the most holy—he hoped thereby to gain the Mystery's blessing in the hunt—but it had been the searing color of Brandy's eyes that he had been trying to duplicate. Now, seeing that Brandy had suffered the same torture, he was willing to forgive her for her attack. He smiled and strode across the tepee, then knelt beside her. "So that is why you are so angry. You think I stayed away by choice."

Brandy wished he weren't so close. His heat, his intoxicating scent seemed to drown her. And his rare smile had a devastating effect on her, making her feel as if her bones were melting. She scooted back on her pallet and said in a scathing voice, "I suppose you're going to tell me you didn't?"

"No, I didn't. I stayed away because it was the only way I could keep my vow of celibacy."

"What vow?" Brandy asked, hardly believing her ears.

"Every hunter vows to abstain from lovemaking until the big fall hunt is over, so as not to drain his strength."

Swift Rabbit had said nothing about this. Suspicious, Brandy said, "I saw other hunters going to their tepees at night."

Flaming Arrow smiled again, this time derisively. "Yes, I know. It seems those men do not find their women as tempting as I find mine. Either that, or they have better restraint."

Although Flaming Arrow's words had a hint of possessiveness about them, a little thrill ran through Brandy when he referred to her as his woman. She wondered what that meant. Did it mean he loved her? Or was it still just a matter of passion? Even if it was only passion, there was a certain amount of satisfaction to be gained by his admission. She knew Flaming Arrow was not a man to admit to it easily. Undoubtedly, he considered his unrestrained hunger for her a weakness, and she knew he scorned weakness. She looked up, saw the wary glint in his dark eyes, and knew he feared he had revealed too much. Suddenly, she realized that her fierce, powerful savage was vulnerable, and that by commanding his pas-

sion, she held just as much power over him as he did
her, that he was as much her captive as she was his.
But instead of reveling in her surprising discovery, as
the old, selfish Brandy would have done, she felt such
a tremendous surge of love for him that she thought
she would burst with the emotion. She slipped her
arms around his neck and pulled him down over her
on the pallet, raining kisses over his face before she
muttered in a husky voice, "Don't say another word.
Just love me."

Brandy never realized that she had stepped back
for her man and, by doing so, had bonded him even
closer to her. Flaming Arrow realized that he had left
himself terribly exposed, an error that as a trained
warrior horrified him, and he had feared that Brandy
would throw his weakness in his face. To his desire
for her was added a sense of immense gratitude,
which so tempered the raging passion he had felt
when he had first stepped into the tepee that his first
kisses were incredibly sweet and tender, his lips
softly eloquent as they moved back and forth against
hers. Brandy felt as if she were melting in a sweet
languor and parted her lips in silent invitation, wanting more intimacy. To her frustration, Flaming Arrow continued his excruciating play at her lips,
gently biting them, then cupping at the sensitive corner of her mouth until Brandy was seething with
hunger, her nails digging into the hard muscles on his
shoulders. Finally, he gave her what she wanted; his
warm tongue slipped into her mouth, tasted it slowly,
savoring its flavor, and delicately stroked her tongue
with the tip of his own.

A moan rose in Brandy's throat, and she pulled
Flaming Arrow even closer, her fingertips tracing

the hard muscles on his back, then closing over his tight buttocks and pressing him even closer and arching her hips into his. She thrilled at the feel of his hard, throbbing flesh that pressed between their abdomens and made a mockery out of her blanket and his breechclout. Then as the ache between her legs burst into a scorching need, she rubbed herself against him.

Flaming Arrow sucked in his breath sharply as an electric shock ran up his spine. Suddenly he didn't want anything between them. He broke the kiss, bringing a moan of protest from Brandy, and sat back on his heels by her side. He skimmed the blanket that covered her down. Like a man starved, he devoured her loveliness, thinking each curve a hallow perfection. Her flawless skin seemed to glow with a rosy life of its own as it reflected the light of the remnants of the fire.

Brandy felt no shame when Flaming Arrow stared at her, his look hot and hungry. Knowing he thought her beautiful and desirable made her feel she was. But she felt cheated. She wanted to see all of him too. "Take off your breechclout."

When Flaming Arrow loosened the string that held the cloth in place and the material fell at a soft heap between his legs, his manhood sprung free. Brandy's mouth turned dry and her heart raced in anticipation as she stared at the rigid proof of his desire for her, standing long and full and bold before her. But before she could reach for him, Flaming Arrow bent and his tongue flicked out like a wet whip against her rosy nipple. She gasped at the hot shot of sheer pleasure that ran through her, and then his mouth closed over hers.

He kissed her as if he were a part of her, and Brandy felt that searing kiss flow through her, over her, inside her, on and on and on, seeming to scorch her lungs and sear her brain. Her senses were spinning wildly when he dropped his head, nuzzled her breasts, and breathed in their fragrance. Then he laved them with his wet, rough tongue and flicked at the nipples with quicksilver movements, slowly descending, kissing, nipping, licking her silky, sweet skin, taking fierce delight in her moans and soft cries of pleasure. He lingered at the insides of her thighs, awed by the incredible softness of her skin there, his senses spinning as he breathed deeply of her intoxicating womanly essence. Then he slid back to feast once more at her breasts, his fingers stroking the dark curls at the apex of her thighs before slipping downward.

Brandy felt his fingers plunging into her damp heat; electric sparks danced down her spine. When he began to move his hand, she cried out, "No! I want you inside me." She reached down and took his hot, throbbing erection in her hand. "I want this!"

A long shudder ran through Flaming Arrow at the feel of Brandy's hand squeezing the ultrasensitive flesh. A sheen of perspiration broke out on his forehead. How like Brandy, he thought. Not asking but boldly demanding. But this time he was determined that he would set the pace, that he would be the master. He reached down with his free hand and pried hers loose, saying in a ragged voice, "You can have both, my little wildcat, if you'll just be patient." He nuzzled her neck and whispered, "Now relax and allow yourself to feel."

Brandy had no recourse. Flaming Arrow's fingers

were already sliding in and out of her, his thumb circling and massaging the tiny ultrasensitive bud. The exquisite tremors began, growing more and more powerful. When his mouth closed over hers and his tongue darted into her mouth like a flaming torch, she convulsed, heard a roaring in her ears and saw fireworks exploding behind her eyes.

Her response brought tremendous satisfaction to Flaming Arrow. He relished the feel of her spasms of delight around his fingers until he became unbearably excited himself. When he felt as if he would burst, he quickly withdrew his fingers and positioned himself between her thighs.

Brandy was still dazed when she felt the hot, rock-hard tip of Flaming Arrow's erection where his fingers had just been. She felt lifeless, totally drained by her recent explosive release, thinking herself incapable of any feelings. She discovered how wrong she was when he drove into her with a powerful thrust, sending a bolt of flame racing up her spine. Her breath came in quick gasps as shock after shock ran through her. Flaming Arrow drove at her with the force of his passion, savage and demanding one minute, then gentle and with great sensitivity the next, then withdrawing and teasing her with the tip of his manhood, making her sob for more, then demanding and pounding again. A sheen of perspiration broke out on her, her heart pounding so hard she feared it would burst, her body consumed with an excruciating need for release.

She dug her nails into his shoulders, sobbing, "Stop! You're killing me!"

But Flaming Arrow wasn't about to stop. This was the closest he had ever come to mastering her. As he continued his tender-savage assault on her senses, Brandy seriously doubted that she would survive. She strained against him, clinging to his wet, slippery skin for dear life, then fiercely held him in her when he began to withdraw with a strength born of desperation. The tightening of her hot, velvety muscles around him, squeezing him so tightly he thought she would crush him, pushed Flaming Arrow's passion over the edge. He no longer cared if he mastered her or not. He caught her to him in a bruising embrace, consumed with his own hot urgency, his teasing and taunting forgotten. He drove them both up that breathless, spiraling ascent, recklessly riding the wild wind. Brandy climaxed first, her body convulsing as she cried out and was flung into a fiery starburst. As the muscles surrounding his rigid length inside her contracted, Flaming Arrow felt it coming, and that incredible surge of power swept over him like a monstrous, scorching tidal wave, sucking the breath from his lungs, making his heart stop for a heartbeat—and it exploded in his brain as he poured himself into her and cried out her name.

Slowly they drifted back down from those rapturous heights, breathless and still trembling. They dozed, then Flaming Arrow made love to her again, and again. Much later in the night, while Brandy lay sleeping in his arms, Flaming Arrow wondered at his hunger for her. He was a man who took pride in practicing moderation, and he had never had any trouble controlling his appetites in the past. But that was before Brandy had come into his life with her flaming hair, her searing blue eyes, her exciting passion, her bold manner that shocked, irritated, and stimulated him. He had never dreamed women like her existed, and he seriously suspected that she was one of a kind.

Brandy stirred in his arms, nuzzled closer, and muttered, "Are you awake?"

"Yes," Flaming Arrow admitted.

After just the briefest pause, she asked in a throaty tone of voice, "Are you too tired for—for this?"

Flaming Arrow jerked at the feel of Brandy brushing her soft thigh against his manhood. Then, as the member hardened and rose in anticipation, he was utterly amazed. He could have sworn he was totally spent, but he'd never had such amazing recuperative powers. He should refuse her, he thought. It was the man's place to initiate lovemaking. Yes, she was much too bold. But Flaming Arrow found he couldn't resist. What he had feared had happened. He was totally besotted with her. In his own way he was as much her captive as she was his.

With something akin to helpless, Flaming Arrow turned to her, and she greeted him with open arms.

15

The next day the Dakotas left
their hunting camp on the wide open prairie and
made the return trip back to the Big Horn Mountains. They traveled past the rolling foothills where
their summer camp had stood and climbed higher
into the mountains themselves. There, standing on
rocky crags or picking their way up the steep
mountainsides, Brandy saw for the first time the big
shaggy sheep with their monstrous curved horns for
which the mountains had been named. She also got
her first glimpse of a grizzly bear. The huge, lumber-
ing animal was a frightening sight even though it was
crashing through the underbrush some distance
away. And she heard her first scream of the mountain
lion, a bloodcurdling sound that made the hair on the
nape of her neck stand on end. Finally, in a protected
valley that was cradled by a high bluff on one side

and surrounded by a forest on the other three, they set up their winter camp, the tepees scattered far apart for privacy during the upcoming long winter.

Brandy placed Flaming Arrow's tepee beside the fast-flowing mountain stream that meandered through the valley beneath the shade of several quaking aspens. The trembling leaves for which the trees were named were a striking golden color and, dry now that fall had arrived, made a soft rustling sound that was soothing in the gentle evening breeze. Here they had an excellent view of the woods across from them. The scattered oaks and maples were spectacular with their brilliant red and orange leaves, and the pine, fir, and spruce were a deep, verdant green.

Brandy had thought that the great buffalo hunt was the last of the winter preparations, but she discovered much to her dismay that the hardest and most feverish labor was still ahead of her. The jerky that had been braided into long strips was pounded with fat and chokeberries into a mash called pemmican, the main staple of the plains Indians, and it was stored in bags made from buffalo bladders and stomachs. Day in and day out, Brandy knelt before a flat stone and pounded, her arms, shoulders, and back aching, and her knees so stiff when she finally arose that she could barely walk. As soon as that awesome chore was finished, she set to work tanning four buffalo hides. Again on her knees, she scraped the flesh from the inside of the hide and the hair from the outside, smeared the smelly concoction of brains and fat on, then once more pounded it to soften the dried skin. When that backbreaking job was done, she almost cried when Swift Rabbit instructed her to take the new hides she had worked so hard on and replace the yellowed skins around the smoke hole on the tepee with them. Brandy had hoped to make a tunic for herself out of at least one of them, or some new moccasins. It was then that she learned that the smoke waterproofed the hides and those skins made much better winter moccasins and leggins.

Still the work was not done. Brandy spent the better part of her day in the woods searching for seasonal berries that could be dried, wild gourds, and acorns—the better part of the nuts were ground into a meal for making a type of flat bread. She gathered enough firewood to last the winter, then stacked it inside the brush enclosure that she had erected as a windbreak next to the tepee. Then she dressed and smoked the turkeys and deer that Flaming Arrow brought her, all the while doing her day-to-day chores too.

During this time, Brandy and Flaming Arrow's relationship changed very little. At night, he was a passionate, often surprisingly sensitive lover. But other than that he paid very little attention to her, particularly in public, which irritated Brandy no end, despite what Swift Rabbit had told her about the Dakotas' customs on the mixing of the sexes. To her way of thinking, there was no reason for Flaming Arrow to treat her like a maiden when he knew all too well she wasn't. The tribe surely knew by this time that they were intimate. Nor was Brandy willing to accept that married couples displayed aloofness in public, since any show of affection between a man and a woman was considered bad taste after the male had reached adolescence. Sons were not even permitted to hug their mothers or grown brothers their sisters. No, despite everything she knew of the Dakotas' reserved nature, Brandy still came to the unwarranted conclusion that Flaming Arrow treated her so coolly in public solely because she was nothing but a lowly captive. She came to another conclusion too—that even if he should come to love her, as she was desperate to make him do, marriage to a white captive was taboo and she was doomed to a lifetime of being nothing but Flaming Arrow's mistress and housekeeper. That she could never hold a respected position in his life, and that he failed to tell her he loved her, ate at her. While she could never get the strength to refuse his exciting lovemaking, she was often irritable and cross with him.

Brandy would have been surprised to learn that although Flaming Arrow appeared to ignore her in public, he was always acutely aware of her, much more than he would have liked to admit. No matter where he was in the camp, his eyes drifted to where she was working. Secretly, he was proud of how well she performed her duties, of her strength and determination. He knew his tribesmen had also taken note of her surprising attributes, and their respect—although it was grudging for the better part—pleased him. But what Flaming Arrow couldn't understand was Brandy's quicksilver moods. She seemed to be two different women: one snapping and shooting daggers at him, the other wildly passionate. Whenever he puzzled over her conflicting behavior, he was always left to conclude that she had become his mistress simply to make life easier for herself, that although she enjoyed his lovemaking, she really cared very little for him, and his pride, too, suffered. It never occurred to him that Brandy might be hurt that he did not profess his love. In the first place, Flaming Arrow had yet to admit it to himself. In the second, it wasn't within his Indian nature to do so. Love was expressed in actions, not words. And so Flaming Arrow didn't understand Brandy any better than she did him, and although they shared a remarkably intense physical intimacy, they were still very much at odds with one another.

Winter—caused by what the Dakotas called the Cold Maker—came suddenly that year. One day they awakened to leaden skies with snow flurries, and within hours the storm had turned into a full-fledged, howling blizzard. Brandy had dreaded the coming of winter, thinking that it would be terribly cold with only the buffalo hides to protect them and the small fire to warm them, but she discovered that the tepee was amazingly toasty and cozy. To be perfectly honest, she was more comfortable there than she had been back in her home in St. Louis, where if she got too far across the room from the fireplace, it was freezing. The skins seemed to reflect the heat, turning it back inward, while the brick and wood of her old home absorbed it and then dispersed it outside into the cold. As the blizzard continued and the snow piled up against the sides of the tepee, creating insulation much like an igloo, the inside was even warmer.

The warmth was a pleasant surprise to Brandy, but the isolation wore on her nerves, and by the third day of the blizzard, Brandy thought she would go out of her mind if she had to spend one more minute in the close confines of the tent. She exploded with a suddenness and unexpectedness that made Flaming Arrow jump where he sat across the fire from her. "I can't stand it! I'll scream if I have to stay one more day in this little tent!"

"You'll get used to it," Flaming Arrow replied, recovering from his surprise at her outburst.

His calm reassurance irritated Brandy all the more. Didn't anything ever get on his nerves? she wondered. Did he even have any nerves? If he did, they seemed to be made of steel. "No, I won't get used to it!" she flared out. "I'll go stir crazy. Stark, raving mad! I'm used to activity."

A sudden warmth came into Flaming Arrow's eyes, and he smiled. "We could make love again."

Brandy stared at Flaming Arrow's lips. He smiled so rarely that it always took her somewhat aback when he did, but this was such an enticing, crooked little smile that it tugged at her heartstrings and made her feel as if she were melting inside. That he could reduce her to putty with just a smile irritated her all the more. "My God! Is that all you can think of? Making love? That's all we've done since it started snowing."

Flaming Arrow's smile spread across his face. "That is why my people call winter the lovemaking season."

"Well there must be something better than that to do," Brandy threw back without even thinking.

The smile on Flaming Arrow's face disappeared in a flash, and his look turned as hard as steel. "I didn't notice you objected," he replied in a cold voice. "If I didn't think you enjoyed it, I wouldn't have bothered you."

Brandy couldn't deny that she enjoyed it. For two days they'd had a sensual feast, making love over and over, and she'd behaved like a total wanton. But something in Flaming Arrow's voice had caught her attention, and something besides total honesty made her answer as she did. She realized she had hurt his feelings, and felt a twinge of deep regret. "I did enjoy it. But this is going to be a long winter, and not even you can keep us occupied all the time."

"What do you mean, not even me?"

"Well, you do have remarkable—staying power," Brandy admitted, a flush rising on her face at her own boldness in discussing Flaming Arrow's performance so frankly. "I don't know where you get the strength and endurance."

Brandy's oblique compliment on his sexual prowess soothed Flaming Arrow's bruised ego, for he was a typical Indian male who took pride in his masculinity. "What about those doeskins I gave you to make a new tunic and skirt? You could sew on those."

"That will occupy my hands but not my mind."

"We could gamble," Flaming Arrow suggested, a sudden glow coming to his dark eyes.

Brandy recognized that glow. She had discovered that the Dakotas dearly loved to gamble, even the women. It wasn't at all unusual to see the women crouched in a circle, one shuffling three walnut halves on the ground while the others tried to guess which half the seed was under, or tossing dice that their men had picked up at a trading fair. They could play for hours and hours on end if they didn't have something more pressing to occupy them, and they often kept a game going on the side while they cooked or sewed or nursed their babies. And the men were even worse. Several feverish games were always in progress. They even gambled on the many horseraces and wrestling matches they had, as well as

betting on who would bring home the biggest buck
or the most turkeys. Yes, Brandy thought, undoubtedly there were fierce gambling games going on in a
good many of the tepees at that very minute, but she
didn't share the Indians' fascination with the sport.
After a short time, she got bored, even if she won. "I
suppose we could," she replied reluctantly, then
couldn't help but add, "every now and then. But I
was thinking of doing something mentally stimulating."

"Like what?" Flaming Arrow asked, stymied by
her suggestion.

"Like talking."

"We talk."

"No, we don't!" Brandy answered emphatically.
"When we're alone, you sit and work on whatever it
is you happen to be doing, and I work on what I'm
doing—mostly in silence. We've never really talked.
If we had a language barrier, it might be different,
but we don't, and we didn't from the very beginning.
Yet we've never really exchanged ideas or discussed
anything at length. The only time we seem to communicate is there," Brandy ended bitterly, pointing
to the pallet she and Flaming Arrow shared.

Flaming Arrow scowled. He was by nature a quiet,
thoughtful man who felt perfectly at ease with his
silence and his own company. He spoke when he had
something important to say, never just for the sake of
talking, which had earned him a considerable respect from the others. When he spoke, they listened.
And he could go for days and days in perfect solitude
without feeling in the least lonely, as he often had in
the winter. Flaming Arrow had always been in such
perfect accord with himself and nature that he didn't

need others, and if the urge to socialize should happen to hit him, his brother and other male friends were always there. All he had to do was walk from his tepee to theirs, and he was always welcome. But Flaming Arrow had never sought out a woman's company for any reason other than to satisfy his physical needs. While he had come to accept the fact that Brandy held him to her by strange ties, he had never considered discussing things with a female, actually exchanging ideas with one. That was something one did with friends. A woman was an entirely different matter. Wasn't it?

While Flaming Arrow silently pondered Brandy's suggestion, Brandy grew impatient and said in a huff, "Well, all right, then! It's obvious you don't care to carry on a serious conversation with me. I suppose you don't think I've got anything intelligent enough to say!"

"I did not say I did not wish to talk with you," Flaming Arrow answered in exasperation. "You have a bad habit of jumping to conclusions. Either that, or you simply like to argue. It's just that I can't imagine what you might want to talk about."

"What?" Brandy asked in disbelief. "Why, anything! Everything! We come from two entirely different worlds. There's a lot I still don't know about your world, and you know absolutely nothing about mine."

"I have no wish to know anything about the white man's world," Flaming Arrow answered stiffly.

"But there might be things that you could learn from us, things that might make your life much easier."

"I do not consider my life hard. I am not like the

reservation Indians, who have grown soft and weak because they have forsaken the old ways, who have given up their freedom to live like the white man because of the white man's empty promises. Look at what it gained them. They die like flies from the white man's diseases; they starve trying to grow crops on miserable plots of land meant for grass and not corn, using the flimsy tools doled out to them by your Indian agents. They freeze in the winter because the hides on their tepees and their backs have become thin with age, and the white man does not allow them to hunt buffalo. They drown their sorrow at losing their old way of life in your firewater, which addles their senses and further robs them of their ambition and their pride. No, I want nothing of the white man!"

"I'm not saying that everything the white man does might be good for your people, and I'm not suggesting you give up your freedom. I know my people haven't been very fair with yours, that we've been greedy, and that too many times the Indian has suffered. But that doesn't mean that there aren't things the white man does or uses that you could benefit from if you knew about them." Brandy paused and looked about her, then said, "Like your Winchester. That's a white man's invention. And you use it because it is superior to your weapons."

"I would not need the Winchester if it were not for the white man," Flaming Arrow pointed out. "I can kill a buffalo with an arrow. You saw that for yourself. No, I need the white man's gun because he has them, to protect myself against him, not because I prefer them."

"What about your knife? That's a white man's

knife. I know because the handle has John Russel Company imprinted on it, the name of a manufacturer back east. Are you going to claim that you have it solely for protection?"

Flaming Arrow frowned. His people had adopted the white man's knife with its steel blade long before the white man himself had come to this country. The fur traders had brought it with them, and the Indian had quickly recognized it as superior to the bone knives they used.

"And are you aware that the white man brought the horse to this country?" Brandy continued.

Flaming Arrow quickly corrected her. "No, the Kiowas brought them, many, many years ago. I know because the elder storytellers said so, and they are never wrong."

"I don't doubt your storytellers," Brandy answered diplomatically. "But it was Spaniards—white men— who originally brought the horse to this continent, to a land far to the south of here. The Indians who lived there stole them from the white man and brought them north."

Flaming Arrow knew that the Kiowas were a southern tribe and that they were rumored to be very successful horse thieves. They were also renowned for their trading skills. It was the Kiowa who had developed the Indian sign language that all the different tribes used to communicate with one another at their trading fairs. His scowl deepened. "How do you know all this?"

"Some I was taught when I went to school. Some I read in books."

"I have seen one of your books. Crooked Nose had one. He said it told a story, but I thought he lied.

There were no pictures in it. I looked. All I saw was small, strange-looking markings."

"Those small, strange looking markings were letters of the alphabet, which are combined to make words, which in turn can be read." Brandy picked up a small stick from a pile of nearby kindling and said, "Here, let me show you what I mean. I'll write your name on the ground."

Flaming Arrow was amazed when Brandy scratched his name into the ground and identified each letter. He gazed down at it and asked, "And you say a white man invented this alphabet?"

" Yes, but not any white man in this country. The ancient Phoenicians devised the alphabet, many, many thousands of years ago, so long ago that their civilization has disappeared from the earth. But the alphabet was a good idea, so it survived all this time. That's what I mean when I said that you might find some benefit in some of the white man's ways. Oh, not all, I'm sure. God only knows, we've made our share of mistakes. But you can keep what you like, what's useful to you, and discard what you don't like. You should never close your mind to new ideas. I've learned so much since I've been with your people that it's incredible. Your ways are so different. You have survival down to a fine art, and yet everything you do seems to be in perfect accord with nature. I feel that being here with you has made me grow, made me into a much stronger, much more self-sufficient person."

Brandy suddenly became aware that Flaming Arrow was staring at her strangely, and she felt very self-conscious. A flush rose on her face, and she said nervously, "My goodness! What got into me? Why, I sound like a pompous schoolteacher lecturing her pupils. I'm sorry. I didn't mean to get so carried away." She glanced around her. "And look! It's dark, and I haven't even begun my evening meal yet."

As Brandy hurried to add wood to the fire and begin the meal, Flaming Arrow thoughtfully scrutinized her. She obviously had been well educated and knew much more than he about the outside world, perhaps more than many whites. A lesser man might have felt intimidated by her knowledge. Still, Flaming Arrow felt that his informal Indian education taught survival just as well, if not better than, anything Brandy had learned in the white man's schools or books. No, Flaming Arrow was more impressed with Brandy's logical thinking than with the content of what she knew, and he was pleased that she had admitted that she had learned much from his people and that her own people were capable of mistakes. He had not expected such openness, such honesty from her, and being the fair man that he was, he thought she deserved the same. Thinking back over the exchange, he discovered that he had actually enjoyed it.

From then on, whenever Brandy and Flaming Arrow were snowbound, they spent a good deal of their time exchanging information and ideas. Although Flaming Arrow found nothing in the white man's life that he wanted, he still found many things Brandy told him interesting, if not fascinating. And Brandy came to understand better the Indians she lived with, their deep religious beliefs, their mysticism, their complexity.

Even when Brandy and Flaming Arrow weren't conversing, their being together took on a new, deeper meaning. Each came to feel perfectly at ease with the other's company. At those times Flaming Arrow would lean back on his willow backrest, smoke the fragrant *kinnikinick* in his pipe, and gaze at Brandy across the fire. No matter what she was doing —whether it was sewing beads on a pair of moccasins, flattening porcupine quills with her teeth and dying them to decorate a buckskin skirt for him, or stirring the pot over the fire—he was mesmerized both by her beauty and by her gracefulness. He couldn't keep his eyes from her. Without realizing it, he was becoming more and more deeply enmeshed in the silken web she was weaving.

16

Flaming Arrow and Brandy weren't confined to their tepee the entire winter. Between snowstorms, they—like everyone else in the village—ventured out. The women combed the woods for newly fallen firewood and set snares for rabbits and traps for ermine and mink. The furs that were not saved to be traded later were used for extra warmth in the calf-high winter moccasins—except for the prized black-tipped ermine tails, that is. Those were saved for decorations, to be sewed on the Indians' clothing, dangled from their braids and scalp locks, or tied to their horses' manes and tails along with their colorful feathers. While the women were occupied with their chores, the men, wearing a strange contraption that reminded Brandy of a tennis racket strapped to their feet, trudged farther up into the mountains in search of deer and mountain sheep. If the hunters were really fortunate, they would find a few stray buffalo to kill. Not only was the fresh meat a welcome change after weeks of a steady diet of pemmican, but the winter kills resulted in thick-haired hides, from which the Indians made their buffalo robes, their winter coats.

One day when Brandy was setting a snare on a hillside overlooking the village, she gazed at the snowy scene around her in appreciation. The newly fallen snow on the ground and piled on the pine and fur boughs was pristine white, and a few flakes were still drifting down from a leaden sky here and there, one or two so large that she could actually see their unique, delicate pattern. Below her, smoke curled lazily in the sky from the tepees scattered in the valley, and the fire inside the shelters gave the hides a faint rosy glow. On a hill across from her, children were racing down the steep rise on sleds made from buffalo ribs, their squeals of delight shattering the crystal silence. It was a beautiful, peaceful winter scene that rivaled any that Brandy had seen either personally or hanging in any home or art gallery.

Her eyes swept over the lovely landscape once more, then came to rest on two women chopping down a beautifully shaped pine. Each blow of the ax sent the snow that had collected on its limbs flying through the air. Suddenly, a wave of melancholy swept over Brandy. The winter scene reminded her of home, the children reminded her of her own carefree childhood, and the cut evergreen the Indian women were dragging away to chop into firewood reminded her of Christmas. What was the date? she wondered. Surely Christmas must be near. Memories of Christmases bombarded her. She could almost smell the aroma of the fresh-cut pine boughs that she and her mother strung up the staircase and across the mantel and the spices coming from the kitchen where Molly, their cook, baked fruitcakes and cookies; hear the carolers singing and the bells on the sleighs tingling outside their house; see the myriad gaily wrapped presents beneath the Christmas tree with its colorful ribbons, strings of cranberries and popcorn, painted ornaments, glittering tin stars, and glowing candles; taste the chestnut dressing, the mashed potatoes with giblet gravy, the glazed ham, and her very favorite of all—mincemeat pie swimming in rum sauce.

Memories of Christmas brought back memories of her brother, for Paul shared her love for the season just as he shared so many of her likes and dislikes. They had been more than just brother and sister. They had been fast friends, so fiercely loyal to each other that they would gladly take the blame and the punishment for something wrong that the other had done. And there was nothing, absolutely nothing so private, so personal that she couldn't confide in her brother, or he in her. She could reveal her most secret thoughts and know, no matter how shocking they might be, that he would still love and accept her. Suddenly, Brandy missed her brother's company, his warm understanding, his unwavering support. She missed him something terrible, for she desperately needed someone to confide in. Keeping her love for Flaming Arrow a secret was a heavy burden on her heart, a burden she longed to share with someone.

Awash in an heart-aching homesickness and a terrible yearning for her brother, tears welled in Brandy's eyes, and she fled through the thick snow to the privacy of Flaming Arrow's tepee.

That was how Flaming Arrow found her when he returned from hunting an hour later: sitting on their pallet before the small fire with tears streaming down her cheeks. Her tears alarmed him, for although he had seen the glitter of moisture in her eyes before, he had never seen her openly cry. He shrugged off his buffalo robe and dropped to his knees beside her. "What's wrong? Why are you crying? Are you hurt?"

Brandy might have denied she was crying, knowing that Flaming Arrow considered it a weakness, but seeing the genuine look of concern in his eyes made her forgo all pretense. At that moment she didn't feel at all strong or the least stoical. Her homesickness and her longing for her brother were so powerful that there was an aching in her chest. She reached up, caught his buckskin shirt in both hands, and pulled him closer, pleading, "Please! Take me back to my people."

Her entreaty touched a chord deep within Flaming Arrow. He felt her pain almost as if it were his own. But although at that moment he would have done almost anything to spare her her unhappiness, he couldn't grant her request. He hardened his expression and answered, "We have been through this before, and nothing has changed. I will never take you back. Never!"

"I don't belong here. Our ways are too different, and I miss my people, especially my brother. You see, we were very close. If you care anything for me at all, please, take me back."

At that moment, Flaming Arrow knew that it was

no longer a matter of pride or saving face with his people that prevented him from taking Brandy back to her people. It was because he cared too much. He had fallen in love with his captive. Somehow or another, she had captured his heart. He couldn't bear to give her up. The realization came somewhat as a shock to him, and for that reason his words were sharper than he meant them to be. "No! I will not take you back. And do not ever ask me again. I grow weary of you badgering me."

At Flaming Arrow's brittle rebuke, Brandy turned away from him to hide the fresh tears that spilled over. Knowing that he had only added more anguish to what she was already feeling, Flaming Arrow felt a strange twisting pain in his chest. He shouldn't be so hard on her, he thought. Wanting to return to her people was only natural, particularly in view of the fact that she didn't feel the same way about him that he did about her. If she did, she wouldn't be asking to go back. And it wasn't her fault that he had fallen in love with her. He had only himself to blame for that. He should have taken her back, there at the very beginning, before he fell under her spell.

Flaming Arrow sat down beside her and turned her to face him. Cupping her chin in his hand and forcing her to look him in the eye, he asked, "Why are you asking this now, after so long?"

"I saw some of the other women chopping down a tree, and suddenly I thought about Christmas and home."

Flaming Arrow frowned, then asked, "What is Christmas? I can't recall Crooked Nose ever mentioning this word."

"It's a religious holiday where we Christians cele-

brate the birth of Christ, a man we believe to be the
son of God."

Brandy went on to tell Flaming Arrow the story of
the birth of Christ and how her people celebrated it,
including the cutting and decorating of the tree.
Flaming Arrow listened attentively. He had no trouble accepting her Christian beliefs. Unlike the mis-
sionaries, she wasn't attacking his own, for Brandy's
beliefs were simply an extension of his own. Nor did
he question a virgin giving birth, for he knew anything was possible with the Mystery. He even accepted the tree as part of the white man's celebrating their feast, for a tree played a very important part
in the Dakotas' major religious ceremony—the Sun
Dance. But Brandy had no way of knowing Flaming
Arrow's thoughts. As usual, his face betrayed nothing, and he made no comment when she finished.

It wasn't until the next morning, when she awakened, that Brandy realized how seriously Flaming
Arrow had taken her. There, across from their pallet,
a small, perfectly shaped spruce was leaning against
the side of the tepee. Brandy stared at the tree in
astonishment, but saw that Flaming Arrow was not in
the tepee. She knew that only he could have brought
the tree. Then tears came for the second time, but
not because the spruce reminded her of home. This
time she cried because the Dakota's unexpected
thoughtfulness had touched her deeply.

Later that morning, when Flaming Arrow stepped
into the tepee and tossed aside his buffalo robe,
Brandy knew he had been to the village sweat lodge
both by his near nakedness—for he was only wearing
his breechclout and moccasins—and the hint of rosi-
ness beneath his bronze skin. The discoloration was

caused not by the steam that was generated from
sprinkling water on hot rocks, but by Flaming Arrow's rolling in the cold snow when his steam bath
was finished. That method of bathing was one Dakota
custom Brandy had elected to forgo, although even
as a captive, she could have bathed in the women's
sweat lodge. While she had become accustomed to
stripping and bathing before the other women, she
couldn't whip up the courage to roll stark naked in
the snow. Just thinking about it made goosebumps on
her skin. Her bathing had been limited to sponge
baths in the privacy of their warm, cozy tepee. That
was what she was doing at that moment, just finishing
her bath, and usually when Flaming Arrow caught
her in the middle of her morning ablutions, he stared
avidly at her nudity, making Brandy feel a little embarrassed. But for once, Flaming Arrow didn't even
glance at her. His full attention was on the tree that
Brandy had decorated with strings of trading beads
and stars made from porcupine quills twisted together.

Brandy tossed down the piece of trading flannel
that served as her towel and quickly wrapped a blanket around her. It wasn't her nakedness that made
her feel vulnerable; she was afraid Flaming Arrow
would laugh at the way she had decorated the tree or
in some way belittle her beliefs, even though it was
he who had brought it to her. After all, she was a
Christian, and he was a heathen. A tremendous wave
of relief washed over her when he turned to her and
said, "It looks very pretty. I have some shells that I
picked up at a trading fair several years ago that you
might like to string for it. Would you like to use
them?"

When Brandy recovered from her surprise, she asked, "Is that where you get the sea shells for your necklaces and earrings? A trading fair? I wondered, since there are no oceans around here."

"Yes, tribes from all over come to the fairs, those who live far to the west, those from far to the south, those from Canada, those—"

"Canada?" Brandy asked in surprise, cutting across the rest of Flaming Arrow's sentence. Then she laughed at herself. "How silly of me. Of course there are Indians in Canada."

"Yes, Ottowa, Assiniboine, a few Dakota tribes, Blackfeet. That blanket you are wearing was brought to the trading fair by a Blackfoot. It is not a thin blanket that your American traders use, but a Hudson Bay trading blanket."

Brandy ran one hand over her shoulder, feeling the thickness and softness of the blanket. It was a much better quality than the other blankets Flaming Arrow had. "I thought the Blackfeet were your enemies."

"They are."

"But you traded for this blanket with one."

"It does not matter who your enemies are at the trading fairs. It is the only place where all the tribes mingle with no animosity. We are there to trade, nothing else." He paused, then smiled and said, "Perhaps I will take you to one someday. You would not believe the things you can find to be bartered there. The northern tribes bring blankets, walrus tusks, seal skins, furs, Hudson Bay blankets; the eastern tribes bring dried corn, melons, fine tobacco, beads, knives and kettles; the southern tribes, silver jewelry, copper and leather goods, guns and ammunition; the western tribes, shells of every shape and size; the plains tribes, horses and beautifully decorated buckskins and buffalo robes. I cannot begin to list everything."

Brandy could hardly believe that all the tribes, including those that were ancient, bitter enemies, would actually put their hatreds aside to just trade. It seemed completely at odds with their warlike nature. Yes, she would have to see that to believe it.

While she was thinking this, Flaming Arrow was wondering why he had suggested taking Brandy to a trading fair. The men in his tribe usually did not take their women to fairs, since they usually took place in far-distant areas and trading was done by the men. Yet Flaming Arrow had wanted to take her simply to show her the excitement of the fair, the unbelievable array of goods. Since he had learned to share his thoughts with this woman who had captured his heart, he seemed to want to share all his experiences with her.

But it was impossible that they marry. He would never offer marriage to a woman who didn't feel as strongly about him. His pride would never allow that. Besides, he had vowed never to marry. Marriage and his commitment to becoming the best warrior in the tribe weren't compatible. He would likely die an early death if he continued to volunteer for every dangerous raid and foray, and Flaming Arrow had not wanted to leave a wife and children behind for whom his brother would have to assume responsibility, as was the Dakota custom. But what would happen to Brandy if he were to die? Flaming Arrow asked himself. He had refused to take her back to her people, first out of pride and now because he couldn't bear to give her up. But he had really never considered her welfare. In the event of his death, would the men in his tribe consider her up for grabs since she was a captive with no social standing and no rights? The thought of Brandy being used to satisfy some man's lust or to slave for his family was appalling to Flaming Arrow. No! he vowed fiercely. She wouldn't be left defenseless and at the mercy of the others. He would see that arrangements would be made for her in the event of his death.

Flaming Arrow tore his mind from his distressing thoughts and turned his attention back to Brandy, sitting on their pallet with the blanket still wrapped around her and brushing her hair. He sank down beside her and watched as firelight picked up the reddish highlights and the long tresses cracked with electricity. When she put the brush down, parted the hair at the center with her fingers, and started to braid one side, he caught her wrist and said, "No, leave it as it is. It's beautiful hanging around your shoulders."

As Brandy dropped her hand, Flaming Arrow ran both hands over the length of hair that cascaded down her arms. He picked up a strand and marveled at how it twined about his hand as if it had a life and will of its own, then lifted it to his mouth, breathing deeply of its sweet fragrance before he kissed it. The incredibly tender act stunned Brandy. Then he raised his head and gazed deeply into her eyes, and for just a split second, he allowed the depth of his feelings for her to show. At that moment, Brandy knew he loved her, and a monumental wave of happiness rushed over her. Sudden tears welled in her eyes.

Seeing the tears, Flaming Arrow asked, "Now why are you crying?"

"Because I'm so happy," Brandy muttered. Seeing his look of disbelief, she laughed shakily. "Sometimes white women cry when they're happy, too, as well as sad."

"What are you so happy about?"

Brandy couldn't tell him it was because she knew he loved her. She wasn't sure Flaming Arrow had even realized it himself yet. "It doesn't matter." Then seeing him open his mouth, she placed her fingertips against his lips and said, "No, don't ask me any more questions. Just kiss me."

Brandy didn't have to repeat her request. Before the tears had come, Flaming Arrow had been fantasizing what it would be like to make love to her with her long hair loose about them like a silken curtain. He kissed her, long and slow and incredibly sweet, then fierce and demanding. As he drank deeply of the nectar of her mouth, his tongue sliding in and out in a sensuous pattern of giving and taking, Brandy gloried in her new knowledge, feeling as if she were drowning in joy and clutching him to her with fierce possessiveness. When he lay her back on their pallet, pushing the blanket aside to rain kisses over her face, neck, and shoulders, then placing little love bites over her breasts, the realization that he loved her increased her physical awareness. It made her feel as if he were making love to her in bright, swirling colors, every kiss, every nip, every caress such an excruciating pleasure that she wondered if she could bear it.

His teeth ever so gently raked a turgid nipple, then took it into his mouth, his tongue swirling around the throbbing peak before he suckled her, and she gave herself up to sensation. But even then everything took on new dimensions. The fire he lit in her blood flared brighter than ever before, the tingles that ran up her spine more electrifying, the warmth that rushed to her pelvis more scalding.

She reached between their bodies where Flaming Arrow lay half over her, found the string that held his breechclout, and jerked on it. As his manhood sprang free, she took him in her hand, taking immense satisfaction in finding him ready for her, the velvety skin stretched taut over the steel of his erection, the rounded tip bathed with the moisture of his desire. She guided him to her, not relinquishing her hold on him until she felt him enter her.

Blue and black eyes locked, smoldering with passion, Flaming Arrow slowly slid into her, inch by magnificent inch. She was acutely aware of him filling her with his immense, swollen manhood, and he was aware of her soft, tight heat surrounding him. Each saw the other's awareness of their joining in their eyes, increasing the breathtaking sensation twofold. Then Flaming Arrow lowered his head and softly kissed her lips, a kiss so sweet it brought new tears to her eyes. His first movements were slow, masterful, and exquisitely sensuous. Increasing in tempo, his strokes became bolder, more powerful, deeper and deeper as their bodies rocked in an erotic dance as old as time itself. Even when her body was consumed with the fire and every nerve was drawn taut with expectation, she remembered he loved her, and every sensation was magnified, so that when she climaxed, it was the most intense she had ever felt, making her actually lose consciousness.

Later, as Flaming Arrow dozed with his head nuzzled in the soft valley between her breasts, Brandy cradled his dark head with her hands, holding it against her just as fiercely as she held the knowledge that he loved her to her heart. Someday he would tell her, she thought. And she desperately hoped it would be soon. Knowing he loved her was no longer enough. She wanted him to acknowledge it in the open, to himself as well as to her, for she was determined not to tell him of her own love first. He had stolen her freedom, her body, her heart, her soul. Her pride was all she had left.

But much to Brandy's disappointment, Flaming Arrow never said the words during the long winter months that followed. She might have thought the loving look she had seen in his eyes that night nothing but a figment of her imagination, had it not been that she had caught him gazing at her with the same warm look on several other occasions, but only when he thought she wasn't aware. His refusal to speak the words puzzled and frustrated her, for she wanted so badly to tell him of her love that it was a physical ache in her throat.

Spring came at the end of March. The warm Chinook winds swept over the Rockies and made the area look like a brown and white patchwork quilt as the winds melted the snow in some places and left it still sitting in others. For days they could hear the soft "plops" of snow falling from the branches of the trees in the forest across from them, and the sound of the ice breaking in the stream beside them was startling, rather like the sound of gunshots.

Several weeks later, when Swift Rabbit was visiting, Brandy asked the old woman, "Was there something exciting that happened in the village this morning?"

The old woman frowned. "Why do you ask that?"

"Because a young girl came to our tepee and summoned Flaming Arrow. I don't know what she said to him because I was collecting firewood in the forest, but I saw him rush off with her."

"Oh, yes, that must have been Moon Woman. She is Yellow Fox's second wife. She—"

"Second wife?" Brandy asked in surprise, interrupting Swift Rabbit.

"Did you not know that a Dakota can have more than one wife?"

"Yes, I know. Flaming Arrow explained that it is done because so many women are left with no one to protect and provide for them, since so many men are killed in warfare. It was just that Flaming Arrow never mentioned that his brother had more than one wife."

"Well, he does," Swift Rabbit replied matter-of-factly, "and that was probably why Moon Woman summoned Flaming Arrow. To tell him that Morning Star, Yellow Fox's first wife, had gone to the birthing lodge and that his brother was about to become a father."

Brandy had known nothing of the expected event. Even though Flaming Arrow frequently visited his brother, he never spoke of him or his family, much less asked Brandy to accompany him on one of his visits. "Then this is his brother's first child?"

"Yes, and since it is a boy, Flaming Arrow will sing over the infant and paint its stripes on it."

"How do you know it's a boy?"

"It was born shortly before I came to visit you. The village crier announced it. Didn't you hear?"

"Yes, but I didn't know what *hunka*, what child, he was talking about. And why should Flaming Arrow sing over it and paint it?"

"Because he is the boy's uncle and more than likely will be his godfather, and that is one thing a godfather does. Among the Dakotas, the godfather is the most important person in the boy's life, even more important than his father. It is the godfather who will teach the child how to ride, how to hunt, and to whom the child will go when he is in need of counseling. His godfather even helps him seek his vision when he comes of age."

Brandy thought over what the old woman had revealed to her. Would the birth of his nephew mean she would see even less of Flaming Arrow? She fervently hoped not. Already she felt left out, not only by Flaming Arrow never speaking to her in public, much less asking her to accompany him when he went to visit his brother, but ignored by the entire tribe. Only Swift Rabbit had befriended her; she visited sometimes now to chat and pass the time of day instead of teach her, and while Brandy was grateful for the old woman's friendship, she yearned to have female companionship of her own age, to be socially acceptable, to belong to the tribe, to be more of a part of Flaming Arrow's life.

But Brandy knew that she had no hope of being accepted into the tribe. As a captive, she would always be an outsider. Unless . . . Brandy's hopes soared at the thought—but she hesitated, wondering if she dared question Swift Rabbit. Still, she had to know where she stood. She gathered her courage and asked, "Can a Dakota marry his captive?"

Swift Rabbit shot Brandy a penetrating look. "Are you talking about yourself and Flaming Arrow?"

A flush rose on Brandy's face, but it was pointless to lie. "Yes. I have reason to believe he loves me."

The old woman nodded gravely, making her gray braids bob. "Yes, I have seen that he loves you. And yes, a Dakota can marry his captive. However, you must remember that you are not Indian, like other captives. You are white—our enemy. To make you his wife, Flaming Arrow would risk the tribe's disapproval, and I do not think he would do that. Remember what I told you? Someday he will be chief."

"He has never mentioned to me that he hopes to become chief," Brandy threw back, not liking what Swift Rabbit was telling her. It had dashed her hopes to the ground.

"Nor have I. Flaming Arrow is a very private man. He keeps his thoughts, his dreams to himself. But even if he has no aspirations for chieftaincy, he will be offered the position, and soon. When one of the older war chiefs accepts that he is too old to lead men into battle any longer, he will step down in favor of a younger, more able man. Then the council will turn to Flaming Arrow because he is skilled in warfare and much respected by all. He knows how to lead men, even the most headstrong of our warriors, and he has shown sound judgment in the past. When he is offered chief, he will accept because he is a man who takes his responsibilities to the tribe very seriously, and that is another reason the council will choose him. So you see, it does not matter if Flaming Arrow personally desires chieftaincy or not. By giving him all the qualities needed to become a great chief, the Mystery has made it his destiny."

"So there is no hope of his marrying me because I'm white," Brandy muttered bitterly. "Only an Indian bride will do for a chief."

Swift Rabbit knew by the expression on Brandy's face that she was crushed, and her heart went out to the girl. "Flaming Arrow may never marry," Swift Rabbit pointed out. "He never has before. Is it not enough to know he loves you, that you are his woman, his only woman?"

Brandy remembered the time when she was in the badlands and thought she was facing death. At that time she had thought she would be happy only to be Flaming Arrow's lover, and he had made her that. Then she wanted his love—and that, too, she had gained. But knowing Flaming Arrow loved her was no longer enough. Nor would his telling her be, if he ever did. She wanted more. Much more. She couldn't stand the thought of always living on the fringes of his life, an outcast among his people. She didn't want to walk in the shadows of his life as a hidden-away mistress, no matter how much he loved her. She wanted to be his wife, to share in all of his life, his public as well as his private, to have their love out in the open and acknowledged by all. "No, it isn't enough," she answered. "I want more."

"You have much to learn about life," Swift Rabbit answered in a firm but gentle tone of voice. "There is a big difference between what you want and what you get from life. You must learn to accept what the Mystery gives you. Only then will you find happiness. That is a truth every Dakota knows."

After Swift Rabbit left, Brandy sat in the dim light

of the tepee, feeling very lonely and very sad. She remembered what Flaming Arrow had once said about the whites: that they always wanted more. No, she wasn't Dakota, and she would never be. She was white to the bone. She still wanted more. She wanted what she couldn't have.

17

Several days later, a rider came
tearing into the village. His arrival caused quite a stir,
for no sooner had he disappeared into Chief Crazy
Horse's lodge than the chief called an immediate
council. Flaming Arrow's presence was requested at
the meeting. When he returned to their tepee several hours later, he was agitated about something—
his face was as dark as a thundercloud.

"What's wrong?" she asked, then seeing him shoot
her a furious look, said "And don't look daggers at me
like that! I didn't do anything."

"Didn't you? You're white!"

"And what in the devil does that have to do with
anything?"

The fury in Brandy's blazing blue eyes brought
Flaming Arrow to his senses. He realized he was taking his anger out on her simply because she was the

only white available. How often had her people
treated his so unfairly, blaming any and every Indian
for the crimes of others. He sighed deeply. "I am
sorry I was so sharp with you. Your people have declared war on the Dakota nation."

"Declared war?" Brandy asked in surprise. "But
how did that come about? When did it happen?"

"Shortly after our meeting with your commissioners last fall, when we refused to sell the Black Hills."

Brandy remembered her premonition that the
commissioners would seek vengeance for the Dakotas' embarrassing and refusing them, but she
couldn't believe they would be so blatantly open
about it. Fear of criticism from the American public,
or of foreign censure, would surely restrain them.
"You mean, they declared war just like that, right out
of the blue?"

"No, it was more contrived, as is the white's way.
Always, they try to fool themselves in justifying steal-
ing our land," Flaming Arrow answered with a contemptuous sneer.

Brandy would have liked to deny his accusation,
but deep down, she knew it was true. Her government did make excuses to try to justify their attacks
on the Indians, and in general, the American public
accepted what the government told them without
question. As the whole, the nation held the red man
in contempt and thought him little more than an
animal with no rights. Unlike Brandy, they had not
lived with the Indian and realized he was as human
as the next person, with feelings and emotions,
dreams and disappointments, joy and sorrows;
much less had they come to appreciate his unique

strengths. A feeling of shame on behalf of her people again crept over her.

Flaming Arrow had no idea she was feeling shame in her silence. He misinterpreted her failure to ask further questions as approval of what her government was doing. Again his anger rose, and he said in a brittle voice, "You did not ask how your government contrived to make war on my people, but I will tell you anyway. In the moon your people call November, the Commissioner of Indian Affairs issued an ultimatum that all Indians on Dakota land must come to the reservation and report to their agencies at once. It was a flagrant violation of the Fort Laramie Treaty. Your government has no right to restrict our use of any of the land granted us in that treaty, either the reservation land or the unceded territory. That in itself was a blatant enough transgression. But even if we had wanted to comply, we couldn't have possibly done so in dead-winter. It would have been foolhardy to have attempted to move our women and children across the open plains that distance in blind ing blizzards, with no forage for our animals. But then, maybe that was what the white man was hoping—that we would commit suicide for them and save them the trouble of killing us."

Brandy felt sicker at heart, knowing that that accusation, as shocking and terrible as it was, was probably true. How often had she heard her people say the only good Indian was a dead Indian?

"By the end of deadline, only one tribe had complied," Flaming Arrow continued. "Now the matter has been turned over to your army. According to the messenger from Red Cloud, we have been issued yet another ultimatum. Either we surrender and go to the reservation, or we will be annihilated."

Brandy didn't have to ask what choice the Dakotas would make. She knew they would fight to the death for their freedom. She could only hope that it wasn't the beginning of the end for the proud Dakota nation.

The next day, a sudden late blizzard caught the village off guard. The sun had been shining so brightly that everyone had assumed winter was over. Then, even after the blizzard had passed, the cold was intense for days, and it was several weeks before the snow melted again, turning the ground to a morass of mud.

A second messenger arrived, and his racing horse's hooves splattered mud everywhere as he tore through the village. Another hurried council was held, and again Flaming Arrow was summoned to Crazy Horse's lodge. But when he returned to the tepee this time, he was beaming and eager to impart the news to Brandy.

"There has been an important battle," he began. "Several weeks ago, General Crook marched from Fort Fetterman with a big army into the Powder River Country in search of Dakotas. Shortly after the big blizzard, his horse soldiers came across an Indian camp on the Powder River and, without even attempting to find out what tribe it was, attacked it. It was the village of Two Moon, who with some agency Dakotas was on his way back to the reservation. They had taken refuge from the storm beneath the bluff beside the river. Your horse soldiers are fools, and I fear they will rue the day they mistook Two Moon for us and attacked him. He is Cheyenne, not Dakota, and was friendly to your people until then. Now he and his warriors are as fierce enemies of the Americans as the Dakotas. The Cheyenne and Dakota warriors quickly rallied and turned the battle around. They pursued your horse soldiers until the next morning, recovered all their ponies, and sent General Crook's expedition back to the fort to lick its wounds. News of the victory is spreading all over the Indian territory, and the entire Dakota nation is rallying. Agency Dakotas are swarming from the reservation and into the Powder River Country to join Sitting Bull and Crazy Horse. Never have the Dakotas been so united. The next time your army comes, we will be ready for them."

When Flaming Arrow had mentioned Fort Fetterman, Brandy had wondered if her brother had been with the cavalry that had attacked Two Moon and his Cheyennes, and she felt sudden concern for him. Seeing the frown on her face, Flaming Arrow scowled and said in a scathing voice, "I see you do not like hearing that your soldiers have been beaten back. You would prefer that the Indians had been beaten instead?"

Brandy didn't want to go back to being enemies with Flaming Arrow. She didn't want to take either side. "No, I don't want to see either side beaten. I'd give anything if our peoples could be at peace with each other, to be rid of all of this hatred, this misunderstanding between us. I was just thinking of my brother, wondering if he took part in the fight, and if so, if he was wounded or"—Brandy had to force the word out—"killed. He and I were very close."

Flaming Arrow had spent his entire life preparing

for warfare and had always counted the whites as his bitter enemies, but he found himself wishing their people could mend their differences too. If that obstacle between them were removed, maybe Brandy would come to love him. He felt a momentary stab of jealousy for her brother, a man who could command such deep affection from her; then, quick on its heels, he did a complete turn-around, wanting to reassure her of her brother's well-being. "I understand there were very few casualties. In all likelihood, your brother is alive and well."

"And in the next battle? What might happen to him then?"

"Perhaps there will not be a next battle. Maybe when your government hears of the victory, they will relent and leave us in peace, particularly when they realize we are uniting."

For a long moment Brandy held her silence, then said sadly, "I wish that were true, but I know my people too well. They won't relent. Crook's defeat will only make them more determined."

Shortly thereafter, the Dakotas moved their camp back down to the Powder River basin and threw themselves into a frenzy of preparations for the army's next move against them. During this time, Brandy hardly saw Flaming Arrow. He was busy from dawn to dusk drilling the warriors who had been put under his command by Crazy Horse. His drilling bewildered the other war chiefs, who fought by the Indians' traditionally independent methods and scorned practicing cavalry tactics and unit discipline. At night, Flaming Arrow was in council with the tribal leaders, planning their strategy for when the army came. The weeks passed and the army made no new expeditions into Indian territory, and Brandy began to hope that the American government might have relented after all. Her loyalties were clearly divided, and she would give anything if a bloodbath between the two could be avoided.

One night, Flaming Arrow came home earlier than usual. After a brief greeting, he sat on their pallet beside Brandy and gazed into the flames of the fire, a thoughtful expression on his face. He maintained this pensive pose for so long that Brandy finally asked, "What are you thinking about so hard?"

Flaming Arrow tore his gaze away from the fire and looked at her for a long moment. He wondered if he should answer her. Had Brandy been Indian, she wouldn't have even asked—Dakota women knew their place. But Brandy was Brandy, and she could be very persistent. If he were to have any peace, he had to answer. "I am trying to come to a decision. I have been offered a position as war chief."

Brandy had known it was coming, not just because Swift Rabbit had predicted it, but because Crazy Horse had obviously been grooming Flaming Arrow by putting him in charge of his own band of warriors and including him in all the tribal councils. But deep down, she had hoped that he wouldn't be asked. Then, just maybe, he might ask her to become his wife. Trying very hard not to show her disappointment, she said, "Why, that's wonderful. You must be very proud of yourself. Which chief is stepping down?"

"None. There has been such an influx of Dakotas from the reservation to join Crazy Horse that he feels he cannot lead them all and do justice to his position and their trust in him. He wishes me to lead the new men and, of course, any warriors in my present band who wish may join me."

"So you will be a full chief?"

"Yes."

Suddenly Brandy's disappointment was replaced with happiness for Flaming Arrow. He was an extraordinary man, a cut above all others, and he deserved to be chief. She was filled with pride for the man she loved. "You will accept, won't you?"

"I don't know. As I said, I need to think about it."

"But what is there to think about? Isn't it something you've always wanted?"

"I suppose, deep down, it is what every Indian male wants, but I had never *really* considered it. My only ambition was to follow my vision, to be the best warrior in this tribe."

"But it's your destiny," Brandy objected, repeating what Swift Rabbit had said. "Surely you must realize that."

"I realize nothing of the sort. There was nothing in my vision about being chief."

Brandy gazed deeply into Flaming Arrow's eyes and saw no pretense or guile there. He meant it! she thought with amazement. He had really never had any driving ambition to be chief. He was simply following the course laid down for him by the Mystery. His humility touched Brandy deeply. She had not expected this any more than she had expected his acts of tenderness, and yet both enhanced rather than detracted from his strength. A fierce determination to see him chief, to see him in his rightful place, was born within her. "But what else could your vision mean? The natural end to being the best warrior in the tribe would be chieftaincy. That's the only thing it could possibly lead to."

"There was nothing about chieftaincy in my vision," Flaming Arrow repeated.

"From what you've told me, the only thing in your vision was a flaming arrow. Its meaning was interpreted by a medicine man. Maybe he was wrong in his interpretation."

"The medicine man is never wrong."

"Why are you being so stubborn about this?"

"I am not being stubborn. I am being careful to make the right choice. There is a heavy burden of responsibility with becoming a chief. Lives are at stake."

"You have responsibility for lives of your men every time you lead a raid," Brandy pointed out.

"Warriors' lives. As chief, I would be responsible for the lives of women and children, too, and not just during a raid. All the time. With your army coming down on us, bent on the annihilation of our race, that is a tremendous responsibility. I am not sure I am up to it."

His refusal to see his own capabilities, his greatness, frustrated and infuriated Brandy. "All right then!" she cried out in exasperation. "Refuse! See if I care!"

"Why should you care? It is no concern of yours. It is a tribal affair."

Indeed! Why should she care? Brandy thought. If he accepted, she would be doomed to spending the rest of her life on the fringes of his. But what was advantageous for her no longer mattered now. All she cared about was what was right for Flaming Arrow. "I care because I know you are wrong. Deep down in my heart, I know you were meant to be chief. And Crazy Horse and the others must know it too. Otherwise, they wouldn't have asked you. If you won't trust my judgment, trust theirs."

It was a point well taken, for Flaming Arrow had a profound respect for Crazy Horse, his mentor. Again he gazed into the fire, deep in thought. The minutes ticked by while the flickering firelight sent eerie shadows dancing across the tepee walls. Finally, after what seemed an eternity to Brandy, he said, "Perhaps you are right. Perhaps there is more to my vision than I saw." He turned his head and looked Brandy once more in the eye. "We leave tomorrow to meet with the other Dakota tribes for our annual Sun Dance. I will dance and seek the Mystery's guidance in this. Hopefully, my vision will reappear, and if there is more to it, as you think, I will see it."

"I'm glad," Brandy replied, but deep down she wasn't glad, not entirely. Although she wanted Flaming Arrow to accept because it was right for him, there was a part of her that didn't want to let go. Her feelings were ambiguous. She had both won—and lost.

18

The next day, the women in the village packed up, and the band left for the Sun Dance. The long trek to the site of the ceremony reminded Brandy of the full buffalo hunt: the men rode in front of the procession, and the women and children brought up the rear with their heavily loaded travoises. The long poles scraped the still tender shoots of buffalo grass from the ground and left a cloud of dust in the tribe's wake. On the third day, they passed the remains of another Indian campsite—yellowed circles of grass were scattered over the prairie—and then about a mile from the site, she spied a burial platform.

Brandy rode her pony closer for a better look and stared at the scaffold. It looked lonely and forlorn, standing in the wide-open prairie with only the moan of the wind and the faint rustling of the grass to keep it company. Looking closer, she saw the body. It had been wrapped in a red-dyed buffalo skin and securely tied, its feet facing east. On an upright pole above it dangled the deceased's medicine bundle, his tobacco pouch, his shield, his lance, his bow and arrows, his . . . Brandy stared, hardly believing her eyes. When Swift Rabbit rode up and came to a stop beside her, she asked, "Is that what it looks like? A horse's tail?"

"Yes. It is the tail from the warrior's war horse."

"They cut off its tail?" Brandy asked in horror.

"The pony was already dead, if that is what is bothering you. Its throat was cut."

"But why would they kill a perfectly good horse?"

"The warrior's spirit needed his mount to reach the eternal country, just as he needed his weapons and other belongings."

The Dakotas' beliefs were somewhat like the Egyptians, Brandy thought, and their religion went as far back in time, if not farther. "Why don't you bury your dead in the ground?"

"Wild animals would dig up the body and scatter parts of it everywhere before the spirit has had time to reach the afterworld, particularly the scalp. We believe that the hair is an extension of one's soul. A person who has lost their scalp cannot enter Mystery Land. They are doomed to haunt the earth forever. That is why we scalp our enemies—to deny them entrance into the eternal world. That is why our warriors often bring back the scalps of their friends who were killed in battle—to give to their relatives for safekeeping. They in turn bury them, thereby releasing the soul."

Brandy was surprised to learn that scalping was a

spiritual act. She had always thought it done for pure fiendishness. "So you never cut your hair?"

"Only in mourning, just as we might cut a finger from our hand or slice a piece of flesh from our bodies. But usually it is done only by wives mourning husbands, to honor them by showing their deep respect for them. You see, a Dakota values respect over love."

Brandy glanced down at Swift Rabbit's left hand. She had noticed that the little finger was missing and had assumed it had been accidentally severed when Swift Rabbit was butchering something. Now she knew the old woman had purposely amputated it in mourning for her husband. Brandy was horrified at the self-mutilation, but she held her tongue. She had too much respect for Swift Rabbit to let the old woman know how strongly she felt about her beliefs.

The next day, they reached the spot that had been chosen for the annual ceremony. There, in a wide expanse of prairie beside a fast-flowing stream known as Rosebud Creek, they made camp. During the next few days a steady stream of Dakotas and their Cheyenne allies arrived and pitched their tepees in a great circle. They left a large wide-open area in the center where the Sun Dance lodge was to be built. Brandy had never thought of Indians as a gregarious people, not even after having lived with them for almost a year, but she found that she was mistaken. It soon became apparent that this was above all a social gathering, one very much anticipated, as the members of the various tribes mingled and feasted one another. It was like one huge family reunion, with everyone laughing and filling the other in on what had happened to them during the past year, and there appeared to be no strangers. There was such a feeling of festivity and camaraderie that, for once, Brandy didn't feel left out.

On the first day of the ceremony, the entire encampment was in a frenzy of activity, and the excitement level was so high that the air fairly crackled with electricity. The painted warriors who were to take part in the ceremony mounted their painted, befeathered, and beribboned ponies, and everyone, dressed in their very finest, followed them from the camp to the stream, where a special cottonwood had been marked and the underbrush beneath it cleared away.

Swift Rabbit accompanied Brandy and explained that the cottonwood was believed sacred by the Dakotas because when cut, the grain revealed a five-point star. This particular tree had been chosen because it was the tallest and its trunk the straightest— therefore it would make the best center pole of the lodge. When everyone was gathered around the tree, the warriors pretended to attack it. Twice they swooped down on it, yelling their bloodcurdling war cries, lashing at it with their axes and hatchets, and shooting it with their arrows. But not until the sun was directly overhead did they actually fell it. As the big tree toppled over with a swoosh and hit the ground with a resounding thud, the crowd let go with a victorious cry that was so loud, Brandy could have sworn it was heard back in St. Louis. Then as each branch was cut from the trunk, red paint was dabbed on it to resemble a wound.

The warriors mounted their horses once again, and the pole was dragged back to the center of the camp.

The crowd again followed, this time singing. When they reached the open area where the lodge was to be built, effigies of a buffalo and a human were tied to the top of the pole, as well as a bundle containing other religious offerings known as the Thunder Bird Nest. Then the pole was raised with another tremendous cheer. By this time, the sun was going down, and everyone sat around the moonlit pole and feasted, except those who were going to take part in dance. Separated from the others in a special lodge, they were fasting and going without water in preparation for the major ceremony.

On the second day, the altar at the base of the Sun Dance pole was built and surrounded by painted buffalo skulls. The eye sockets and mouths had been filled with balls of sage; a bag of tobacco had been tied to the tip of each south horn and a piece of deer hide to each left horn. While the altar was being prepared, a circular framework of posts was built around the sacred center pole and covered with green tree branches to form a roof.

At dawn on the third day, the day the main ceremony was to begin—the actual dancing—Brandy stood with Swift Rabbit and the rest of the onlookers on the fringes of the Sun Dance lodge and watched the warriors who were scheduled to dance walk from the lodge where they had been purified and painted. Brandy stood on her tiptoes and craned her neck, trying to see over the heads of the crowd, hoping to get a glimpse of Flaming Arrow. She had seen nothing of him since they had left their old camp, and she would have been bewildered or hurt by his conspicuous absence had Swift Rabbit not explained that celibacy was required for the participants of the Sun

Dance as well as the fall hunt. But much to Brandy's disappointment, all the warriors weaving their way through the crush of the crowd looked alike. They all wore a simple, undecorated breechclout and moccasins and were painted exactly the same from head to toe. The only difference was the feathers that dangled from their scalp locks, and Brandy had not yet learned the fine art of reading feathers to differentiate one honor from the other. Then Brandy did notice a difference. One man stood taller and straighter than the others, and when she saw his walk, she knew it was Flaming Arrow. No other man's stride was as graceful, as sure, as confident as his. She stared hungrily at him.

While the men took their places around the altar and center pole, Swift Rabbit explained the meaning of the paint they wore: the solid red paint from the waist up represented all that was sacred; the black circle around their faces, the spirit who has no end; the four black vertical lines on the chin represented the four directions; the black bands around their wrists, ankles, and upper arms were symbolic of the bands of ignorance that tied the dancers to earth. Each man wore a wreath of sacred sage on his head and had sage tied to his wrists, and every man carried a special eagle whistle with a white plume at its end. A root dangled from their necks to relieve their thirst, and another at their ankle to ward off weariness.

Brandy had to turn her head when two slits were cut in Flaming Arrow's chest just above his nipples and wooden skewers were forced beneath his skin. It wasn't that it was such a bloody procedure, for surprisingly, the wound bled very little, but just knowing that it must be terribly painful made her stomach churn. When they made two slits on his back as well and tied buffalo skulls to them, Brandy asked Swift Rabbit sharply, "Why are they doing that to Flaming Arrow? None of the others are having it done on both their chests and their backs."

"It is being done to him because that is how he wishes to dance. He wants to double his offering to the Mystery. Only the strongest warriors will attempt it. The skewers are placed beneath some of the back muscle, as well as the skin, and it takes them longer to tear."

Again Brandy was horrified at the Indians' self-abuse. She might have turned and left except that those behind her had crowded in so close, it would have been next to impossible for her to squeeze her way out. She was forced to watch as the long pieces of rawhide that were tied to the top of the center pole were attached to the skewers on Flaming Arrow's chest. Then he began to dance, bending, then rising on his toes and pulling on the thongs, blowing on his whistle and gazing at the medicine bundle at the top of the pole.

An hour passed, then two, then three. The crowd of onlookers sat cross-legged and watched solemnly in perfect silence. The only sounds were those of the whistles being blown and the thump of the dancers' heels on the packed earth. The summer sun climbed higher and higher in the sky, and the heat in the lodge rose. A fine sheen of perspiration covered the dancers.

"How long does this continue?" Brandy asked Swift Rabbit.

"Until either the skin or muscle tears, or the next sunrise."

"Sunrise?" Brandy asked in shock. "Why, that would mean they would dance twenty-four hours nonstop. That's impossible, particularly since they've been fasting and without water for days. They're already in a weakened condition. They'll collapse!"

"Yes, a few will before it is over. This is an endurance test as well as a religious feat."

Brandy saw that every eye was on the dancers. She misinterpreted their solemn concentration as avid interest and could no longer contain her disapproval of what she thought was a grisly, disgusting ritual. "And I suppose that's what everyone is waiting for?" she asked harshly. "To see who collapses first? Like a bunch of vultures? My God, I can't believe this! It's like something out of the Dark Ages, sitting around and watching men suffer, waiting for them to drop from exhaustion. I'm not going to watch any longer. I'm leaving!"

Swift Rabbit caught Brandy's arm as she tried to rise and said, "No! You do not understand. They take no pleasure in seeing these men suffer. That is not why they are here. They are friends and families of the dancers. They watch because it is the only way they can give their support. And if you care anything for Flaming Arrow, you will do the same."

When Brandy made no comment, Swift Rabbit said, "He knows you are here. He knows you watch. Will you let him down? Will you let the others call you a weak, cowardly white woman?"

At that point Brandy couldn't have cared less what the others thought of her, but she couldn't let Flaming Arrow down. That was a part of loving someone

—being there when they needed you. It didn't matter if there was nothing she could do to ease his pain or his thirst, or even that she violently disapproved of the ceremony. All that mattered was being there for the man she loved with her heart and soul.

The rest of the day and the night was an agony for Brandy. She felt each painful tug of the thongs as if it were she and not Flaming Arrow jerking to free himself, the throbbing ache of his leg muscles as if it were she dancing on the hard, packed earth and not him. A cold sheen of perspiration broke out on her forehead, her head pounded, and her tongue cleaved to the top of her mouth from thirst. An incredible weariness invaded her, but she forced herself to remain upright, her eyes locked on Flaming Arrow as she tried desperately to infuse him with what remained of her strength. She became so involved with his ordeal that she became a part of it. Tears streamed down her face, and she furiously wiped them away until there were no more tears left. She wasn't aware when some dancers either collapsed in exhaustion or finally broke their bonds and left the lodge in the company of their loved ones. Nor was she aware when Flaming Arrow finally tore the skewers in his chest loose. As he danced to free himself of the buffalo skulls hanging from his back, arching his body backward and shaking his back, she sat trancelike, tied to him by some strange spiritual bond that surpassed any physical joining they had ever had.

Suddenly one of the buffalo skulls hanging from Flaming Arrow's back fell to the ground and broke in half. A moment later, the second fell. For a split second, the only sound was that of the popping logs in the fires the Indians had built before the altar; the absence of the shrill sound of the eagle whistle was so conspicuous that the sudden quiet seemed eerie. It was the near silence that brought Brandy from her trancelike state. She glanced about her, feeling confused and dazed, and saw that Flaming Arrow was the last dancer to complete his ordeal. The hour was very late, but the lodge was still crowded with onlookers who had sensed the unusual drama taking place between Brandy and Flaming Arrow and had stayed to the end. Many of the women held children sleeping with their heads in their laps or on cradle boards across their knees. The chiefs of all of the various tribes had stayed, sitting cross-legged to one side of the lodge, the long tails of their war bonnets curled around their shoulders and lying in their laps like shawls. Only the immediate families of the other participants had left.

Then Brandy saw Flaming Arrow standing before the altar. He was so exhausted that he was swaying, and sweat dripped from his body to the ground. His eyes were glazed over, and Brandy feared he would pass out at any moment. She started to rise to go to him, but Swift Rabbit pulled her back down. "No, not yet. Not until they have cut the strips of thorn skin from his chest and back and put them on the altar as his offering."

Brandy waited while the medicine men performed this gruesome task. Then Flaming Arrow turned and walked weakly away from the altar, and the crowd rose, parted to clear a path for him, and stood in respectful silence, their dark eyes glowing with admiration. Brandy scurried to her feet and would have pushed her way through the crowd to support him had Swift Rabbit not again stopped her by saying, "You may go to him, but you must not try to help him. If at all possible, he must make it to his tepee of his own accord. He has performed a remarkable feat here today. Do not ruin it for him."

Brandy obeyed. With Swift Rabbit, she followed Flaming Arrow as he weaved his way through the maze of tepees to his home with only the light of the full moon to illuminate his way. He staggered like a drunk man, and several times stumbled, but he always managed to regain his feet. If he knew the women were following him, he gave no sign. Brandy was so busy watching him that she startled when a man stepped up to her.

"I'm sorry," Yellow Fox said. "I did not mean to frighten you. I thought you knew I was behind you."

"No—no, I didn't," Brandy answered, her heart racing from the fright he had given her.

"I came to offer my assistance in case you needed help in getting my brother back to his tepee," Yellow Fox explained. "But I do not think I will be needed. Once again, Flaming Arrow has shown his amazing endurance and made his family proud of him. I am very fortunate to have such an illustrious godfather for my son to emulate." Yellow Fox glanced over to the side and saw Flaming Arrow pushing the hide covering over the door to his tepee aside "I will leave now so you can tend him. Tell him I will visit in a few days, when he has regained his strength."

As Yellow Fox walked away, Swift Rabbit said, "I will leave now too." She untied two leather pouches hanging from her belt and handed them to Brandy. "Use the leaves in the beaded bag to make a poultice for Flaming Arrow's wounds, and simmer the root in the other with meat to make a broth. It will help him regain his strength quickly. If you need me for anything further, you know where my tepee is."

"Thank you," Brandy answered. "Thank you for the healing herbs, thank you for staying with me today, and"—sudden tears swam in Brandy's eyes—"and thank you for being my friend."

But before Swift Rabbit could respond, Brandy turned and hurried off. The old woman stood and watched the white girl disappear into Flaming Arrow's tepee, feeling the sting of tears in her own eyes. She, too, had been proud of Flaming Arrow. Once again, he had proven what an exceptional man he was. But she had also felt proud of the way Brandy had handled herself. In all the *ne-wä-gwa-wa-che-pes* she had watched over the years, Swift Rabbit had never seen anyone throw themselves so totally into giving support to their loved one, not even the most devoted wives. That she knew the white-eyes scorned their ceremony only made Brandy's gift of herself so much more astonishing.

Swift Rabbit turned and saw the pearly glow on the eastern horizon that preceded the sunrise. She stopped to say her prayers to the one above, to the sun, to the Four Old Men—the four directions. Then she glanced over her shoulder and saw the full moon. The glowing globe seemed to hang over Flaming Arrow's tepee. It was an unusual sight: the sun rising in the east, and the moon simultaneously setting in the west. It reminded her of her people's belief that the sun was a man who came from his lodge in the east each morning and made his daily trek across the sky, until he entered his tepee again and darkness fell, and that the moon was his wife and waited for him. Yes, she thought, Flaming Arrow was the sun, powerful, shining in glory, his destiny of reaching greatness as sure as that of the sun crossing the heavens. What a shame that the white girl who waited for him couldn't be his moon.

Her heart heavy with sadness, Swift Rabbit turned and walked to her tepee.

19

When Brandy entered the tepee, she found Flaming Arrow lying on his stomach on their pallet. Because his eyes were closed and his arms and legs were flung out as if he had just collapsed, she assumed he had passed out. Quickly she lit a fire and put a pot of water over it. While the water was heating, she took the leaves from the beaded pouch Swift Rabbit had given her, placed them in a small wooden bowl, and poured a small amount of warm water from the pot over them. While the leaves were soaking and softening, she knelt beside Flaming Arrow and dipped a rag into the pot of warm water. She bathed the dried blood, sweat, and dust from his back.

The leaves had turned to a pastelike concoction. Scooping them up with two fingers, she prepared to apply it to one of the wounds. Looking down at it, sudden tears came to her eyes, for although the area of torn skin was not particularly wide or long, the wound was deep, and she knew it must have been terribly painful. Tears welled in her eyes, then spilled over, and one fell on Flaming Arrow's back.

"Why are you crying?"

Brandy jumped at the sound of Flaming Arrow's voice. She glanced up and saw him looking over his shoulder at her. "I thought you were—" Brandy hesitated. She didn't want to say unconscious for fear he would think she thought him weak. "I thought you were asleep."

"No, I was just resting. But that does not answer my question. Why are you crying?" Flaming Arrow held his breath, hoping she would say that she was crying because she loved him and couldn't stand to see him in pain.

But Brandy had promised herself that she would not divulge her feelings before Flaming Arrow admitted to his love. "I'm crying because I'm angry," she lied.

"Angry?" Flaming Arrow asked in surprise.

Suddenly Brandy *was* angry—angry that he had unnecessarily subjected himself to so much pain and agony. "Yes! Angry! White women cry when they are angry as well as sad or happy."

"But why should you be angry?"

"Because what you did was so stupid! Abusing your body that way. Inflicting pain on yourself. It's disgusting! It's sickening! And for what? Nothing! I would have thought you had more intelligence."

Flaming Arrow's entire body stiffened. His dark eyes glittered. "It was *not* for nothing! I sought my vision. I asked the Mystery to reveal my destiny, to guide me onto the right path. For this, I sacrificed a small portion of myself. I thought you knew why I was dancing and understood."

"You expect me to understand a flesh-and-blood sacrifice? No! I neither understand your rationale, or approve. The entire ritual is barbaric!"

"Christians do not believe in sacrifice?" Flaming Arrow asked in a voice as heavy with contempt as Brandy's had been. "You give nothing in return to the Mystery who gives you your life, this world to live in, the food you eat, the water you drink, everything?"

Like a bolt out of the blue, Brandy remembered Christ's crucifixion. Not only had the son of God allowed himself to be bound to a cross made from a tree, to suffer for an explicit purpose, but He had given more than just a few strips of his skin. He had given the supreme sacrifice, his life. It was a startling realization: that Flaming Arrow's beliefs were so close to her own. Why, she had thought of him as a heathen, but in all probability he was closer to God than she. He didn't just worship on Sundays, as her family did. His beliefs were an integral part of his everyday life, and like his unexpected acts of tenderness and humility, his sincerity enhanced his strength in her eyes.

"You did not answer my question," Flaming Arrow pointed out when Brandy remained silent.

"My faith does practice sacrifice, but usually not as profoundly as yours. We believe in giving to the poor."

"That is also a part of the *ne-wä-gwa-wa-che-pe*. When the individual dancers have finished, there will be a time set aside for those who wish to make public gifts to the poor and for parents to offer out-grown clothing of their children to others."

Yes, Brandy conceded, now that she thought about it, she had never seen anyone go without food or clothing while she had lived with the Indians. And there was no such thing as an orphan. The Dakotas loved each child in the tribe as if it were their own, protected it, provided for it if need be. To be perfectly honest, they cared for their own people much better than her people did. Then she asked, "Did you have your vision?"

Her question surprised Flaming Arrow. He had felt her presence so strongly while he was dancing that he almost thought she would have seen the vision too. But now that he knew she hadn't, he was glad. He had been given what he had prayed for—something that might reveal the destiny the Mystery had chosen for him and help him to come to a decision. While he had danced, he had strongly felt that the Mystery wanted him to be chief. It was something he had sensed rather than envisioned. Then at the very end of the dance, right before he shook loose the last buffalo skull tied to his back, he'd had a vision that disturbed him deeply. Now, he had to make a second decision, one that was much more personal, one that would affect Brandy's future, and for that reason he needed time to think it over without her interference.

"Did you hear what I asked?" Brandy questioned. "Did you have a vision?"

"Yes," Flaming Arrow answered, laying his head back down, "but I am too weary to speak of it."

"But—"

"No! I am too tired. We will discuss it later. Now I only want to sleep."

Flaming Arrow slept until evening. Over the next two days, whenever Brandy approached the subject of his vision, he adroitly turned the conversation to something else. With the medicinal herbs Swift Rabbit had given Brandy, both his wounds had healed, and he had regained his strength amazingly swiftly. Then on the third evening, he announced that he was going for a walk.

When he returned, Brandy was occupied with sewing some beads on a new buckskin shirt she was making for him and did not hear him come in. While her head was bent and she couldn't see his face, he looked at her lovingly, slowly taking in each feature as if he were committing it to memory. Then he sat down beside her and announced with a calmness that belied his inner turmoil, "I am going to take you back to your people."

Brandy's head came up like a shot. She couldn't have been more shocked if he had thrown a bomb in her lap. She stared at him for a moment, totally dumbfounded, then asked, "But why?"

"I have my reasons."

"What reasons?"

"They are not important to you."

He planned to take her back to her people, sever her from his life forever? A terrible fear seized her, followed by anger. "The devil your reasons aren't important to me! I want to know why. No!" she amended with a fierce expression on her face. "I *demand* to know why!"

"You are in no position to make demands," Flaming Arrow replied, his lips tight set.

"Because I'm a captive, or because I'm a woman?" Brandy asked hotly. But before he could respond, she continued. "You can forget it! Either way, I'm not going to sit meekly back and have you decide my future for me without even consulting me. Now, why are you taking me back?"

No, she wouldn't accept anything meekly, Flaming Arrow thought in growing exasperation. Not Brandy. Not his feisty white-eyes. She was the most obstinate, argumentative woman he'd ever had the misfortune to meet, and she was determined not to make this difficult task any easier for him. He might as well be honest with her—up to a point. "Now that your country has declared open war on us, it is too dangerous for you here."

"What will the others in the tribe think? Won't they laugh at you for taking your captive back?"

"It does not matter what they think. My concern is for your safety."

He was putting her safety above the opinion of the tribe, something that he valued highly, Brandy thought. No, she hadn't mistaken his look that day. He loved her. But, damnit, why wouldn't he say it? "Since when doesn't their opinion matter?"

Brandy waited, desperately hoping Flaming Arrow would admit he loved her, but he grimly held his silence. "All right, then!" she cried out in angry frustration. "So it no longer matters what they think. But I'm not going back—and you can't make me!"

Flaming Arrow was so surprised that he drew back as if she had slapped his face. "First you beg me to take you back to your people. Now you refuse to go. I think you only like to argue with me, to fight."

"You can think any damn thing you like!" Brandy answered hotly, tossing her sewing aside and coming to her feet. "But I'm not going back!"

Flaming Arrow slammed to his feet and glared at her. "Why not?"

"I have my reasons."

"What reasons?"

"There're not important to you," Brandy answered, throwing his own words back at him.

Flaming Arrow moved with the swiftness of a striking snake. He caught Brandy's arms and jerked her full force against his body, bringing her to her tiptoes. "You will answer me. I asked why."

The words were said softly, but there was steel beneath them, and the look on his face was one of fierce determination. Suddenly, the burden of trying to hide her deep feelings from him became too much for Brandy. Tears sprang to her eyes, and she sobbed, "Damn you! Because I love you!"

Flaming Arrow felt as if he had been struck by a thunderbolt. He stared at her in utter disbelief, then asked, "What did you say?"

Brandy was a little shocked herself. She hadn't meant to blurt it out like that. "No, I won't say it again. Not until you tell me."

The moment of silence that followed seemed like an eternity to Brandy. Then, with a perfectly emotionless expression on his handsome face, he asked, "Tell you what? That I love you?" The smile that spread across Flaming Arrow's lips and the warm look that came to his eyes made Brandy feel as if her bones were melting. His voice dropped to a husky timbre. "Yes, I love you."

Fiercely, he embraced her, and Brandy hugged him back just as tightly as both savored their happiness. For a long moment, they stood that way, content to just bask in the warm, wonderful feeling of knowing their love was returned, for neither had ever dreamed that such sublime joy was possible. Then they pulled back and looked deeply into each other's eyes, as if to read the love there and to confirm what they had finally admitted with their lips.

It was Brandy who spoke first, her happiness and the tremendous relief she felt finally spilling over. She dropped her head on his chest and sobbed, "Oh, God! I thought you would never say it, that you would never tell me you loved me."

Flaming Arrow nuzzled the top of her head and placed a quick kiss there. "I didn't because I didn't know how you felt." Then, as reality took hold, he felt a deep regret and sighed. "But it doesn't change anything. I'm still taking you back."

Brandy's heart skipped a beat, and she jerked her head up so suddenly that it gave Flaming Arrow a good clip on his chin. "But why?"

"As I said, it would be too dangerous here for you, with no one to protect you."

"But I'd have you to protect me," Brandy objected.

"For how long? A few weeks? A few months?"

An icy shiver ran over Brandy. "Why are you talking so strangely?" Seeing the closed expression coming over his face, she said fiercely, "No! You won't lock me out. Not this time! Tell me why you said that."

When Flaming Arrow stubbornly held his silence, she said, "We love each other. There should be no secrets between us."

It wasn't the matter of sharing confidences with a woman that held Flaming Arrow back—Brandy had broken down that barrier long ago. No, what held him back was the urge to protect her from something unpleasant. But she had proved over and over that she was strong. He nodded his head gravely and said, "Sit down. I will tell you of my vision."

The ominous tone to Flaming Arrow's voice made another shiver run up Brandy's spine. When they were both seated on the pallet, he said, "The vision came as it did in the past, a flaming arrow emerging from a dark cloud laced with lightning and streaking across the sky. But this time I saw something more. Suddenly, the arrow snapped, and the flaming end fell to the ground."

Brandy waited for something more. "That's all?"

"Yes." When she continued to stare at him, Flaming Arrow said, "Don't you see? The arrow snapping in two and the flaming end falling to the ground can only mean one thing. My death."

Brandy didn't see this new part of Flaming Arrow's vision as necessarily ominous. "But everyone has got to die sometime," she reasoned.

"Yes, and I always thought I would meet an early death because I sought the warrior's life so avidly. That is why I never planned to marry. I didn't want to leave a wife and children for my brother to have to care for. But now, with war looming over us, I feel my death is even more imminent. That is why I must take you back to your people. I do not want to leave you unprotected."

"But you don't know that the arrow snapping meant death," Brandy objected. "That's only the way you're interpreting it. It might mean something entirely different."

"Like what?"

"I don't know! But I do know one thing. It changes nothing for me. I'm still not going back."

"You do not realize just how dangerous things are at the present time. A few days before we made camp here, word arrived that another army has left Fort Fetterman, one even bigger than the first. That is why so many of the warriors danced in this *ne-wä-gwa-wa-che-pe*—to appeal to the Mystery for power in the upcoming battles. Your army is marching down on us right now, bent on destroying us. In a few weeks, I could be dead."

The thought of Flaming Arrow dying was so painful, so horrible, that Brandy refused to even consider it. "No, I refuse to believe that's what your vision means. Sitting Bull saw a great victory in his vision today. He saw soldiers falling in his camp."

"Where did you hear that?" Flaming Arrow asked in surprise.

"Your brother dropped by while you were gone to tell you the exciting news. I thought maybe you had run into him."

"No, I walked down by the stream. I hadn't heard."

Flaming Arrow turned thoughtful. Sitting Bull's vision of victory seemed to be at odds with his, and Sitting Bull was a great chief. Surely the Mystery spoke more profoundly to him than to a mere warrior. Perhaps he *was* misinterpreting his vision. But even if he wasn't, even if he did get killed, it still wasn't too late for Brandy to return to her people.

His brother, who had an uncanny way of staying out of the thick of fights and undoubtedly would live to be a ripe old age, could see to that. Yellow Fox would have only to take her within a few miles of her army and point her in the right direction. Flaming Arrow didn't want to part with Brandy, particularly now that he knew how she felt about him. For the first time in his life, he felt selfish. He wanted every bit of happiness he could find with Brandy before he went to the Mystery Land, whether it be weeks or years.

Brandy had no idea what thoughts were going through Flaming Arrow's mind, and she was determined she would not go back. She broke into his thoughts and said with a fierce gleam in her eyes, "I'm not going back, no matter what you say!" As Flaming Arrow turned his head and she gazed into his dark eyes, all of the love she felt for him came rushing to the surface. She framed his face in her hands and said in a voice full of anguish, "Please, don't ask me to leave. Ask anything, but not that. I couldn't bear living without you. Life would be meaningless for me."

Flaming Arrow cupped one of Brandy's hands in his own and brought it to his lips, kissing the palm while his eyes still held hers. "Life would be meaningless for me too. You can stay."

He bent his head and kissed her, softly, tenderly, eloquently telling her of his love, and Brandy felt so incredibly happy, she thought she had died and gone to heaven. Then he drew back and pulled his knife from the scabbard that was tied to his waist. As he held the point of it against her thumb, she jerked back her hand and asked, "What are you doing?"

"We have openly professed our love for one another. Now I will make you my wife. I will make a small cut on your thumb, then mine. Then we will join them, so our blood can mingle and we can become one."

Brandy had known Flaming Arrow loved her, but she had never expected him to marry her. She stared at him in disbelief, then as he picked up her hand again, she jerked it back the second time. "No! I won't let you do it."

"It will just be a small nick. It won't hurt that much."

"That's not what I mean. I'm not afraid of the pain. But I won't let you throw away your chance to become chief because of me. I know how the tribe feels about white-eyes. They will never approve of me. You don't have to marry me. I'll be happy just to be with you."

Flaming Arrow had not even considered that his marriage to Brandy might jeopardize his becoming chief. But he found he didn't care. More than anything in this world, he wanted her to be his wife, to place her at an esteemed position at his side. "Always I have served my tribe. I will continue to do so in whatever way they ask of me, whether it be as chief or as a simple warrior. But I will not let them influence my decision concerning this. For once in my life, I seek my own happiness, and I feel I have earned this right. I want to marry you very, very much."

Brandy was filled with wonder that Flaming Arrow loved her so much. Knowing the depths of his love only made hers swell to new, even greater, dimensions. She offered him her hand, and with it gave her heart, her soul, her very life.

True to his words, Brandy hardly felt the small cut Flaming Arrow made in the fleshy part of her thumb. Then he did the same to his thumb and pressed it tightly against hers, his long, slender fingers interlacing with hers and curling around her hand as he did so. As their blood mingled, she looked down at their hands and thought the Dakota custom of joining a man and a woman beautiful in its simplicity. They didn't need pomp and pageantry, or even a minister. The only other being they needed was there with them. She could feel the Mystery's presence, blessing their union.

Flaming Arrow looked deeply into Brandy's eyes and said softly, *"Tecihila, micante."*

I love you, my heart, Brandy thought, mentally repeating Flaming Arrow's fervent vow. She was so filled with happiness that she thought she would burst.

Flaming Arrow withdrew his hand, then wrapped a small strip of trading cloth around both her thumb and his to stanch the bleeding. As he stood and brought her to her feet with him, she asked, "Where are we going?"

"To the stream, to fulfill the rest of our marriage ceremony."

Seeing Flaming Arrow pick up the pieces of flannel that they used for their towels, she asked, "We're going to bathe? Now? In the middle of the night?"

"It is more than just bathing," Flaming Arrow answered as he picked up a blanket and tossed it over his shoulder. Brandy opened her mouth to ask yet another question, but he placed his fingertips over her lips and said, "No more questions. I will explain everything when we reach the river."

As they stepped from the tepee, the camp was illuminated with the soft light coming from an enormous full moon. Most of the tepees were dark, and she assumed that the majority of the tribe were at the lodge where the *ne-wä-gwa-wa-che-pe* ceremonies were still taking place. Taking her hand in his, Flaming Arrow led her away from the encampment and through the woods, the ground there dabbled with patches of moonlight that filtered through the canopy of leaves above them. The soft murmuring of the stream guided them to it. When they stepped from the woods to the wide sandy bank and Brandy saw it, her breath caught. The evening breeze made the water ripple, and the small, undulating movements reflected the moonlight and made the river look as if thousands of glittering stars were floating in it, twinkling here, then there, then here again.

For a moment Brandy stood in the hushed silence and took in the breathtaking view. Somewhere in the woods behind her, honeysuckle was blooming, and its sweet fragrance drifted in the night air. Flaming Arrow dropped her hand, walked a few steps away, and spread the blanket on the ground behind her. As he walked back up to her, Brandy heard his soft footsteps and closed her eyes. She saw him in her mind as he approached her with his graceful, feline stride. A warm curl formed deep inside her.

Flaming Arrow stood behind her and gazed at the river. "It's beautiful, isn't it? A fitting scene for our wedding night."

But the beauty of the night was lost on Brandy. Her full attention was on the man standing behind her. His deep voice was a sensual caress to her ears, and she could feel his body heat surrounding her like a warm cocoon. She could smell his unique scent, a scent so masculine and exciting, it always sent her senses reeling.

Flaming Arrow's warm fingers brushed her throat as he pushed aside her braids. Then he bent and softly kissed the nape of her neck. Brandy's desire, which always seethed just below the surface for Flaming Arrow, rose hot and urgent, and she trembled with need. As his lips slipped to the side of her throat, she arched her neck to him, hungry for the feel of his mouth there. When he slipped his arms around her, one hand cupping, then stroking her breast through her buckskin dress, her bones melted and her heart quickened.

She turned in the circle of his arms and looked up to see his eyes were smoldering with a look that promised heaven and more and that made her heart race even faster. Sliding her arms around his strong neck, she lifted her head, her lips aching for the feel of his. Flaming Arrow's warm mouth covered hers, his tongue playing teasingly at the corners before he slipped inside to gently ravish the heady sweetness there. Sensation erupted in Brandy. A moan of raw desire rose from deep inside her as she pressed her body even closer to the flame that was threatening to consume her. She wanted this kiss to last forever.

While he was kissing her, Flaming Arrow deftly untied the lacings at the neckline of Brandy's dress and slipped it down her arms to drop in a soft heap at her feet. Then he stood back, his eyes hungrily sweeping over her body, her pale, satiny skin reflecting the bright moonlight and making it look as if it were glowing with a light of its own. Even her hair had taken on the color of the moon, shining like highly polished silver. She was beautiful, he thought in awe. Every curve and hollow was a perfection, a silver goddess of love. *His* goddess of love.

Brandy felt Flaming Arrow's warm, ardent gaze to the bone. Then, wanting to see all of him, she stepped forward and untied the string that held his leggins, skimming them down his long, corded legs. The feel of her fingers brushing against his thighs made Flaming Arrow's breath catch. As she removed his moccasins, he stepped from one, then the other, untying the rawhide string that held his breechclout in place as he did so. As Brandy sat back on her heels and caught sight of him standing before her totally naked, her heart seemed to skip a beat, and then it hammered wildly against her chest. Tall, proud, fierce, with his powerful, muscle-ridged body bathed in moonlight, he looked wonderfully savage and utterly magnificent.

Her eyes swept hungrily over him, and Brandy saw he was at full arousal. The sight of his splendid erection excited her incredibly, and she reached for him. Flaming Arrow brushed her hand away, caught her arms, and pulled her to her feet. As she reached for him the second time, he said in an urgent, ragged voice, "No, don't touch me! Not yet. A Dakota bathes his woman before he makes love to her the first time."

"This isn't our first time." Brandy wanted desperately to forgo the bath and get on with the lovemaking. She was primed and ready, her need to feel his rigid strength inside her so intense, she could almost taste it. She stepped closer and slipped her arms around his shoulders.

Flaming Arrow sucked in his breath at the feel of

her breasts pressing against the heated skin of his chest. He clenched his teeth, fighting for control, then pried her arms loose, saying in a firm voice, "But it will be our first time. The first time I make love to my wife."

His wife, Brandy thought, a thrill racing through her and reminding her of her new position in Flaming Arrow's life, the one she had so coveted. Yes, this night was special, she admitted. Surely she could put her passion aside for a while. They'd have the rest of their lives to make love, but only one wedding night. This was the time for promises and commitments. The other could wait.

Brandy put up no resistance when Flaming Arrow led her into the river until the water hit her at midthigh. Dipping his hand in the liquid, he lathered her body with a sliver of soap he had brought with him. As he washed her, the expression on his face deadly earnest, Brandy realized that his bathing her was symbolic. He wasn't just cleansing her in preparation to making love to her, he was ministering to her. It was his first act as her husband of caring for her, of providing for her, and by virtue of it being so very personal, he showed that there was no task too menial, no action too intimate, for him to undertake on her behalf. Brandy was deeply touched, and the fact that he was an Indian, one of a breed of men who did not believe in pampering their women, made it even more so.

But as Flaming Arrow continued to wash her, the Dakota ritual became an agony for Brandy. She knew it had spiritual meaning, but his previous lovemaking had sensitized her to his touch, and her body responded to the feel of his hands circling her breasts, smoothing across her belly and hips, then down her legs with a will of its own. By the time Flaming Arrow was pouring water over her shoulders to wash away the soapsuds, she was burning with need, and her legs felt so weak, she feared she would collapse.

Flaming Arrow swept her up in his arms and carried her to the river bank, and Brandy muttered, "What about you? Don't I bathe you too?"

"No, only the husband does the bathing."

Brandy was vastly relieved. She seriously doubted if she'd have the strength to reciprocate.

Flaming Arrow lowered himself and Brandy to the spread blanket. For a moment he hovered over her, drinking in her naked beauty with his hot eyes. Then, spying a drop of water on the tip of one nipple, sparkling in the moonlight like a diamond, he bent his head and licked it away. Brandy gasped, feeling as if a bolt of fire had shot to her loins. Then he raised his head, and just before his mouth closed over hers in a long, demanding kiss, Brandy saw the fire burning in his dark eyes. As his tongue softly plundered the nectar in her mouth, Brandy answered his kiss ardently, kissing him back, her tongue an instrument of exquisite torture that drove him wild and made every muscle in his body tremble with intense anticipation.

Pulling his mouth from hers, Flaming Arrow broke the fiery kiss, then dropped soft kisses over her face and eyes, down her silky throat to her breasts. There he dallied, licking the moisture that clung to the soft mounds away, then followed a trickle of water down her rib cage, across her flat abdomen, to the indentation of her navel. The feel of his tongue lapping at the small pool of water there, then darting and flickering as it traced intricate patterns over her abdomen, lower and lower, make the flame that was already burning in Brandy's blood flare even brighter and hotter. The feel of him placing tiny, biting kisses on the tender skin on the insides of her thighs, so close to where she wanted him inside her, made her writhe in frustration. "Please," she begged, almost incoherent with need, "please."

Flaming Arrow rolled over her and positioned himself between her legs, then slid his hands beneath her to cup her buttocks and lift her. Brandy cried out in relief and eagerly arched her back to receive him. Then seeing him lower his head, the long hair at the sides of his head brushing the insides of her thighs before he kissed her there, she stiffened in shock, then cried out "No!" when his tongue flicked out like a fiery dart.

Flaming Arrow raised his head and said in a thick voice, "This, too, is Dakota custom, that the man's tongue would know his woman the same as his loins."

Brandy's white sensibilities were shocked to the core. "No, it's wrong. It's too—too intimate."

"Nothing is too intimate between a husband and his wife." Flaming Arrow's dark eyes caught hers in a piercing gaze. "You are my wife. For months I have longed to taste your nectar there. Now it is my right, and I will not be denied."

Flaming Arrow dropped his head, ignoring her frantic pleas for him to stop and holding her hips firmly so she couldn't squirm away. His tongue laved the warm lips, swirled around the bud of her desire, then dipped to taste her sweetness and returned to tease and tantalize the burning core of her womanhood. She tried to fight the ripples of pleasure, but she was helpless against his exciting, erotic ministrations and his artful tongue. As the sweet ripples turned to tidal waves of sheer ecstasy, she gave up her resistance and spread her legs, opening up to him as a flower offers its nectar to a honey bee.

Brandy was whirling in a maelstrom of sheer sensation as Flaming Arrow mastered her with his lips and tongue. Her blood surged through her veins like liquid fire; her skin burned with a million tiny fires; every nerve in her body tingled. She moaned, thrashed her head from side to side, writhing beneath him, thinking she would die if he didn't stop this exquisite torture. It was too much to bear. Then as his hands slipped from her buttocks, up her sides, to cup her breasts, his thumbs brushing across the nipples, she climaxed, her body convulsing in a long shudder and her back arching.

She opened her eyes to see Flaming Arrow smiling down at her. "And now what do you think of our Dakota custom? Did I not give you pleasure, as well as show my willingness to take every part of you as my wife?"

Brandy couldn't possibly deny that he had given her pleasure. She had behaved like a total wanton, glorying in his shocking lovemaking. But she still wasn't convinced it was right. Anything that felt that good had to be forbidden. "Yes, it was"—she hesitated, not wanting to appear too enthusiastic, then finished in the Dakota tongue,—*"waste."*

Flaming Arrow cocked one dark eyebrow and asked, "Good? Is that all you can say?"

"Wasteste."

Flaming Arrow chuckled. "I think it was more than very good. I think you loved it. And someday you will do the same to me. You will take the seed that clings to the tip of me in your mouth, to show your desire to preserve life—your life, my life, all life."

Again Brandy was shocked. She'd never be able to do *that* to him, she thought. Then remembering the pleasure he had unselfishly given her, she found that not only did she want to return those exquisite feelings, but the thought of making love to him that way was actually exciting. She stroked his broad shoulders and answered, "No, I won't do it someday. I'll do it now."

Her willingness greatly pleased Flaming Arrow. His smile spread, but he shook his head and said, "No, not tonight. Making love to you that way excited me unbearably. I had no idea it would be so stimulating. I don't think I could stand to have you do it to me. I already feel as if I'm about to burst. I want to be inside you when it happens."

So did Brandy. "And that's where I want you. Inside me." A sudden urgency swept over her. "Now!"

Their eyes locked, Flaming Arrow entered her slowly, each very much aware of the significance of their joining. Then when he was buried deep inside her, they lay perfectly still and savored their union, their perfect oneness. Brandy didn't think she could contain her happiness. When Flaming Arrow tenderly kissed her lips, then muttered against them, *"Tecihila,"* the tears spilled over, and she returned his vow of love in a voice choked with emotion.

For once, Flaming Arrow didn't question her tears. He could see happiness shining in her eyes. He bent his head and kissed her, a slow, sweet kiss that grew steadily warmer and warmer, and their passion ignited like a firestorm. Then he led her up those glorious heights, their hearts thundering and their bodies straining, taking her in a sweet-savage storm until he brought them to that mindless, searing explosion of passion that hurled them among a starburst of flaming colors.

Later, as Flaming Arrow held her in his strong arms and dozed, Brandy gazed up at the full moon, feeling wonderfully content. To her amazement, she had gained all she had ever secretly hoped for. Not only had Flaming Arrow finally admitted he loved her, but he made her his wife—something she had thought would never happen. Her happiness was sublime. There wasn't another thing in this world that she could possibly want.

20

Flaming Arrow and Brandy returned to their tepee before dawn, and later that morning, while Brandy was sleeping after their long night of lovemaking, Flaming Arrow went to the *ne-wä-gwa-wa-che-pe* lodge, where the festivities were still taking place, to inform Crazy Horse and the council of his marriage. If they desired to withdraw their offer because he had married a white woman, they would have time to do so before the last day of the ceremony, when the new chiefs were announced.

If Crazy Horse was disappointed in the man he had personally groomed and championed for chief, he showed no sign. His expression was so devoid of any emotion that his face could have been made of stone. His only comment was, "If the council decides the offer still stands, you will accept?"

Flaming Arrow was still having trouble understanding his recent vision. A part of him stubbornly clung to the belief that the flaming end of the arrow falling to the ground signified death was near. It was a feeling he couldn't shake. But even if he might not have long to serve in the office that had been offered to him, that was no reason for him to refuse. The warriors who had fled the reservation and flocked to the side of Crazy Horse still needed a strong leader of their own, and if he became chief, he would not be like one of those chiefs who watched the battle from a safe distance. He would fashion his style of fighting after that of Crazy Horse, a war chief who not only led his warriors but fought beside them, who placed himself in the thick of the fighting, in the greatest danger. Almost without exception, war chiefs of that caliber met an early death. To some degree, if he died in the upcoming battle, he would only be doing what was expected of him. "Yes, I would accept," Flaming Arrow answered gravely.

Crazy Horse made no comment, but simply nodded his head, and Flaming Arrow knew he was being dismissed.

As Flaming Arrow walked back to his tepee, he pondered over what might happen. He sensed that Crazy Horse still wanted him to become chief, despite his marriage to a white-eyes, one of the enemy. But Crazy Horse was an usually perceptive man and had an uncanny knack for reading the true character of a person. Did he not object to Brandy because he knew of her special attributes? And if that were the case, would Crazy Horse use his influence with the council on Flaming Arrow's behalf? Flaming Arrow strongly suspected he would but he knew that the council might not agree. There were men on it whose hatred of the white-eyes ran very deep, particularly since their newest treachery in breaking their treaty. Then again, there were those on the council who had a grudging respect for Crazy Horse's skills in warfare but were wary of the chief on a more personal basis. Many considered him strange because of his intensity and his religious zeal, and a few even considered him fanatical. No, just because Crazy Horse championed him was no reason the council would be in agreement. The Dakotas were as independent in their thinking as they were in their fighting.

When Flaming Arrow reached his tepee, he found Brandy missing. He was wondering whether he should search for her in the woods or wait for her to return when she walked into the tepee. "Where have you been?" he asked.

"I went to tell Swift Rabbit about our marriage."

Flaming Arrow didn't have to ask how the old woman had taken the news. He knew by the happy sparkle in Brandy's eyes. But then, he wasn't particularly surprised that Swift Rabbit had approved. He knew she had come to appreciate the white girl long ago.

When Flaming Arrow made no comment, Brandy said, "I hope you don't mind me telling her, but I wanted to share my good news with her. She's become very dear to me."

Flaming Arrow understood. He, too, wanted to share his happiness with those closest to him. That had been his intention when he had rushed back to the tepee. "No, I don't mind. And now I won't have to ask the village crier to announce the wedding.

Undoubtedly, she'll spread the news much faster," he added with a wry twist of his lips. "But it does mean we will have to hurry to do what I intend."

"And what is that?"

"To tell my brother the news and introduce you to his family. We don't want them to hear it through the village grapevine. They might be offended."

Brandy heartily agreed that the family should be the first to know. She'd had no idea that Flaming Arrow would feel the same, that he would make their marriage so public so soon, much less that he would be eager to introduce her to his family.

Brandy had wanted very much to be a part of Flaming Arrow's life outside the privacy of their tepee, but as they hurried across the village, she became more and more apprehensive. What if his family refused to accept her? After all, she was a white-eyes, their enemy. And even if they accepted her, would they be ashamed of her? Would they look upon her and Flaming Arrow's marriage as a humiliating embarrassment? By the time they reached Yellow Fox's tepee, Brandy's nerves were crawling and her knees were shaking so badly, she could hardly stand.

They found Yellow Fox sitting on a blanket outside his tepee, soaking up the warm midmorning sun and smoking his pipe. A surprised expression came over his face when he saw Brandy with Flaming Arrow. Before his mind could fathom what it meant, Flaming Arrow announced their marriage.

Brandy held her breath, dreading Yellow Fox's reaction. She had no way of knowing that Yellow Fox had always been a little intrigued with her, that he had hoped she could give warmth and a new meaning to his brother's life, that he had watched her

closely and had secretly come to admire her. Therefore, she was stunned when a broad smile spread
across his face and he jumped to his feet, clapping
Flaming Arrow on his shoulders and saying, "Congratulations! I had almost despaired of you ever coming to your senses. You have chosen wisely."

A wave of relief washed over Flaming Arrow. He
didn't care what the rest of the village thought—he
had only wanted his brother to approve. Not only
was Yellow Fox his only living kin, his blood link to his
ancestors and his roots—something very important
to every Dakota—but his older brother was his best
friend, too, probably because there had never been
any sibling rivalry or competition between them.
Yellow Fox had always been content to sit on the
sidelines and let his brother do the excelling for the
family, to play the role of Flaming Arrow's confidant
and companion.

Yellow Fox turned to Brandy. "As the elder
brother, I wish to welcome you to our family." He
grinned, slicing Flaming Arrow a teasing look. "Secretly, I have always wanted a sister. I was very disappointed when Flaming Arrow was born and I discovered he was male."

Brandy was speechless. Not in her wildest dreams
had she expected such warm acceptance, nor had she
thought Yellow Fox would possess a sense of humor.
All of the other warriors seemed so dour. She struggled to find her tongue, then muttered, "Thank you."

Yellow Fox turned and called to his wives inside
the tepee, telling them to step outside. As the two
young women emerged, Brandy could see a strong
family resemblance in the sisters. Noting that there
was absolutely no expression on their faces, her ap-

prehension rose again. Desperately, she wanted their approval, perhaps even more than Yellow Fox's. She was hungry for female companions of her own age, friends with whom she could gossip and share personal confidences, young women who shared the same interests. She wanted to be silly sometimes, to giggle for no good reason, to feel free and lighthearted, and she knew the younger Indian women did this. She had seen them. And as fond as she was of Swift Rabbit, this was one craving that the older, more mature woman couldn't satisfy.

Then Brandy caught sight of the baby in the cradle Morning Star was carrying, and all thought of the two young women vanished. At that moment she only had eyes for Flaming Arrow's godson. "Oh, he's beautiful!" she cried out softly, then held out her arms. "Can I hold him?"

Unknown to Brandy and Flaming Arrow, Morning Star and Moon Woman had observed Brandy during Flaming Arrow's Sun Dance. Like so many others in the tribe, they had been impressed with her courage in lending him support despite the obvious pain it was causing her. They had also come to realize that she loved him deeply. For those reasons, they held no animosity toward her, despite their stony faces. But when Brandy called the baby beautiful and held out her arms, both young women's hearts melted. Mothers were mothers the world over, and none could resist having their child called beautiful. Moon Woman loved the baby as if it were her own. The two beamed with open pleasure, and Morning Star held the baby out to Brandy.

Brandy accepted it gingerly, for she had never held a baby of any kind, but the cradle board gave

her something substantial to hold and she felt less
awkward than she would have holding just the baby.
Dark, sober eyes gazed up at her from a round face.
"What's his name?" she asked.

"Deer Runs Fast."

Brandy knew that it was customary for the Dakotas
to give male infants a silly or inconsequential name
because it was only a temporary name. When the
boys were old enough to seek their vision, they
would be given their adult name at the naming ceremony and throw away the birth cords they wore
around their necks, which symbolized cutting themselves from their childhood.

Everyone sat down, the women in a tight little
circle, and the two men a few feet from them.
Brandy couldn't take her eyes from the baby in her
lap. She stroked his head, which was covered with a
thick mat of black hair, and said in an awed voice,
"His head is so soft. I've never felt anything so soft."

The two sisters smiled and nodded in perfect
agreement.

As Brandy trailed a finger down the side of the
baby's face, he reached up and caught her finger
with one of his chubby hands, then smiled. It was the
same little crooked smile that Flaming Arrow gave
her every now and then, and her deep-seated mater-
nal urges surged to the surface. Suddenly, she was
filled with a powerful yearning. She wanted Flaming
Arrow's child so badly, it hurt.

Then Brandy had to smile at her own perversity.
Flaming Arrow's family might have accepted her as
one of their own, but she was still very much a greedy
white. Just the night before she had thought her happiness sublime, that there was nothing more that she

could possibly want. But it wasn't true. Now she wanted Flaming Arrow's child. Always, she wanted more.

Flaming Arrow and Brandy were still visiting with Yellow Fox and his family when Crazy Horse suddenly appeared and announced that the council had chosen Flaming Arrow as war chief for the newly arrived Dakotas. Flaming Arrow was stunned, then dropped his voice so Brandy couldn't hear and remarked, "I didn't think they would still want me."

Crazy Horse shot Brandy a quick look over Flaming Arrow's shoulder. "Because of your marriage to the white-eyes? No, they saw how brave she was when you danced at the *ne-wä-gwa-wa-che-pe*. The majority of the council withdrew any objections they might have had. You know how strongly they admire courage. Also, it is common knowledge in the tribe that she has accepted our ways, as difficult as they might be for her. She has shown an unexpected strength and determination."

Flaming Arrow was glad that others in the tribe had noticed Brandy's strengths, but he didn't know what Crazy Horse was talking about when he referred to Brandy's courage during his dance. He had been too involved in his agony to notice hers, but he didn't feel this was the time to ask. Besides, something was bothering him. "You said the majority didn't object to my marriage. What about the others?"

"The decision of the council does not have to be unanimous," Crazy Horse pointed out. Seeing the frown still on Flaming Arrow's face, he said, "It will be up to you to convince them that the others chose wisely, that your marriage should have no bearing on how you handle your new position as war chief. Keep that in mind."

With that, Crazy Horse walked away. Flaming Arrow turned to his brother, who was grinning from ear to ear. "It's about time," Yellow Fox said. "I was growing weary of waiting for you to become chief."

"Then you knew they were considering me?"

"I have known since the first day you picked up a bow and arrow that someday you would be chief. Since then, it has only been a question of when. You have done our family proud."

Brandy, too, was proud—so proud she thought she would burst. And she was relieved. She knew then that if Flaming Arrow had been denied his rightful place, she would have never forgiven herself. But she wanted to run to him and hug him so badly, it was an agony for her, but she knew she couldn't do it. It would be unseemly for even a wife to show that much emotion in public. All she could do was smile at him.

But Brandy put everything she felt into that smile, and Flaming Arrow knew exactly what she felt. He smiled back, and for all practical purposes, the others might as well not have been there. Their happiness crossed the space between them, and once again, they were united in a strange, mystical bond that seemed to defy time and space.

"Have you finished your war bonnet?" Yellow Fox asked, shattering the spell between Flaming Arrow and Brandy.

"What?" Flaming Arrow asked in a dazed voice, his attention still on Brandy.

"I asked if you have completed your war bonnet. It

would be unseemly for you to accept such a prestigious position with half the feathers you have earned missing."

"No, I haven't finished it," Flaming Arrow admitted. "I didn't feel it was that important."

"Ah, just as I thought!" Yellow Fox muttered, throwing his hands up in despair. "Sometimes you carry humility too far. I won't have the family disgraced because of your lack of pretense. A chief would be naked without a war bonnet. Come, we will go to your tepee and work on it together. That way we will have it finished by tomorrow night."

Yellow Fox hurried off. Flaming Arrow turned to Brandy and asked, "Can you find your way back to our tepee by yourself?"

"Yes, but maybe I should leave too."

"No, you can visit for as long as you like. Making a war bonnet is men's business."

As Flaming Arrow walked off, Morning Star asked Brandy, "Does Flaming Arrow have a fine pair of buckskins, a shirt as well as leggins and a breechclout? One that is decorated appropriately for a chief?"

Brandy was taken by surprise. "Well, I was sewing on a new shirt for him, but—well, I didn't know he would have to have special clothing now that he's chief."

"He won't have to have special clothing except for the ceremony," Morning Star informed her.

"And he will need a new quill breastplate too," Moon Woman added.

Brandy looked at the two young women in dismay. "But I can never get all that made by tomorrow, not even with Swift Rabbit helping me."

"We can help, too," Morning Star answered, her dark eyes glowing with excitement.

"Thank you," Brandy whispered.

"We are your family now. You do not need to thank us. It is our place to help one another," Morning Star answered. "Now, go and bring Flaming Arrow's buckskins and your sewing things here. If he and Yellow Fox are working on his bonnet there, there won't be room for all of us in the tepee. Besides, those soft down tufts that they use to cover the quill of the eagle feathers on the bonnets make me sneeze."

That day and into the next, the four women worked feverishly to complete Flaming Arrow's clothing for the ceremony the next night. Their fingers flew as they applied the intricate beading and quills to the buckskins. Even his moccasins and breechclout were beaded, a chore so time consuming that Brandy didn't even return to her own tepee that night but took only a short nap. As they worked, Brandy discreetly observed her two new sisters-in-law. She had always been curious to know if women married to the same warrior weren't jealous of one another. She had been told that the women were glad to have someone to split their chores with, as well as to keep them company when the men were gone for long periods of time, but it didn't seem natural to share a man's affections, to say nothing of his bed. But from what she could see, Morning Star and Moon Woman were perfectly happy with the arrangement, and they both doted on Deer Runs Fast. But Brandy knew she herself could never accept such an arrangement. If Flaming Arrow ever tried to take another wife, she'd scratch his eyes out, after she'd denuded him of every hair on his head. In that way, she was still white to the core—terribly possessive, as well as greedy.

The night of the big ceremony came, and it seemed that everyone in the huge encampment attended. The closest she and Flaming Arrow's family could get was the very fringes of the open-sided lodge, and Brandy had to stand on her tiptoes and crane her neck to see. She didn't understand any of the ceremony. The words were drowned out by the sound of the medicine men's rattles as they chanted over the new chiefs, but Flaming Arrow looked magnificent. It was not because he was arrayed in his new finery and his impressive war bonnet, whose double tails dragged the ground. No, it was the splendid man himself who shone. He stood tall and proud and looked every inch the powerful chief.

It wasn't until the feast after the ceremony that Brandy was reunited with her husband. She saw him shoving his way through the crush of the crowd all around her and was so proud of him, she thought she would burst with the emotion. Every fiber in her body yearned to throw her arms around him and hug him. But of course she couldn't. Indians frowned on public emotional displays, particularly between men and women, so much so that couples who were courting had to hide beneath a blanket thrown over their heads when they danced or strolled through the camp. Then, only adding to her frustration, she and Flaming Arrow were separated again after exchanging nothing more than a smile, and Brandy was forced to endure hours of feasting and watching the Indians dance around a huge bonfire, sitting discreetly behind her husband and the other chiefs with their wives and families. Had it not been for Yellow Fox and his witty remarks to entertain her throughout the long evening, she would have probably screamed in boredom.

Finally, when the hour was very late, the Dakotas brought the *ne-wä-gwa-wa-che-pe* to a close for that year. Its end was marked when Sitting Bull was carried on his litter from the center of the encampment to his tepee, for after sacrificing fifty pieces of skin that had been sliced from his arms and chest, he was too weak from loss of blood to walk. From the day the tree had been cut to its end, the annual Dakota ceremony had lasted ten days.

After her limited sleep the night before and the lengthy ceremony, Brandy was so weary, she could barely walk to their tepee. It took a supreme effort to put one foot before the other and to keep her eyelids open. But she wasn't so tired that she couldn't muster the energy to congratulate her husband. As soon as they stepped into the tepee, she hugged him and said, "I'm so proud of you."

While they were making his war bonnet, Yellow Fox had told Flaming Arrow of Brandy's courage the day he had danced. He was equally proud of her. He gave her a fierce hug back, swept his war bonnet from his head, and tossed it aside. Then he lifted her in his arms and carried her to his pallet, his heart already racing in anticipation of making love to her. As he stood over their pallet, he wondered why she felt so heavy and why her arm was hanging limply to the side. Peering closer, he saw her eyes were closed, and he realized with dismay that she was so exhausted, she had gone to sleep in his arms.

Feeling a deep regret, he gently placed her on the pallet. For a moment, he considered undressing her, then decided against if for fear it would disturb her sleep. He stripped off his clothing and lay beside her.

Instinctively, Brandy snuggled up to him, then roused herself just enough to mutter, "If you ever take another wife, I'll kill you both. I won't share you."

Flaming Arrow was so surprised by her unexpected vow that he was momentarily stunned. Then he chuckled to himself, thinking how typical it was of his fierce, outspoken white-eyes. Only she would dare to issue a chief an ultimatum. He nuzzled the top of her head and answered, "You don't have to worry about that happening. I'm afraid you're all the woman that I could possibly handle."

Flaming Arrow waited for some response. It wasn't like Brandy to let him have the last word on anything, regardless of how tired she might be. When none came, he assumed that she had fallen back asleep before he had even answered.

But that was not the case. If there had been just a little more light in the tepee, Flaming Arrow would have known Brandy had heard. Her eyes were closed, but there was a very smug smile on her lips.

21

The next morning, when Brandy and Flaming Arrow were eating their breakfast, she found it hard to believe that the handsome Dakota sitting across from her was both her husband and a new chief. She wondered if his new position would demand much of his time and if she would see even less of him. Curious, she asked, "How big will your tribe be?"

"I'd estimate approximately three hundred warriors and their families. That includes those men from Crazy Horse's tribe that wish to join me."

"I was under the impression that chiefs gauge their power and importance by how many men follow them. I know Crazy Horse planned on you taking the better part of the reservation Indians who have joined him, but won't he get upset if some of his old warriors leave him in favor of you?"

"A lesser man might, particularly one of the chiefs that are so fiercely protective of their image among the other tribes, but Crazy Horse has never been power hungry. He's always contended that it isn't the size of the fighting force but its quality that matters. Besides, even if my expectations are met, Crazy Horse will still have over a thousand warriors at his command."

Brandy knew that there had been a large gathering of Indians at the *ne-wä-gwa-wa-che-pe*, but she hadn't stopped to consider numbers. Crazy Horse was just one great chief. There were many others. A shocked expression came over her face.

Seeing it, Flaming Arrow asked, "Is something wrong?"

"My brother said there weren't a thousand warriors in the entire Powder River Country."

"Your brother is incorrect. There have always been many more Dakota and Cheyenne in the Powder River Country than your people thought. I'm afraid the army marching down on us is going to be in for a big surprise if they find us, particularly in view of all of the reservation Indians that have joined us."

Brandy had completely forgotten about the new army expedition against the Dakotas, what with her sudden marriage and then the frantic preparations for Flaming Arrow becoming chief. Her thoughts turned to her brother. Had he survived the battle with the Cheyennes that spring, and if so, was he in the new expedition? "Do you have any idea how large General Crook's army is?"

"According to our scouts, over a thousand men. That does not include their Crow and Shoshone allies."

Brandy did some quick mental computing. If the Dakotas and the army were to come to grips, they would be pretty well matched as far as numbers were concerned, but she hoped it would not come to that. She loved Flaming Arrow with her whole heart and soul, but she loved her brother too. She was torn between two allegiances. She said a silent, fervent prayer that General Crook and his army would never find the Dakotas.

But Brandy's prayer wasn't answered. Six days after the *ne-wä-gwa-wa-che-pe*, word arrived at the Indian camps on the Rosebud that General Crook and his army were less than a day's ride away. As soon as he heard the news, Flaming Arrow rushed off to confer with the other chiefs, leaving Brandy to pace apprehensively in their tepee.

Flaming Arrow returned late that afternoon and didn't leave Brandy in suspense long. Almost as soon as the hide flap over the entrance had fallen back into place behind him, he announced, "Crazy Horse, a Cheyenne chief, and myself are riding out with our warriors to attack General Crook and his army. We'll leave as soon as our men can make their preparations."

"You mean you're not going to wait until morning?" Brandy asked, stunned.

"No. The warriors are so optimistic about a victory because of Sitting Bull's vision that they're eager for battle, so eager that Crazy Horse and I couldn't hold them back if we wanted to. But we're in perfect agreement. Now is the time to strike, when the officers mistakenly think we're not aware of their presence and that they can catch us by surprise while we're still in our camp. They don't expect *us* to attack *them,* particularly from this distance. If we ride all night, we can catch them unexpectedly shortly after daybreak and turn the tables on them."

While he was talking, Flaming Arrow was on his knees and groping in his parfleche for something. As he pulled out a buckskin shirt, Brandy wondered why he would wear it in summer. The most she had ever seen him wear in warm weather was his breechclout and leggins. She had never seen the garment before, nor was it an ordinary shirt. It was almost knee length, the upper half painted blue, the lower yellow, and decorated with much beading and quilling. As Flaming Arrow pulled it over his head, she realized that it wasn't sewn together at the sides but was tied with strips of rawhide.

Seeing her puzzled expression, Flaming Arrow explained, "This is my war shirt. It's left open at the sides so it will be cooler and less restrictive during battle It has as much medicine as the pouch I carry."

Flaming Arrow wore a medicine pouch on the rawhide string that supported his breechclout. He never went anywhere without it, and when he was sleeping, it hung on a pole over their pallet. Brandy had no idea what was in it. He had made it known from the very beginning that its contents were se cret.

Still stunned by the sudden turn of events, Brandy watched while Flaming Arrow tied a tomahawk next to the scabbard that held his knife, then added his pipe bag, whetstone bag, and strike-a-light bag to the belt under his shirt. After slashing his face with paint, he stepped outside to paint his war horse and saddle it.

Brandy saw that the entire camp was in a frenzy of activity as the warriors prepared for their departure. Boys ran through the camp, leading the men's mounts from the huge herd that grazed to one side of the village, the excited camp dogs barking and nipping at their heels. Men rushed here and there to gather their weapons, and a few even took the time to purify them in smoke over fires hastily built for that purpose. The medicine men rushed from man to man to bless them and their horses, wildly waving their rattles and chanting. Then across the camp, she saw Crazy Horse, with streaks of lightning painted on each cheek, throwing handfuls of dirt over himself and his horse. "What in God's name is he doing?" she muttered, half to herself.

Flaming Arrow glanced in the direction Brandy was looking. "He's anointing himself and his mount. He always does that before he goes into battle."

No wonder some people thought he was strange, Brandy thought.

When she turned, Flaming Arrow was wearing his war bonnet and carrying his Winchester. He flew onto his saddle with a graceful leap. Looking up at him, Brandy thought he looked every inch the dangerous savage with his dark eyes glittering with anticipation, his chin and lips set firmly with purpose, his high cheekbones and forehead slashed with paint. The feathers on his magnificent bonnet fluttered in the breeze, and his painted war horse pranced, then pawed the ground, as anxious for action as its master. As the light from the setting sun caught the barrel of the Winchester he held in his hand and the metal took on a reddish gleam, the full impact of what was happening hit Brandy. Flaming Arrow was going off to war. Fast on its heels, she remembered his vision and that he had interpreted it as meaning death was near. An icy fear clutched her heart; the blood drained from her face, leaving it ashen. A sudden weakness invaded her, and her knees trembled. She opened her mouth to speak, but her tongue felt paralyzed. Finally, she managed to whisper, "Be careful." Then feeling stronger, she stepped forward, caught his rock-hard thigh in one hand, and said in a much louder and clearer voice, "Oh, God, *please* be careful."

Unlike Brandy, Flaming Arrow had been very much aware of his vision from the moment word had arrived that the army was so near. Brandy's reassurance and Sitting Bull's vision had never really convinced him that his interpretation was incorrect. He had merely set his ominous feelings aside while he was preoccupied with his new duties as chief. Now, gazing down at Brandy and seeing the raw fear on her beautiful face, that terrible feeling of foreboding bore down on him more heavily than ever. For the first time in his life, he really didn't want to go into battle. It wasn't that he was afraid to die. It was simply that since Brandy had come into his life, he had so much to live for.

Flaming Arrow heard the sudden thundering of hooves and felt the ground shake as Crazy Horse raced his warriors from the camp. He knew without even looking around that his men were mounted and eagerly waiting for him to give the order to leave. He could feel their dark eyes on him, as well as those of everyone in the camp. But his gaze was locked on Brandy. It was as if she and he were locked in a strange vacuum of time and space, as if the rest of the world had temporarily ceased to exist. With something akin to desperation, he wished he could make love to her just one more time.

Then Flaming Arrow did something that surprised the village and caught Brandy completely off guard. Throwing his Dakota upbringing that prohibited any public display of affection between men and women to the wind, he leaned from his horse, caught Brandy's shoulders in his hands, lifted her to her tiptoes, and kissed her, long and hard, putting everything he felt—his total love, his adoration, even his regret that this might be their last—into that fierce kiss. Then with a guttural sound that was torn from the depths of his soul, Flaming Arrow released her, raised his Winchester into the air, waved it, and gave his mount a swift kick with the heel of his moccasins. As his war horse raced off, weaving its way through the maze of tepees, Flaming Arrow's warriors fell in behind him, yelling at the top of their lungs while everyone else cheered.

It took a moment for Brandy to recover from Flaming Arrow's unexpected and profound kiss. When she did, she tore out after him, fully prepared to beg him on her knees not to go, for she had sensed a finality about his good-bye that had terrified her even more. By the time she raced from the village into the open prairie around it, the huge war party was racing up the hill that overlooked the camp, the manes on the horses' outstretched necks whipping around the warriors' bronze faces as they rode low in the saddle. The pounding of thousands of hooves on the ground left a huge cloud of dust in their wake.

Realizing she was too late to stop Flaming Arrow, Brandy fell to her knees. She held the painful stitch in her side and took in deep breaths of fresh air mixed with anguished sobs as tears streamed down her face. Then through the blurry moisture, just as the three chiefs' horses crested the hill, she saw Flaming Arrow, the long double tails of his war bonnet spread out in the air around him like wings and the setting sun casting him and his racing mount in a rosy color. Furiously, she wiped the tears from her eyes and stared, willing him at least to turn his head and give her one last look.

On the hill above, Flaming Arrow wanted to turn his head for a last look, but he didn't dare for fear he'd falter and turn back. It took every ounce of his steely control to keep his eyes locked on a point between his mount's ears. When his horse topped the crest and raced down the other side of the hill, the two were encased in a deep purple shadow. Flaming Arrow knew he had reached the point of no return. He had hoped he would feel relief at putting the excruciating parting behind him, but what he felt was not relief. He was glad for the rapidly falling darkness as the sun dipped below the horizon. Something was happening to him, something that would shock his warriors if they saw, something that should leave him feeling unmanned and deeply humiliated but didn't. The tears that had suddenly loomed in his eyes had spilled over, and all he felt was a profound sadness at his loss. Fervently, he wished destiny hadn't asked so much of him.

Back on the prairie beside the sprawled Indian camps, Brandy lay in the grass in the dark, crying until there were no more tears left. Much later in the night, Swift Rabbit found her, spent and sleeping in exhaustion, her buckskin dress damp with dew.

While they were walking back to the village, Brandy told the old woman of Flaming Arrow's vision and explained why she was so frightened. "I'm afraid he was right, that it did mean death was imminent, that I'll never see him alive again."

"And do you think any of the other women feel any differently?" the old woman asked in a gentle, yet firm tone of voice. "That because you are white you feel things more deeply? If you do, you are wrong. They are all afraid for their loved one's lives. They do not need any visions to arouse that fear. They know war and death go hand-in-hand, and not a one has not already lost one of their male relatives. Each time their husband or father or brother or son rides off to war or a raid, they wait, terrified the worst will happen. That has always been the Dakota woman's lot in life—to wait and agonize. But you must not show your fear. That is not our way, and you are one of us now."

Brandy had never stopped to think what the other women might be feeling. She had been too engrossed with her own terror. "I don't know if I can do that. I was brought up differently. I wasn't taught to suppress my emotions, and despite everything you say, I'm still white. Marrying Flaming Arrow didn't change that."

"Your skin is still white. That is the only thing that will never change. But the way you think, the way you behave can change. You are a Dakota woman now, by choice. And you are the wife of a chief. You have a role to play. Otherwise you will disgrace Flaming Arrow, and I know you love him too much to knowingly do that. You must not show your fear to the others. And if you must cry, do so in the privacy of your tepee." The old woman paused and saw doubt in Brandy's eyes. "You do not give yourself credit for having the strength and the determination to change, but I know you have it in you. You have already changed from the girl you were when Flaming Arrow brought you to our camp. And I am not saying that I expect you to become like the Dakota women in all ways. You could never be meek or retiring, and to be perfectly honest, now that I have come to know you, I would not like you that way. There is within you a vital force that cannot be suppressed. And that is good, for it is the source of your strength. But sometimes strength must be tempered with wisdom. The same is true with emotions. I am not telling you to stop feeling. That would be as impossible as trying to keep the sun from setting or the rain from falling. We are all human; we all feel. I am only cautioning you to hide your emotions from the others, to behave with the dignity that befits the wife of a chief destined for greatness."

After Swift Rabbit had left her in her tepee, Brandy lay on her and Flaming Arrow's pallet for a long time thinking about what the old Indian woman had said. There was one word that hung in her mind: *dignity.* For the first time she had an inkling of what the Dakotas were striving to attain when they kept their feelings to themselves and put on their stony expressions. But it was more than a brave front they presented or an impressive manner of stoicism. For the Dakota, dignity was also a way of thinking. It was the mark of maturity. She certainly hadn't been acting very adult, wearing her feelings on her sleeve and crying at the drop of a hat. Why, she had lost her composure so often, it was a wonder Flaming Arrow wasn't ashamed to be seen in public with her.

Brandy couldn't stand the thought of Flaming Arrow being ashamed of her. No, it had always been his admiration that she had fervently sought. She firmly vowed she'd try her very best to hide her feelings and behave in a more Dakota-like manner, that she'd be dignified and composed—even if it killed her!

After a few hours of sleep, Brandy joined Morning Star and Moon Woman in their tepee, hoping that being in their company would help keep her mind from the terrible danger Flaming Arrow was facing. But it soon became apparent to Brandy that the two young women were just as worried about Yellow Fox's safety. Of course, neither woman came right out and said so. Nor did their manner reveal it, for both had broad smiles on their comely faces and they carried on a steady stream of light conversation as they performed their household duties. But Brandy sensed their fear, thought their front too deliberately brave to be believable, and her heart went out to them. But her own compassion had to be hidden, too, making the burden of acting mature and composed doubly difficult.

It was an excruciatingly long day, and by the time Brandy returned to her tepee that night, her stomach felt as if it were tied into a million knots and her nerves were crawling. She stripped off her clothes, lay down, pulled the blanket up over her, and curled into a tight ball, trying desperately not to give way to the terrible fear inside her. Then, catching a whiff of Flaming Arrow's scent that lingered there, the small vestige of composure she had broke and a flood of tears came, accompanied by gut-wrenching sobs. Hours later, she finally fell asleep in utter exhaustion. Her last glum thought before her eyelids drifted down was, Well, so much for dignity. She was going to make a miserable Dakota wife.

22

While Brandy underwent her ordeal of waiting, Flaming Arrow and his warriors were racing to do battle with Crook's army. Just as the three chiefs had planned, the war party rode all night and, shortly after dawn, made contact with Crook's Crow and Shoshone scouts near the headwaters of the Rosebud. The army scouts' bronzed faces drained of all color, for the sight of over a thousand furious Dakota and Cheyenne warriors was enough to make their blood run cold. They turned tail and raced back to warn the soldiers, the war party fast on their heels and whooping at the top of their lungs.

Within minutes, Flaming Arrow and his men got their first sight of the hated white-eyes, a force of some thirteen hundred men still in marching formation. The infantrymen were mounted on undisciplined army mules that went berserk at the unholy sounds coming from the attacking warriors and promptly dumped the better part of their riders in the dust. Seeing the wave of Dakota and Cheyenne coming down on them, the force split into roughly three groups. Crook took some of his infantry onto a bluff overlooking the creek; two companies of his cavalry rushed to a hill on the opposite side of the creek; and the rest of the force disappeared somewhere off in the opposite direction. Racing beside Flaming Arrow, Crazy Horse cried out, "Come on, Lakotas, it's a good day to die!"

Flaming Arrow had heard the chief's famous war cry more than once. Crazy Horse always used it to exhort his men to greater feats, and the mention of death never gave them pause. To die honorably and bravely in the midst of battle was every warrior's dream, for he knew he would be taken straight to the Mystery Land. But for once, the stirring cry didn't light a patriotic fire in Flaming Arrow's blood. He didn't want to die. He had too much to live for.

For that reason, Flaming Arrow fought harder and fiercer than he ever had, unwittingly inspiring his men with his bravery and boldness and infusing them with his iron determination to win. It was a mad, swirling fight—actually three battles in one—and Flaming Arrow and the other chiefs kept a constant pressure on the troops, fighting in a very un-Indian way, riding right down among them and at some points splitting the soldiers into even smaller disorganized groups. At one point, Flaming Arrow and a score of his men caught a group of Crow and Shoshone scouts trying to make their way to General Crook and his men on the bluffs overlooking the creek. The two enemy Indian groups came to a com-

plete halt and stared at each other with unmitigated
hatred before they engaged in a savage hand-to-hand
combat, furiously swinging knives, battle axes, and
tomahawks. Those that were unseated rolled in the
dust and clouds of drifting powder smoke, while the
petals shaken loose from the wild plum and crab-
apple trees around them drifted down and their fragrance filled their nostrils. Emerging victorious from
the bloody violent confrontation, the Dakotas flew
into their saddles, many carrying fresh scalps, and
raced behind Flaming Arrow to join in yet another
howling sweep on the enemy's lines.

The battle went on and on, and during the day,
several other Dakota chiefs whose smaller tribes
lived nearby joined in with their men. Finally, early
in the afternoon, the warriors began breaking off
fighting and drifting away. Crazy Horse, Flaming Arrow, and several other chiefs rode in among them
and managed to get them to return to battle, but it
was short-lived. After hours of constantly attacking in
a very un-Indian manner and keeping Crook and his
men pinned down and helpless against their on-
slaught, the Indians' strong individualism came to
the fore. Like warriors since the beginning of time,
the warriors gave their chiefs only so much control
over them. Ultimately, each and every man made his
own decision, and now the warriors were simply
tired and hungry and ready to go home. Total annihilation of the white-eyes could wait for another day.
So after a fierce, final sweep on the army's positions,
they turned and rode away. Their leaders had no
choice but to follow.

Ordinarily, Flaming Arrow might have been frustrated by his warriors' refusal to fight any longer.

Like the other chiefs, he knew that if they had continued their assault, they would have completely defeated the enemy. But Flaming Arrow felt no disappointment. He was elated that the battle was behind him and that he was still alive. And while they hadn't gained total victory, Flaming Arrow knew they had given Crook's army such a severe beating that he'd be forced to retreat again. By the time he was reinforced, hopefully summer would be past and it would be too late to march against the Dakotas before winter set in. Flaming Arrow realized he might only be buying time, but life had become so dear, so sweet to him, that he'd gladly settle for anything he could get. Every moment with Brandy was precious.

For that reason, Flaming Arrow couldn't wait to get back to her. He gave his men only a few hours to eat and rest. Then, coercing them with promises of a great celebration when they reached the main camp, he drove them once again all night. Only Yellow Fox guessed that Flaming Arrow had an ulterior motive for wanting to get back to camp so quickly, other than to claim the glory he had covered himself in that day, but Flaming Arrow's brother had no objections. The sooner he put distance between himself and the enemy, the happier Yellow Fox would be. For once he hadn't hung back on the fringes of the battle and given it only his half-hearted efforts. Yellow Fox had fought as fiercely and bravely as everyone else, and he had done it more for Flaming Arrow's sake than his. He had not wanted to embarrass his brother, who was now chief, by appearing any less eager than the others. But that didn't mean that Yellow Fox particularly wanted to continue playing the role of a courageous warrior who laughed at death.

He, too, valued life, and while he had been proud that Flaming Arrow had been made a chief, he was beginning to have some regrets. As much as he wanted to lend support to his brother, deep down he knew that he was not hero material and that his chances of continuing to survive many ferocious battles like that were very slim.

Brandy was still sleeping early the next morning, when Flaming Arrow and his warriors rode into the camp. Their faces were painted black for victory, and many waved the still-bloody scalps they had taken over their heads. She was awakened by the sounds of the horses' hooves pounding on the packed ground, the men's triumphant shouts, and the villagers answering with wild cheers. Groggily, she sat up and shook her head, trying to wake herself. Then, when the flap over the door was suddenly thrown aside, she sat bolt upright in her pallet.

Flaming Arrow stepped into the tepee, his dusty buckskins splattered with blood and half an eagle feather in his scalp lock shot away. Like the others, his face was painted black, which made the whites of his eyes stand out. For a moment, Brandy stared at him in disbelief, for she had never dreamed he would return so soon. As the full impact hit her—he was alive!—she gave a jubilant cry and jumped to her feet. Then, realizing that he could be injured, she asked anxiously as her eyes quickly skimmed over him, "Are you all right?"

"I'm fine."

"Oh, thank God," she answered, feeling weak with relief. "And thank God you're back. I was so worried. And I missed you so—"

Flaming Arrow stepped forward and placed his fingers over her lips to silence her. "That can wait until later," he said in a voice that throbbed with need. "Right now I need you."

He pulled her into his arms with such force that it knocked the breath from her. Then he was kissing her, deeply, passionately, holding him to her fiercely with one arm, while his free hand ran over her soft, pale skin, caressing her back, her hips, stroking her thigh, then rising to cup one breast possessively. And all the while, Brandy's hands were busy frantically undressing him, wanting desperately to feel his bare skin against hers. His leggins and breechclout fell away, and she fumbled for the ties on his war shirt. Then, having loosened them, she stepped away from him and pushed the shirt up. With one swift movement, Flaming Arrow pulled it over his head and tossed it aside, and just before he took her in his arms again, she got a brief glance of his magnificent male body.

Flaming Arrow drew her to the pallet with him. Their kisses were urgent and feverish one minute, deep and consuming the next. Hungrily, their hands swept over each other, re-exploring, rediscovering. He marveled at the silkiness of her skin, and she thrilled at his hard-muscled sleekness. It was as if they had been separated for years, instead of just hours; and in truth, it had seemed a lifetime to both. They couldn't get enough of the taste and the feel of each other as they kissed and licked and nipped the entire length of the other's body, their hands everywhere, caressing, smoothing, fondling, both totally oblivious to the black paint from Flaming Arrow's face that was being smeared all over them.

Then, with a small growl, Flaming Arrow rolled Brandy to her back and plunged into her warm depths in one smooth, strong thrust that was as true as one of his arrows, and Brandy felt as if she were suddenly riding a bolt of lightning. Sparks raced up her spine and exploded in her brain. She cried out—but not from pain. She was more than ready for him. She cried out in sheer joy, arching her hips and bringing him even deeper. And that still wasn't enough. She clutched him frantically, desperately wishing she could take all of him into her and hold him there beneath her heart forever.

As Flaming Arrow began his movements, his mouth crashed down on hers in a deep, searing kiss that scorched her lungs and seemed to suck her very soul from her. Brandy wildly kissed him back, straining against him and meeting each breathtaking, masterful stroke with one of her own.

Their movements became frenzied as they gave of themselves with unbridled passion and total abandon, and yet deep down, both knew that this lovemaking was an expression of much more than just their need for physical fulfillment. It was an affirmation that Flaming Arrow had returned alive and whole, a celebration of their triumph over death, and neither would allow themselves to think of the future. The present—that moment—was all that mattered.

They soared into a burst of exquisite ecstasy, their joyous cries mingling and reverberating in the air around them. Even after they had drifted down from the rapturous heights, they held each other fiercely. Finally, Flaming Arrow fell into an exhausted sleep, his dark head cradled in the valley of Brandy's breasts, his arms still twined around her.

It was then that Brandy glanced down and saw the black paint smeared all over their bodies. She thought to rise and wash, then quickly decided against it. She wasn't ready to give Flaming Arrow up yet, not even briefly. She held him to her, glorying in the feel of his broad chest rising and falling against hers, his powerful heart pounding against hers, the corded muscles on his back rippling beneath her fingertips—all tangible proof that he was alive. Then slipping one hand up to his head, she threaded her fingers into his dark hair around his scalp lock, and closed her eyes, holding him close to her heart as she, too, slept.

That evening, the Dakotas and their Cheyenne allies held a victory celebration, and although Brandy would have preferred not to, she attended. It was, as Swift Rabbit had said, her duty as the wife of a chief, and she was determined she wouldn't let Flaming Arrow down.

She sat, as she had before, with the other wives and families of the chiefs behind the leaders, in what was considered by the Indians a place of honor. A huge bonfire lit the area; its flames leaped high into the dark sky and sent shadows dancing eerily over the tepees. The large crowd of Indians who had gathered chatted excitedly, creating a steady drone that hung in the air. Then Sitting Bull, still lying on his litter, was brought from his lodge and the litter placed among the other chiefs who sat cross-legged before the fire.

The ceremony began with a feast. The women

brought around willow baskets piled high with a flat, round bread made from grinding the prairie turnips with wild grasses and geraniums and huge wooden platters with roasted meats: venison, rabbit, sage hen, pheasant, turkey, buffalo steaks, mutton from the mountain sheep. Then after everyone had eaten their fill, wooden bowls of fresh strawberries and roasted nuts were passed around.

Once the feast was finished, the chiefs pulled out their pipes and pouches of *kinnikinick* and lit up. The sweet, pungent tobacco smell drifted in the air and mingled with the lingering odors of the roasted meat and woodsmoke. Then as the drums began to beat and the musicians standing in a circle around the fire began to shake their rattles, Brandy saw a large group of young women leading the dancers to the cleared area around the fire. The girls' faces were painted a brilliant vermilion and a few even dressed in warriors' clothing, something that surprised Brandy in this culture that she had thought geared so much to the male. Then as the women drew back and left the black-faced warriors standing in a circle around the fire, Brandy stared in horror at the scalps the men carried in their hands, for this was the first victory dance she had attended and she hadn't known that it was to be a "Hair Kill" dance.

The next three hours were an agony for Brandy. The sound of the drums beating, the rattles rattling, the whistles blowing, the dancers' feet pounding a wild tattoo on the hard ground created a terrible din, but to make matters worse, each dancer was singing his own individual war song, and the songs didn't match the rhythm of the beating drums. Brandy's head was pounding. The sight of the men waving and wildly shaking their scalps above their heads while they gyrated, leaped in the air, and furiously beat on the ground with their moccasined feet made her stomach churn, for she couldn't help but wonder if one of those scalps belonged to her brother. Remembering what Swift Rabbit had told her about not betraying her emotions, she pasted a stony expression on her face and stared not at the dancers but at the tip of a feather on one of the war bonnets ahead of her, fighting down the gorge that threatened to rise in her throat.

Finally, the dance ended when Sitting Bull motioned for his litter to be lifted and carried back to his lodge. The older chief was still weak from his ordeal at the Sun Dance, some of the Indians might have been disappointed at having the celebration called to an early end, but for Brandy it was a blessed relief. She walked with Flaming Arrow back to their tepee in silence, still deeply disturbed.

It wasn't until they were in their tepee and Flaming Arrow had lit a fire that he said in a matter-of-fact tone of voice, "The dance upset you. I assume it was the scalps."

Brandy thought it pointless to lie. "Yes."

"We do not scalp just to mutilate the bodies."

"I know that. It's just that I couldn't help but think that those were scalps from my people."

"You are not very observant. If you had looked closer, you would have seen that those scalps had scalp locks. They were Indian scalps, both those taken in yesterday's battle and in others. As a rule, the Dakotas disdain white scalps. They are worthless. They have no coup value, like an Indian scalp."

Later, after Flaming Arrow had fallen asleep,

Brandy lay with her head on his shoulder and stared at a lone glittering star she could see through the smoke hole. Knowing that the scalps had been Indian hadn't made the dance seem any less macabre, nor had it relieved her worries about her brother. She still didn't know if he was alive or dead, and as glad as she was that Flaming Arrow had survived the battle, she was disturbed that he had killed some of her people. Their marriage hadn't changed the fact that their nations were still enemies, and she wondered if she hadn't made a mistake when she had refused Flaming Arrow's offer to take her back to her white world. Despite what Swift Rabbit had said, she didn't think she had it in her to be a good Dakota wife. Perhaps, if she really set her mind to it, she might learn to accept some of their more gruesome customs, like scalping, but she didn't think she would be able to stand living in constant fear for Flaming Arrow's life, going through hell every time he rode off to battle or on a raid. She didn't know how the Indian women bore it, always waiting and worrying. Just this taste of it had wrought havoc on her nerves.

Nor could she help feeling torn. Despite what Swift Rabbit had said, she was still white, not just in the color of her skin but in all ways. And yet the thought of leaving Flaming Arrow, of going back and walking out of his life forever, was unbearable too. She was standing on a shadowy line between two worlds. She had only to make a choice and step over into one or the other. But the problem was that she no longer knew to which world she belonged.

23

Early the next morning, Flaming Arrow woke Brandy by shaking her shoulder and announcing that they were moving their camp.

Still groggy, Brandy sat up and wiped the sleep from her eyes. Briefly she wondered why Flaming Arrow hadn't mentioned anything about leaving the night before. Then she asked, "Are we going back to where we camped last summer?"

"No, that place is to the south of here. We are moving west, through a pass in the mountains to a place we call Greasy Grass and your people call the Little Bighorn River."

Again, Brandy pulled down their tepee and packed up their belongings. It appeared that every tribe that had gathered to celebrate the Sun Dance had decided to leave that morning, and the noise and frantic activity that usually accompanied the break-

ing of camp was even worse than usual. Unlike the
other treks she had made in the past year, this time
she and Swift Rabbit traveled with Morning Star and
Moon Woman instead of at the back of the column of
women and children, as had befit a captive and an
old woman silly enough to befriend her. By midmorning, Brandy saw no particular advantage in
their new position other than the company the two
young women gave them and the opportunity to
hold Deer Runs Fast every now and then. It was just
as hot and dusty.

As they wound their way up into the broad mountain pass, Brandy glanced over her shoulder, then
brought the horse she was riding to a halt. In surprise, she turned in her saddle and looked over the
pile of household goods and hides on her travois at
the valley below her. She had expected to see the
tribes leaving the huge campsite in different directions, going the same ways they had come, but there
was a steady stream of Indians lined up behind them,
looking, from that height and distance, like a trail of
ants winding their way up the foothills. Brandy had
been with the Indians long enough to know that different tribes didn't ordinarily travel together, much
less make their summer camps together. It simply
wasn't practical. Their huge pony herds would
quickly eat off the surrounding grass and the hunters
would strip the area of all game.

That evening, when they had made camp, Brandy
asked Flaming Arrow, "Are we all going to the same
place, or are the other tribes going to split off from us
somewhere along the way?"

"No, the chiefs have decided that we will all make

our summer camps together this year in view of the white threat."

"But I thought you said you had beaten General Crook and his army so thoroughly, you didn't think they would be a threat for the rest of the summer," Brandy objected.

"It is not General Crook who is the threat. He has retreated to his supply base, and the Dakotas in that area will keep him occupied for a while. No, it is the other two armies that we are concerned about."

"What armies?" Brandy asked in surprise.

"A month ago, before Crook set out the second time, a large army under the command of General Terry left Fort Abraham Lincoln. Another under Colonel Gibbon left Fort Ellis. Our scouts have been keeping an eye on their progress, and recently they have come close enough to become a threat to us. We know they had made their supply base on the Yellowstone, at the mouth of the Powder River, and then early this morning, before daybreak, Crazy Horse received word that a part of the army was probing in the vicinity of the Rosebud. That is why we left so abruptly this morning. And it appears we left none too soon. The dust had barely settled after our departure than the army appeared."

Brandy's heart leaped in fear. "Then they're following us?"

"No. We assume they were simply scouting. They are traveling back north to the Yellowstone."

Brandy felt it had been a little too close a call for comfort. "How much farther is it to Greasy Grass?" she asked, wrinkling her nose at the Indians' name for the Little Bighorn River.

"One more day's march."

"It doesn't seem as if we're putting much distance between them and us," she said in an anxious voice, the army's close proximity making her feel very threatened.

Flaming Arrow saw the fear in her eyes. He reached across the small space that separated them with one hand and tenderly trailed his fingers down the side of her face. "Why are you afraid? Do you not know that I would protect you with my life?"

Brandy saw the naked love in his eyes and could almost feel his strength, his confidence, infusing her where his fingertips touched her skin. "Yes, I know," she admitted, closing the distance between them and slipping her arms around his waist. "It's just that I thought we could travel a little farther west."

Flaming Arrow put his arms around her and cradled her protectively against him for a moment. "We cannot go much farther, or else we would be in Crow country." He paused thoughtfully for a moment, then said, "At Greasy Grass we will make our stand, if there is one to be made. We are the strongest we have ever been, our numbers the greatest. Not even during Red Cloud's War were we this united. The white man has pushed us as far west as we will go." He drew back and looked her in the eye. "You see? We stand ready. There is no reason to fear," he reassured her. Then he bent his head and kissed her.

The next day they continued their trek across the Wolf Mountains, a low range that was actually a spur of the Big Horn Mountains, and late that afternoon reached their destination. Greasy Grass, a wide, rather shallow river meandered through an area where the fringes of the Great Plains broke against

the mountains. The land was furrowed, cut by many
ravines and creeks and wrinkled by hillocks and
ridges. On the west bank of the tree-shaded river, the
five tribal councils of Dakota and one of Cheyenne
settled down in a string of camps that stretched for
three miles along the watercourse and contained
well over fifteen hundred lodges and brush enclo-
sures and twelve to fifteen thousand Indians. Of
these, well over four thousand were warriors in their
prime, for more reservation Indians had joined them
daily after hearing the news of the victory at the
Battle of the Rosebud. The Cheyennes, under Two
Moon, set up their camp at the northern end, and
Chief Gall, King Crow, and Sitting Bull at the southern. Crazy Horse, Flaming Arrow, and the other Dakota chiefs threw up their tepees between the two.

On the third night, when Brandy and Flaming Arrow were preparing for bed, Flaming Arrow suddenly asked her, "What do you know about Long
Hair?"

The unexpected question took Brandy by surprise,
but there was no doubt in her mind that Flaming
Arrow was referring to Colonel George Custer. The
newspaper reporters who glorified the notorious Indian fighter were just as likely to refer to him as Long
Hair—the name given to him by the Indians because
of his long blond hair—as his given name. "Why do
you ask about Colonel Custer out of the clear blue?"

Flaming Arrow frowned. "Are you sure we're talking about the same man?"

"I'm positive. Long Hair is Colonel Custer."

"I thought he was a general."

"He was, during the War between the States, but
like everyone else who stayed in the army, his rank

was reduced after the war ended." Brandy paused, giving Flaming Arrow a piercing look. "But you still haven't told me why you asked about him."

"Do you remember I told you about the two armies that are searching for us?"

Brandy nodded.

"Well, they have left their base at the headwaters of the Powder River. One, under Colonel Gibbon, is marching up the Yellowstone. The other, under Long Hair, is marching down the Rosebud Creek. With Long Hair is Major Reno, the officer who led the scouting party I told you about the other day."

Brandy wasn't particularly alarmed at the news. They weren't camped on either the Yellowstone or the Rosebud, and she personally thought their new location so isolated and well hidden in the rugged territory that the armies would have a difficult time finding them. But there was something she was curious about. "I can understand how you know when the armies march and where they are. That's just a matter of observation. But how do you know the names of the officers?"

"We have friends, trappers like Crooked Nose, and men your people call mountain men, who are free to come and go at the forts. Their skin may be white, but their spirits are Indian. They tell us the names. And they know we are particularly interested in the whereabouts of Long Hair."

There was a dangerous glint in Flaming Arrow's dark eyes that made a shiver run up Brandy's spine. "Why Custer? My brother says he's not really that great an Indian fighter, although he claims to be."

"There are several reasons why Dakotas particularly hate him. First, it was Long Hair who led the horse soldiers who protected the party who surveyed the proposed route of the Northern Pacific Railroad. They were on Indian land and in violation of the Fort Laramie Treaty. We had several clashes with them, and they withdrew. Then the very next year, Long Hair led the expedition into the Black Hills, again in violation of the treaty, but the horse soldiers were in and out before we even knew they were there. Otherwise, we would have sent them running from there too. But we know for a fact that it was Long Hair who brought the wave of greedy prospectors down on us. We were told by a trapper friend that before he even left the Black Hills, Long Hair sent his scout to Fort Laramie where the nearest telegraph was to announce to the world that there were veins of gold on the side of almost every hill and that nuggets could be found among the roots of the grass. You saw those mountains. You know for yourself that was not true. He lied, and because of his lies, we now must fight again for our hunting ground. That is why the Dakotas are particularly interested in Long Hair. We have an old score to settle with him "

Brandy could have pointed out that General Sheridan had ordered Custer to violate the treaty, but she couldn't deny that Custer had played a big role in making the country burn with gold fever by his premature and much-exaggerated claims. What the trapper had told the Dakotas had been true. Custer hadn't been able to wait until he returned to his fort to spread the news about the discovery of gold in the Black Hills. Not only had he endangered the soldiers on the frontier by putting them in the precarious position of trying to turn the tide of greedy whites flooding into Indian territory, but he had also set into motion the events that had put the entire Dakota nation at risk.

With these thoughts in mind, Brandy responded, "Custer has a reputation for acting rashly. According to my brother, the other officers don't care for him or trust him. He's a terrible braggart, and the way he woos the press and seeks public attention disgusts them. They consider his behavior below that of an officer and a gentleman, particularly a West Point graduate. They all pretty much agree that he's nothing but a glory seeker, and none of them likes the way he sets aside rules for his own benefit. Paul said he brings an old Negro cook and a huge cast iron stove with him, even in the field, to say nothing of dragging an unruly pack of hound dogs everywhere he goes. And he seems to think that his wife should have privileges that other officers' wives don't. He takes her into the field with him, too, as well as younger male relatives he always has visiting him, so they can get in on the excitement. And as if he's trying to deliberately set himself aside from the other officers, he rarely wears a regulation uniform but instead a flamboyant one he's designed himself."

"Yet your people think of him as a great war chief?" Flaming Arrow asked in bewilderment. An Indian leader who behaved in such a manner would quickly lose his warriors' respect and his powerful position. "That is what out trapper friends tell us."

"Yes, he is thought of as a great military leader." Brandy gazed off into space for a moment. "It's really strange. The majority of the men he serves with have decided reservations about him, if not out-and-out dislike, but the American public adores him. They have ever since he caught their attention during the war, when he was made general at the age of twenty-three. They called him the boy general, and his acts of daring and bravery aroused their excitement. To give the devil his due, I suppose he does have a certain charisma about him. It seems that people either love him or hate him."

"Why did your brother say the other officers do not trust him?"

"Because of something that happened in a campaign Custer was leading against the Southern Cheyennes. It seems that one of his officers, a Major Elliot, and his company were cut off from the rest of the army. Had Custer gone looking for him, he could have saved the company from disaster, but he didn't. Elliot and his entire command were killed. Oh, Custer managed to come up with some excuse that satisfied his superiors, but since then, the other officers have never trusted him. Nor do his men like him. They call him Old Iron Butt because he's so hard on them. Once he was court-martialed and suspended from duty for an entire year for marching his troops beyond their endurance and abandoning two men who were later killed by Indians."

"Yet you said he is brave."

"Yes, according to all accounts he is. In battle, they say he's fearless—but terribly reckless," Brandy added as an afterthought.

Flaming Arrow carefully took note of everything Brandy had said about his hated enemy, particularly the last. He knew that reckless men often make mistakes, and if the mistake was lethal, it didn't matter how brave the man was.

* * *

Two days later, in the early hours of the afternoon Brandy was tending her cooking fire and talking to Swift Rabbit, who had dropped by for a visit. All around them, other women were tending their fires, while children played their games between the tents and the camp dogs dozed lazily in the afternoon heat. When Brandy heard the sound of hoofbeats, she turned to see a rider tearing down the side of the riverbank, frantically weaving his way around the women who were doing their washing there and yelling something unintelligible to Brandy. But apparently the women he had almost run down had heard. They dropped the trading blankets they were beating against the rocks or spreading over nearby bushes to dry and raced back up the bank to the camp, spreading the alarm that they were about to be attacked by the enemy.

The news momentarily stunned Brandy. She had no idea who the enemy was—the army or an unfriendly tribe. By the time she recovered, the entire camp was in a turmoil. Everyone ran here and there, as warriors dashed for their weapons and women frantically gathered their children. Then she saw Flaming Arrow running toward her. Without a word, he tore past her and into their tepee. Brandy followed him, but just as she bent to enter the tepee, he emerged wearing his war shirt and carrying his rifle.

"What's happening?" she asked.

"Sitting Bull's and Gall's camps are about to be attacked by horse soldiers coming up the river from the south. Stay here in our camp. We should be able to repulse them. You will be in no danger here."

As Flaming Arrow ran away to fetch his horse from

the huge herd grazing to the side of the long encampment, Brandy could hardly believe her ears. She could have sworn they had found a safe hiding place. Then seeing Yellow Fox running after his brother, she suddenly remembered something. She whirled around and muttered, "Oh, my God!"

Swift Rabbit had followed Brandy and was standing right behind her. Even though Brandy had muttered the words in English, the old Indian knew by the fearful expression on Brandy's face that something was terribly wrong. "What is it?"

"Flaming Arrow said the army is about to attack Sitting Bull's and Gall's camps. Morning Star and Moon Woman are down there, on the river."

"But why would they go there?"

"They said the water in the river here was too muddy to really clean their blankets. They wanted to go beyond where the camps lay, where there was no one and the water was still clear." Brandy turned and tore off, calling over her shoulder, "We've got to warn them!"

Brandy ran as fast as her legs would carry her. Swift Rabbit lagged behind despite her valiant efforts to keep up with the younger woman. They raced through the string of camps beside the river, dodging other Indians running helter-skelter here and there, and they were almost run down several times by warriors on their horses speeding to do battle with the intruders. When they reached Sitting Bull's camp, they kept on running, right through the line of warriors who were racing their horses back and forth to throw up a dust cloud to screen their preparations for the upcoming battle. As they came around a bend in the river, Brandy spied the two young Indian women kneeling beside the river in the distance and washing their blankets, totally oblivious to the danger they were in and the chaos in the camps upriver from them. Behind them, his cradle board propped against a rock so he could watch while they worked, Deer Runs Fast laughed and gurgled and waved his fat little fists in the air.

Then Brandy saw something that made her blood run cold. She missed a step and stumbled. Coming around another bend was a line of blue-coated cavalrymen, and waving above their heads was a swallow-tailed pennant with the red numeral seven on its bottom half. She thought of the shocking stories Swift Rabbit had told her about attacks by her army on Indian camps, of how the cavalrymen had slaughtered defenseless women and smashed their babies' skulls in with the butts of their guns. She knew that if she could see the soldiers, they could see the two defenseless women on the river bank.

Raw fear sent adrenaline flowing through her veins and gave her the strength to run even faster. Her moccasins sent the sand on the bank spraying out in a golden arc behind her as she yelled at the top of her lungs, "Look out! Run for your lives!"

Hearing her, Morning Star and Moon Woman looked up. The puzzled expressions on their faces told Brandy that they still hadn't realized the danger they were in. "Look behind you!"

The two girls turned and saw the soldiers coming down on them at a fast trot. Finally galvanized, they dropped the blanket they were washing, and Morning Star swooped up the baby's cradle board. Within seconds the two women, their dusky faces blanched of all color, came abreast of Brandy, who turned and

ran with them back down the riverbank. Behind
them, they could hear the pounding of the horses'
hooves.

They met Swift Rabbit just as they came around
the bend in the river, the old woman limping and
breathing hard. Brandy caught her arm and whirled
her around, jerking her hard, then pulling Swift
Rabbit after her as she ran. The four women tore
through the thick cloud of dust the warriors had
raised with the soldiers fast on their heels. Then bullets were flying everywhere as the Indian defenders
and the army suddenly came face to face.

"Get down!" Brandy yelled, for fear they would be
struck by a bullet in the cross fire.

Morning Star, Moon Woman, and Swift Rabbit sank
to a crouch, but Brandy pushed them facedown in
the dirt one by one. Then she threw a protective arm
over Morning Star, who was holding Deer Runs Fast
beneath her, and lay down beside them. Bullets and
arrows whizzed through the air over their heads;
dust and gunsmoke rolled all around them, and more
than once they were almost trampled by a horse's
sharp hooves. The noise of the battle invaded their
ears: the sharp crack of rifles, pounding hooves,
grunts and cries of pain, Indians yelling their blood-
chilling war cries, and cavalrymen cursing. A body
came flying down on them as a horse charged past
and landed beside Brandy with a loud thump. She
looked to the side and saw a dead trooper sprawled
on his back beside her, the feathers on the long lance
buried in his chest still quivering from the impact
and a look of horror frozen on his face.

Brandy didn't have time to feel anything for the
fallen soldier. She looked up and saw another caval-

ryman sitting on his horse above her, his rifle pointed
directly at Morning Star's back as his mount shied
nervously from all the noises. Brandy reacted instinctively, to protect both Morning Star and the baby
who lay beneath her. She grabbed the rifle the fallen
trooper had dropped, jumped to her feet, and fired.
The bullet hit the cavalryman square in the chest,
sending blood and tissue flying everywhere as he
flew backward from being hit at such close range.
The missile from his gun flew harmlessly into the air
as his skittish horse reared in fright. The rifle was still
smoking when Brandy saw Swift Rabbit rise to a
stand beside her, a quizzical look on her wrinkled,
leathery face. It was then that reason returned, and
Brandy realized she had killed one of her own people. But she felt no remorse. She was too incensed
that the trooper would try to kill an unarmed woman
and a helpless baby.

Then Brandy noticed that the cavalry was in a
frantic retreat. The howling, angry Dakotas were
racing after them, and she and the others were left in
a choking cloud of dust and gunsmoke. Curious to
know what was going on, she gave Morning Star and
Moon Woman strict orders to return to their camp.
Then, with Swift Rabbit stubbornly insisting upon
going with her, she made her way back to the bend in
the river, side-stepping bodies of the dead that were
strewn all over the battlefield.

At the bend of the river, the two women crouched
in the thick underbrush beneath a cottonwood tree.
Here they could see the battle line the cavalry had
drawn not far from where Morning Star and Moon
Woman had been washing their blankets. The
soldiers had dismounted to fight on foot, with their

right flank resting on the river and their left stretching toward some low hills. Beyond them, horse holders led their mounts to the protection of the thick woods.

For thirty minutes, Brandy and Swift Rabbit watched the battle, and it was clear from the very beginning that the army was fighting against fearful odds. The Dakotas charged again and again, putting constant pressure on the thin line of troops. Then it became obvious that the Indians were making their way around the left flank.

"Do you think they're going to attack them from the rear?" Brandy asked Swift Rabbit.

"I think they have in mind to stampede their horses. Then the horse soldiers will be trapped."

The old woman had hardly gotten the words out of her mouth when Brandy noticed that a large number of troopers were leaving the battle line and going to the rear. She assumed that the officer in charge had guessed what the Indians had in mind and had sent a part of his men to guard their mounts. But that left a gap in the battle line that the rest of the soldiers had to try to fill. There simply weren't enough men to do the job. The left flank was pushed back, and the Dakotas galloped around to the rear of the soldiers, and again the soldiers were forced to fall back, this time into the thick woods.

From then on, Brandy and Swift Rabbit couldn't see much of the battle—the thick underbrush and woods obscured their vision—but they could hear it. Roughly an hour after the cavalry had charged the Indian camp, Brandy saw the cavalry, once again mounted, coming from the woods. They tried to cross the river, but the Indians pursuing them were so close on their heels that they had to forsake that plan of action. The last Brandy saw, what was left of the cavalry force was racing down the river bank with the Dakotas nipping at their heels.

Brandy and Swift Rabbit stayed where they were for about thirty minutes, waiting to see what might happen next. They knew a furious fight was taking place farther down river, for they could hear the almost steady gunfire. Suddenly, the sounds dwindled until just a sporadic crack of a rifle could be heard. Then, much to Brandy's surprise, she saw the Dakotas rushing madly back up the river bank. The long column was riding so close together that she couldn't tell if Flaming Arrow was with them or not. She waited, filled with dread, thinking the cavalry must have received reinforcements and were in pursuit, but when no soldiers appeared, her dread was replaced with puzzlement.

"Where do you think they were going in such a hurry?" she asked Swift Rabbit. But the old woman was just as baffled as she and answered with a shrug of her shoulders.

Then Brandy heard it—a slight rustling of leaves in the underbrush in the woods beside them. Swift Rabbit heard it too. She picked up the gun Brandy had put down and cautiously rose to her feet. As she crept into the underbrush, Brandy rose and followed her, whispering, "Where are you going?"

"The white-eyes must have left their wounded when they retreated. I think the sound we heard was from one of them. We will find him and take him back to our camp to torture."

Brandy was horrified. Killing a man to protect those she cared for was one thing, but torturing someone was something she could never do. She quickly followed Swift Rabbit, determined to stop her before the old woman could find the wounded man if that was indeed who had made the noise. But following the old woman through the thick, thorny underbrush wasn't easy, and by the time she caught up with her, Swift Rabbit was pushing aside the limb of a bush with one hand.

Brandy came to halt, her eyes widening when she saw the soldier lying behind the bush where he had collapsed. His left pants leg was covered with blood, and he was unconscious. "No!" she whispered in a voice filled with horror.

"Are you talking about torturing him?" Swift Rabbit asked, a disgusted look on her face. "I had hoped you were truly one of us when you shot that other white-eyes, but I guess you're still squeamish in some things." She pointed the rifle at the soldier and said, "Then we will just kill him."

"No!" Brandy cried out, pushing the barrel of the gun aside.

"If we do not kill him, the others will find him and torture him. It will be an act of mercy."

"Then help me hide him, quickly before they come!" When Swift Rabbit just stood and stared at her, Brandy pleaded, "Please help me! If you care anything about me at all, help me." Tears welled in her eyes. "That man is my brother!"

24

When Brandy had seen her brother lying beneath the bush, she had been bombarded with a series of emotions coming so rapidly on one another that it was hard to tell where one ended and the other began. First she had been filled with utter disbelief to find her brother there, for she had thought he was with General Crook's army far to the south, then horror when she had seen the blood all over him, then fear for his life when Swift Rabbit had pointed the rifle at him. Now, kneeling beside her beloved brother and looking down at his handsome, familiar features, she was filled with love and an incredible happiness at seeing him again. She was so caught up in her joy that she momentarily forgot the danger he was in, until Swift Rabbit reminded her by saying, "If we're going to hide him, we had better hurry."

Brandy scrambled to her feet, then bent, saying, "He's too heavy for us to lift. We'll have to drag him. I'll take one arm and you the other."

Swift Rabbit helped Brandy drag her brother to a ravine studded with thick brush and place him in a cavelike depression that had been hollowed out beneath the roots of a huge cottonwood during one of the times the deep gully had flooded. The move exhausted both women, for Paul had been dead weight, and it took them a few moments to regain their breath and their strength. Then Swift Rabbit said, "If we do not stop the bleeding in that leg, your brother will die anyway."

The old woman's ominous words gave Brandy the impetus to act. She rose from where she had collapsed beside her brother, knelt on her knees, and quickly cut away the material of his pants with her skinning knife, revealing the gaping bullet hole in Paul's thigh. "Do you think the bullet is still in there?" she asked Swift Rabbit.

"Look at the back of his leg. If you see a hole there, then the bullet went through."

Thankfully, the bullet had gone through, and Swift Rabbit helped Brandy apply a tight bandage made from the material of Paul's coat to stay the bleeding. That done, the old woman calmly announced that she thought the bone was broken, and she fashioned a splint of small limbs to support the leg. During this time, the two women could hear gunshots in the distance and knew another fierce battle was being fought. What they didn't know was where, for it was difficult to tell which direction the sounds came from in the dense woods.

After the two women had finished with the splint,

Brandy sat back on her heels and looked her brother over more closely. He was breathing, but his face was terribly pale, and she feared they were too late to save his life. An icy feeling surrounded her heart, and tears swam in her eyes. To have miraculously found him, and then lose him, would be a terribly bitter pill to swallow. Then Paul aroused enough to mutter, "Water," and Brandy was so relieved that she cried out softly, "Oh, thank you, God!"

With hands that shook from the release of the tension she had been feeling, Brandy removed the canteen that hung on Paul's belt and uncapped it. As she lifted his shoulders to place the canteen against his lips, she realized it felt light. She shook it, then said to Swift Rabbit, "It's empty."

"Give it to me. I will take it down to the river and fill it."

A moment after Swift Rabbit had left the shallow cave, Brandy saw Paul's eyelids flutter open. She leaned over him as he looked up at her in a daze, then asked in a disbelieving voice, "Brandy?"

"Yes," Brandy answered with an elated half-sob.

"Oh, my God, it's really you!" Paul cried out, his eyes lighting up with happiness. "I thought I was hallucinating."

"Yes, it's really me," Brandy replied with a shaky voice. Tears that had been hovering in her eyes spilled over and ran down her cheeks.

Despite his weakened state, Paul slipped his arms around Brandy and hugged her tightly, saying in a rush of words, "I still can't believe it. I had almost given up hope of ever finding you. I was so worried about you, but I absolutely refused to believe you were dead. I couldn't have stood that. Oh, God, I'm so happy to see you! I didn't think I ever would again."

Brandy hugged him back just as fiercely and said, "I didn't think I would ever see you again, either, and I've missed you so much."

Paul pulled back and said with an earnest look on his face, "I looked for you. I volunteered for every patrol the army sent out against the Kiowas, but you were in none of their villages."

"I knew you would search for me."

"You're damn right I did! I was prepared to search to the ends of the earth for you. I'd planned to leave the army as soon as my enlistment expired this fall so I could spend all of my time just searching for you." He dropped his arms and lay weakly back down, his eyes skimming over her Indian dress. "But I'll have to admit, I never would have thought to look for you among the Sioux. How did you get here? We thought the Kiowas wiped out that company of men you were traveling with."

"It *was* the Kiowas, but I wasn't with the soldiers when the Indians attacked. I was off in some woods, where I hid. Later, the leader of a Dakota raiding party found me and made me his captive."

Paul had known Brandy was a captive from the very beginning, and it didn't matter if she was a Kiowa captive or a Sioux—her fate would have been the same. Being forced to look at all the terrible things it entailed had not been easy for him. Thinking of Brandy as someone's slave, working herself to the bone, being deprived of food and perhaps shelter, being scorned, possibly beaten, had filled him with anger and pain. But what had really agonized him was wondering if she had been sexually defiled.

To him, that was a special hell set aside for women, and the thought of her suffering that pain and that terrible degradation was almost more than he could bear. Now that he had found her—or rather, she had found him—he had to know. "Did he—" Paul hesitated. He hated to use the word *rape*. It had such an ugly sound to it. But then that was what the act was— ugly and brutal. "Did he harm you?"

Brandy knew what her brother was asking. They were so close, they could almost read each other's minds. "No, he didn't harm me in any way."

Paul felt immense relief. Brandy certainly didn't look as if she had particularly suffered. He had never seen her looking so beautiful. Even her unladylike tan couldn't detract from it. If anything, it only made her remarkable blue eyes stand out even more.

Having reassured himself of her good condition, Paul struggled to his elbows and looked about him. Since he didn't remember the cave, he assumed that Brandy had dragged him here and bandaged his leg. Then seeing the splint, he asked, "Is it broken?"

"Yes, I'm afraid so."

"No wonder it hurt so damn much. I couldn't bear to walk on it." Paul gazed off, a furious expression coming over his face. "That goddamned Custer! If I could get my hands on him right now, I'd kill him!"

"He was leading the army that attacked the village?"

"No, Major Reno was. Custer ordered us to attack and promised he'd back us up. That lying bastard! He deserted us!"

"Wait a minute," Brandy said in a gentle voice she hoped would calm her irate brother. "Back up, please. There are some questions I need answered.

What are you doing here with Custer and the Seventh Cavalry? You were in the Third Cavalry. I thought you were with General Crook."

"I was transferred last winter, when Sheridan was planning this expedition against the Sioux. He was trying to shore up the Seventh. He had enough recruits to fill the ranks, but not enough officers." A look of pure disgust came over Paul's face. "I don't have to tell you how I felt about being transferred. Of all the goddamned officers I could have been assigned to serve under—-Custer! And it turned out everything I always suspected about him was true. He's the most arrogant bastard to ever walk the earth. Before we marched away from our supply base, General Terry suggested that Custer reinforce his column from Colonel Gibbon's, but Custer refused. He claimed that the Seventh was such a closely knit group that reinforcements from another unit would add nothing to its strength. That's a bunch of hogwash! Like I said, a good deal of the Seventh is made up of raw recruits who have never seen action, much less fought together before. Then Custer refused Terry's offer of three Gatling guns, saying they would embarrass him. God, what I would have given for a Gatling a few hours ago!"

Paul paused to catch his breath, then lay back down and stared at the dirt ceiling of the shallow cave for a long moment. Then he continued. "Refusing to accept reinforcements and those guns was contemptuous enough, but then Custer turned around and disobeyed orders. General Terry had explicitly told him before we left the Yellowstone that if he picked up an Indian trail on the Rosebud going west across the Wolf Mountains, he was *not* to follow it.

Instead, he was to follow the Rosebud south past its headwaters, then swing west and come up the valley of the Little Bighorn, while Gibbon's army marched from the opposite direction. Custer ignored Terry's orders and made his own plan of operation. Instead of following the Rosebud south, we followed the Indian trail west over the mountains. Custer knew it was a big band we were tracking. Hell, any idiot would have known that from all those hoofprints and travois markings. Then this morning, the Crow scouts confirmed from a high point in the mountains they call the Crow's Nest that there was a huge Sioux camp beside the Little Bighorn. Custer rode up there and had a look himself, but by that time a haze had covered the valley, and he couldn't see anything. Custer told us he didn't think there were any Indians there. It wasn't until we discovered several Indians watching our movements that we realized there *were* Indians in the vicinity, and once more, they knew of our whereabouts. Custer decided to attack at once. Then he did something that he would have court-martialed any of us junior officers for doing. He split his column—not once, but into four different groups. He sent Captain Benteen and his men southwest to investigate some bluffs and any valleys that might be beyond them. Then he split what was left between Major Reno, himself, and a pack train. He took the north side of a creek that the Crow scouts said emptied into the river, and we took the south bank, with the pack train and the better part of our ammunition trailing way behind Custer."

"But I thought you said Custer ordered you to attack the village," Brandy objected, interrupting her brother's story for the first time. "How could he do that if you were separated?"

"He sent his adjutant, Lieutenant Cooke, over to give the order to Major Reno. I was beside the major and heard the order. Cooke said, 'General Custer directs that you take as fast a gait as you deem necessary and charge the village, and you will be supported by the entire outfit.' "

"And you really believe Custer deliberately abandoned you?"

"I know he did!" Paul answered, his face contorted in fury.

"But how can you be so sure?"

"Shortly after we had ridden into battle, I looked up, and through a break in the bluffs along the river, I saw a part of Company E, the Gray Horse Company. You know how the cavalry separates the different companies by designating a certain color horse to each company. Well, Company E was with Custer, and if I could see them, they could see us. Custer knew the desperate position we were in and abandoned us, just as he'd done before. That goddamned bastard! He didn't want to share the glory with the others. That's why he disobeyed orders. And he'd always bragged that the Seventh could beat any Indian force on the plains. He thought the Seventh was invincible, under *his* command. Well, you saw how invincible we were. Christ, it was a slaughter! There must have been hundreds of warriors in that village."

"No, thousands."

A shocked look came over Paul's face. "You're joking."

"No, there must be between four and five thousand warriors in the various camps. They knew you were coming, you know. They knew when you left the Yellowstone. They were waiting for you, although I'll have to admit that they didn't realize you were going to attack this afternoon until you were almost upon us."

Paul was pensive for a long moment as he absorbed what Brandy had told him. Sheridan had hoped to catch the Indians in their camps by surprise, to catch them napping if possible and wipe out every man, woman, and child. Instead, the Sioux had turned the tables on them.

It was Brandy who broke the silence. "I have one more question. Did you know there were women and children in that camp when you attacked it?"

Paul shot Brandy a quick glance, then finding he couldn't look her in the eye, he averted his and answered in a hard voice, "This is war, Brandy. It isn't pretty."

"The struggle between the states was war, too, but you didn't attack towns and villages indiscriminately. Even after you verified that the enemy was actually there, you gave the women and children a chance to escape before you attacked."

"Dammit, we were ripped to ribbons this afternoon!"

"That's beside the point! I'm talking about what your intention was. Did you think that camp was unprotected? Did you think the men were away hunting? Did you mean to ride in and murder helpless women and children? I've heard stories since I've been with the Indians that that's what the army does, and I want to know the truth."

"Custer gave the order. I don't know what his intentions were. But I do know a lot of good soldiers are dead now because of him."

Brandy thought her brother's answer evasive. She could have pointed out that a lot of good Dakotas were dead because of Custer, too, Indians who had been minding their own business.

Paul cocked his head at a sound. "That's gunfire. Can you tell which direction it's coming from?"

Brandy strongly suspected Paul was trying to change the subject, but she didn't object. She thought it pointless to pursue the conversation they had been having. She had found out what she had wanted to know. "Not really. But I do know I saw the rest of Reno's men retreating the way they came after they came out of the woods."

"Yeah," Paul muttered, remembering the battle. "God, it was a nerve-wracking fighting in those woods. The Indians were all around us, shooting from behind every bush and tree, hitting both men and horses. Reno gave the order to mount. It was a verbal order, and a lot of men didn't hear him. Just then, several Sioux burst into the clearing we were standing in and let go with a volley. One of the bullets caught me in my mounting leg and another hit Bloody Knife, Custer's favorite scout, in the head. He was the only Indian who didn't desert us when he heard we were going to attack the Sioux, and he was standing so close to the major that the bullet splattered blood and brains all over Reno. It upset the major so badly that it addled him. He gave the order to dismount, then to mount again, but before I could try to drag myself up to my saddle, my horse broke loose from me and ran off. I thought it was all over for me for sure, but I guess the Sioux figured I wouldn't

go anywhere and I could wait. They all took off after
Reno." Paul paused and listened. "Damn, I wish I
knew what was going on out there."

At that moment, Swift Rabbit appeared, and Paul
gasped in surprise when he saw her. "There's nothing to be alarmed about," Brandy assured him.
"That's Swift Rabbit. She's my friend."

"Friend?" Paul asked in a scornful tone of voice.
"She's a squaw!"

"Don't use that term!" Brandy said in a firm voice,
her blue eyes suddenly flashing. "It's derogatory and
hateful. She's my friend, and if it weren't for her, you
could well have bled to death by now. She was the
one that bandaged and set your leg, after she helped
me drag you here to hide you from the others."

Paul gave Brandy a long, piercing look. "You've
changed."

"Yes, I have. I've grown up in the past year, and
Swift Rabbit played a very important role in that.
And I don't hate Indians anymore. So don't insult
them in my presence."

Paul didn't know what to say. The fierce young
woman beside him suddenly seemed like a stranger.

Swift Rabbit handed the canteen to Brandy. "We
must go. The sun will be setting soon, and Flaming
Arrow will return to camp. If he does not find you
there, he will come looking."

Brandy had completely forgotten about Flaming
Arrow. The last she had seen him, he had been riding
off to do battle with the soldiers coming down on
them. But strangely, she wasn't in the least frightened for him. Briefly, she wondered if it was because
she had such total confidence in his ability to take
care of himself, or because she had seen how badly

the new recruits were shooting and knew that there had been few Indian casualties. Then pushing those thoughts aside, she asked Swift Rabbit, "Then you won't tell him about my brother?"

"No, I will not tell. But you must not come back here. It would be too dangerous."

"But my brother will need more water, and food. I'll have to come back."

"It would be very risky. If the others should find you hiding him—"

Swift's Rabbit's voice trailed off. But she didn't have to finish her sentence. Brandy knew what would happen to her if the others discovered she was hiding one of the enemy. That would be considered treachery, punishable by death. No, not even the fact that she was a chief's wife would save her. She would just have to be very cautious.

Brandy turned to her brother, helped him to a semisitting position, and placed the canteen against his lips. She said as he drank, "I've got to go, before Flaming Arrow returns and finds me missing."

Paul finished drinking and took the canteen from Brandy. "Flaming Arrow? Is that the name of the man who captured you?"

"Yes," Brandy answered, easing him back down to the ground.

"Stay here," Paul said, catching hold of one of Brandy's hands with his. "Hide with me. Colonel Gibbon and his army are bound to show up sooner or later."

"No, I can't."

"Why not? Because she'll tell?" Paul asked, motioning to Swift Rabbit, who was already backing down the incline of the ravine beside the cave.

"No, she promised she wouldn't tell. But he'll come looking for me. And he'll find me too. I know because he tracked me down once before, in an area much more rugged than this."

Paul wondered at her captor's possessiveness, and yet she had said he had not harmed her.

Brandy pried her hand loose. "I'll come back, when it's safe. In the meanwhile, keep very quiet. There are other women out in these woods looking for white survivors from the battle. I don't have to tell you what they will do to you if they find you."

A shiver ran over Paul, and for the first time, he realized just how fortunate he was that Brandy and her friend had discovered him first. He watched as Brandy pulled some grapevines over the entrance of the cave to conceal it, then listened to her footsteps as they grew fainter.

Then the only sound was that of the gunshots in the distance, and the darkness seemed to intensify them. God, Paul thought, he wished to hell he knew what was going on out there.

25

No one paid any attention to Brandy and Swift Rabbit as they made their way back through the line of camps to their own. It was assumed that they were doing what so many of the other Indian women were doing—rushing from camp to camp trying to collect news of the fighting. By the time Brandy reached her tepee, dusk was falling, and she barely had time to get a fire going before the guns in the distance fell silent.

She expected to see Flaming Arrow ride in at any moment, particularly after she saw some of the others returning, cheering and waving their rifles over their heads, a few even discharging bullets into the air. Then, just when she was beginning to get a little apprehensive, he appeared. Quickly she scanned his body to assure herself that he was not wounded; then

seeing he was unharmed, her eyes shone with relief
and happiness.

The same look was mirrored in Flaming Arrow's
dark eyes. For a moment he sat on his mount and
stared at her, his look so warm and loving that
Brandy thought her heart would melt and her bones
turn to water. Then, remembering his displeasure
with her, a scowl crossed his dusty face.

Brandy saw the deep frown. It puzzled her, for she
thought he would have been elated at the Dakotas'
victory. As he dismounted beside her, swinging from
his mount in a graceful arc that belied his exhaustion,
she asked, "What's wrong? You seem unhappy about
something."

He towered over her, and the look on his face
would have made his strongest warrior cringe. "I am.
I thought I told you to stay in this camp."

Brandy assumed that he had found out about her
brother some way or another, and she couldn't hide
the guilty flush that rose on her face. Her heart thud-
ded in fear of what he would do, not to to her, but to
her brother.

"Morning Star and Moon Woman told me what you
did. That was very brave—and very foolish."

A wave of relief washed over Brandy when she
realized he didn't know about her brother. "Oh,
that."

"Oh, that?" Flaming Arrow thundered, remembering the terrible fear he had felt when the two
young women had told him the story. "Is that all you
can say? Don't you realize you could have been
killed?"

Suddenly, Brandy realized why Flaming Arrow
was so upset. He was afraid for her life. Knowing he

cared that deeply sent a little thrill running through her, for Brandy had not grown so accustomed to his love that she took it for granted. But it didn't make his anger any less unreasonable. "And would you have had me do any differently?" she asked. "Should I have just let them and your godson be killed?"

"You could have sent someone else."

"Who? All the warriors had ridden off with you."

Brandy saw a helpless expression come over Flaming Arrow's face, and she knew she had made her point. She slipped her arms around his waist and leaned her head on his chest, not caring in the least if the dust and gunpowder there rubbed off on her. "Don't be angry with me," she said softly. "I didn't really have any choice, any more than you do when you ride off to battle." She lifted her head and looked him in the eye. "Now maybe you know how I feel when your life is in danger."

Flaming Arrow didn't know what to say. Brandy had disarmed him completely with her logic. But still, just the memory of his fear left him feeling weak.

Brandy turned back to her fire and dished up a bowl of stew from a pot hanging over it, then handed it to Flaming Arrow. "Now, eat, before it grows cold. Then you can tell me what has been going on."

After they had eaten, Flaming Arrow told Brandy about the battle just outside Sitting Bull's camp and how they had forced the army to retreat. Brandy didn't point out that she had been there and seen it. She thought it prudent not to remind Flaming Arrow of her close call with death.

"Then we received word that there was another

column of soldiers to the east of the river, and we left a few of our men to pursue the first column while we attacked the second," Flaming Arrow continued, solving the mystery for Brandy about why the warriors had suddenly rushed off. "Gall and his warriors crossed the river and hit them from the south, while Crazy Horse, Two Moon, and myself led our men in a sweep to the north. The column was caught between us. The horse soldiers managed to make it to a ridge, where they tried to set up a battle line, but their situation was hopeless. Not only were they facing overwhelming odds, but because of all of the gullies and hills, they were forced to dismount and fight on foot. They didn't have a ghost of a chance. They were in the wide open, and most of their horses had stampeded, so they couldn't even use them as breastworks. They fought back to back, the cluster of men growing smaller and smaller, for we had them completely surrounded. In the end, it was a fierce hand-to-hand combat among the thick swirling dust and drifting gunsmoke, and a total victory for us. Every white-eyes was killed."

"Every single man?" Brandy asked in a shocked voice.

"Yes. Over two hundred horse soldiers. But I must admit they fought bravely. Not a single one tried to escape. Nor did they beg for their lives. Each and every one fought to the bloody end." Flaming Arrow paused, then said, "We stripped them and left them lying there. We had hoped to find Long Hair among them, but there was no man there with long blond hair. We assume he was leading the column of men who reinforced the first column we sent fleeing back down the river."

From what her brother had told her, Brandy knew
the cavalry column the Dakotas had wiped out had to
be Custer's. He and his men had been on the east side
of the river. But what had happened to Custer if he
hadn't been found with the other dead? she wondered. Had he deserted them, too, and run for his
life? And if his column had been totally annihilated,
the cavalry column that had reinforced Reno's must
have been Benteen's. "Where is the army now?"

"On some high grassy hills overlooking the river,
about halfway between the thick woods where they
first retreated and the creek that they followed here.
The two columns are digging in there, trying to make
a breastwork out of saddles and anything they can
find that will stop a bullet."

And probably wondering where Custer's column
was, Brandy thought.

"At daybreak, we will attack them again," Flaming
Arrow continued, "and hopefully claim another complete victory. They are in as desperate a situation as
the column of horse soldiers we caught out in the
open. They're surrounded, without water. Their ammunition won't hold out forever. It will just be a
matter of time."

The thought of a second slaughter sickened
Brandy, and yet she couldn't in her heart feel anger
at the Dakotas. The army had come looking for a
fight, had attacked them without provocation. The
Indians had just been protecting their homes. No, if
anyone was to blame for the terrible defeat the army
had suffered that day, for the needless bloodshed of
so many men, it was Custer. Damn, where in the
devil had the arrogant bastard gone? If she knew,
she'd go after him herself.

* * *

Dawn came early the next day, the second-longest day of the year, particularly in that high latitude. Brandy was glad when Flaming Arrow and the others rode out a little after three in the morning, for a good many of the warriors had danced the entire night and the wild beating of the tom-toms and their repetitious chanting and bloodcurdling yelling had not only kept her awake but wrought havoc on her nerves. But Brandy didn't try to catch a few hours of sleep. While Flaming Arrow was gone, under cover of the grayness that preceded the dawn of the new day, she slipped away from the camp and into the woods where her brother was hidden.

By the time the sun came over the horizon, Brandy had reached the cave. As soon as she pushed aside the thick screen of grapevines and Paul realized it was she, he said, "Thank God you're back. I've been going crazy in here wondering what's going on out there. I heard the first shots a while ago."

Brandy sat beside him and handed him a piece of roasted rabbit from the basket of food she had brought with her. "Those shots are coming from some tall hills to the south of here, where Reno fled after he left these woods. He was reinforced by another column of men, who I assume must have been Benteen's."

"Then Custer never came back with his column of men?"

"He couldn't, or rather, they couldn't. His entire column was wiped out. It happened shortly after Reno fell back from these woods."

Paul was stunned. For a moment, he just stared at

Brandy. Then he asked in a voice that cracked with emotion, "Every last man?"

"Yes, I'm afraid so."

"Where in the hell were they?"

"To the east of the northernmost end of the Indian camps, in a wide-open grassland where they had no protection. The Indians came at them from both the north and the south and caught them in a vise."

For a long moment, Paul silently mulled over the disastrous news. Then he said in a bitter voice, "Well, I guess Custer's little brother and nephew got to see the excitement he brought them along to see. God-damned fool! Dragging youths along on an expedition to round up Indians! Somebody should have put a stop to it. And he shouldn't have brought along that newspaper reporter, either, but you know how Custer loved to be in the limelight. He wanted a firsthand account of how he'd whipped the Indians. Well, he gained immortality, all right, but that reporter won't be writing the story, the poor bastard."

"Flaming Arrow said Custer wasn't with them, that there was no man there with long blond hair."

"Custer didn't have long blond hair. Not yesterday. Before we left Fort Abraham Lincoln, he ran the horse clippers over his head and sheared his hair off to the scalp."

"Then you think he was with the others?"

"Why do you ask that?"

"You said Custer had deserted his men before and that he knew Reno's column was in a desperate situation. I thought he might have realized what a terrible mistake he'd made and run off."

Paul thought over what Brandy had said, then remarked, "I don't think Custer would go that far. He was arrogant, impetuous, high-handed, but I don't think he was a coward. Did Flaming Arrow say anything about a man in a fancy buckskin suit? That's what Custer was wearing."

"No, he didn't. But then, I wouldn't have asked a question like that, even if I had known. I wasn't supposed to know it was Custer's column, remember?"

Paul's brow furrowed. Then he commented, "I've been thinking about the man who captured you. You said he had followed you and found you before. You tried to escape?"

"Yes."

"And what did he do to you when he found you? Did he punish you?"

"No."

Paul gave Brandy a long hard look, then said, "I find that strange. From what I've seen of Indians, they can be very harsh. Just who is this man?"

"He's a Lakota chief."

A look of relief came over Paul's face. "Oh, I think I understand. He's a much older man. He looks upon you like a daughter, or a granddaughter, perhaps."

Brandy laughed. "Not hardly. He's young, handsome, and very virile."

Again Paul's brow furrowed. "Then what is your relationship with him?

"He's my husband."

Paul felt as if he'd been kicked by a mule. He sucked in his breath sharply. When he had recovered from the shocking news, he said, "I thought you said he hadn't harmed you."

"He hasn't. He's never hurt me in any manner."

Paul stared at Brandy for a moment, then took her hand in his and said in a gentle voice, "Brandy, it's okay. I understand. He forced you to—lie with him. I know it's not your fault. You can be honest with me. I don't blame you. You've nothing to be ashamed of. He's the one who behaved like an animal."

Fury rose in Brandy. She jerked her hand away and said angrily, "He's not an animal! He's a man. A wonderful man! And he didn't force me. I wanted him to make love to me. I wanted to marry him." She paused to give her words emphasis. "I love him."

Seeing the horrified expression coming over Paul's face, Brandy continued in an angry voice, "Don't look at me like I've lost my mind! I know perfectly well what I'm saying. I'm not a spoiled little girl anymore. I'm a grown woman who knows what she wants. And I'm proud to be Flaming Arrow's wife."

The look of horror on Paul's face was replaced with one of contempt. As he opened his mouth to speak, Brandy cut across his words. "No! Don't say anything. I know what you're thinking. That I'm the lowest thing on earth because I consort with an Indian, an 'animal,' as you called him, a 'savage.' Well, let me tell you something. Not only is Flaming Arrow just as human as you, but he's more man than any white man I ever met. He's as strong as a rock, the most self-assured person I've ever met, brave and dedicated, yet sensitive and gentle. He's as honest as the day is long, and he doesn't know the meaning of conceit or selfishness." Brandy paused, seeing yet another expression on her brother's face: disbelief. She slammed to her feet and walked to the entrance of the cave. "I'm wasting my breath talking to you. You've already formed your opinion. Think what you like!"

As Brandy started to step from the cave, Paul

called out, "No, wait!" Brandy turned, her body rigid with anger. "Everything is coming at me too fast. And I've never seen you like this—so—so intense."

"That's because I've never felt this strongly about anyone else. I told you. I love him."

"Then come and sit down beside me and tell me about it. From the beginning."

"That might take a while."

Paul smiled and answered, "I'm not going anywhere. I have all day."

It was the smile that did it. It was so warm and genuine that Brandy couldn't hold on to her anger. She walked back and sat beside her brother. She was still talking hours later, relating how she had shared Flaming Arrow's experience in the Sun Dance. Both were so involved in her story that neither noticed that the gunshots in the distance had dwindled away to almost nothing. Then a shadow fell across the mouth of the cave. They both gasped as they looked up and saw Flaming Arrow standing in the entrance, a furious look on his face.

Terrified he might do something to Paul, Brandy jumped to her feet and put herself between the two men, crying out "No, don't hurt him! He's my brother!"

"I know who he is!"

Flaming Arrow's answer stunned Brandy, until she spied Swift Rabbit standing behind him. "You promised you wouldn't tell!" Brandy said in an accusing voice.

"I had to tell," the old woman answered, stepping from behind Flaming Arrow. "You would not want to be left behind, would you?"

"What are you talking about?"

"Word has arrived that there is a big army coming down on us from the north," Flaming Arrow informed her. "The chiefs have met and decided that we will not make another stand here. We are running low on ammunition. We are leaving immediately!"

As Flaming Arrow moved toward Paul, Brandy caught his arm. "No, please, don't hurt him. If you care anything about me, don't harm him."

Flaming Arrow jerked his arm from her grasp and answered in a tightly controlled voice, "I do not harm unarmed men. I am going to move him."

"You mean take him prisoner?" Brandy asked, switching from the Dakota tongue to English. "That's worse than killing him right on the spot."

"I do not want him as a prisoner. I am moving him from the woods to the river, where he won't be caught in the prairie fire we intend to light between us and the army that is marching down on us." Flaming Arrow pushed Brandy to the side, saying gruffly, "Now, move aside. You are slowing us down."

Flaming Arrow knelt on one knee beside Paul, then took one of Paul's arms and placed him over his broad shoulder. As he came to a stand, Paul objected. "I can walk if you'll just support me."

"That would take too long," Flaming Arrow answered. "I told you. We are in a hurry."

Flaming Arrow carried Paul from the cave, down the ravine, and through the sun-dabbled woods, with Brandy and Swift Arrow hurrying behind. Paul was amazed by the Dakota's strength and the speed with which he walked. He had no idea that Flaming Arrow was accustomed to carrying deer across his shoulders that weighed not much less. When they cleared the trees, Flaming Arrow stopped and looked both ways down the river. Then, seeing no one, he carried Paul to the edge of the water and set him down.

A piece of paper fluttered by, and Brandy reached down and caught it. "What's this money doing here?"

"It was all over the battlefield yesterday," Flaming Arrow informed her, "and today it is blowing all over the camps."

Brandy turned to Paul and gave him a questioning look. "It must have come from Custer's men," Paul answered, "since the wind is blowing from that direction. You see, we didn't get paid until we were one day out of Fort Abraham Lincoln. Custer took it upon himself to hold our pay back. He didn't want the men spending it in the fleshpots in Bismarck."

And now they would spend it nowhere, Brandy thought sadly.

Ever since Brandy had planted the seed of suspicion in his mind about Custer running and deserting even his own column of men, Paul hadn't been able to forget it. Now, before, Flaming Arrow left, he had to know. "You were at the massacre yesterday, weren't you?"

Flaming Arrow stiffened, and his black eyes flashed. "It was *not* a massacre! It was a battle in which your men were outnumbered and outfought. There was no mutilations, and very few scalpings."

"All right," Paul said in tone of voice meant to soothe Flaming Arrow. "I didn't mean to upset you. But there is something I want to know. Did you see a man dressed in buckskins among the dead? Not ordinary buckskins. The jacket was double-breasted."

"Yes, I saw that scout before another Dakota

stripped him. He had been shot in the head and chest and was lying beside a red and blue flag with white-crossed sabers."

"Christ! That wasn't a scout. That was Custer! That was his personal pennant."

"No, it was not Long Hair," Flaming Arrow objected. "That man's hair was so short that he was almost bald. No one even bothered to scalp him, although he fought bravely. With no hair, his scalp was worthless."

"Custer ran horse clippers over his head before we rode out on this expedition. He was almost bald except for a stubble."

Flaming Arrow remembered the blond stubble on the man's head. A sudden light came into his eyes, and a smile spread across his lips. "So Long Hair, our old enemy, is dead," he muttered. "Yes, yesterday was a good day for the Dakotas."

Paul heard Flaming Arrow's words and answered grimly, "No, Flaming Arrow, you're wrong. You're dead wrong. Yesterday was the worst day in Sioux history."

"You are insane! We killed our old enemy, Long Hair. We won a great victory."

"Precisely. That's my point. You won *too* great a victory. Never has the American army been beaten so badly, so totally by any Indian force. The American people will never forgive you for that. If you had left just a few men alive, it might have been different. But your victory was too complete. The people will be shocked when they hear the news. And the timing is very bad. Right now our country is celebrating its centennial, its hundredth birthday. Patriotism is running very high. The newspapers will call it a massacre. Then the people will cry out in outrage for vengeance, and the army will be more than happy to punish you, for this terrible defeat will embarrass them. As for Long Hair? Killing him didn't help you any either, at least not as far as the American public goes. They've always been blind to his faults, and now that he's added tragedy to his legend, he'll be even more of a hero. Your nation is doomed, Flaming Arrow. You'll never know another minute's peace. You'll be hounded, chased until there is no place to run. And still that won't be enough to satisfy the American people. They'll want to wipe you from this earth, just as you did that column of men. No, yesterday was not a great day. It was the beginning of the end for your nation."

Paul knew by the sober look that had come over Flaming Arrow's face that the chief was giving all he had said serious consideration. He paused for a moment to give the Dakota time to digest it all, then said, "You don't want Brandy living like that. Being chased like a wild animal. You don't want her to share your fate. Let her stay here with me so I can take her back where it's safe."

Flaming Arrow sensed that everything Paul had said was true, and at that moment his perplexing vision was very much in mind. As much as he hated to give Brandy up, he knew it would be for her good. He turned and looked at her, his dark eyes so full of love and longing that it tore at Paul's heart. Then he said, "Your brother is correct. It is too dangerous for you to stay with us any longer. You will go back with him."

For a moment Brandy couldn't believe her ears. Then a sudden fury filled her, and she exploded.

"The devil I'll go back with him! We've already been through this! I told you weeks ago I wasn't going back!"

"Things have changed."

"Nothing has changed! I'm not going back, and that's final!"

Flaming Arrow looked at Paul and said, "Perhaps you can persuade her." A self-derisive smile played on his lips. "I'm afraid I haven't had much success in controlling her. She has a mind of her own."

Any animosity Paul might have felt toward Flaming Arrow had fled when he had seen the blatant love for Brandy in the tall Dakota's dark eyes. Now, as he admitted to helplessness with Brandy, Paul felt a certain kinship. "No, I won't be able to change her mind," Paul answered with a wry smile of his own. "I never could do anything with her either. She's as stubborn as a mule."

The two men's eyes met across the distance in perfect understanding, while Brandy seethed on the sidelines. Then Flaming Arrow turned to Brandy and said, "I'll leave you two to say your good-byes. But do not dally. The other tribes are already breaking camp."

As Flaming Arrow and Swift Rabbit walked away, Brandy sat beside her brother on the river bank. For a moment they sat in silence, neither knowing a painless way to say good-bye. Then Brandy asked, "Will you tell the soldiers about me when they find you here?"

"No, I don't think so."

"How will you explain your splint, how you got from the woods to the river?"

"I'll tell them an old Indian woman found me and took pity on me."

"Are you ashamed of me? Is that why you don't want to tell them the truth?"

"I'm not ashamed of you, Brandy. I'm proud of you. And I don't have any hard feelings toward Flaming Arrow, either, not since I've met him. You were right—he is a cut above other men. I sensed it. And I'd have known he was a chief even if you hadn't told me. It's written all over him. But I don't think the others would understand. They'd be like I was at first. And I won't stand by and watch them scorn you."

"And Mother and Father? What will you tell them?"

"I don't think I'll tell them anything, either, for the same reasons. Besides, they're pretty much reconciled to the fact that you're dead. That was easier for them to accept than to worry about what terrible things might be happening to you. If I told them the truth, they'd be right back where they started, worrying about you."

"Yes, I suppose you're right," Brandy agreed sadly.

Paul gave Brandy a long pensive look, then asked, "What about you? If Flaming Arrow is killed, will you come back?"

It was a possibility that Brandy had not been willing to face before, and now for the first time, she gave it serious thought. She was surprised when she realized that the answer was no, that she'd stay. This was her world now, not just Flaming Arrow's, but hers. The Dakotas were her people now. She wondered when she had made the choice, when she had switched her allegiance from one nation to the other. Had it happened that day when she had shared in

Flaming Arrow's spiritual experience at the Sun Dance? Or had it happened yesterday, when she took up arms against her own countryman to protect Morning Star and Deer Runs Fast? Or maybe it had been even later, when Paul had called Swift Rabbit a squaw and aroused her anger, or when he'd refused to meet her eyes when she had asked if he knew there were women and children in the village. No, it hadn't been any one of those things. It had been a combination of all of them. In essence she had been making the transition from the minute Flaming Arrow had brought her to live with the Dakotas. She had not simply stepped from one world to the other. It had been a long, very determined walk.

Brandy looked Paul deeply in the eyes and answered, "No, I won't go back. Not now, not ever."

"Somehow I knew you were going to give me that answer. And now there's something I want you to know. My enlistment is up in September. I'm not going to re-enlist."

"Why? Because you don't want to come face to face in battle with Flaming Arrow?"

"I admit that occurred to me, but it goes deeper than that. I was already considering it last night, before I even knew he was your husband. Sitting in that dark cave, all alone, not knowing if the rest of the army was dead or what, I got to thinking. What in the hell are we doing here, anyway? This isn't our land. And the Dakotas haven't done anything wrong. We're the ones breaking the treaty. And that question you asked me: Did I know there were women and children in the village? That really got to me. I couldn't kill women and children, and still keep my self-respect. No, I want out of this damned army now, before I do something I can't change, something that I'll always be ashamed of."

Brandy placed her hand to one side of his jaw and answered softly, "I'm glad you made that decision— for myself, for my adopted people, and for you." She leaned forward and kissed him on the cheek. "Good-bye."

Tears stung behind Paul's eyes. "Good-bye."

Brandy rose and walked sadly away while Paul watched. Then, just before she rounded a bend in the river, he called, "Tell Flaming Arrow I said good luck!"

She turned, waved, and called back, "I will!"

Just before Brandy stepped around the bend, Paul realized he was indeed proud of her. His little sister had turned out to be quite an extraordinary young woman.

An hour later, Paul was found by a scouting party that Reno had sent out and was taken back to the hills where the ragged remnants of Custer's illustrious Seventh Cavalry were entrenched. There, with the other officers, he watched the Dakota tribes pull out, one by one, with the precision of a cavalry unit— thousands and thousands of men, women, and children, some mounted, others walking, their ponies dragging travoises heavily laden with household goods and tepee skins. The last Paul saw of his sister and the tribe she had adopted was from behind a curtain of billowing, black smoke as the Indians slowly wound their way up the foothills to the snowy peaks of the Big Horn Mountains.

26

The Dakota tribes didn't stay to
gether when they reached the Big Horn Mountains
after their victory at Greasy Grass. They split up,
fanning out in every direction. Flaming Arrow
aligned himself with his old mentor, Crazy Horse,
and the two tribes crossed the Powder River Basin
and settled down a few miles from the south fork of
the Grand River, north of the Dakotas' beloved Black
Hills. There they spent a relatively quiet summer,
oblivious to the furor they had created in the rest of
the country with their victory, while Generals Crook
and Terry, their armies hastily reinforced by a furious Sheridan, crisscrossed the Powder River Country
over and over in a fruitless search for the Dakotas.

In August, Flaming Arrow entered their tepee,
and Brandy knew by his long face that he had re-

ceived bad news. "Sit down beside me" she said, "and tell me what is bothering you."

Flaming Arrow sank to the pallet. "There has been another treaty made with the reservation chiefs. The white-eyes have gained what they wanted all along, what we fought so hard at the Battle of the Rosebud and Greasy Grass to protect. In this treaty, they have taken back the entire Powder River Country, along with the the Black Hills and its adjacent lands." Flaming Arrow slammed his hand down on the ground between them and said in an angry voice, "Those chiefs had no right to make that agreement! It is illegal. The Fort Laramie Treaty clearly states that it can be changed only by the vote of three-quarters of the adult males in *all* of the Dakota tribes."

"Don't you suppose the chiefs were put under a great deal of pressure by the commissioners from Washington?"

"Yes, I know they were both bribed and threatened. But still . . ." His voice trailed off.

Brandy took his hand in one of hers. "It doesn't matter what the chiefs do or don't do, so don't waste your energy getting angry at them. The Americans will get what they want, regardless. And they don't need a treaty to do it."

"I know. It's just that I feel those chiefs have betrayed all the Dakota warriors who died in those battles."

"Perhaps they have. But it's on *their* conscience, not yours."

"Yes, and it changes nothing for me either. I am still a free Dakota. I will live and hunt where I want."

* * *

A few weeks later, a Dakota courier came racing into their camp with the alarming news that the neighboring village of Chief American Horse was under attack. Flaming Arrow and Crazy Horse quickly mounted a force to go to their aid. Unfortunately, by the time they arrived, the village had been captured and the army had received reinforcements, enough that the two chiefs didn't dare engage in battle. They returned to their camps and again moved.

In October, Flaming Arrow and Crazy Horse received word that Sitting Bull and Gall had been approached by General Miles—who had replaced General Terry—about surrendering and going to the reservation. A council had been arranged, but it had broken up and ended in a battle. From then on the army seemed to have a particular vendetta against the Dakotas, harrying the tribes at every turn and carrying the war on into the winter months, something they had never done before.

Then, in November, a pitiful, ragged bunch of Cheyennes appeared in Crazy Horse's camp asking for refuge. They were what was left of Dull Knife's tribe, who had been camped in the Big Horn Mountains when the army had set upon them, killing most of the tribe and destroying their village. That night, after Flaming Arrow had returned from Crazy Horse's tepee, he sat for a long time and brooded darkly. Finally he asked Brandy, "Have you ever heard of a Colonel MacKenzie?"

Brandy searched her memory, then answered, "Yes, I believe I have. He's a cavalry officer of some notoriety as an Indian fighter and known for his aggressiveness. He's reputed to be the man who brought about the Comanches' downfall. Why do you ask?"

"He was the officer who led the attack on Dull Knife's camp. They say he has taken over command of Crook's horse soldiers. They call him Bear's Coat, because of the heavy furs he and his men wear." Flaming Arrow paused. "The Cheyennes claim he did not seem interested in forcing them to surrender, that he appeared more bent on total destruction. Many were killed, some women and children, and their tepees, with all their belongings, were burned to the ground. The horse soldiers even slaughtered their ponies."

Later that night, after Flaming Arrow had gone to sleep, Brandy lay musing over this news. From what she remembered, MacKenzie had broken the back of the Comanches by hounding them and keeping them constantly on the move, so that they didn't even have time to hunt for food, wearing them down while they slowly died of starvation. Then she remembered something that made her blood run cold:" *"If you want to kill the lice, kill the nits."* Had Sheridan or MacKenzie said that horrible thing about how to effectively fight Indians? It really didn't matter which man did. One was the superior officer doing the ordering, the other the man in the field. Brandy felt sick. It was as the surviving Cheyennes from Dull Knife's decimated tribe had claimed. The army wasn't interested in surrender, nor was it seeking to just punish the Dakotas. They wanted total annihilation of the Dakota nation—men, women, and children—and as much as she hated to admit it, she feared the American people were giving them their complete support.

In the months that followed, the army harried the nontreaty Indians who had refused to go on the reservation relentlessly. Crazy Horse and Flaming Arrow seemed to be the main target of their hunt. It seemed that no sooner did they settle down than they had to flee, over and over and over. Then on January 8, the army discovered their camps in the Wolf Mountains during a raging snowstorm.

Flaming Arrow and Crazy Horse quickly mounted their men and rode out to meet the soldiers, and even over the howling wind, Brandy could hear the crack of rifles and the awesome sounds of the army's artillery. The running battle went on all day in the swirling snow. Then Flaming Arrow and Crazy Horse sent back word for the women to break up the two camps and pull out while they covered their escape.

It was a night Brandy would never forget, trudging through the darkness in knee-high snow trying to lead the horse that was pulling her travois. The swirling snow stung her face, her hands were numb with cold, and her feet felt like two blocks of ice despite the fur-lined moccasins she wore. Several times, she handed her reins to either Moon Woman or Swift Rabbit, who were leading their horses on each side of her, and went back to the travois to check on Morning Star and Deer Runs Fast, who were huddled in the buffalo hides there. Every time she saw Morning Star hovering over the baby's cradle board, trying to protect him from the icy winds, Brandy became incensed all over again, thinking it would take cruel, heartless men to attack a peaceful

village in the dead of winter, sending women and
children out into the wilderness in a raging blizzard.
It was her fury that kept her going that night.

Morning came, but the light was no help. The snow
was falling so thickly that Brandy couldn't see more
than a few feet in front of her. Fleeing blindly
Brandy had no idea where they were, but she sensed
they had left the mountain pass they had been traveling through because the wind was much stronger
here, blowing so hard that it seemed determined to
push her back, and it no longer howled. It shrieked
like a demented woman.

Suddenly, Brandy sensed that Swift Rabbit was no
longer walking beside her. She stopped her horse
and slowly retraced her steps, crouching as she
walked and groping in the madly swirling snow.
Then she stumbled on something half-buried in the
snow, she cried out in relief and frantically pushed
the snow aside.

As Brandy knelt beside Swift Rabbit and pulled her
up, cradling her against her chest, the old woman
muttered, "No, do not stop for me. You will get lost
from the others. Go on. Leave me."

"I'll do no such thing!"

"I am old and tired. I will slow everyone down. Go.
Leave me. It is the Indian way."

"I'm not an Indian, remember?"

"But you are. Every day you are more Dakota."

"I'll never be so Indian that I'll leave a friend to
die, no matter how old she is!" Brandy replied fervently.

Ignoring Swift Rabbit's objections, Brandy struggled to help the old woman stand, then held her
firmly around the waist with one hand and groped

with the other until she found the pile of buffalo skins on Swift Rabbit's travois. It took some doing to untie the rawhide strings that held the skins in place—the rawhide was frozen stiff, and Brandy's fingers were numb—but she was finally successful in getting the old woman bundled down among them.

"You cannot lead your horse and mine," Swift Rabbit said. "Leave me here. I will not freeze now. When the blizzard has passed, I will catch up."

"I told you, I'm not leaving you here."

"You are the most stubborn person I have ever met!" Swift Rabbit said in exasperation. "It is Morning Star and Deer Runs Fast that you must concern yourself with. Their lives are in your hands. I am just an old useless woman."

"You're not useless. I need you."

"You no longer need me. I have taught you everything I know."

"There are other ways of needing people. I need you because—I love you."

The only thing that Brandy could see of Swift Rabbit was her eyes. Like her and the other women, the old woman had wrapped a trading blanket around her head and the lower part of her face. Brandy saw a tear spill over from one eye and then freeze on her high cheekbone. "You're crying!" she said in amazement.

Furiously, Swift Rabbit wiped a tear from the other eye before it could spill over and said in an emotion-choked voice, "Yes, but you must promise never to tell anyone. They all think I'm so stern."

Brandy smiled beneath the blanket wrapped around her lower face. What Swift Rabbit had said was true. Every woman in the tribe stood in awe of her, and if truth be known, Morning Star and Moon Woman were just a little afraid of the tough old woman. Brandy gently brushed the frozen teardrop from the old woman's leathery cheek. "I promise I won't tell anyone. It will just be another of our secrets. That's what friends are for."

Brandy tucked the buffalo skins more tightly around Swift Rabbit, then trudged through the snow past the old Indian's waiting horse and picked up its reins. It was then that she noticed that the wind had fallen and that the snow was not coming down so thickly. She could even see the vague, shadowy outline of her travois and horse ahead of her. She plowed through the snow until she came abreast of her travois. Then, after checking to make sure Morning Star and Deer Runs Fast were all right, she made her way to the head of her horse and picked up its reins.

It was difficult to lead two horses, for both were exhausted, cold, and reluctant to go any farther. More than once, the animals stopped and pawed at the snow until they had uncovered a patch of brown grass, and Brandy was forced to wait while they ate— something she really couldn't begrudge them, knowing that it would give them strength to go on. She just wondered where she herself was going to get the strength. All she wanted to do was lie down in the snow and go to sleep.

About midday, the sky cleared and the bright sun shone down on them, creating a painful glare as it reflected the white of the snow. Shading her eyes with her mittened hand, Brandy could see that the women with their horses and travoises were scattered all over a broad plain and that there wasn't a tree in sight. Nor was there any sign of the warriors.

"What will we do now?" Morning Star asked Brandy from the travois.

"How would I know?" Brandy threw back.

"You are the chief's wife," Morning Star pointed out.

"Well, that doesn't mean I'm in charge," Brandy answered, feeling a little panicky for fear it did.

"There is a good campsite up in those hills over there, with wood and water," Swift Rabbit said, climbing from her travois. "We have made our winter camp there before." Swift Rabbit walked up to Brandy and held out her hand, saying, "I will lead my horse now. I am fully rested."

Brandy handed the reins to her and called out to the group, "Head for those hills!"

The words were still echoing in the crisp, crystal-clear air, when Brandy leaned over and whispered to Swift Rabbit, "See? I told you you weren't useless. We would have been totally lost without you."

At that moment, the old woman very much felt the burden of her years, but nonetheless she beamed with pleasure.

Shortly after the women had set up camp in the hills, Flaming Arrow, Crazy Horse, and their warriors rode in, looking exhausted and half frozen, their eyebrows beneath their fur caps covered with frost and their faces blackened with gunpowder. As Flaming Arrow swung down from his mount, Brandy tried to keep her eyes from the string of horses being led past their tepee. She knew the rolled buffalo hides flung across their backs contained the bodies of those slain in battle, for the Dakotas retrieved their dead as well as their wounded whenever possible. Flaming

Arrow rushed her into their tepee, anxious for its warmth, but Brandy did not miss the piercing wail of a woman who had discovered her husband was one of the dead. The sound tore at Brandy's heart, and as soon as they were inside their lodging, she clutched him to her frantically, as if she were afraid death would try to steal him away from her.

Later, Flaming Arrow told her the snowstorm had covered their tracks and that he doubted that the army would be able to find them the second time. But as the days passed, Brandy felt no security in their new home. She was terrified that a sentry would race into the camp at any minute, telling them another cavalry column was riding down on them. She was sick to death of being hounded, of always being on the run, of never knowing a moment's peace. The entire tribe was exhausted and on the brink of starvation, for they'd had no relief from being chased and hadn't been able to make a fall buffalo hunt. But strangely, it wasn't the emptiness in her stomach that bothered her as much as the constant anxiety. She longed for a peaceful place, a place where she could be free from fear. The yearning became so intense that it was all she could think of, day and night.

One night, when they sitting around their cozy fire in their tepee, Flaming Arrow suddenly announced, "I am going to seek my vision again."

Brandy was stunned. "But why?"

"I have come to believe you were correct, that the flaming end of the arrow breaking off and falling does not signify my death. Since the Sun Dance, I have been in many battles. Always I was in the thick of the fighting. Men fell all around me. And yet I have not received so much as a scratch. I think the arrow breaking has another meaning, and in these trying times, I need the Mystery's guidance. Hopefully, this time, it will become perfectly clear what He wants of me. So tomorrow I will go to seek my vision again."

"Tomorrow?" Brandy asked in a shocked voice. "Why, it's freezing out there!"

"It was at this time of the year that I sought my first vision, and I was hardly more than a boy. And the place where I had my first vision is not far from here. That is why I have such high expectations. I am duplicating both the place and the time of year."

Flaming Arrow left the next morning, taking only his knife, flint, and medicine pouch with him. To Brandy's dismay, he didn't even take a buffalo robe or blanket but wore only his buckskins. She worried about him. But strangely, not because of how exposed he was to the elements. She was terrified that an army patrol might stumble across him, alone and unarmed.

On the fourth evening he returned, appearing in their tepee with a suddenness and unexpectedness that startled Brandy. But she knew from the moment she looked at his face that he had been successful. The lines of tension that had been there for months were gone, and she had never seen him looking more relaxed.

As he bent his head to kiss her, she stepped back and said, "No! First, tell me what you saw."

Flaming Arrow chuckled at her impatience. "Sit down with me."

They sank to their pallet, and Flaming Arrow's

dark eyes glittered with excitement. "My vision came this morning, just as the sun was rising. I saw a flaming arrow come from a dark cloud laced with lightning and streak across the sky. Then the flaming end of the arrow broke off and fell to the ground."

"Yes, yes, I know of all of that," Brandy interjected anxiously. "But there was more, wasn't there?"

"Yes, there was. I suppose it was there before, but I never noticed it. My attention was always on the flaming end of the arrow. But this time I saw that the rest of the arrow continued to streak across the sky until it disappeared in the sun, and that the arrowhead wasn't barbed, but smooth. It had become a hunting arrow, not a war arrow."

"I never knew there was a difference."

"Yes, the war arrow is barbed to make it more difficult to remove."

"But what do you suppose that means?"

"I do not suppose. This time I know its meaning, without a shadow of a doubt. At first it was meant for me to be a strong warrior, a war chief. I have fulfilled that part of my vision. But now the Mystery has other plans for me. The hunting arrow is a sign of peace. From now on, I must serve my people in that capacity."

"Then you're going to surrender, to let them put you on a reservation?" Brandy asked, feeling keen disappointment. Flaming Arrow's fierce independence was one of the things she loved the most about him.

"No, I did not say that. I will never give up my freedom, nor do I believe the Mystery wants that from me."

"Then what *do* you plan?"

"I will move my tribe to Canada. It means we will have to give up our prized hunting grounds here in the Powder River Country, but we will still be free and no longer hounded by the army. The Great Mother in Canada has always been much kinder to Indians than the leaders of this country, and the tribes get along well with her red-coated horse soldiers. They are not like the soldiers in this country, who cannot understand that we want to be free. The Mounties, as I believe you call them, are like our trapper friends, kindred spirits."

To Brandy, it sounded like the answer to her prayers. "And Crazy Horse? Will he and his tribe move too?"

"No. I have already told him of my decision, and he said he will not leave the Powder River Country. He loves our old hunting ground too much. But he holds no bad feelings against me. He will tell those in his tribe that any who wish to go with me to a new home in Canada may do so, and I will tell those in my tribe that any who wish to remain can stay with him. Our parting will be as our relationship always has been, amicable and respectful of the others' wishes."

Flaming Arrow circled Brandy's shoulders with one arm and hugged her to his side. "So what do you think of my plans?"

Brandy's eyes shone with happiness. "I think they're wonderful."

"Then you're prepared to pack up tomorrow for the long trek?"

"Tomorrow?" Brandy repeated in surprise. "But it's still winter. Aren't we going to wait for spring?"

"No. The army will not expect us to do something like this in the middle of winter—move that distance in the snow and intense cold. If we wait until spring-time, they will be patrolling the border to keep us from escaping. We are very low on ammunition. What we have left, I wish to use for hunting, not fighting."

It made good sense to Brandy, and the sooner she could stop worrying about an unexpected attack, the better. "Yes, I agree, and we certainly couldn't possibly run into a blizzard any worse than the one we went through. If we could survive that, we can survive anything."

She looked up and saw the warm glow in Flaming Arrow's dark eyes. Her heart skipped a beat before it raced. She knew what that look meant, and she was as hungry for him as he obviously was for her.

He rose, pulled her to her feet with him, then slowly undressed her, kissing each inch of skin he exposed. Each touch of his lips, each caress of his hands heightened her desire. Then he unbraided her hair and spread the long tresses out around her like a cape. For a moment he stood, awed by the sight of firelight playing over the reddish-brown tresses, then spied one pert, rosy nipple peaking through the strands that lay across her breast. He bent and licked it, the warm, wet lash making Brandy's breath catch and her legs tremble.

When he lifted his head, Brandy saw that the warm glow in his eyes had turned to a blazing fire. "You have bewitched me," he muttered in a ragged, roughened voice. "I am totally besotted with you."

And he stepped forward to take her in his arms, Brandy pushed him gently back. "No. I want to see all of you too."

Flaming Arrow stood frozen to the spot as she

slipped his buckskin shirt over his head, deliberately brushing her naked breasts against his chest as she did so and taking delight in hearing his breath catch. Dropping the garment to the floor, she traced the powerful muscles on his chest from his shoulder to one dark nipple, then lazily circled it until she saw it harden. Leaning forward, she licked the hardened bud, just as he had done hers, and heard his moan of pleasure. Smiling with self-satisfaction, she untied the string that held up his leggins and pushed them down, thrilling to the feel of his thigh muscles contracting beneath her fingertips. Kneeling, she slipped her hands beneath the flap of his breechclout, then founded his erection through the material. She saw him clench his hands just before she pulled on the string there.

As the breechclout fell away, she sat back on her heels and looked up at him. Flaming Arrow stood like a magnificent bronze statue. The firelight playing over him accentuated every ridged hollow, every corded sinew. He was the human male animal in its perfection, she thought, proud, commanding, every powerful muscle primed for action—including the splendid one between his legs. A shiver of anticipation ran through her.

Flaming Arrow dropped to his knees beside Brandy and drew her to the pallet with him. But to his surprise, she caught him by the shoulders and rolled him to his back, saying, "I'm going to make love to you this time. I don't want you to do anything but just lie there."

It was a shocking proposition to a Dakota warrior, that he take the passive role in lovemaking. He had been taught to be the aggressor in everything he did.

And yet deep down, Flaming Arrow was intrigued. His moment of hesitation was his undoing, for by that time Brandy was already kneeling beside him and taunting him with featherlike strokes, caresses that left a trail of fire in their wake. Her fingers lightly explored his chest, teasing both flat nipples until they were hard buds, then smoothing across his taut abdomen, lower and lower, brushing back and forth across his groin, taunting close to the rigid column of flesh that ached for her touch, then down his corded thighs, the hard, horseman's muscles there jerking in response to her touch. Still stroking the inside of one thigh, she lowered her head and dropped tiny kisses over his neck, his shoulders, his chest, and down his abdomen, her tongue flicking, then circling his navel. Her hand moved from his thigh to stroke the velvety skin of his erection, while her lips moved lower and lower, sweeping in an arc back and forth between his hip bones, nibbling and licking.

Flaming Arrow sensed what she was about to do, but he was already so wildly excited that he didn't think he could stand any more of her erotic ministrations. "No," he muttered weakly, "that's enough," then sucked in his breath at the feel of her dropping light kisses over the hot tip before she took him in her mouth. Then he was too weak to further object. The feel of her lips and tongue working their devilish magic there made him feel as if his muscles were melting from his bones, while his breath turned shallow and ragged.

Brandy had heard Flaming Arrow's muttered objection, then smiled as he arched his hips to give her even better access to him in a silent but eloquent plea for more. But Brandy didn't want to bring him to fulfillment with her mouth. She wanted to share that climactic experience with him, and arousing him had excited her unbearably. She lifted her head, swung one leg over him, and rose over him.

Through passion-dulled eyes, Flaming Arrow saw Brandy rearing over him and realized her intent. For her to bring him to fulfillment with her mouth was one thing, but for him to passively lie beneath her while she rode him was quite another. That would be carrying her aggressive role a little too far. He caught her hips to roll her to her back and put things back in their proper perspective.

But as she lowered herself over his rigid length with her reddish-brown hair shimmering in the fire-light and her proud, milky breasts impudently jutting out, Flaming Arrow remembered that this was Brandy, his bold, outspoken, fiery white-eyes, and that no matter how good a Dakota wife she might become, she would never be a meek, manageable, submissive mate. And he didn't want her to be— ever! For without her exasperating traits, she wouldn't be the woman who fascinated him and excited him, the captive who had captured his heart and soul.

Then as she paused in her descent, their eyes met, his like black glowing coals and hers a searing blue. Brandy sensed that Flaming Arrow was relinquishing a part of his age-old belief that professed the male was superior and dominant in all things. She knew she had won a battle of sorts, and a triumphant smile spread across her lips. Then, as he exerted just the hint of pressure on her hips and she descended yet another inch, she sucked in her breath sharply at the feel of his scorching, swollen flesh inside her.

Flaming Arrow curtailed his caresses to just stroking Brandy's sides and thighs as he allowed her to
ride him. She did so magnificently, her first movements slow and exquisitely sensuous; then, as her
own pressing need came to the fore, she swiveled her
hips and moved faster and faster. Flaming Arrow
gave himself up to sheer sensation as she took them
higher and higher on that dizzying ascent, his excitement becoming unbearable and his arousal so acute
it was almost painful. He was beginning to fear he
wouldn't be able to hold back any longer, when
Brandy suddenly came to a halt, stiffened, and threw
back her head. A glazed look came over her eyes.
Knowing she was teetering on the shattering brink,
Flaming Arrow let out an exalted cry and allowed
himself release. His scalding seed deep inside her
pushed Brandy over that quivering peak to her own
blinding white-hot climax.

Brandy collapsed weakly over him, her head buried in the warm crook between his neck and shoulder. Flaming Arrow stroked her back and tenderly
kissed her forehead and temple, whispering endear-
ments and love words. Brandy felt too blissfully relaxed and contented to even move or kiss him back.
Then his hands stilled, and she knew by the sounds of
his deep breathing that he had fallen to sleep.

For a moment, she felt a little twinge of regret. She
had hoped they could make love again. Then remembering that he had probably had no sleep since
he had left to seek his vision, she felt ashamed of
herself. They'd have the rest of their lives to make
love.

Careful not to wake him, she rolled from Flaming
Arrow and pulled the blanket up over them, then

snuggled back up to him, pillowing her head on his shoulder and placing her hand on his chest over his heart, relishing the feel of its strong, steady beat. Then, remembering where another, much tinier heart beat, her hand left her husband's chest to tenderly cup the little bulge of her abdomen.

"Micinksi," she whispered—my son. For there was no doubt in Brandy's mind that it was a boy. She wondered if she should tell Flaming Arrow. She had held back the news, knowing that he had so many pressing things on his mind, but suddenly, she couldn't keep her wonderful secret a second longer. No matter how exhausted Flaming Arrow was, she had to tell him. She had to! Otherwise, she'd burst.

She rose so that she hovered over him and gently shook his shoulder. Flaming Arrow awakened with a start, looked from side to side, then asked in a bewildered voice, "What's wrong?"

"Nothing is wrong," Brandy answered softly. "It's just that I have something very important to tell you, and it can't wait another moment."

His curosity aroused, Flaming Arrow asked, "What?"

A secretive little smile spread across Brandy's lips. Then she said, "No, I won't tell you. I'll show you."

She took his hand and placed it over her lower belly and watched the expression on his face turn from puzzlement, then to wonder, then to pure joy as it dawned on him what her secret was.

His dark eyes shining with happiness, he looked her deeply in the eyes and said in a voice choked with emotion, "I thought I knew every curve and hollow of your body as if it were my own, yet I never guessed. Why didn't you tell me sooner?"

"You had so many things on your mind, and I wanted to pick a special time."

Gently, almost as if her body was made of crystal and not flesh and bone, he rolled her to her back, then bent and softly kissed her there, an act so tender and so touching that it brought tears to her eyes. Then he took her into his arms and once more looked her in the eyes, saying earnestly, "I will love and cherish you both always. And I will find a safe home for us in Canada. You will never have to fear or go without again. I promise."

His powerful arms closed around her so tightly that Brandy feared for her ribs, but nonetheless, she embraced him back, her tears of happiness spilling down her cheeks. She knew Flaming Arrow would keep his promise. He always had. They would have a wonderful life together and live to a ripe old age. She smiled, thinking that she had gotten everything she had hoped for. She had captured her magnificent savage, and in him had a virile, exciting lover and a strong, caring husband. She had wonderful friends, a place of respect among the tribe, and Flaming Arrow's child. And now the last of her dreams was coming true. Soon, she'd have a safe, peaceful home.

Her greedy white heart had finally been satisfied. She had it all.

Joanne Redd is a native Texan currently living in Missouri City. A longtime obstetrics nurse, Joanne is the author of many critically acclaimed historical romances, including *Apache Bride, Desert Bride, Chasing a Dream,* and *To Love an Eagle,* which won the *Romantic Times* award for Best Western Historical Romance. She is currently at work on her next historical romance for Dell.

FREE FROM DELL

with purchase plus postage and handling

Congratulations! You have just purchased one or more titles featured in Dell's Romance Promotion. Our goal is to provide you with quality reading and entertainment, so we are pleased to extend to you a limited offer to receive a selected Dell romance title(s) *free* (plus $1.00 postage and handling per title) for each romance title purchased. Please read and follow all instructions carefully to avoid delays in your order.

1) Fill in your name and address on the coupon printed below. No facsimiles or copies of the coupon allowed.

2) The Dell Romance books are the only books featured in Dell's Romance Promotion. Any other Dell titles are not eligible for this offer.

3) Enclose your original cash register receipt with the price of the book(s) circled plus $1.00 **per book** for postage and handling, payable in check or money order to: Dell Romance Offer. Please do not send cash in the mail.

    Canadian customers: Enclose your original cash register receipt with the price of the book(s) circled plus $1.00 **per book** for postage and handling in U.S. funds.

4) This offer is only in effect until March 29, 1991. Free Dell Romance requests postmarked after March 22, 1991 will not be honored, but your check for postage and handling will be returned.

5) Please allow 6-8 weeks for processing. Void where taxed or prohibited.

Mail to: Dell Romance Offer
        P.O. Box 2088
        Young America, MN 55399-2088

NAME_____

ADDRESS_____

CITY_____STATE_____ZIP_____

BOOKS PURCHASED AT_____

AGE_____

(Continued)

Book(s) purchased:_____

_____

_____

I understand I may choose one free book for each Dell Romance book purchased
(plus applicable postage and handling). Please send me the following:

(Write the number of copies of each title selected next to that title.)

MY ENEMY, MY LOVE
Elaine Coffman
From an award-winning author comes this
compelling historical novel that pits a
spirited beauty against a hard-nosed
gunslinger hired to forcibly bring her home
to her father. But the gunslinger finds
himself unable to resist his captive.

AVENGING ANGEL
Lori Copeland
Jilted by her thieving fianceé, a woman
rides west seeking revenge, only to wind up
in the arms of her enemy's brother.

A WOMAN'S ESTATE
Roberta Gellis
An American woman in the early 1800s
finds herself ensnared in a web of family
intrigue and dangerous passions when her
English nobleman husband passes away.

THE RAVEN AND THE ROSE
Virginia Henley
A fast-paced, sexy novel of the 15th
century that tells a tale of royal intrigue,
spirited love, and reckless abandon.

THE WINDFLOWER
Laura London
She longed for a pirate's kisses. . . even
though she was kidnapped in error and
forced to sail the seas on his pirate ship,
forever a prisoner of her own reckless
desire.

TO LOVE AN EAGLE
Joanne Redd
Winner of the 1987 *Romantic Times*
Reviewer's Choice Award for Best Western
Romance by a New Author.

SAVAGE HEAT
Nan Ryan
The spoiled young daughter of a U.S. Army
General is kidnapped by a Sioux chieftain
out of revenge and is at first terrified, then
infuriated, and finally hopelessly aroused by
him.

BLIND CHANCE
Meryl Sawyer
Every woman wants to be a star, but what
happens when the one nude scene she'd
performed in front of the cameras haunts
her, turning her into an underground sex
symbol?

DIAMOND FIRE
Helen Mittermeyer
A gorgeous and stubborn young woman
must choose between protecting the
dangerous secrets of her past or trusting
and loving a mysterious millionaire who has
secrets of his own.

LOVERS AND LIARS
Brenda Joyce
She loved him for love's sake, he seduced
her for the sake of sweet revenge. This is a
story set in Hollywood, where there are two
types of people—lovers and liars.

MY WICKED ENCHANTRESS
Meagan McKinney
Set in 18th-century Louisiana, this is the
tempestous and sensuous story of an
impoverished Scottish heiress and the
handsome American plantation owner who
saves her life, then uses her in a dangerous
game of revenge.

EVERY TIME I LOVE YOU
Heather Graham
A bestselling romance of a rebel Colonist
and a beautiful Tory loyalist who
reincarnate their fiery affair 200 years later
through the lives of two lovers.

Dell

TOTAL NUMBER OF FREE BOOKS SELECTED _____ X $1.00
= $_____ (Amount Enclosed)

Dell has other great books in print by these authors. If you enjoy them, check
your local book outlets for other titles.